If Memory Serves

Also by Vanessa Davis Griggs

Ray of Hope

The Truth Is the Light

Goodness and Mercy

Practicing What You Preach

Strongholds

Blessed Trinity

Published by Kensington Publishing Corp.

If Memory Serves

VANESSA DAVIS GRIGGS

Dafina
BOOKS

Kensington Publishing Corp.
http://www.kensingtonbooks.com

DAFINA BOOKS are published by

Kensington Publishing Corp.
119 West 40th Street
New York, NY 10018

All Kensington titles, imprints, and distributed lines are available at special quantity discounts for bulk purchases for sales
promotions, premiums, fund-raising, and educational or in-
stitutional use. Special book excerpts or customized print-
ings can also be created to fit specific needs. For details, write
or phone the office of the Kensington Special Sales Manager:
Kensington Publishing Corp., 119 West 40th Street, New York,
NY 10018. Attn: Special Sales Department. Phone: 1-800-
221-2647.

Dafina and the Dafina logo Reg. U.S. Pat. & TM Off.

ISBN-13: 978-0-7582-1737-0
ISBN-10: 0-7582-1737-4

First trade paperback printing: October 2008
First mass market printing: May 2010

10 9 8 7 6 5 4 3 2

Printed in the United States of America

*Dedicated to my children Jeffery, Jeremy, and
Johnathan Griggs;
in loving memory of Joshua and Jarrod Andre Griggs
(one of whom I was able to hold in my arms for a few
precious minutes;
both of whom I will forever hold in my heart);
and all who know and understand what
loving someone is truly all about.*

Acknowledgments

I can never begin this process without first acknowledging and giving thanks to my Heavenly Father who loves me and shows it with every breath I take. To my mother Mrs. Josephine Davis and my father Mr. James Davis Jr.: I am more than blessed and greatly honored to call you *my* parents.

I truly have a remarkable family. To my husband Jeffery; children Jeffery Marques, Jeremy Dewayne, and Jonathan LeDavis Griggs; grandchildren Asia and Ashlynn; sisters Danette Dial and Arlinda Davis, sister-in-law Cameron; brothers Terence Davis and Emmanuel Davis: I love and thank you all for blessing my life in so many ways. We've been together through thick and thin, and we're still standing.

To my cousin Mark Davis and a host of fantastic friends (too many to name) but especially Rosetta Moore, Vanessa L. Rice, Zelda Oliver-Miles, Linda H. Jones, Bonita Chaney, and Ella Wells: I thank you for all that you bring to my life. To Stephanie Perry Moore: It's been such a pleasure having you as a fellow author as well as being a special friend. I know God has some awesome things in store for you. I'll always be in your corner, enthusiastically cheering you on. To the members of The WBRT Society book club, GAME book club, and the many other book clubs that choose or have chosen my book(s): Thank you so much. To the members of Delta Sigma Theta Sorority Birmingham Alumnae Chapter: You do so much for so many and I humbly appreciate the way you've embraced, supported, encouraged, and shown me so much love.

To my editor Rakia A. Clark: Thank you for who you are and all that you do. I appreciate you. Thanks also to the wonderful staff of Kensington/Dafina for the awesome work all of you do from my gorgeous covers to the distribution of all our books.

To those of you who are choosing to read *If Memory Serves*, I thank you so much! I don't now and never will take you for granted. When I write, please know that I'm thinking of you, desiring with every stroke of the keyboard and my pen that I give you my very best. I consider this a deal of sorts that you and I have entered into together, and I want more than anything to always uphold my end of this deal. With this book (as you take this reading journey along with me), I ask that you resist any and all urges to turn to the end of the book. And yes, there will be times when I believe it might be difficult and you may feel you can't take knowing (or not knowing) any longer. I only ask that you trust me and trust this experience I've worked so hard to bring to you.

I love hearing from you. I'd also like to thank you for helping me spread the word about my books. May you walk in God's exceedingly, abundantly, above-all-you-can-ever-ask-or-think blessings!

Vanessa Davis Griggs
www.VanessaDavisGriggs.com

Chapter 1

Memory, who was going by the name of Elaine Robertson and had asked Johnnie Mae Landris to just call her Elaine instead of Ms. Robertson, sat on the bed in the room Johnnie Mae said would be hers for as long as she stayed. Certain that she was alone, she picked up the phone and dialed. "Hi, Sam," she said with a grin. "It's me—Memory."

Johnnie Mae had just finished showing her two bedrooms, in both of which the beds were low and close to the floor. The first room had a queen-size sleigh bed with stone-top nightstands set on each side.

"What's the name of this collection?" Memory had asked, attempting to show she was *somewhat* knowledgeable about life's finer things. Fine furniture always had a name.

"The Amherst collection—it's English inspired," Johnnie Mae said with a smile. No one had ever asked her that before. She was impressed Memory had, but even more impressed that she'd recalled the collection's name to be able to answer her.

"They certainly crafted some exquisite pieces," Memory said, leisurely strolling around the room, touching and tracing various intricate details lightly with her fingers for an up-close-and-personal feel. Fully aware Johnnie Mae had another bedroom she wanted her to see, Memory wasn't trying to be snooty or picky. She'd just never been this close to a setup so nice and was determined she would experience this on her own terms without rushing or glossing over it in order to appear even more refined.

Memory touched the antique brass hardware, felt the smoothness of the cherry-finished wood . . . the coolness of the stone-topped nightstand. She marveled at the overlaid carving on the bed's head- and footboard and the doors of the large, three-drawer armoire. Yet nothing she'd seen rivaled the swirling, hand-carved pilasters that topped the nine-drawer dresser's mirror and the armoire that stood catercornered between two walls.

Easing down gingerly on the cushioned bench at the foot of the bed, she looked around again, taking a visual inventory of the entire room. "This is lovely," she said. "So lovely. It's warm and engaging. Feels like . . . home." She nodded. "Yes, like home."

"Thank you," Johnnie Mae said as she quickly glanced around the guest bedroom. It was a place she rarely came into and—with the exception of having to periodically dust the furniture and hardwood floor covered largely by a maroon Oriental rug—really had no reason to. "Before you get *too* comfortable," she said, "don't forget there's one other bedroom I want you to see. Then you can decide which of the two you prefer."

Memory stood up. "This one's fine. In fact, it's *better* than fine. I keep trying to tell you that I'm not sure I'll even be here long enough to need a place to lay my head."

"Look, Elaine, you can at least stay the night," Johnnie Mae said. She hadn't had a chance to call Sarah Fleming yet, so she wasn't sure what the plan for Memory would be. She just knew she needed to keep her close until she could relay her suspicions to Sarah and find out how she wanted to proceed from here.

Memory strolled toward the doorway and looked back at the room as she and Johnnie Mae stepped into the all-white carpeted hallway. They walked two doors down, passing the opened door of a large bathroom accentuated with gold fixtures and faucets.

Johnnie Mae opened the door to another bedroom. This was the room her mother usually stayed in whenever she came over (which had only been a total of three times since they'd moved into their newly built house back in August 2004).

"Oh my goodness," Memory said, gasping aloud as she scanned the bedroom with one quick swoop. "This is breathtaking . . . absolutely breathtaking! Whose collection is *this*? Not that I'd ever be able to afford anything this grand, but, still, I can certainly brag about having seen it."

"It's called the Royale collection," Johnnie Mae said, then leaned over and whispered, "and it's really not *that* expensive." She flashed Memory a warm smile.

Memory began to walk around the room. "It has a sort of architectural feel to it."

Johnnie Mae was slightly taken aback. "That's exactly what the woman at the furniture store said when we were looking at it." Each piece had elements found in medallions, crown moldings, and various ceiling tiles (often used throughout Europe) embedded in it. "You're really quite good at this," Johnnie Mae said, again impressed.

Memory noted the low poster bed with its smoky cherry tone. She sat down on the mattress, bounced on it, then stood up—just to see how easy it would be to get in and out of it. That was one thing, at almost seventy, she and people her age cared more about these days: whether they could get in and out of bed without having to climb up or slide down. This bed was perfect, as was the one in the other room. She walked toward the dresser that proudly boasted twelve drawers: three small ones across the top, nine large dovetailed ones below. Her attention darted from the dresser to the armoire to yet another piece of furniture in the room that was too large to be a nightstand yet too small to be any type of dresser.

"What's this called?" Memory asked as she glided her worn, wrinkled fingers across the furniture's gold-painted shells, leaf moldings, and scrolls while noting how the details on it were identical to the other pieces in the collection.

"Oh, this? It's called a demilune. It has shelves inside," Johnnie Mae said, opening its door to show Memory the three shelves now filled with various books.

"A demilune?" she repeated with a look that indicated more information was needed.

"Yes, demilune—for the crescent or half-moon shape of the furniture's top."

"Oh," Memory said, tapping its top with her fingers. She walked back to the dresser, fascinated by how much the design resembled the cherrywood tiles she'd seen on the ceilings of expensive homes in a magazine she'd thumbed through just the other day. The medallions on it—as well as the ones on the armoire, mirror, and dresser—favored floral rosettes. The furniture was visibly solid. A baby blue chaise longue in front of a white-mantelled fireplace seemed to commandeer attention to the large sitting area.

"We can put my things in here," Memory said, deciding on the Royale room. "But again, I want to make it perfectly clear that I don't wish to impose on you or your family. Of all the things I intended today, believe me, this was *not* one of them."

Johnnie Mae nodded. "Oh, I know. But as I've told you already, you won't be imposing. You can clearly see for yourself, we have more than enough room here."

Memory smiled. "I do thank you for this time to, at least, regroup. I still need to decide where I should go and what I should do next." Memory looked at the French-style telephone on the nightstand. "Would it be okay if I use your phone? I have a calling card, so the long-distance charges won't be charged back to you."

"Of course it's okay. Please make yourself at home. And we have unlimited long distance, so save your calling-card minutes for another time. Feel free to talk as long as you need, to whomever you need." Johnnie Mae headed toward the door. She stopped and turned around. "Can I get you anything? Something to eat or drink, maybe?"

"No, thank you. I'm good for now. Perhaps after I'm finished here, though."

"As soon as Pastor Landris gets home, I'll have him bring up your luggage."

"Oh, I can get them," Memory said as she eased down onto the bed. "With four suitcases, it'll take a few trips, but I'm used to it. I've been dragging those bags around for a while. But I really don't see a reason to bring them up, especially when we're just going to end up having to take them right back to the car, most likely, later tonight."

"Nonsense," Johnnie Mae said. "Pastor Landris will get them. And whether you stay a few hours, a night, or a week, I'm sure there are things in your suitcase you need."

"*Whether* I stay or for how *long* . . . Well, we'll just have to see about that. But please know that I appreciate you." She looked around the room once more. "Truly, I do."

"Again, feel free to call as many people as you need to and talk for as long as you like. When you're finished, you can come back downstairs to the den. Now, there's a private bathroom right there," Johnnie Mae said, pointing to a closed door.

"I was thinking how I might need a map just to find my way around this place."

Johnnie Mae smiled. "You'll be fine. I'll see you downstairs. I'm going to close the door"—she grabbed the door handle—"so you can have your privacy." She stepped out, shut the door quietly, leaned against it, then released a long, slow sigh.

Johnnie Mae couldn't help but think this might be a good time to call Sarah. Only she wasn't sure how much time she'd have before Memory came looking for her. She decided it was best to just wait for Landris to come home. That way, he could keep Memory occupied while she took the time needed to explain everything that was going on to Sarah and whomever else she might have to. Almost two weeks shy of being seven months pregnant, Johnnie Mae waddled slightly as she walked down the winding staircase.

Memory picked up the phone. She'd been quietly listening to make sure Johnnie Mae had indeed gone back downstairs. Johnnie Mae had told her it was okay to use their long-distance service, but Memory figured that would likely leave some type of paper trail. She pulled her calling card out from the purse she'd kept securely underneath her arm, pressed the toll-free number to connect her, keyed in her calling-card number, then the number of the person she was dialing, and waited patiently as it began to ring.

"Hi, Sam," she said with a grin when the familiar voice answered the phone. "It's me—Memory."

"Well, it's about time I finally hear from you," a deep, scratchy voice replied. "I've been worried sick about you. What's going on? Where are you? Are you all right?"

"Everything's fine and going according to plan." Memory glanced around the room. "Well, truthfully, it's going *better* than planned. Would you believe I'm at Pastor and Mrs. Landris's house? That's if it's proper to call a mansion a house."

"You're kidding," Sam said.

"Nope. And get this. I had my choice of two of the most gorgeous bedrooms I've ever laid eyes on. Of course, you know me. I ended up going with the Royale room. It's a gorgeous blue. Johnnie Mae says I can stay for as long as I want. Can you believe this?"

"You're lying, Memory. Stop lying."

Memory lightly brushed her hand over the baby blue, jacquard satin comforter (half of the bed was covered up with baby blue and dark blue shams as well as geometrically shaped designer pillows). "You know I wouldn't lie about something like this. I didn't plan for it to work out this way, but you know what they say about God."

"Memory, now, I done told you—don't be playing with God or His name."

"I ain't playing. I'm just telling it like it is. God really *does* work in mysterious ways. Don't forget, you were the one who reminded me that I'd visited Pastor Landris's church back in Georgia when I stayed with my daughter and granddaughter that time," Memory said. "That *had* to be God. You know how it is when you think you know someone from somewhere but you can't recall when or where it was or whether it's just your mind playing tricks on you? Well, that's how it was when I saw Pastor Landris here. It was you who ended up helping me pinpoint where I'd most likely seen him before."

"Then I guess you should be thankful for me," Sam said in between a hard cough.

"Now, you know I appreciate you." Memory stopped for a second. "And what are you doing for that cold or whatever that is you have? You sound terrible."

"Oh, I'll be fine. You're the one who needs to take care and watch your back."

"I'm doing that. After that no-good Christopher Harris double-crossed me . . ."

"Memory, don't go getting your blood pressure all worked up over him again. God is going to take care of that situation one of these days. And you can believe *that*."

"Yeah . . . Well, God takes a little too long for me. You of all people know how impatient I can be when it comes to having to wait."

"So, what happened with that woman you were staying with last we talked?"

Memory got up and walked toward the closet. The phone wasn't cordless, but the cord was long enough to reach it. She opened the double doors and walked in. The closet was huge. "Arletha was threatening to tell that private detective fellow who's been following me everywhere that I was at her house. I had to get up out of there in a hurry."

"Does she know where you are now?"

Memory came out of the closet and closed the doors. "No. Nobody knows, except for you and the Landrises. And they only know me as Elaine Robertson."

"Well, my lips are zipped. You plan on staying there a little while or what?"

"I don't know what I'm planning to do at this point. As I said, I wasn't expecting any of this to happen this way. But now that this opportunity has practically fallen in my lap, maybe I'll just ride it out and see where it takes me. I just need to think about this a little more, I suppose."

"Memory, I know I don't have to tell you this again,

but I'm going to say it anyway. You *really* need to be careful. Take care of yourself. My friend Mabel died the other night. And you know what they say about death— it always comes in threes."

"Well, don't you worry none about me. I'll be careful. Just because I got saved here recently for real, it doesn't mean I got stupid."

"You just keep me abreast of what's going on," Sam said. "Check in every chance you get, 'cause you know I worry about you when I don't hear from you every few days."

"I know. I'm going to get off the phone now. I'll call you again later and let you know what's happening on my end. 'Bye, dear." Memory placed the receiver on its hook, sat down, then grinned as she looked around the room once more. As she relaxed on the stack of pillows behind her, Memory's grin quickly began to swell into a low, soft chuckle.

Chapter 2

Hope deferred maketh the heart sick, but when the desire cometh, it is a tree of life.

Proverbs 13:12

Landris had come home earlier than was normal for him. In fact, he'd been caught off guard by just how blinding the June sun could be if you happened to be facing west between four and five o'clock in the afternoon. As soon as he walked in the house, Johnnie Mae asked him to get Memory's luggage out of the car and take it to the bedroom her mother generally used. Johnnie Mae, Memory, and Johnnie Mae's daughter, Princess Rose, were all laughing and talking in the den next to the kitchen when Landris came and joined them.

After Johnnie Mae felt certain Landris had Memory's full attention, she excused herself and hurried upstairs to her bedroom to call Sarah.

"Don't be giving me hypotheticals. Bring my child home to me," Sarah said after Johnnie Mae explained the situation as she perceived it. "Catch a plane first thing in the morning, or if you must drive up, then drive. Just bring my child home to me."

"Okay, Sarah. But I need to know how much you want me to tell her about who you really are," Johnnie Mae said.

Going by the name Elaine Robertson, Memory didn't have a clue Johnnie Mae suspected whom she really was.

Then again, Memory didn't know that most of what she believed to be true regarding her own life was, in fact, not the whole truth. If she was truly the Memory Patterson they were seeking, the world as Memory knew it was about to quickly go from flat to round. Johnnie Mae wasn't sure she should be the one telling Memory any of this or whether this was truly the best place for it to be done.

"Tell her whatever you need to tell her to convince her to come. Everything, if you have to," Sarah said.

Johnnie Mae hung up the phone and made her way back downstairs. She walked into the den just as Landris was telling Memory one of his favorite jokes.

"There was a feud between the pastor and the choir director of this church," Landris said, smiling just a tad. "Now, the first hint of trouble seems to have come when the pastor preached on 'Dedicating Yourselves to Service' and the choir director decided the choir should sing 'I Shall Not Be Moved.' Of course, the pastor believed the song had merely been a coincidence, so he put it behind him and didn't think any more about it. The next Sunday, the pastor preached on 'Giving.' After that sermon, the choir members squirmed as the choir director led them into the hymn 'Jesus Paid It All.' By this time, the good pastor was starting to get a bit upset." Landris chuckled a little.

"Sunday morning service attendance was beginning to grow as the tension increased between the pastor and the choir director," Landris continued. "One of the largest crowds the church ever had showed up the next week to hear the sermon, which just happened to be 'The Sin of Gossiping.' True to form, the choir director selected 'I Love to Tell the Story.' Well, it was on— there was no turning back. The next Sunday, the pastor told the congregation that unless something changed, he was considering resigning. The congregation collectively gasped when the choir director led the choir into 'Why Not Tonight?' " Landris struggled to maintain a serious face. He continued.

"Well, of course no one was surprised when the pastor resigned a week later. He explained to the congregation that Jesus had led him there, and Jesus was leading him away. The choir looked at the choir director, who just couldn't resist. Jumping to his feet, he joyfully led the congregation into the hymn 'What a Friend We Have in Jesus.' "

Memory started laughing and couldn't stop. "I've never heard that before," she said, trying to compose herself. "You're really funny. I didn't know preachers were allowed to have a sense of humor."

"Oh, you didn't?" Landris asked. "Well, the Bible says, 'A merry heart doeth good like a medicine.' " Landris looked at Johnnie Mae, who stood by the couch, beaming.

"Pastor Landris can be quite the funnyman when he wants to be," Johnnie Mae said. "He's not stuffy like some preachers can tend to be."

"So I see," Memory said. She looked from Johnnie Mae to Pastor Landris and instantly picked up on an unspoken communication between them. "Miss Princess Rose," Memory began, "you're in school, huh?"

Princess Rose stood up and began to hop on one foot. "Yes, ma'am," she said, then hopped on the other foot. "Today was our last day."

"What grade are you in?"

Johnnie Mae touched Princess Rose to make her stand still. Princess Rose stopped hopping and began to twist her upper body from side to side, causing her two long pigtails to swing the way she loved for them to do. "I'll be in the *first* grade, Miss Elaine," she said, emphasizing the word "first," "when school starts back."

"Oh, you will?" Memory said, glancing at Johnnie

Mae with a smile, then back over to Princess Rose. "How old does that make you? Five? Six?"

Princess Rose held up one hand, showing all five fingers, and the index finger of her other hand.

"Talk, Princess Rose. You know how to talk," Johnnie Mae said, looking sternly but lovingly at her daughter.

"Six and a half," Princess Rose said.

"Then why aren't you going to the second grade when school starts?" Memory asked.

"Her birthday comes late. She was born in December," Johnnie Mae said, answering the question for her daughter. "I considered putting her in private school for a few years so she could be in her right-age grade, but I decided against it."

"Well, I bet you're really, really smart," Memory said, looking at Princess Rose.

Princess Rose started to nod, then stopped when she looked at her mother. "Yes, ma'am. I *really, really* am," she said with a contagious giggle. "*Everybody* says so!"

They all laughed.

"M . . . Ms. Elaine," Johnnie Mae said, having almost slipped and called her Memory, "would you mind if I borrow Pastor Landris for just a few minutes?"

"Of course not," Memory said, immediately taking a swallow of her iced tea.

"I'm sure you're past ready for supper," Johnnie Mae said.

"Oh, no, I'm fine for now. That snack you gave me earlier really did the trick."

"We'll only be a few minutes," Johnnie Mae said with a smile. "I promise." Landris stood up and they went upstairs to their bedroom.

"Okay. What's up?" Landris asked as soon as Johnnie Mae closed the door.

"I spoke with Sarah."

"And—"

"And . . . she wants me to bring Memory to Asheville, North Carolina, tomorrow morning."

He shook his head. "I don't know about that, Johnnie Mae. You're pregnant. I don't think you need to even be considering anything like that." Landris stared firmly into her brown eyes. "Just put her on a plane. It'll be faster that way, anyway."

"Landris, you know how important this is to Sarah. I'm pretty sure that's Memory downstairs. What if she decides to run away again?"

"That's, of course, *if* the woman downstairs really is her. Has she admitted to you that she is, in fact, Memory?"

Johnnie Mae glanced at the floor for a brief second, then back up. "Well, no."

"Then you really can't be certain she's Memory. And you just may have gotten Sarah's hopes up for nothing."

Johnnie Mae looked lovingly into her husband's hazel-brown eyes as she spoke softly. "I know it's her, Landris. I can feel it. So can you. I plan on talking with her and finding out once and for all, though."

"When?"

"As soon as I go back downstairs. I wanted to talk with you first." Johnnie Mae walked toward the door. "I didn't want to do anything before talking with you about it. If my suspicions are correct, then Sarah's long-lost daughter is downstairs in our den at this very moment. Sarah's been searching everywhere for her. You know this. I can't take the chance of losing her before the two of them can meet. And if that means I have to drive her to Asheville, North Carolina, myself, then that's exactly what I'm prepared to do."

Landris came over and pulled Johnnie Mae into his arms. "Now, you know I'm not going to let you go up to Asheville by yourself. You know that. But first things first. You need to be certain the woman downstairs is really Memory Patterson. So tell me. How are you planning on accomplishing that little feat?"

"Now, that much I'm not so sure about yet. She was telling me things at the church earlier today. I don't know whether I should see if she'll tell me on her own who she is, and then I tell her what I know, or whether I should just tell her what I know, and we move on from there. I just don't know."

"And precisely how much are you planning on telling her?"

Johnnie Mae grabbed the door handle. "Landris, I truly don't know. Just pray for me while I do this, okay? Honestly, I haven't a clue what my plans are from here on out. All I know is that something has to be done. And now is the time. I'm just trusting God."

"Do you want me there while you talk to her?"

Johnnie Mae released the door handle, tilted her head, and smiled before rising up on the tips of her toes, caressing his face with both hands, then giving him a quick peck on his lips. "No. But if you could keep Princess Rose occupied for me, that would be such a tremendous help. Princess Rose appears to be somewhat smitten with 'Ms. Elaine,' and I don't want any interruptions when she and I begin our talk."

"Are you sure?" Landris asked. "We both know this is some heavy stuff here."

"I'm sure. It's going to be okay," Johnnie Mae said as she smiled at him.

It was Landris this time who planted a soft kiss on her lips. "Well, whatever you need"—he planted yet another kiss on her lips—"you know I'm here for you."

She nodded, opened the door, and they walked back downstairs hand in hand.

"Princess Rose, how about you and I go to the game

room and watch a little TV on the wide-screen," Landris said as soon as he and Johnnie Mae entered the room. "Or maybe we can play a game. If memory serves, I believe you and I are due for an air-hockey rematch." Straightaway, he noticed how Johnnie Mae's eyes widened right after the word "memory" came out of his mouth. He touched her hand to put her back at ease.

"I'm just going to beat you again, Daddy Landris," Princess Rose said, getting up off the couch and skipping toward him. "I don't know when you're going to ever learn."

"Yeah, well, we'll just have to see about that then, missy, now won't we?" Landris said with a sly grin. Princess Rose grabbed his hand and started pulling him toward the hallway that led to the downstairs game room.

After the room was quiet, Johnnie Mae went and sat down across from where Memory was sitting at the end section of the U-shaped sectional sofa.

"I suppose you want to finish what you and I were talking about at the church," Memory said, releasing a deep sigh. "I did say some things that could cause you to be a bit leery of me right now. Especially considering you've so graciously opened up your home to me—a perfect stranger, in actuality."

Johnnie Mae was still unsure of which direction she should take. Should she let Memory tell her the rest of what she had begun at the church and see whether or not she would tell her the whole truth? Or should she admit to Memory up front what she suspected and tell her the things she knew?

Namely that Memory Elaine Patterson, the daughter of Mamie and Willie B. Patterson, was neither Mamie nor Willie B.'s child, but in fact, the daughter of one prominent and extremely wealthy Sarah Elaine Fleming. Johnnie Mae prayed silently.

Chapter 3

"Elaine, back at the church," Johnnie Mae began, "you were telling me about your family and how you were feeling bad about some things that had happened in your life."

"Yeah. And you probably think I'm a real jerk or something now."

"No. No, really I don't. We just didn't get to finish the conversation, and there appeared to be more you wanted to tell me."

Memory looked at her and frowned. "Yeah. There was more. It's just, now I don't know if I feel so great about telling you like I did earlier."

Johnnie Mae pursed her lips, then nodded one time. "And why is that?"

Memory looked around the rather large area. The kitchen and the den were like one big room since nothing divided the two except for their identifying furnishings. In the den was a fireplace, sectional sofa, and glass-top tables (one with tropical fish swimming inside of it), while the kitchen featured a work island, glass-top table, cushioned bench and chairs alongside normal kitchen appliances like the double oven, steel stove, and refrigerator. A sixty-inch, flat-screen television was mounted on the wall in the den that could easily be viewed from practically anywhere a person might happen to be in either of the two areas.

"Look at all this," Memory said. "You invited me to come and stay in your home. What if something I tell you causes you to believe I'm some horrible person you can't trust? What then?"

"So you're considering my offer to stay a while?"

"Let's just say I'm thinking about at least staying the night. But what if I were to tell you the rest of my story and you decide you want me out of here? Then what do I do?"

"Is that what you think? Is what you've done that awful?"

Memory shrugged. "I took something from my own family when they trusted me to do the right thing. What's to keep you from believing I wouldn't do something like that to you, too?"

"Elaine, please. Whatever it is you wanted to tell me earlier, I'd really like to hear it now. You need to trust someone other than yourself."

Memory stood up and began to walk around the room. "Yeah . . . right." She stopped in front of a painted portrait that hung over the fireplace. She nodded her approval. "Nice painting of you."

Johnnie Mae glanced at it. "Thanks. Pastor Landris painted that some years ago."

"He's a talented man, I see."

"Yes, he is," Johnnie Mae said. "But you're avoiding the subject. Elaine, there are things I need to talk with you about, but first—I need you to come totally clean with me."

Memory turned around and looked in Johnnie Mae's eyes. She released a half grin before walking back and sitting down on the sofa.

"You know, don't you?"

"Know what?"

"Who I am," Memory said.

"And who might that be?" Johnnie Mae asked.

Memory released another sigh as she shook her head. "Look, I'm tired of running. I'm tired of all the deceit and lies. My name is Memory." She looked at Johnnie Mae and started to chuckle. "Just what I thought. You're not the least bit surprised hearing that."

"No."

"So who told you, and how much time do I have before they show up to take me away?"

"Memory, I don't know who you're talking about is coming to take you away."

"Some private detective. He's been looking for me for years, although for the life of me I can't understand why he's still following me. He's definitely relentless. So what was it? Did Arletha Brown call and tell you, and you decided to turn me in, or what?"

"Memory, I don't know an Arletha, and I've not spoken to any private detective."

Memory laughed and shook her head again. "And I'm supposed to believe that?"

"I'm telling you the truth. Listen, there's something I need to tell you. I've not been totally straight with you myself. I figured out who you were because of things you said to me earlier today during your counseling session."

"Things *I* said?" Memory asked, obviously confused.

"Yes. It's a bit complicated. In fact, if I wasn't so involved, I'm not sure I would believe it myself," Johnnie Mae said. She placed her hand on her stomach. Her baby had begun to move what felt to be a bent elbow across her stomach.

Memory's eyes followed Johnnie Mae's hand as she rubbed the georgette top that covered her stomach. She sat back against the sofa. "I'm all ears."

Johnnie Mae readjusted and sat forward. "The truth is, I've met your daughter, Lena Patterson, as well as your granddaughter, Theresa Jordan. It was back in 2001."

"Oh. So you just *happen* to know Lena and Theresa? From a church in Georgia?"

"Kind of. I don't know them that well, although we did travel together to Asheville, North Carolina, in October of that same year."

"Asheville, North Carolina—seems to be a popular town these days. In fact, that's the place the private detective throws around whenever he leaves a message for me." Memory reached down and picked up her glass of tea. She swirled the remaining amount around. "I'm sure you want me to believe you're not working with this man now. But what if you're merely stalling . . . trying to keep me here until he shows up?"

"Memory, trust me; if I was up to something like that, I sure wouldn't be having this conversation with you now. We could have continued on with our little charade, and no one would have been the wiser. But there's more to this story—so much more."

"Then say what you have to say and be done. I'm a big girl. I can handle it."

"It's not whether or not you can handle it. It's whether or not I should be the one telling it."

"Look, Johnnie Mae, I appreciate you for having listened to me earlier today. And I especially appreciate you for having opened up your home to me like you did. But realistically, if you know Lena and Theresa and you were hanging out with them back in October of 2001, then I'm sure you know they consider me a thief." Memory grabbed her purse and stood up. "So if you don't mind, I think I'll get my things and be on my way."

Johnnie Mae struggled to get up off the couch. "Memory, I do know about the Alexandrite necklace, but I can't let you leave yet."

"You can't keep me here against my will." Memory started out of the room. "I'm going up those stairs, getting my suitcases, and getting out of here while the getting is good."

"Memory, I'm not trying to keep you here. There's something I need to tell you."

Memory continued to walk hurriedly out of the room and toward the staircase.

Johnnie Mae walked as quickly as she could after her. "Memory, wait! There's something I need to tell you! It's important."

Memory trotted up the stairs. Johnnie Mae turned around and looked back in the other direction. Landris was downstairs in the game room. She knew she could make her way to the intercom to call him, but it would take a few minutes for him to get upstairs. As Johnnie Mae started to go back in the den, Memory appeared at the top of the stairs with two pieces of her luggage. She set them down, turned around, and went back, returning shortly with the other two.

"Memory, please don't try carrying those on your own. You might hurt yourself." Johnnie Mae started up the stairs.

"You're pregnant, Johnnie Mae." She started down the steps with one of the suitcases. "Don't do anything that might endanger you or your baby. Just let me pass, and I promise I'll leave your home peaceably. All I want is to get out of here—that's all. I'm not trying to cause you any trouble, and I would appreciate it if you'd extend me the same courtesy."

"Where are you trying to go? You don't even know where you are, so what are you planning to do if you leave here? Wander the streets?"

Memory struggled as she carried the heaviest piece of luggage down first. She huffed and puffed, her body wobbling with each step taken. "Is that why you brought me here? So I could become a prisoner in your home? Did you think I wouldn't be paying attention enough not to know where I was?" She now stood face to face with Johnnie Mae. "Please let me pass. I don't want you or your baby to get hurt, okay?"

"I'm not going to let you hurt either of us," Johnnie Mae said as she moved closer to the side of the wall to be sure she was totally out of Memory's way.

Memory reached the foyer, set the suitcase down near the door, and hurried back up the stairs to get another one. "In case you want to know," she said, lifting up the second suitcase, "I do know the address here. You don't honestly believe I've been doing this for this long and don't know how to take care of myself any better than that, now, do you?" She set it down. "I know what street we're on, and, yes, I noted the house's address when you drove in." Back up the stairs, she picked up the last two suitcases and took them down.

"Memory, please stop. If you'll just allow me to finish what I'm trying to tell you, this will all make sense. After I finish, if you still want to leave, I'll drive you wherever you're trying to go myself. I promise."

Memory laughed as she once again walked past Johnnie Mae, who had now made her way to the marbled-floor foyer and was standing next to Memory's other two suitcases. "Yeah, I just bet you will."

"Why won't you trust anyone?" Johnnie Mae asked.

Memory set the two suitcases down, twisted her pocketbook from being pushed to her back, straightened up, then shoved her fists into her sides and said, "Because people somehow always manage to let me down, that's why."

Johnnie Mae reached out to touch her hand. "Please, I'm begging you. Give me five minutes and let me tell you what's really going on. Five minutes. Can we please

go back in the den and talk?" Johnnie Mae began pressing her hand against her stomach.

"You in pain?" Memory asked.

"No, just feeling a bit uncomfortable at the moment.
But I *really* do need to sit down. I'm certain this will
pass, but it's important that I tell you something."
Johnnie Mae became tired . . . out of breath almost, as
she spoke.

Outside, a horn honked twice.

"That's my ride," Memory said as she turned and
opened the door. "They got here a lot faster than I
thought they would. I guess they must have had one already in the vicinity." A yellow taxi sat in the circular
driveway. She beckoned for the driver to come up and
help her as she pulled two of the suitcases outside
using their rollers.

Johnnie Mae didn't know what to do at this point. She
looked around as though she was searching for something to stop Memory. Spinning back toward Memory,
she quickly blurted out, "Mamie Patterson wasn't your
real mother!"

Memory stopped, turned around slowly, and began
to frown at Johnnie Mae. "What did you just say?"

Johnnie Mae let out a sigh. "Mamie Patterson wasn't
your biological mother," she said in a much calmer
tone.

The taxi driver took the suitcases and headed for his
cab.

"Sir, wait!" Memory called out to him. "Give me a
minute, please." She then looked hard into Johnnie Mae's
now-pleading eyes. "Okay," Memory said to Johnnie
Mae. "Start talking."

Chapter 4

*Rise up, ye women that are at ease;
hear My voice, ye careless daughters;
give ear unto My speech.*

Isaiah 32:9

"Well? Does the cat have your tongue?" Memory asked as she patted her foot. "If you have something you want to say, then say it."

"Memory, I really need to sit down. Honestly, I'm not feeling so well."

"Maybe you should let Pastor Landris know so he can see about you," Memory said, clutching her purse strap. "Look, the meter's running. Tell you what. See ya."

Johnnie Mae stood straighter. "Mamie Patterson is the woman you grew up believing was your mother. She wasn't. There's more to this story, but I can't tell it standing here like this. I really need to sit down. Why don't you come inside, and we can go to the den and talk about this in private?"

Memory turned to the taxi driver and told him she wouldn't need him after all. He set the luggage back in the foyer. She paid him what she owed and came back inside.

Johnnie Mae contemplated, as she closed the door, whether she *should* go get Landris to come and help her tell Memory. Things were not going as she'd hoped at all.

Memory walked toward the den. "You want to come

on so you can start explaining this nonsense you're spouting off about Mamie not being my real mother?"

"Sure," Johnnie Mae said, catching up. "Would you
care for some more tea first?"

"From what you're alleging, I'm not sure tea will be
strong enough." Memory walked in and sat down. She
held up her glass for Johnnie Mae to refill.

Johnnie Mae went to the kitchen and put crushed ice
in both her and Memory's empty glasses. She then pulled
two cans out of the refrigerator and went back into the
den area. "Here you go," she said, handing Memory
her glass of ice and one of the cans.

"What's this?" Memory asked, looking at the yellow
can with maroon letters.

"You said you may need something stronger. That's
Buffalo Rock. It's a type of ginger ale, great for reliev-
ing stomach ailments and motion sickness. Personally,
I enjoy its stronger-than-normal ginger taste. You have
to be careful though; it really is strong."

"So you believe I'm going to need something for
motion sickness, huh? You suspecting it might get a bit
turbulent around here?" Memory popped the tin on the
cap, then poured the dark-colored liquid into her glass.
She took a huge swallow in spite of Johnnie Mae's previous warning. "Whoa!" she said, shaking her head a
few times. "Oh, this ought to do the trick. It has a kick
to it, that's for sure!" She only sipped it this time.

Johnnie Mae rubbed her stomach as she poured the
can of Buffalo Rock ginger ale into her glass. Taking
only a sip, she shook her head as though she too was
attempting to dislodge something inside of it. "Is it
okay if I call you Memory?"

"It hasn't stopped you so far. Memory . . . Elaine . . .
Whatever suits you is fine with me. I'd just like for you
to get on with it, though. Time's a-ticking." Memory
pointed at the digital clock on the mantel.

Johnnie Mae took another sip before setting her glass down. "I'd rather this had been handled a different way. Let me begin by admitting that I don't know everything—"

"Just tell me what you *do* know," Memory said with a bit of agitation in her voice.

Johnnie Mae looked seriously at her. "It all started when I met this elderly woman in a nursing home back in 2000. She was living in Selma, Alabama, at the time, but she told me she had originated from Asheville, North Carolina."

"That's where I grew up."

"Yes." Johnnie Mae nodded as she rocked a little. "I know. Anyway, this woman ended up telling me a tale about how her family had been hiding her away for decades, which was why she happened to be in Alabama. She then asked for my help."

"And let me guess. She told you she would tell you something important if you would only agree to help her escape that place?"

"Not exactly. She told me about a baby . . . her baby. How she believed her baby hadn't died as she'd been told when the baby was born. It seems a few villainous members of her family were trying to make her out to be crazy, when, clearly, she was not." Johnnie Mae leaned forward. "Memory, the woman's name was Sarah Fleming."

"I don't know anybody by the name of Sarah Fleming. In fact, I don't know anyone with the last name of Fleming at all."

"Sarah Fleming had a friend named Mamie Patterson."

"My mother. So she knew Mamie. So what? This Sarah woman knew my mother, and now she's trying to say my mother wasn't really my mother just so she can break out of some nursing home. And you fell for *that*?"

"Memory, Sarah Fleming really is your mother."

Memory's body began to shake as she started to laugh. "Yeah, okay. Mamie Patterson, who happened to have had twins, mind you—me and my brother—was not really my mother because some woman you met in an old folks' home, crazy, but not really crazy according to her own diagnosis, says so." Memory stood up. "Okay. I've given you more than five minutes here. You've said your piece. I heard you out. Now, if you don't mind, I'd like for you or Pastor Landris to take me to the nearest bus station so I can get out of here before I end up going crazy." She turned and started walking away.

"Memory, that Alexandrite necklace you took from Lena and Theresa. The one that was in the safe-deposit box at the bank—"

Memory stopped, spun around slowly, and stared at Johnnie Mae. She grinned. "Okay. So now we're finally getting to the real reason that I'm here. There's no Sarah Fleming. That's just something you made up to get me confused and disoriented while you try to find out what happened to that necklace." Feeling a little lightheaded, Memory sat down and began to rub her head. "All right. Let's just do this and get it over with."

"Memory, I'm only bringing up the necklace because I want you to see that it's tied to the truth about your biological mother."

"Right. And that would be Sarah Fleming."

"Please, just listen. The necklace was in a box . . . a box with wings etched on it. In fact, the woman who brought it to Mamie . . . when you were younger, the box that housed the contents you believed belonged to you, that was Sarah's mother—Grace."

"Man, that private detective is good! So, what else did he tell you?"

"Memory, I haven't spoken with a private detective. Your mother, Sarah Fleming, has been looking for you since she first learned for sure you were still alive in 2001."

"Yeah? Let's see. I'm almost seventy, and that would make her about . . . how old now?"

"I believe she turns ninety this year."

"And this woman, this Sarah Fleming, who claims to be my mother, is still living?"

"Yes. In fact, I spoke with her a little while ago. She really wants to meet you."

Memory stood up and walked around. "Sarah Fleming, you say, who is actually my mother, a mother I didn't even know existed, wants to meet me?"

"I know this is hard, and it's a lot to spring on you. Believe me, I really didn't want to do it this way." Johnnie Mae readjusted her body so it would be easier for her to keep up with Memory's wanderings.

"And how exactly were you planning on telling me all of this if you hadn't been forced to do it this way?"

Johnnie Mae relaxed a bit more. "Honestly, I wasn't sure. I wish I could have just taken you to Asheville and let Sarah and Lena tell you everything."

She stopped walking. "Lena knows?"

"Yes."

"And she's met this Sarah Fleming woman? What am I asking? Of course she's met her."

"We all went to Asheville together. That's another story, but, yes, Lena and Theresa both have met Sarah. In fact, had you been there that day, it would have been five generations together in one place, along with your great-granddaughter."

Memory came and sat down. "My great-grand-daughter." She smiled as she rubbed her sagging face with her hand. "And this Sarah lady is back in Asheville now? Not Selma?"

"Yes. She's back in Asheville."

"And you say you talked with her today?"

Johnnie Mae sat back against the sofa. "I called her this evening to let her know that I suspected you might be her daughter. I needed to know what she wanted me to do in case my suspicions turned out to be correct."

Memory nodded. "Is she in a nursing home in Asheville?"

"No. She lives in her own house there. I've not seen her since 2001, but she's a remarkable woman, Memory." Johnnie Mae smiled as she tilted her head. "The two of you have the same gray eyes." Johnnie Mae took a swallow of ginger ale. "I told her I'd bring you to see her tomorrow. We can drive up. It's about a six-hour trip from here."

Memory smiled. "And do I have any say-so about whether I meet her or not?"

"I'm sorry. Forgive me. Of course you do. You're not a prisoner here. We're not trying to keep you in order to turn you over to anybody. I would think, though, after learning this news, you'd want to meet the woman who gave birth to you. She certainly has been praying and waiting a long time to meet you."

Memory took a swig of drink directly from the can this time. "Almost seventy years, according to my calculations. Well, I'll have to think about this. Obviously, she's had more time to get used to the idea than I have. But you say I'm not a prisoner here? And I can leave if I want to? So if I get up and walk out right now . . ."

"I'll not physically try and stop you. I only thought it fair that you know the truth. If you decide to leave or that you don't want to meet your biological mother, that's your choice. I just can't imagine you not wanting to at least meet her," Johnnie Mae said.

"What if I'd prefer calling her first? Talk to her over the phone before we meet?"

"That would be great! I can give you her phone number."

"I think I'd like to have it, if you don't mind. I'm not sure I'll call her, but if you would give me her phone number, I would appreciate it."

Johnnie Mae nodded. "It's upstairs." She stood up. "I'll get it for you."

Johnnie Mae went and retrieved the number. She wrote it down, came back, and handed it to Memory. "I do wish you would call her. I know she'd love hearing your voice. You can talk to her tonight, and tomorrow, if you want, we can go up there so the two of you can meet. I realize I can't force you to call or to meet her. But Memory, she's an old woman and as sweet as she can be. She doesn't have a lot of time left on this earth. I would think you'd want to spend as much of that time with her as possible, now that you know the truth. I know there's so much more about all of this she can tell you."

Memory took the number. "Yeah. There's a lot I still don't know or understand. I think I'd like to call her now. Is it possible for me to have some time here alone?"

Johnnie Mae touched her hand. "Of course. I'll go down and see what Landris and Princess Rose are up to. What do you think? Twenty . . . thirty minutes?"

"Twenty's enough. I don't mean to put you out. And I'm still not sure what I'm going to do. If I call her, what do I say? But I do think calling is what I should do first."

"It's no problem. And you're not putting me out. The phone's right there." Johnnie Mae pointed at the cordless phone. "Sarah will be ecstatic to hear from you." Johnnie Mae smiled, then left Memory in the room alone.

Memory looked at the number, picked up the phone, dialed, then quickly hung up before it could connect. Opening her purse, she put the paper with the number inside of it. After a few minutes, she opened up her purse again, took out the paper, stared at the number, dialed, then waited—practically holding her breath—as the phone began to ring.

Chapter 5

*For Jacob My servant's sake, and Is-
rael Mine elect, I have even called thee
by thy name: I have surnamed thee,
though thou hast not known Me.*

Isaiah 45:4

Johnnie Mae went downstairs to the game room. Landris rushed over to her as soon as she walked in. "How did it go?" he asked.

"I'm giving her some time to process what I've just told her. I think she's going to give Sarah a call."

"Daddy Landris, are you gonna play or what?" Princess Rose asked as she placed the hockey puck on the table and stood in position to slam it to her step-father's side.

"Honey, why don't you go and play the arcade machine while Daddy Landris and I talk for a little while?"

"Okay, I'll go play Ms. Pac-Man or something," Princess Rose said, shaking her head. She dragged over to the arcade machine, climbed up on the bar stool, and pressed the button to start the game. As the familiar music blasted, Princess Rose began moving the joystick.

Landris and Johnnie Mae went and sat down at the table that also doubled as a checker- and chessboard.

"So, what happened?" Landris asked, leaning in close.

"She admitted she's Memory. She thought I was working with a private investigator. At first, she didn't believe me when I told her I wasn't, nor was I trying to trap her," Johnnie Mae said.

"She didn't believe you were being on the up-and-up with her?"

"Not at first. I think she believes me now. I told her a little about Sarah, and we touched momentarily on the Alexandrite necklace."

Landris retrieved the checkers from inside the drawer of the table and placed them on the surface. "Did she happen to mention what became of the necklace?"

"No," Johnnie Mae said, pulling out all the black checkers and lining them up on her side of the board.

"Did you even ask her?"

"No."

Landris stopped and looked at her. "No?"

She widened her eyes and smiled. "No."

He looked at the checkers on her side. "Why do you always get to have the black checkers first every time we play?"

"Who said we were playing?"

He pointed at her side. "You have your checkers lined up like we are."

Johnnie Mae leaned in. "I was busying my hands. Is that all right with you?"

Landris set up the red checkers on his side. "Fine. I was merely asking." After his checkers were in place, he signaled for her to make the first move. "And why are we all down here instead of up there with Memory right now?"

"I'm giving her time to think about what she wants to do, and hopefully to call Sarah. I told her I'd be about twenty minutes, in case she did decide to call and verify what I've told her so far."

"And you told her that Sarah was her real mother?"

"I had to." Johnnie Mae moved another checker piece after Landris moved. "She was trying to leave, so I had to do something fast. She had a taxi here and had managed to drag her luggage down the stairs."

"She lugged those bags down the stairs by herself?" Landris jumped her checker and removed it off the board. "She's pretty tough for an older woman."

"Yeah. She had to make three trips to do it, unlike you, with your strong muscles, who was able to take the four pieces up in two. I started to come and get you, but I didn't want to chance her leaving before I was able to tell her about Sarah. I told her enough to get her attention. She knows Mamie wasn't her biological mother and that Sarah is. She's aware that we know all about the Alexandrite necklace. I figure when she arrives in Asheville, Sarah will fill her in on whatever else she needs or may want to know." Johnnie Mae triple jumped his checkers and removed them.

"You've been down here for about twenty minutes now. Don't you want to go back up and check on her?"

"I don't want her to think we don't trust her," Johnnie Mae said. "Let's give her another five to ten more minutes."

Landris made a double jump. "Crown me," he said with a grin.

Johnnie Mae added a checker on top of the checker that was now in the king spot. She glanced at the Wurlitzer jukebox. Landris noticed she was looking at it. He stood, pulled her up next to him, and with his arms wrapped around her, walked her over to it. Locating the song he was searching for, he pressed the corresponding buttons.

"Unwritten," a song by Natasha Bedingfield, began to play. Princess Rose immediately stopped what she was doing and hopped down off the black swerving bar stool. She began singing the words to the song—a song that was definitely a hit in their house. The entire family loved it. Landris began to twirl both mother and daughter around ever so gently during certain parts of the song. He started "Walking the Floor" with Johnnie Mae, a dance that could be crowned the black waltz. Princess Rose continued to sing her heart out.

When the song ended, all three of them laughed, clapped, and cheered.

Princess Rose jumped up and down. "Play it again, Daddy Landris! Play it again! That's my song!" She began to sing "I am unwritten" without the music, then said, "I love that song! Oh, please, play it again!"

Johnnie Mae smiled, leaned down, and kissed her daughter on the top of her head. "Another time, sweetheart. We have company upstairs. We don't want to be rude and leave her alone too long, now, do we?"

Princess Rose lifted her head high and opened her arms in a dramatic fashion. "Then let's invite Ms. Elaine down here so she can have some fun with the song, too!"

"It's suppertime. Maybe Ms. Elaine will come down afterward and enjoy the song with us. We'll see how things go." Johnnie Mae tapped Princess Rose on her nose and then planted a kiss on it. "All right, let's go." She pointed toward the stairs. "March."

Princess Rose began to step hard in a military-type fashion as instructed, Johnnie Mae followed her, and Landris pulled up the rear.

When they reached the top of the stairs, Johnnie Mae noticed how quiet it was. There was no sign of Memory in the den.

"Where is she?" Princess Rose asked. "Ms. Elaine!" Princess Rose yelled. "Ms. Elaine!"

"Princess Rose, don't yell like that. She's probably upstairs. She may be on the phone up there."

"You want me to run upstairs and get her?" Princess Rose asked, purposely swinging her two plaits from side to side.

"No. You and Daddy Landris go wash up and set the table. I'll go check on her."

Landris reached out and caught Johnnie Mae's hand before she could walk away. He gave her a quick kiss on her cheek.

Johnnie Mae smiled, then continued on. When she reached the bedroom where Memory was staying, she knocked on the closed door. No answer. She knocked again. Still no answer. "Memory . . . ?" Johnnie Mae said, knocking louder. "Are you okay?"

Nothing but silence answered her. She opened the door slowly. Still no sign of Memory. Walking over to the bathroom door, she knocked on it. "Memory? Are you in there?" She wasn't in there, either. Johnnie Mae quickly made her way back downstairs.

"We set the table in the nook area so it would feel a little cozier," Landris said. He stopped and looked at Johnnie Mae. "What's wrong? Is everything all right?"

"She's gone."

"Gone?"

"Yes. Gone. The bedroom's empty. She's not upstairs."

"Maybe she just stepped outside for some fresh air," Landris said.

Johnnie Mae thought for a second, then hurriedly walked back into the foyer. Landris followed her. "Why didn't I see that before?" she said. "Her suitcases are gone. They were right by the door. They're not upstairs. She's gone, Landris." She sighed hard.

"Before you get upset, let's see whether she left a note or something."

Searching in the den where Memory was last, neither one of them found a thing.

"I don't believe this," Johnnie Mae said, disappointed. "How could she just leave like that without saying a word? What am I going to tell Sarah now?" Johnnie Mae shook her head as she started walking out of the den area.

Landris grabbed her by her shoulders. "Johnnie Mae, it's not your responsibility. Sarah hired the best people out there to find her, and look—you came closer to getting her to Sarah than any of them have been able to do so far. You did your best. Now, don't go beating yourself up about it. She may contact us later or just come back on her own."

Johnnie Mae shook her head again emphatically. "She's not coming back." She pulled away from his grasp and continued out of the room.

"What are you going to do?" Landris asked.

"Call Sarah and let her know Memory's gone. I'm sure this is going to devastate her. We were so close, and I allowed her to slip through my fingers."

Johnnie Mae walked up the stairs to her room to get Sarah's number. She sat on her bed then dialed the number.

"Sarah, this is Johnnie Mae. Yes, I know you're excited about the possibility of finding Memory. Well, I did find her. Memory was here at my house when I spoke with you earlier. But something happened since then. I'm sorry, Sarah. I told her the truth about you, but she must not have believed me, because she left. I am *so* sorry, Sarah. So very, very sorry. We were so close, and it looks like I ended up letting her get away."

Chapter 6

L ena was at Sarah's house. She and her husband, Richard, had gotten in their car and driven up to Asheville almost immediately following Sarah's call late that evening.

"I believe Johnnie Mae's found Memory," Sarah had said to Lena over the phone after she hung up with Johnnie Mae. "She was talking hypothetically, but I know better. If it turns out it's her," Sarah said, "Johnnie Mae's going to bring her to me tomorrow."

If this ended up being the case, Lena didn't want Memory arriving at Sarah's without someone present who truly knew Memory. So she and Richard had quickly thrown a few things in a single suitcase and made the four-hour drive in record time from Atlanta to Asheville, arriving a little after eleven o'clock that night. That was when Lena learned Johnnie Mae had called back and confirmed it was, indeed, Memory.

Lying in bed, dabbing her eyes as tears rolled out, it was evident Sarah was tired. Almost ninety years old, her body seemed determined to remind her of that. "There's a problem though," Sarah said, her chest slowly rising, her breathing noisily shallow.

"What?" Lena asked. "Memory's insisting on flying first-class instead of coach?"

"No. When Johnnie Mae called back, she called to say Memory's gone."

"What? Gone? You mean she left to come up here without Johnnie Mae?"

"No. It appears she left because she didn't want to come here at all." Sarah relaxed more into the pillows stacked behind her.

"I don't understand. Didn't Johnnie Mae tell Memory about you?"

Sarah took a deep breath and released it. It was almost becoming work for her to breathe these days. "She told her." Sarah closed her eyes for a second, then opened them and forced a smile. "She told her pretty much everything. That I was her mother, that you and Theresa met me." Sarah then told her everything that Johnnie Mae had relayed to her.

"So, what was it? She didn't believe Johnnie Mae? Did Johnnie Mae not tell her that you're not well?"

"Johnnie Mae doesn't know the status of my health." She smiled, this time genuinely. "I'm old, Lena. When you get to be my age, things start to break down and wear out. This heart"—she patted her chest softly—"has ticked quite a few beats during its time. Yes, I'm a little worn for wear, but I'm still here. Still trusting and believing God."

"I'm sorry. I know how much seeing Memory means to you."

Sarah motioned for the glass of water on the nightstand. She took a sip and handed it back to Lena. "And I am not oblivious to how you feel. You've made yourself more than clear regarding your thoughts about Memory, my dear. But she's still my child. My flesh . . . and . . . blood." Sarah closed her eyes and became eerily silent.

Lena looked down at the elderly woman, her hair completely gray and willowy. She looked so peaceful lying there. Lena could see her chest rising and falling under the blinding white duvet cover. She leaned down and kissed her grandmother on the forehead. Stepping out of the room, she closed the door gently behind her and slowly walked down the stairs to the parlor.

"Is she asleep?" Gayle asked. A slim woman in her early forties with caramel brown skin, Gayle was the nursemaid the family had hired to stay with Sarah. Faithful to Sarah and the family, she'd been a true blessing for the past three and a half years. Gayle didn't look at what she did as a job; it was more of a calling— her ministry.

"Yes," Lena said. "She's asleep. She told me what happened with Memory."

Gayle began to nod her head. "Well, it's good she finally went to sleep," she said. "She was so excited when she thought at long last she was going to get to meet her daughter. She'd picked out what she was going to wear, even down to the jewelry. It appeared for certain it would happen this time. I hate it's turned out the way it has."

"What happened with Memory?" Richard asked, looking over at Lena. "Did that person end up not being Memory after all?"

High school sweethearts, now a cute elderly couple, Richard Jordan and Lena Patterson had married June 22, 2002, as part of a double-wedding ceremony. Their daughter, Theresa, and Maurice Greene had been the other couple who took their vows alongside them. That had definitely been a special day. Lena and Theresa had been the most beautiful brides, and the grooms hadn't been too shabby, either. They married in the church where Bishop Jordan had retired as the pastor years earlier.

"No, turns out it was Memory, all right," Lena said.

"But she did what she's famous for doing—left without letting anyone know she was going or without bothering to say good-bye." Lena was trying, albeit unsuccessfully, not to sound too bitter.

"I'll go check on Miss Fleming while you two talk. Do you need anything before I go?" Gayle asked. At five feet eleven, she towered over Lena, even wearing her signature flat, fuchsia tennis-like shoes.

"We're fine. Thanks, though," Lena said.

"You know where everything is. If I don't see you before you turn in, have a good night."

"Thanks, Gayle. We probably will turn in," Lena said as she yawned. "We're not as young as we used to be. That drive seems to drain Richard and me every time."

"Speak for yourself, Lena girl. I'm ready to go dancing if you want to," Richard said.

Lena fanned her hand at him. "Don't start nothing, Richard." She then turned back to Gayle. "How do you think my grandmother is holding up through all of this?"

"I think she's doing okay. I will admit, though, she was almost a different person when she got that call today. She even called Minnie, the housekeeper, to come back and give the house a once-over again to ensure everything was perfect, just in case company did show up tomorrow. I sure hate she had the rug yanked out from under her yet again."

Lena smiled and nodded without speaking another word. After Gayle left, she turned to Richard. "You ready to go upstairs and turn in?"

"Truthfully, just thinking of those stairs tires me out. I'm almost considering staying down here and sleeping on this fine pink and white couch."

"We could stay in the bedroom down here if you'd prefer. It's not as large as the one we usually stay in upstairs, but if you really don't feel like going up, I can bring some of our things back down here," Lena said.

"You'll do no such of a thing. I'll make it all right. I still have some fire left inside of me."

Lena rubbed his bald head. "Yeah," she said with a smile. "I know."

He stood. "Let's get going." He held out his arm. "Madam, may I have this dance?"

Lena laughed and took his arm. "So now we're going to dance?"

"Yeah," he said. He started walking with her holding onto his arm. "I think they call this the two-step. One-two," he said as he shuffled his feet forward. "One-two."

Lena shook her head. "You're too much."

"And while we're on our way up, you might want to tell me what you're really thinking about Memory."

"Honestly, except for breaking Grandmother's heart, I can't say I'm surprised or sorry she disappeared. I know I'm supposed to forgive her, but, Richard, I don't know if I can. You know the kind of money and wealth Grandmother possesses. I don't know what Memory will do when she finds out about that."

"So Johnnie Mae didn't tell her that part?"

"No. According to Grandmother, Johnnie Mae didn't tell her she was well-off. She only told her that Sarah Fleming was her mother. And you see what she did after she learned that much. Memory—the same old mother I've grown to know."

"I don't know, Lena girl. I just have a feeling, down deep in my bones, something's about to happen around this place. I'm just glad you're here to see about Sarah."

Lena stopped when they reached the top of the stairs and looked directly at him. "And I'm just glad you're here with me to love on me the way you always do."

Richard smiled as he caressed the left side of her face. "Lena girl, there's no other place I'd want to be *except* wherever you are. No other place."

Chapter 7

*Remember ye not the former things,
neither consider the things of old.*

Isaiah 43:18

Lena was up early. She had helped Sarah get ready.
Sarah still liked to dress nicely even if she was only
planning to sit around the house all day. The past few
days, Lena had been thinking of things she could do to
possibly cheer Sarah up and keep her mind off Memory as much as possible. The Saturday started off a
beautiful sunny one.

Richard had gone early to play golf with a group of
men he'd formed a friendship with from earlier visits
to Asheville. They preferred hitting the golf course in
the early morning hours, especially during the summer
months, when midday could be rather hot. All of the
men were in their late fifties and early sixties. Lena and
Sarah were sitting out on the terrace about to eat breakfast when the doorbell rang.

"Will you get that, Lena?" Sarah asked. "It's probably my friend Polly checking up on me. Like clock-
work, she stops by early every Saturday morning."

Polly Swindle was a woman in her mid-fifties Sarah
had met at church when she came back to Asheville to
live. Polly made it a point to stop by frequently. And
when she didn't come, she'd call to check on her friend.
Sarah had left Polly a message telling her she didn't

have to worry about her this week since Lena and Richard were there. Sarah figured either Polly didn't get the message or she just wanted to come by anyway.

Lena hurried to the door. She saw a woman with her back to the door. Lena, smiling, opened the door. The woman faced her; Lena's smile dropped. "*You,*" she said.

"Lena?" the woman said, her head held high. "You look wonderful. I mean, look at you. You got your face fixed and everything!" She smiled as she shook her head. "My, my, no one would ever be able to tell you were once badly scarred in a fire."

Lena's voice was soft as she tried to control her emotions. "What are you doing here? Why don't you just leave now and save everybody a lot of heartache later?"

"Now, why on earth would I want to do a thing like that? I've come to see Sarah Fleming." She turned and beckoned for the cab driver before continuing. "Would you be so kind as to let Sarah know I'm here?" Her voice was soft and nonthreatening.

"Lena, who's that at the door?" Sarah called out as she slowly shuffled into the foyer toward the entranceway. "Polly, dearest, is that you? Your timing is impeccable."

Lena turned around to Sarah as she tried to keep the person at the door out of Sarah's vision. "No, it's not Polly. Why don't you go back out on the terrace?"

"Well, if it's not Polly, then who is it?" Sarah asked as she continued to get closer, attempting to get a better look at the visitor standing in the doorway.

The woman stepped inside the house, politely pushing her way past Lena.

Sarah, now almost face to face with the stranger, stopped and looked at her. "Oh, I'm sorry. I thought you were some—" She began to look closer. "Do I know you?"

"Sarah Fleming?" The woman extended her hand. "My name is Memory."

Sarah placed both hands on her heart. "Memory?" she said. She appeared to be struggling for her next breath. "*My* Memory?" She reached out to her. "Is it really you?" Just then, her right hand clutched her chest as her body crumpled to the floor.

Chapter 8

In those days was Hezekiah sick unto death. And Isaiah the prophet the son of Amoz came unto him, and said unto him, Thus saith the Lord, Set thine house in order: for thou shalt die, and not live.

Isaiah 38:1

Johnnie Mae sat in the window seat in the kitchen nook enjoying the sun early Saturday morning. She was deep in thought. In just two more weeks, she would be entering her seventh month of pregnancy. Her mother was still holding her own, although lately it appeared she was having more bad days than good ones. It was June 4th, four days since Memory had disappeared without a word. Johnnie Mae felt awful having been so close to reuniting Sarah with Memory, only to have it blow away in what amounted to mere minutes.

Sarah had insisted when she and Johnnie Mae spoke four days ago that Johnnie Mae not beat herself up about it. "It wasn't your responsibility, and it's not truly your problem," Sarah had said. "If it's for me and my daughter to meet, it will happen. In God's good time, I have to believe, it will happen. You told her, and either she didn't believe you or she didn't care. Either way, it's not on you. And I don't want you to feel bad about it, do you hear me?"

But Johnnie Mae couldn't help but feel bad. Maybe she hadn't gone far enough with the truth. Maybe she hadn't been convincing enough. Maybe she shouldn't have let

Memory out of her sight until she'd personally delivered her to Sarah's door.

The phone rang, causing Johnnie Mae to jump. She got up and looked at the caller ID. The number was unfamiliar to her.

"Hello?"

"Yes. I'm sorry to bother you so early on a Saturday morning like this, but is Pastor Landris available, please?" The older woman's voice shook as she spoke.

"Hold on, let me check," Johnnie Mae said as pleasantly as she could muster. She wasn't sure if Landris was awake yet or not. She pressed the button to place the line on hold and walked up the stairs to their bedroom.

"Landris?" she said when she walked inside and didn't find him still in bed.

He stuck his head out of the bathroom. "Morning, baby."

"Good morning. The phone's for you. Line one."

"Do you know who it is?" he asked as he walked out of the master bath.

"No. I wasn't sure if you were up yet, so I didn't ask. She's been holding a few minutes." That was his cue to not keep the person waiting any longer than necessary.

Landris walked over to the phone on the nightstand and pressed the button. Johnnie Mae left and headed back downstairs. Now that she knew Landris was awake, she decided to fix him some pancakes and fresh fruit for breakfast. He still liked his cup of coffee every morning, even on weekends, so she started a fresh pot of coffee. She wasn't a big coffee drinker before she got pregnant. Now that she was, she had cut down on her caffeine intake of all kinds to as little as possible.

Landris came into the kitchen just as she was finishing up. He walked up behind her, wrapped his arms around her, and kissed her twice on the cheek. "You didn't have to fix me breakfast this morning," he said.

Johnnie Mae handed him his plate. "Oh, but I enjoy doing things for you," she said. "So, who was that calling so early, if you don't mind me asking?"

Landris bit down on his bottom lip as he went and sat at the table. "That was Reverend Knight's wife. He had asked her to call me. But she was also calling to tell me that the doctors weren't giving him much time left. In fact, they're not expecting him to make it through the day. She didn't want him hearing what the doctors were saying, so she called me from her cell phone."

"Are you going over there now?"

"Yeah. I wanted to get there as soon as possible. But first I'm going to eat this wonderful breakfast"—he waved his hand over his plate—"you so lovingly made me."

She set a cup of coffee down next to him and brushed his dreadlocks with her hand a few times. "You don't have to eat this, if you want to go on over to the hospital now. It's okay. I know how close you've grown to Reverend Knight over this year."

"Yeah." He bowed his head and prayed, then looked back up and started eating some pineapples. "I still need to eat. Who knows how long I'll be, once I get there?"

"Do you want me to come with you?" She sat down across from him.

He took a bite of pancake. "No. I know you're still trying to get over what happened with Memory. Besides, didn't you say your blood pressure was up when you went to the doctor on Thursday, and that your hands and feet were swelling yesterday?"

"Yes. But right now I feel fine."

"Well, I don't want you overdoing it. I don't want to take any chances with you or our baby. So you just rest like Dr. Baker told you. And please quit worrying about Sarah and Memory. I know you, Johnnie Mae. But this battle is not yours; it's the Lord's."

She sighed. "I'm not worrying. I just feel bad about how things turned out."

"Then you need to quit feeling bad. Do you understand me?"

"I know. But we were so close there, and then—"

He took his fork, speared a piece of fresh strawberry, and held it up to Johnnie Mae's mouth—effectively halting her from saying another word as he put the fruit into her mouth. "And then it didn't happen," he said. "So don't worry yourself about what you can't change. You did your best. In fact, you did more than most folks I know would have even attempted to do. You brought Memory to our home. You were going to let her stay here." He shoved some more pancake into his mouth and gulped down his coffee.

"I know, Landris. It's just hard when you come as close as we did and you end up letting it slip through your fingers. But you're right—I can't change what's already passed. We'll just have to keep praying and believing that God is working it all out."

Landris finished the last of his fruit and coffee. "Not *is* working—*has* worked it out. In the spirit realm, it's already done. We just have to walk it out down here. God's will will be done on earth as it already is in Heaven." He grabbed a paper napkin out of the holder on the table and briskly wiped his mouth. Standing up, he then kissed her with a quick peck on her lips. "Get some rest today, okay? If you're going to pray, then stop worrying about it. Just thank God that—"

"It's already done," Johnnie Mae said, finishing the familiar saying. She looked at him and smiled as he put the dirty dishes in the dishwasher. "Give Reverend Knight my love, and tell Mrs. Knight that if she needs anything to not hesitate to let me know."

"I'll tell her. But I'm telling you, I'm not going to let you overdo it. For now, your job is to take care of yourself and our baby." He put his hand on her stomach and grinned.

Landris hurried to Brookwood Hospital. He prayed for his friend as he drove, reflecting back to the first time they'd met in that old rundown building he was looking to lease or buy to begin his ministry in Birmingham. He hadn't been sure whether or not he could really trust Poppa Knight, as the older man preferred being called. But in time, they had become close. By then, Reverend Knight had been diagnosed with lung cancer. Reverend Knight managed to attend their first service in the new sanctuary of Followers of Jesus Faith Worship Center even though he was sicker than he was letting anyone know.

When Landris arrived at the Critical Intensive Care Unit, or CICU, Mrs. Knight greeted him at the entrance of Reverend Knight's room.

"Pastor Landris, thank you so much for coming so quickly," she whispered.

"Who's that?" Reverend Knight asked, his voice muffled by an oxygen mask.

Mrs. Knight nodded and smiled at Landris as she turned back toward her husband. "It's Pastor Landris. He's here to see you. I'll leave you two alone for a few minutes."

"How are you feeling this morning, Poppa Knight?" Landris asked as soon as he was next to the bed. Seeing his mouth covered, he wasn't actually expecting him to talk.

Reverend Knight took the oxygen mask off and tried hard to smile. "Hanging in here," he said, hardly able to speak as he held up his hand to show the IV tubes attached.

"I can't stay long. They're making an exception for

me to visit with you outside of normal visiting hours. But you know I had to come by this morning and see you," Landris said.

Reverend Knight closed his eyes and swallowed. "How long?" he whispered.

"Well, the nurses are pretty strict about these minutes," Landris said.

Reverend Knight opened his eyes wider and shook his head. "No. To live. Doc, the truth." Doc was what Reverend Knight called Landris from time to time.

Landris touched his hand. "Reverend—"

"Don't, Pastor Landris. Please don't. Don't do me like everyone else. Tell me—how long are they saying I have left?" His voice was barely a decent whisper.

Landris moved in a little closer. "Not very long. But you know man doesn't have the final say-so. You recall in the book of Isaiah?"

"Hezekiah," Reverend Knight said, nodding. "He was dying. Isaiah told him the Lord said for him to set his house in order because he was going to die and not live."

"Yes, Hezekiah. Only I was thinking more about the part where Hezekiah turned his face toward the wall and prayed unto the Lord. And God told Isaiah He had heard Hezekiah's prayer and had seen his tears."

"And God added fifteen more years to his life," Reverend Knight said, smiling.

Landris squeezed his hand. "Yeah—that part."

Reverend Knight struggled to speak. "I've already turned and prayed once. And God has given me more time than the doctors originally gave me. I've made my peace; I'm ready to go home to be with the Lord. I just wanted to see you and to thank you while I still could."

"Thank me for what?"

"For helping me to see the error of my ways and getting things straight with so many people before I leave this earthly tabernacle. The relationship I've had with my wife this past year"—he began to gasp for air—"has been such a blessing. I only regret I didn't change sooner so she and I could have experienced this much earlier. All that wonderful time lost because of my arrogance and pride." He touched Landris's hand. "Keep doing what you're doing, Doc. No matter what people say about you—no matter who may try to stop you." He wheezed. "You're making a tremendous difference for the Kingdom. I'm a living example of that."

"Reverend Knight, I feel your heart. Save your strength, okay?"

"Save my strength?" He grimaced. "For what? No, I have to encourage you to keep pressing toward the mark. Still, you need to watch your back and pray. Watch and pray." He closed his eyes. "Will you do one other thing for me?" He opened his eyes. "Will you check on my wife from time to time to ensure she's all right after I'm gone?"

"I'll do that. I promise."

Mrs. Knight came back into the room. Landris looked at her as she stood on the other side of her husband's bed.

Reverend Knight turned to her. "Joyce, I want Pastor Landris to preach my eulogy," he said.

She put her hand on his hand. "Paul, let's not talk about this right now—"

"If not now, then when? I want Pastor Landris to preach my funeral when I'm gone." He took hold of her hand. "Please." He looked at them both.

"Sure, Paul. If that's what you want. But what about Marshall?" she asked, referring to Reverend Marshall Walker. "He's always believed he would be the one who would preach your eulogy if you went before him."

"Call Marshall again for me and ask him one more time to come and see me," Reverend Knight said to her.

The nurse came in. "I'm sorry, but I'm going to have to ask you to leave now," she said, her attention directed at Landris. "We don't want Reverend Knight to overexert himself."

"Of course," Landris said. He turned to Reverend Knight. "I'll be back to see you later, okay?"

Reverend Knight nodded. "Thank you for coming."

Landris patted his hand. "Sure thing, Poppa Knight." He smiled. "Sure thing."

Reverend Knight closed his eyes as though he was trying to hold back tears. He nodded as the nurse placed his oxygen mask back on.

Landris went home.

Later that afternoon, the phone rang. Johnnie Mae answered it. She quickly made her way to the exercise room, where Landris was. "I just got a call," Johnnie Mae said, breathing hard.

"Mrs. Knight?" Landris asked as he continued pumping the bar with its round weights attached to each end into the air. "Has Poppa Knight taken a turn for the worse?"

"No, it wasn't about Poppa Knight. It was Lena Patterson."

"Lena?" He held the bar with the weights high and steady in the air.

"Yeah. She's still at Sarah's house. Memory showed up there this morning!"

Landris set the weights back on the bench holder and sat up. "Memory showed up at Sarah's house? But how? How did she know where to find her?"

"I'm not sure of all the details. But apparently the shock of finally seeing Memory was too much for Sarah. They put her to bed and had to bring her doctor in."

Landris grabbed his towel and wiped some of the

sweat off his muscled body. "Is she going to be all right?"

"They're not sure. But she is conscious. Lena wanted to know what we thought about Memory, since we spent time with her. She asked if I felt Memory could be trusted."

"What did you say?"

Johnnie Mae handed him his bottle of water. "That she seemed to be on the up-and-up with us as far as we could tell. Even her leaving the way she did—she never promised she'd stay or that she would go meet Sarah. I don't know, Landris. I told her she has to pray about it and go with how *she* feels she's being led."

The phone rang. Johnnie Mae jumped. "I'll get it," Landris said as he walked over to the phone on the wall. He spoke for a few minutes, then hung up. "That was Mrs. Knight. Reverend Knight just lapsed into a coma. I'm going to go over to the hospital to make sure she's okay."

"Yes, of course. Do you want me to come with you this time?"

He took her hands and looked at them. They were still swollen. "What I want is for you to go back up those stairs and get off your feet. I'm going to shower and change. I'll bring you and Princess Rose something for lunch when I come back." He kissed her and began walking with his arm around her expanded waist as they made their way up the stairs together.

Johnnie Mae leaned in closer to him. "You're soaking wet," she said.

"Yeah. It's called sweat. That's why I'm taking a shower." He hugged her tighter. "Oops. I guess that makes you wet now."

She pushed him away from her in a playful manner. He stopped walking, leaned down, and gave her yet another kiss.

Chapter 9

Put Me in remembrance: let us plead together: declare thou, that thou mayest be justified.

Isaiah 43:26

Thirty-five-year-old Theresa Jordan married forty-three-year-old Maurice Greene on June 22, 2002. It had been quite sentimental, with her and her mother, Lena, marrying on the same day in a double-wedding ceremony. Mauricia, Theresa and Maurice's baby girl, had been born on September 11, 2001. Almost a year after they wed, Theresa learned she was pregnant again. A healthy, seven-pound-six-ounce baby boy was born to the two of them on February 16, 2004. She and Maurice had disagreed from the start what his name would be. Maurice wanted him to be a junior or the second, and Theresa didn't think that was such a great idea in the least.

"Then we'd have Mauricia and Maurice. People might mistake them for being twins or something," Theresa had argued.

"So," was all Maurice had said in defense of it. "Who cares what other people think? This is my son, and I'd like him to be named after me. Who knows when we'll have another boy," he said as his counterargument.

"Oh, I can tell you. This is *it* for me. I'm getting too old to be running around behind children," Theresa said.

So the baby was named Maurice Gilead Greene the Second.

Now the sixteen-month-old toddler, whom they most times called M-double-G or MGG, was being hurriedly placed in his car seat as Theresa rushed to leave for Asheville, North Carolina. Theresa had asked Maurice to come with her, but he couldn't get Monday off from work. If he went with Theresa, they would have to return on Sunday night. Theresa wasn't certain of all that was awaiting her at Sarah's house, so she didn't want to be obligated to come home that quickly in case there was a need for her to remain longer.

"Didn't you tell me your parents are there?" Maurice asked.

"Yes," she said, wringing her hands.

"Look at you, Theresa. You're a nervous wreck," Maurice said. "I really don't want you driving to Asheville alone, not when you're like this. So here's what we'll do. I'll drive you up there, and if you decide you need to stay longer than Sunday night, I'll leave you there. You can either ride back with your parents, or I can come back and get you next weekend. Flexibility— yet another advantage to being a stay-at-home mom."

"You'd do that, Maurice? Because I really don't want to go up there alone. I honestly don't know how I'll react to seeing Memory again."

"I know. I saw you almost falling apart when you hung up from talking with your mother after she told you Memory was there."

"I don't understand how she could just show up without warning like she did."

"Well, Theresa . . . now, your great-grandmother *has* been searching for her. This is what Sarah's been praying a long time to happen."

"Yeah, but Memory could have called and prepared her by letting her know she was coming instead of just

showing up on her doorstep the way that she did. All I
know is that if Memory serves to hurt either her or my
mother again . . . I just don't understand what moti-
vates Memory to do what she does. That's all. I just
don't understand."

Maurice threw enough things in a duffle bag to last
the weekend, and off they went to Asheville. They arrived late Saturday afternoon.

"Hi, Mama," Theresa said to Lena as the two of them
hugged at the door. "How are you holding up?"

Lena shook her head. "Let's not ruin this moment
just yet." She hugged Mauricia and made a fuss over
her before reaching for the baby to come to her. "Look
at both of you! You've both grown just in the past few
weeks since I saw you last," she said.

Maurice Senior kissed his mother-in-law on the
cheek, then carried their things upstairs to their usual
bedroom.

Lena and Theresa exchanged pleasantries, and Lena
got to spend a little more time fussing over her grandchildren as they sat in the parlor. Maurice came downstairs and sat next to his wife. M-double-G toddled
over to his father and scrambled up into his lap.

"Do you want to go up and speak to your great-
grandmother now?" Lena asked Theresa. "She's awake."

"How is she doing?" Theresa asked.

"The doctor says she's much better. It wasn't bad
enough for him to have to put her in the hospital. She
just got a little too excited, I guess. It put a strain on her
heart and the rest of her system. He wants her to take it
easy and not overdo it. They're closely monitoring her
blood pressure, as well as other things. She's getting
top-of-the-line care."

"And Memory?" Theresa asked, looking as though
she'd eaten something nasty.

"She's upstairs . . . with Sarah."

"Of course. And you left Great-grandmother alone with her?"

"Yes," Lena said. "It's what Sarah wants."

Theresa began shaking her head. "I just don't believe this."

Lena touched Theresa's knee. "It's not like we weren't expecting one day for this to happen. Sarah has paid tons of money to find Memory. This day was inevitable."

"Yeah, I know. But I guess, deep down, I was hoping . . ."

"What? That Memory would never show up?" Lena asked as she smiled and cocked her head to the side.

Theresa rolled her eyes and sighed. "No. I wanted Great-grandmother to get to meet her. I'm sorry, Mama, but I just don't trust Memory. Okay, there—I said it. I don't want Great-grandmother to end up hurt."

"You mean like you and I ended up hurt?"

Theresa leaned her head back and placed her hands on her face. "Yes, like you and I ended up hurt." She looked at Lena. "Mama, we put ourselves as well as our hearts out there for Memory, and look what she did to us. Look what she did to you, her own child. She left you when you were a child. And when you needed her most, she came back after your grandmother died . . . or should I say Mamie—"

"As far as I'm concerned, Mamie was and always will be considered a grandmother to me. I'm not disrespecting Sarah in any way by saying that. Mamie raised me. People say that blood is thicker than water, but love is thicker than them both. Big Mama loved me. She loved Memory, too, in spite of all the awful things Memory did."

"I still can't believe how they pulled that off," Maurice said, chiming in. "Sarah having a baby on the same day Mamie Patterson had hers. In order to save Sarah's baby from Sarah's half-brother, Heath, Sarah's mother,

Grace, got Mamie, a stranger, to pretend she'd given birth to twins, a boy and a girl, and then raise Sarah's child as her own. Truth can definitely be stranger than fiction."

"And that's the point here we must remember. Memory is Sarah's child," Lena said. "There's no denying it. My goodness, you can look at the two of them and see that."

"Great-grandmother has gone through so much during her lifetime," Theresa said as she picked up MGG, who was standing before her with his arms raised high. "I just can't sit back and allow somebody like we know Memory to be to come in and possibly do the exact same thing to her that Sarah's family did all of these years."

"Memory claims she's changed," Lena said.

"Yeah? Now where have we heard that before? Oh, that's right. At my house. Right before she *lied* and *stole* the Alexandrite necklace right out of our safe-deposit box from a bank *vault*, no less! I can't possibly fathom why we wouldn't believe her now."

"Theresa, there's no need in you getting all upset about it. Sarah is fully aware of what Memory did and how we feel about her for that. But the bottom line is that Memory is her daughter . . . her only child . . . her flesh and blood. And we know how a mother can be when it comes to her own."

"Oh, yes. Tee, of all people, should identify with how motherhood changes you," Maurice said, using the name he sometimes still called her. "She lets our two darlings get away with all sorts of things."

"I do not," Theresa said as she continued to turn her face away from the hard pats MGG was inflicting on it simultaneously with both his little hands.

"M-double-G, stop that," Maurice said sternly. Maurice the Second turned, looked over at his father, and started laughing as he unexpectedly reared backward. "See what I mean?" Maurice said, pointing at Theresa. "There's no way Theresa would have *ever* stood for something like that before she had Mauricia and Maurice. No way." He laughed.

Theresa put MGG on the floor. He ran over to Mauricia and started trying to take away a toy she was playing with. "I suppose I really need to go speak to Great-grandmother," Theresa said. "But honestly, I don't feel like seeing Memory just yet."

"Well, hello, Theresa," a voice said softly from the arched entranceway.

Theresa looked in that direction. "Memory," she said, acknowledging her grandmother with barely an audible word and a nod.

"It's good to see you," Memory said as she came closer. "And *these* two beauties *must* be my great-grandbabies." She headed more in the direction of the children. "They are beautiful!" Memory said, smiling at them. She glanced over at Theresa.

Theresa found herself just staring at Memory. The closer she was getting to her and her children, the more Theresa's jaw had tightened. The rage she thought she'd gotten under control was rapidly beginning to make its way to the surface. Theresa turned away from Memory and looked at Lena, who, she quickly discovered, was watching *her*.

It was all but apparent to Theresa: being around Memory, in the same room with her, in the same house with her, in the same city with her, in the same state, was going to be a lot harder than she ever thought. A *lot* harder!

Chapter 10

Can a woman forget her sucking child,
that she should not have compassion
on the son of her womb? Yea, they may
forget, yet will I not forget thee.

Isaiah 49:15

Theresa stood up, leaned down, and kissed Lena. She picked up little Maurice, grabbed Mauricia by the hand, then walked toward Memory. When she reached her, she turned back to look at Lena and Maurice. "We're going up to see Great-grandmother now."

"Theresa," Memory said as she reached out and touched her arm.

Theresa looked at Memory's hand. "Please don't ever do that again," Theresa said.

Memory removed her hand. "I'm sorry. Theresa, I'm sorry about everything."

Theresa laughed and shook her head. "Yes. I'm sure you are." She then left and went upstairs.

When Theresa reached the top of the stairs, she let out a long sigh. She took her hand and wiped away the tears that, despite her best efforts to keep them at bay, had somehow managed to squeeze out and down her cheeks. She took a deep breath, knocked softly on the door, and walked in with all smiles, into Sarah's bedroom.

"Well, well. Look who's here," Sarah said. "Gayle told me you all were here. I was wondering how long it would be before you would come up to see me. Come give Grammy-grand a kiss," Sarah said with a smile. Grammy-grand was what her great-great-grand-children called her.

Mauricia didn't talk much. She was shy and, most times, had to be coaxed into interacting with others. "Mauricia, give Grammy-grand a hug and a kiss," Theresa said, giving her daughter a little push toward the bed.

"Hi, Grammy-grand," Mauricia said as she gave Sarah a halfhearted hug and a carefully placed kiss on the cheek.

Theresa leaned MGG down so he could kiss Sarah. "Mmmm-mmmh!" MGG said as he kissed her.

"Wow! That was some good sugar," Sarah said. "I have a present for you two."

"You do?" Mauricia said, her face lighting up now. "What is it? Where is it, Grammy-grand?"

Sarah laughed. "Oh, so you're only as quiet as you want folks to believe you to be, I see," Sarah said to Mauricia. "Miss Gayle, will you take them down to the playroom and give them their presents from me?" Sarah said to her nursemaid.

"Sure thing, Miss Fleming. Come on, kids. Let's go see what Grammy-grand got for you," Gayle said, knowing Sarah was really trying to garner some alone-time with Theresa.

After the room was cleared out, Sarah motioned for Theresa to sit down in the chair next to the bed. "Why so much sadness? Why the down face?" Sarah asked.

"I'm sorry. I must be tired from the ride. I didn't realize I appeared down."

"Oh, you don't. In fact, you're doing a terrific job faking that smile to show just how peachy keen things are. You forget though . . . I have a gift to see beyond all of that. So tell me. What's wrong?"

"Nothing really."

"Theresa, I know you're not happy about Memory being here. I know Lena isn't, either. I'm sorry about that. You both brought your cases against her to me from the very beginning. And believe me, it's not that I'm being insensitive to your and Lena's feelings or discounting what she did to you both. But she's *still* my child—my only child."

"Great-grandmother, please don't let the way I or my mother feels affect you and your happiness. We truly don't mean to dampen this joyous occasion for you."

Sarah smiled. "I'm well aware you don't trust Memory any farther than you can throw her. But Theresa, in loving Memory I must move past the things she may have done in her past. For this to work, I have to give her a fair shake now. I want to know her for however much time I have left on this earth. I have to do all I can to make every second of our time together count for something good. Do you understand?"

Theresa took her great-grandmother's hand. "I understand, and I won't ruin this for you. But will you do just one thing for me?"

"What's that?"

"Be careful. Memory may be trying to convince everyone that she's changed, but I don't want her to hurt you. That's all. In loving Memory, I don't want *you* to get hurt."

Sarah squeezed Theresa's hand slightly. "Theresa, what can Memory do to hurt me? Honestly? What do I have that she can take that's not already hers? I know I just met her today, but she's the true heir to all of this," Sarah said, making a sweeping gesture with her hand. "She doesn't have to take what's already hers. All I want is her heart and to give her mine. That to me is more important than these temporary material things."

Theresa relaxed in the chair and sighed. "You know,

you are *so* wise. You almost make me feel bad about being angry with her about a *thing*."

"Be angry, but sin not. Theresa, you know you weren't really angry at her about that Alexandrite necklace. The necklace was a mere symbol, that's all it was. Both you and your mother were hurt because she took your heart and your love, and to you, she stomped all over it without any regard to what she was doing. She made you feel your love was nothing to her. That's the thing you and Lena will have to find your way back from. You trusted Memory with your heart, and she didn't take care of it the way you thought she should have. You gave her your love, and it appeared she didn't return that love or respect back to you." Sarah began coughing uncontrollably.

Theresa immediately jumped up and poured water into her glass. She handed it to Sarah and helped her hold it as she drank. "Do I need to get Gayle for you?" she asked.

Sarah sipped the water and released a sigh, then a smile. "I'm okay. Maybe a little tired now. It's been a long day, to say the least. A good one, but a long one nevertheless."

Theresa took the half-empty glass and set it back on the nightstand. "Do you need me to get you anything else?"

"Would you mind sending Memory back up here for me?" Sarah said as she closed her eyes. "I'd like to see her again."

"Of course, Great-grandmother." Theresa leaned down and planted a kiss on the matriarch's forehead. She appeared in such perfect peace. "Of course," Theresa whispered so as not to wake her.

Chapter 11

I will go before thee, and make the crooked places straight: I will break in pieces the gates of brass, and cut in sunder the bars of iron. . . .

Isaiah 45:2

Memory had gone in and sat in the light pink wing-back chair near Lena. She looked at her, then smiled. "So, you had plastic surgery done on your face?" she asked.

Lena looked at her, shook her head, and smiled. She still found it hard to believe just how insensitive her mother really could be. "Yes, I had plastic surgery. But not for the reason you may think."

"How could you possibly know what I'm thinking?" Memory asked. She could see the tightness in Lena's demeanor. "I think you might be a wee bit too sensitive still."

Lena laughed. "See there, the same old Memory."

"I'm not the same, Lena. I told you that. At least I've tried to tell you that, but you refuse to spend any time in the same room with me long enough to hear me out." Memory leaned forward. "I'm not the same person I was the last time you saw me."

"Yeah. Well, I find it interesting how pleased you seem to be about my face."

"I'm pleased because you're so beautiful."

Lena began to nod her head and prim her mouth even

more. "And I suppose I wasn't *so beautiful* when you saw me last."

"Look, Lena. I'm sure you still have a lot of mental issues about your face. But I haven't done anything to merit your attacking me like this. Frankly, I didn't care what you looked like the last time I saw you."

Lena shook her head slowly and smiled. "That's right. You didn't care what anybody looked like the last time we were together. You were only interested in getting your hands on that Alexandrite necklace. Well, I hope it was worth it." She looked right in Memory's face. "And for your information, I had the plastic surgery not because I cared so much about how I look, although I'm sure you have a problem with that statement. I had it done because of medical problems it was causing with my eye and that side of my face. It was for health reasons, not vanity."

"Lena, I was merely pointing out how good you look. It was meant to be a compliment. And as for the comment you just made about the necklace, let me say it here. No, Lena, it was not worth it."

Just then the doorbell rang. Lena looked at her watch. "That's probably Richard finally getting back from his outing. Excuse me," she said as she made her way toward the door.

Richard stepped in the foyer. "Sorry I'm so late getting back. After we finished playing golf, we decided to have lunch at the club. We got to talking . . ." He looked at his wife. "Lena, what's wrong?"

"Memory's here."

"Here as in this house?"

"In the parlor," she said as she took a few steps away. Richard set his golf clubs out of the way and followed Lena. They walked into the parlor together.

Memory looked up, saw Richard when he entered,

and smiled. "Well, well. It's good to see you together. I guess this means the two of you finally got hitched?"

"We're married, if that's what you're asking," Richard said with a puzzled look. He could tell he'd walked in on something; what that something was, wasn't quite clear.

"Memory was just about to tell me how taking the Alexandrite necklace like she did hadn't been worth it. Come in, Richard. Have a seat." Lena led him to the sofa, and they sat down practically in sync. "Please, Memory. Do continue."

Memory shook her head. "Lena, I'm sorry for what I did that ended up hurting you and has caused you to distrust me so right now."

"Who said anything about distrusting you now? Did you, Maurice?" Lena glanced over at Maurice and flashed a smile. "You, Richard?" She touched his hand. "Oh, that's right. You just got here, so it couldn't have possibly been *you*. I suppose that leaves . . . me." She looked at Memory as her smile dropped. "No, I don't suppose I do trust you."

"You don't, and I can't say I blame you for being skeptical. But I'm a different person now. You see, there was this church I was attending in Birmingham, Alabama—"

"That's where you were hiding out," Lena said.

"Birmingham is one of the cities I stayed in, but I've graced a few places over these past years. I'm certain you're aware of that fact since I'm sure Sarah kept you informed of the times she'd just missed me. Sarah thinks the world of you, dear."

"And I think the world of her. She's a good woman," Lena said. "A real good woman. A strong woman who has survived a lot. And I'm telling you here and now— I won't allow you to come in and hurt her." She shook her head slowly. "I won't."

"You mean . . . the way that I hurt you?" Memory asked.

"What makes you think you hurt me? I knew what was up with you when you showed up on Theresa's doorstep in Atlanta that day. All you did was prove me right."

"Okay, so I lived down to your expectation, which wasn't that high to begin with."

"O-kay, ladies," Richard said, holding up his hand as though he was directing traffic. "I'm sure you're both pretty hot with emotions right now. What say we grab something to eat and table this discussion until cooler heads prevail?"

"We're not emotional," Lena said. "Memory's my mother. She's Sarah's daughter. Sarah's been actively looking for her since October of 2001. And today . . . today Sarah's prayers were answered. As we can all see, Memory's here now. This is a joyous occasion. Memory says she's here with the right heart and with the right spirit. Granted, all we have is her word, but her word should be enough." She looked at Memory, scarcely blinking as she spoke. "Right, Memory?"

Maurice got up and left out of the room.

"I never claimed when I was in Atlanta that I wasn't there to get back what I believed was rightfully mine. That Alexandrite necklace belonged to me, Lena. I heard that woman, Grace, who—as it turns out—was actually my grandmother . . . my *grandmother*." Memory began a nervous laugh. "My goodness, the more I think of what's happened . . . how out of control this all got . . ." Memory placed her hand to her face and sucked in a long, deep breath before noisily exhaling it.

Lena looked at Memory and couldn't help but feel a little sorry for her. She seemed sincere enough. Lena realized this part truly had to have shocked Memory's system. Learning, after all these years, that Mamie wasn't her real mother. Hearing from strangers that her biological mother was alive and had been searching for her for years now. Then to show up at a mansion and discover your mother is not just light-skinned as she probably assumed upon seeing her, but white and quite financially well-off. All of this had to be difficult for her to process in such a short amount of time.

"Richard's right," Lena said, getting to her feet. "Why don't we go in the kitchen and get something to eat? Sarah had all this food brought in, and nobody's eaten much of it." She looked at Maurice, who was just walking back into the room with a plateful of food. "Well, almost nobody."

Maurice sat down and took a big bite of his shredded barbecue pork sandwich. The sauce oozed out onto his finger as he bit. He licked the sauce off and bit again. "Mama, I'm still a growing man," he said, talking with his mouth full. "Besides, I didn't have time to eat anything before we left. I'm starving!"

"Yeah, you're still growing all right—out. I think it's safe to say that your vertical growing days are long behind you." Lena patted his stomach, then started out of the room. "The kitchen's this way," she said to Memory, who hadn't ventured much farther than the upstairs area, mostly in Sarah's bedroom after they managed to get her up there and in the bed. "Later, I'll show you the rest of the house if you like. Grandmother asked if I would take you on a tour. . . . When you're ready, of course."

"It's quite *impressive* just from what I've seen so far," Memory said, looking around from where she remained.

Lena stared at her. The way Memory emphasized the word "impressive" caused Lena to be even more determined than ever to keep an eye on her.

Just to be on the safe side.

Chapter 12

Like as a woman with child, that
draweth near the time of her delivery,
is in pain, and crieth out in her pangs;
so have we been in Thy sight, O Lord.

Isaiah 26:17

Seeing his wife twisting and turning on top of the bed, Landris walked hurriedly to her and leaned down. "Johnnie Mae, what's wrong?" he asked, immediately noting that her hands and feet seemed to have swollen even more.

"I'm not sure. All of a sudden, I started feeling sick," Johnnie Mae said, rubbing her head with one hand while her other hand rested on her basketball-looking stomach.

"Are you in any pain?"

"My head hurts a little. But babywise, I'm not hurting . . . just feeling really uncomfortable for some reason. It came down on me all of a sudden."

He stood up. "I'm calling your doctor. Where's her phone number?"

"In my purse. . . . It's over there on the coffee table by the chaise longue." She pointed toward the sitting area.

Landris brought her purse to her. She took out a business card and handed it to him. Landris called the number, which was immediately routed to the doctor's answering service. Ten minutes later, Dr. Brenda Baker called him back.

"Take Johnnie Mae to the hospital," Dr. Baker said. "I'll meet you there."

Landris did as he was told.

Dr. Baker examined Johnnie Mae soon after she arrived.

"I'm going to have to admit you," she said in her calm, soft-spoken voice.

Johnnie Mae swallowed hard. "Is the baby okay?"

"For now, the baby's fine. But your blood pressure is dangerously high. Dangerously high. You've developed what we call preeclampsia."

"Is that the same as toxemia?" Johnnie Mae asked, clarifying the terminology to ensure they were talking about the same thing.

"Yes, toxemia. Johnnie Mae, I'm not going to sugarcoat this. Preeclampsia or toxemia can put both you and your baby at risk."

"What risks?" Landris asked.

"For the mother, the most serious is brain damage," Dr. Baker said. "There's also the possibility of blindness, kidney failure, and liver rupture. The baby is at risk of premature birth, which, as you're both aware, can carry its own complications."

"Then what do we do to fix this?" Landris asked as he looked from Johnnie Mae to Dr. Baker.

"We're going to put her on bed rest here and monitor both her and the baby. Our first course of action is to get her blood pressure down." She then looked at Johnnie Mae. "Where it is right now, you're at risk of having a seizure or, worse, a stroke. Of course, even doing this, we still have to be careful. Lowering your blood pressure can decrease the amount of blood that gets to the baby. If that happens, the baby could end up deprived of oxygen, which can cause brain damage as well as other things." Dr. Baker began alternating her attention between Johnnie Mae and Landris as she continued. "But if we can't get your blood pressure under control and keep it that way, you could progress to true eclampsia. And should that happen, we'll have no other choice except to take the baby."

"I'm not yet seven months. If you put me in labor or take the baby this early, that will really put our baby at risk." Johnnie Mae looked directly at Landris. "I don't want to do anything that will harm or cause us to lose this baby. I don't."

Dr. Baker touched Johnnie Mae's hand. "For now, we're going to see if we can't get you stabilized using medication. If we're successful, none of this will be an issue. But Johnnie Mae, as your doctor, my first responsibility is to ensure *your* well-being."

"And my baby's," Johnnie Mae said, her voice pleading as she said it.

"We're going to do all we can to ensure the well-being of you both. But Johnnie Mae, I want you to know. Should it come down to saving your life or allowing this pregnancy to continue for the sake of the baby, as your doctor, I'm going to do what's necessary to save you." She looked intensely, seriously, and directly at Johnnie Mae.

"Dr. Baker, I understand what you're saying, but we have to make sure this baby is all right." Johnnie Mae caressed her stomach. "I'll stay here at the hospital for as long as you like. I'll do whatever you tell me to do, exactly as you tell me to. But if it comes down to me or this baby, we've got to give this baby a fair chance. We just have to."

Dr. Baker glanced at Landris, then back at Johnnie Mae. She managed a comforting smile. "Let's not give so much attention to the negative at this point," she said, her voice even softer than usual. "What say we just concentrate our attention on getting you better? That will be the best for all concerned. Okay?"

Johnnie Mae nodded slightly as she looked down at her now-clasped hands.

Dr. Baker glanced at the two nurses who had just entered the room. "The nurses need to do a few things to get you settled in. They're also going to move you to a permanent room," Dr. Baker said to Johnnie Mae, patting her hand twice. "Pastor Landris, will you walk out with me while they do what they need to?" She picked up Johnnie Mae's chart and headed to exit the room.

Johnnie Mae looked first at Dr. Baker, who was waiting to leave, then at the slightly worried expression in Landris's hazel-brown eyes.

Landris leaned down and kissed her softly on her forehead. "I'll be back as soon as they're finished. Okay?" He looked lovingly at her and smiled. She smiled back, giving him a nod of confidence.

When Dr. Baker and Landris were far enough away, Dr. Baker stopped and turned to him. "Pastor Landris, I know this is hard. I've seen this happen more times in my eighteen years of practice than I care to think about— a mother insisting on sacrificing herself for the life of her baby should it come to that. I'm certain this would be the case with Johnnie Mae. I assure you, I plan to do all I can to help this pregnancy reach full-term. It's a known fact that the longer a mother carries a baby inside the womb toward the forty weeks, the better. But please make no mistake about this. What's happening here is not something we want to play around with. For now, Johnnie Mae's condition is preeclampsia. That's for now. If her condition turns into eclampsia, that's almost always fatal. This is as direct and honest as I can put it for you. With all the advances in medicine we have today, a premature baby has a higher rate of survival than ever before. We have a terrific neonatal unit and staff here. Be assured that your baby would receive top-notch care. I need you to understand everything that's going on because, honestly, if we have to move, we'll need to move quickly and without hesitation. We can't allow time and indecision to become our enemy."

Landris looked at her with a puzzled stare. "So what you're saying is that it really could come down to a question of doing something that will save Johnnie Mae's life, yet put our baby's life in danger, or losing Johnnie Mae in order to save the baby? You're telling me it's possible I may have to choose between my wife and our unborn child?"

"I hope and pray it doesn't come to that. But I need you to know, at this point, there's a strong possibility this could well be the case," Dr. Baker said. "For now, though, it's imperative that we keep Johnnie Mae as calm and experiencing as little stress as humanly possible. That can make a world of difference. Couple that with the medication I'm prescribing for her, and I'm optimistic this just may do the trick and put us all back on track for a normal, healthy, full-term-delivery scenario."

Landris shook his head, mostly in disbelief. "In essence, what you're really telling me is this is spiritual warfare, and I need to be doing some serious, fervent praying *before* this battle gets an even greater foothold."

She looked back at him, and, without any hesitation whatsoever, she said, "Yes, Pastor Landris. I suppose that's *exactly* what I'm telling you."

Chapter 13

*But now, O Lord, Thou art our father;
we are the clay, and Thou our potter;
and we all are the work of Thy hand.*

Isaiah 64:8

Johnnie Mae heard a knock on the half-closed hospital door. "Come in," she said. A smile came across her face. "Charity!" she said when Charity Morrell walked in.

Charity came and gave her a hug. "How are you?" she asked, almost gushing.

Johnnie Mae repositioned her body. "I'm feeling much better, thank you. But how did you know I was here?"

"They announced you were in the hospital in church on Sunday. It's also posted on the church's Web site." Charity sat down in the chair next to the bed. "I still keep up."

"I am *so* happy to see you. Look at you! You look absolutely wonderful!"

"That's what everybody keeps telling me," Charity said. "Things are going well. But what's going on with you? No one's saying what's happening with you, just that you're in the hospital and that you'll likely be here for the remainder of your pregnancy."

Johnnie Mae smiled through the thought of her rather distressing prognosis. "The doctor calls it preeclampsia, but you may have heard it called toxemia."

Charity glanced at the monitor that displayed various readings. She was familiar with some medical readouts. "Your blood pressure's up quite a lot," she said.

"Yeah, but it's better than it was when I came in on Saturday, thank the Lord."

"Well, the entire church is praying for you." Charity sat back against the chair. "I'm glad I got to see you. I was afraid they wouldn't let me in. Pastor Landris requested that we pray for you but for us not to come by or call because you need lots of rest."

"But you came anyway," Johnnie Mae said with a grin.

"Yes. I hope you don't mind. I don't intend to stay long. I just had to come see you. I know how much it meant to me when you would come by and see me."

"Of course I don't mind. I'm glad you came." Johnnie Mae pushed her body up straighter. "Tell me, how are things with you? Really."

Charity smiled. "I'm really doing well. Really, I am. I'm back in my own house again. Both Dr. Holden and Sapphire say it looks like I'm conquering my disorder. In fact, neither Faith nor Hope has made an appearance of any kind in months now. We're *all* encouraged by that."

"Does that mean you're completely cured?" Johnnie Mae asked.

"I don't know if we can go *that* far yet. As a matter of fact, I have an appointment with Dr. Holden at one PM. But I *can* say I've unearthed a lot about myself. I still can't recall what happened that caused me to split my personalities the way I did in the first place. And now that Faith appears to be gone for good, I'm not sure if I'll ever know."

Johnnie Mae readjusted her body yet again. It was hard for her to get comfortable.

"Do you need me to get something for you?" Charity asked, rising to her feet.

"No, I'm fine. It just gets tiring lying in a bed all day and night, being in one position all the time. I try and make a point to move myself around and reposition my body to keep my blood circulating. Please go on; I didn't mean to interrupt you."

Charity sat back down and continued. "Faith refuses to come back and cooperate with either Sapphire or Dr. Holden. For reasons I can't explain, Faith seemed to prefer Dr. Holden. She just didn't care to talk to Sapphire. That's why I've been seeing both of them. I see Sapphire only weekly now, and Dr. Holden once a month. I did ask Dr. Holden about possible hypnosis, but he's not too keen on doing that. He and Sapphire both prefer the route we're taking. So I'm meeting Dr. Holden today to see what else, if anything, we might discover about my life and/or 'Trinity' "—Charity crooked her fingers and pumped them to quote the word "Trinity"—"that hasn't been uncovered already."

Johnnie Mae smiled. "Still calling the three Trinity, huh?"

"Sometimes I do. It just makes it easier than saying or trying to explain Faith, Hope, and me." Charity sneaked a quick glance at her watch. Timewise, she was doing okay. "How's your mother?" Charity asked.

Johnnie Mae's countenance quickly changed. "Physically Mama is fine; her mind, *not* as sharp. Still in and out of real time. With me being here now, I don't know what's going to happen. And I told you my oldest sister, Rachel, moved; then, just as quickly as she left, she ended up moving back."

"When she moved, where did she go?" Charity asked.

"Columbus, Georgia. She was only there for about two weeks, though. My baby brother, Christian, is in the military. He just returned from Iraq. He and his family will be stationed there for the next year. They just bought a big new house, which is why Rachel went there. But with this Iraq war still going on, he may have to go *back* to Iraq again."

"That doesn't seem fair. Why does he have to go back if he's been there once?"

"It has something to do with the commitment of tour they make. They may only stay a year, but they signed up for two. So when they come back to the States, they can be sent back to finish out the rest of the tour they didn't serve already," Johnnie Mae said.

Charity let out a sigh. "You know, I miss your mother. I wish I could see her."

"I know. Mama really enjoys your company. You have such a way with her. But with me being in here for who knows how long . . ."

"Oh, you don't have to explain. I'm aware that the rest of your family is not too enthusiastic about me being anywhere near her," Charity said. "They've all made that abundantly clear."

"Well, I know you'd never do anything to harm her. Those are my siblings, though. Who can say what will happen now that I'm temporarily out of commission?"

Charity could tell this conversation was bringing Johnnie Mae's spirits down. Looking at her watch again, she stood up. "I guess I should get going. I don't want to be late for my appointment. I'll continue to pray for all of you, just like y'all prayed for me."

"Please do."

Charity stepped up closer to the bed. "If it's okay, I'd like to come back and see you again. I can sit over there in the corner and not talk if my talking bothers you. But I really care about you, and I care what happens to you and your family."

"I'd like that—you coming by. And I love talking to you, Charity, so you can forget about that sitting-in-some-corner-and-being-quiet nonsense. I'll let Landris and the hospital staff know that you're welcome to visit me anytime you want."

Charity smiled. "Well, you get some rest and make sure you do what your doctor tells you." She headed toward the door, then turned back around. "Johnnie Mae, would it be okay if you and I have a word of prayer before I leave?"

Johnnie Mae smiled. "I would like that." She reached her hand out to Charity.

Charity came back over and grabbed her hand, holding it as they prayed for healing and health for them, as well as for the health of the baby Johnnie Mae was carrying.

Chapter 14

*And it shall come to pass, that before
they call, I will answer; and while they
are yet speaking, I will hear.*

Isaiah 65:24

Dr. Holden was in his office. Charity was his first
appointment of the afternoon, although he wasn't
sure whether there was anything more he could do to
help her. She'd made tremendous strides in her recovery over the past few months. He thought back to when
they seemed closest to getting into the mind of one of
her personalities . . . back when Faith wanted to talk to
him and only him.

Faith had been something else that day. She'd tried
her best to get to him—going as far as turning the tables
on him . . . pretending to write things in a notebook,
evaluating him the way he was supposedly evaluating
her. He thought about that notebook. He'd originally
placed it in his desk drawer. Later he had looked at it,
only to find the pages she'd written were childish doodling—scribbles, just as he'd suspected.

Inspired to find the notebook to see what, if anything, Faith may have hidden that he might have originally missed, Dr. Holden opened his desk drawer and
rummaged through it. Locating the notebook, he looked
at the doodles. Nothing. Flipping past those pages confirmed only blank pages. Determined to check every
page all the way to the end, he continued to turn. And

that's when he saw it—a page where Faith had actually written words. He began reading, engrossed by what were five pages of actual words.

The intercom buzzed, interrupting him. "Dr. Holden, your one o'clock is here," his secretary announced.

"Would you ask her to wait a few more minutes, please," Dr. Holden said. He finished reading Faith's words, then closed the notebook. Picking up the phone, he pressed the speed-dial number to Sapphire's private line.

"Sapphire, this is Dr. Holden. I know this is short notice, but is there *any* way possible you can get away for about ten minutes and meet with me in my office?"

"I'm really swamped today. What about in the morning?" Sapphire countered.

"It's about Charity Morrell's case. I've discovered something, and I'd like you in on it. She's here for her appointment now, but I was hoping to let you see this first."

There was a moment of silence. "I can't possibly come now. My next patient is already here and waiting. Is it something you can tell me over the phone?"

He flipped back to the pages of words. "I'd prefer not to," Dr. Holden said.

"Are you planning on sharing this with Charity today?" Sapphire asked.

"I believe this is going to help her. So, yes, I definitely plan on showing it to her. If you like, I can see about rescheduling her for a time when you *can* be here."

"Dr. Holden, I realize you're being polite wanting me in on this. But please feel free to do what you believe is best to help Charity. You can fill me in later."

Dr. Holden glanced at the first page of writings once again. "I think I'll go on and move on this. I'll let you know what happens." He closed the notebook, said good-bye, and hung up. Pressing the intercom button, he told his secretary to send Charity in.

A minute later, Charity walked cheerfully into his office. "It's good to see you again, Dr. Holden." She shook his hand. "So . . . you ready to get this show on the road?"

He gestured for her to sit as he picked up the notebook. "Charity, do you recall some months ago when you were here in my office and Faith made an appearance?"

Charity looked in Dr. Holden's face, trying to figure out where he was going with this. "You mean the one and only time, and, as far as I know, the last time anyone has seen or heard from her?" Her eyes widened. "Unless you know something I don't."

"As far as we can tell, it was. But I started thinking back to that day and how Faith had written some things in a notebook. This notebook." He held up the steno pad.

"Do you remember it?" he asked. She nodded. "Well, I decided to pull it out a little while ago. Originally, I thought Faith had written things about me since that's what she claimed she was doing. I believe she was trying to distract me during that session. Upon my examination of the notebook, I saw she'd been doodling, which only confirmed my initial suspicion. The rest of the notebook appeared to be blank, which is why I didn't even bother to place it in your file. As it turns out, I was mistaken." He leaned forward.

"Charity, Faith wrote things in here I believe will be the key to helping you. To see what she wrote, you'll have to flip closer to the back of the notebook. She was quite sneaky yet clever in doing that. That's why I missed it." He held the notebook out to her.

Charity stared at it as though it were a poisonous snake.

Dr. Holden studied her, making note of her hesitance. "What is it? Tell me."

She shook her head slightly. "I'm just not sure I want to see it," Charity said as she slowly took the notebook. "You know what it says, and you believe I'll be okay?"

"Yes. Trust me. If I felt you couldn't handle it, I wouldn't be doing this. I did call Sapphire before you came in to see if she might be available to come over while you and I were in session this afternoon, but she had a patient and couldn't come today."

Charity flipped open the notebook, saw what was all-too-familiar childish doodles and scribbles, and just as quickly closed it. "I can't," she said. "Not now."

"Yes, you can. Charity, you can do this. It's time for you to face those demons of the past that have been haunting you for so long. You need to move forward in a positive way in your life. I believe what's written in there will push you toward the place you truly need to go. I'm here for you; so is Sapphire. We'll help you through this."

"I'm sorry, Dr. Holden, but I just can't do this right now." She rubbed her head. "All of a sudden, I'm not feeling so well." Charity reached down, picked up her purse off the floor, and stood up, rubbing her head once more. "I think I'm going to cut my session short and go home and lie down." She turned and hurriedly walked toward the door.

"Are you experiencing one of your headaches?" he asked. She shook her head slowly without turning around. "Charity, I'd really prefer you read that here. In fact, I insist. It will make me feel better knowing that you're not alone when you see it."

She turned around and faced him. "Dr. Holden, I'm never alone. And trust me, before I read this, I'll have prayed mightily to ensure the Holy Spirit . . . my Comforter is there with me *to* comfort and guide me. You see, for the first time in my life, I truly do believe I can do all things through Christ who strengthens me. This is something I need to do on my own . . . without any crutches. I know I'll be all right." She smiled.

"Will you at least call me and let me know how you're doing after you read it? No matter how you're feeling— good or bad? And if you need to see Sapphire or me, I don't care when or what time, you'll let us know no matter how booked or busy we might be?"

"I will. I promise. But Dr. Holden, there are just some things we have to do ourselves," Charity said. "You understand." She then opened the door and walked out.

Chapter 15

*Woe unto them that call evil good,
and good evil; that put darkness for
light, and light for darkness; that put
bitter for sweet, and sweet for bitter!*

Isaiah 5:20

Montgomery Powell the Second stood as she entered the room. "Thank you so much for agreeing to see me," he said, extending his hand to her.

"You made it sound like it would be worth my while," Memory said as she shook the hand of the dirty-blond-and-gray-haired white man who looked to be in his sixties.

He gestured for her to have a seat on the green brocade, French-styled couch. "As I told you over the phone, I believe this could be a win-win situation for us all."

Memory sat down. "You said this concerns the welfare of my family. In your letter, you said the least I could do is talk to you." Memory was referring to a letter he'd written and sent to Sam's house a few years back when she was once hiding out there. Memory didn't know why she'd kept that letter in her purse, but she had. His phone number was on it. She'd called him from Sarah's shortly after Theresa went back home.

"I was starting to believe I'd never hear from you. It's been some time since I sent that letter," Montgomery said. "I'm thankful you got in touch with me when you did."

"Mr. Powell, if you don't mind, I'd like to get to the point of why I'm here," Memory said. "In your letter, you mentioned you have something I might be interested in getting back. When I received this letter, I'd never heard of you and couldn't imagine anything you might have of mine I'd want, let alone want back. But since I just happen to be visiting your fair city, curiosity has gotten the best of me. So tell me, Mr. Powell the Second, what on God's green earth could you and I possibly have to do with each other?"

He turned over a clean glass and began pouring brandy into it. "Memory." He glanced at her as he poured. "Is it okay if I call you Memory?" He was prim and proper.

"Memory's fine."

"And you can call me Montgomery." He held up the crystal decanter filled with brandy. "Care for something to drink?"

"No, thanks. It's a bit too early to be drinking."

He took his glass in his hand, swirled the brown liquid around, sniffed, exhaled loud and slow, then sat in the solid, hunter green wingback chair next to the couch. "Trust me, my dear, it's never too early for good brandy." He took a sip, then exhaled again. "So tell me. How much do you know about Sarah Fleming?"

"Not much. In fact, I just met her for the first time in my life a week ago."

He nodded slowly while gazing at her. "It's quite astounding how much you two actually look alike. There's no disputing you're her child. Well, Memory, when I first heard she had a child, of course, I didn't believe it."

"Excuse me, but I suppose I'm missing something somewhere. Now, how exactly is it you happen to know my mother?"

"Sarah's family. Her half-brother, Heath, was my father, making her my aunt."

"Forgive me," Memory said, cutting him off yet again. "But I'm still a bit confused. Your last name's Powell— hers is Fleming. She never married to change hers."

"Allow me to clarify. My father's mother was married to another man when she conceived him. Reportedly, it was common knowledge that she and Victor Fleming had a deep love for one another that lasted for many years. Forgive me for not divulging all the details. Rumor also has it that my grandfather was quite the ladies' man. I'm sure you can relate. Things weren't as easy for people like my grandmother as they can be today."

"Okay, so what you're saying is your grandmother was fooling around on her husband while still married *to* and living *with* him, ended up knocked-up—excuse me, I meant with child by another man—and, let me guess, probably passed the baby off as his?"

He turned up his nose, then forced a smile. "My grandmother was trapped. She did what she had to. When my father was born, yes, she was still married to her husband, thereby my father's name, Montgomery Heath Powell. Everybody called him Heath. However, six months after my father's birth, her husband died. A month later, she married Victor Fleming. Tragically, she died days after giving birth to her second son, Victor Fleming Jr. My father's name was never legally changed to Fleming, I suppose due to my grandmother's own untimely death, after which Grandfather married Grace, and they had Sarah. My father died twelve years ago, two years after Uncle Vic. I, being the next male in line, was appointed in my father's will to take over and manage the family's home and all family affairs in Aunt Sarah's stead, while she was . . . away."

"And why exactly was she 'away?'" She placed emphasis on the word "away."

He rubbed his temple. "Oh dear. No one's told you?"

He began to stroke his chin. "You know, I was afraid of that. Let's just say Aunt Sarah has had serious challenges for many, many years now, and we'll leave it at that."

"Oh, you're dying to tell me. So, do . . . tell. What kind of *challenges*?"

"I see you don't know how to leave well enough alone." He drained his glass dry, then stood up and poured himself another. "Aunt Sarah hasn't always been stable, mentally that is. She's a dear, sweet woman, and we as a family unit have done as much as we could to get her the help she needs. I must say that I'm impressed with how well she's held up while searching for you. You are a slippery one. At her age and in her fragile state, it's a wonder the two of you *ever* got to meet."

"But as somehow you already knew before I arrived here, we did," Memory said.

"Yes, and I don't know if anyone, other than Aunt Sarah, is happier about that than I. But I'm also astutely aware of the riff caused, shall we say, by a certain piece of Russian jewelry." He walked over and opened the drawer to the sofa table. Taking out a flat black velvet box, he handed it to Memory as he took a sip from his glass. "Open it," he said.

Memory took the box and did as instructed. She looked up at him with a frown. "Where did you get this?"

"I bought it. But, of course, you should know that. It's the Alexandrite necklace you sold, for a handsome price I might add, about four years ago. It's a shame, too. I mean a shame that I had to buy it back, considering it already belonged to our family to begin with." He sat back down, glass in hand as he swirled it, while staring into her eyes.

"That necklace was given to my mother. . . ."

"You mean Mamie Patterson?"

"Yes . . . Mamie."

"That's something, isn't it? The way everybody was deceived. Aunt Sarah made to believe her child—you— had died all of those years ago. It's no wonder she stepped off the deep end. That was all Grace's doing. Personally, I believe she wanted to drive her own daughter crazy to keep her from the inheritance." He took another swallow as he peered over the glass rim before setting it on the coffee table. "You know Grace—again, that was Sarah's mother in case no one besides myself has told you that—was in on the whole baby-deceiving scheme from the start. I suspect she didn't want a half"—he paused, then continued—"black child in the family. You understand. She was also the one who took that necklace. We concluded it was merely a payoff to keep Mamie Patterson's mouth shut. Anyway, that's how the necklace came to leave our family in the first place."

"I wouldn't say it *left* our family," Memory said as she relaxed against the sofa.

"That's right. You ended up taking it back. I think that was quite brilliant—the way you tracked it down and all. I'd almost resigned myself to the fact that it was lost to our family forever." Montgomery crossed his leg. "Then all of a sudden, I get a call, out of the blue, in September of 2001—that the necklace had been located and was on its way via a special courier. I paid two million dollars to get that little jewel back. But as you can see, it's worth every penny." His eyes appeared to twinkle as he spoke.

Memory recalled how the reward paid had been a million dollars. *So, he'd paid two to get it back?* "What makes you think I was the reason it came back to you?"

"Memory, please, let's not play games. We're both too old to play games. You're here now, and you're learning the truth. The truth that who you thought was your mother all those years really wasn't. . . . That

Sarah Fleming was and is the woman who gave birth to you." He stopped briefly and grinned. "Now *that* must have been a true shocker. Lies and deception from your own family. But from all indications, now it appears you have a credibility problem because of that magnificent piece of jewelry you hold in your hands."

"And how would you happen to know about my issues?" Memory asked.

"Oh, I have my ways. Aunt Sarah, bless her heart, believes in you because she loves you. But your daughter . . . it's Lena, isn't it? And your granddaughter, sweet little Theresa, both find it hard to trust you. Or at least I would imagine they do. But you know what they say. 'Oh, what a tangled web we weave.' " He smirked again. "Well, you know the rest. Now, who could have predicted things would turn out the way that they have?" He reached forward and retrieved the necklace from her. "Stunning piece of work, don't you think?"

Memory's eyes began to bore a hole in him as she stared him down. "Let's just cut to it, okay? What do you want?"

"Me? Why, I just want you and your family to get along better. I want to work something out so you can give your daughter this necklace back, and the two, or I should say three, of you can mend your fences and become a happy family again. This should be a joyous time for all of you. There should be no strife or animosity between mothers and daughters . . . or granddaughters, for that fact." He smiled. "Family unity. Forgiveness. That's what I want. For y'all to be one big, happy family—what Sarah wants most."

"And why don't I believe you?"

He set the box with the necklace down on the coffee table in front of her. "Maybe because we tend to see our own selves in others. Meaning you can't trust yourself, so you can't possibly trust others for seeing who *you* are, and not who *they* really are." He sat back against the chair. "I'm offering you a way to make up for what you did to your own flesh and blood. Consider it as my early seventieth birthday present to you. And as I'm sure you've already learned, that necklace was technically yours anyway. In truth, you had a right to take it back and sell it, which, we can see, you clearly did." He pointed at it. "I had a right to buy it, which, as we can also see, I did. Now I'd like to figure out a way to return this necklace to its rightful owner—you."

"What makes you so sure that necklace ever belonged to me? And who said I received any money from the sale of it?"

He began to swing the crossed leg that rested on top. "According to family legend, that necklace was your inheritance anyway. It was designated to go to the first-born grandchild. That's you. Grace made sure no one messed with that when she gave the necklace to Mamie to hold for you. Unfortunately, others decided to take matters into their own hands, namely, Lena, and keep what was rightfully yours." He grinned slightly, then sucked his bottom lip. "At least, that's the story I was told. How am I doing so far?"

Memory rolled her hand in a circular fashion, indicating he should continue.

"As for how I know you received the money from the sale, I know the money was paid to your friend . . . what was his name . . . ?" He tapped his right temple several times with his index and middle fingers. "What was his name?" He got up, walked over to the sofa table again, opened the drawer, took out a folder and opened it, then closed the drawer. "Ah, yes! Christopher Harris," he said, returning his attention to Memory.

"Well, since you think you know so much, do you know that Christopher Harris double-crossed me? That the little weasel left me high and dry?" Memory's tone was harsh and slightly laced with anger. "Left me with nothing except a slew of folks looking for me. Which now I can see, apparently, you were one of them."

"Hmmm, it is a shame, isn't it? How there's just no honor among thieves these days. Which is why I have a legally enforceable business proposition I think you'll be most interested in." He sat down and handed her a sheet of paper from the folder. "I'm willing to let you have that Alexandrite necklace, and all you have to do is agree to sell me the house my aunt Sarah lives in after she passes on."

Memory almost laughed out loud. "Sell you the house?"

"Yes. I have it on good authority that you're going to inherit the house upon her death. I'm sure you don't care anything about that old place. I'm not asking you to give it to me; I intend to pay you its fair-market value. You're not going to get gypped in the deal." He leaned in closer to her. "All it will take is your signature on that agreement"—he pointed at the paper she held—"witnessed by a notary public or a lawyer, which— believe it or not—my lawyer just *happens* to be here, waiting in another room. If you sign that piece of paper today, you can have the Alexandrite necklace . . . free and clear today."

She snickered. "I can have it? And it won't cost me one red cent, you say?"

"Not one red cent," he said, practically mocking her.

"And the only thing I have to do is sign this paper stating I'll sell you the house once my mother dies, should I inherit it—which neither one of us can be certain will end up being the case," Memory said. "Looks to me you're taking quite a risk here."

"Trust me—you're the main heir to my aunt's vast fortune." Montgomery began to stare off into the distance. Returning his eyes to her, he said, "And there's quite a fortune to be had. I should know. I was the one managing things. That's until Aunt Sarah came back four years ago and commandeered almost everything I and my family have worked so hard to keep and acquire completely away from me." There was a twinge of anger in his voice this time. He suddenly began to chuckle quietly to himself.

"And how do I know for certain you have the funds to purchase her house, *should* I inherit it and decide to sell it to you as you're asking *here*?" She shook the paper.

"I assure you, I still have plenty of money." He took out a pen and laid it on the table. "However, the agreement states I'll purchase the house at fair-market value, and if I can't, then I don't get it. It's as cut and dry as that. This won't cost you a thing. The way I see it, you're not going to want to keep that old house anyway. This makes it easy for you to take the money, a quite substantial amount of cold, hard cash, in fact, and do whatever you want. See the world, share the money with your family . . . buy yourself a nice home wherever you'd really like to settle down—whatever you want to do. All I want is the house and all of its contents. When the time comes, you sell it, take the money, and walk away . . . free and clear. In the meantime, your having the necklace makes things right with your family. A win-win situation for everyone. So, shall I call my lawyer in now?"

"And why do you want that house and its contents so badly?"

"Pure and simple—sentimental value. That house and all the things inside of it have been in our family for generations now."

"Oh, just say it. You believe you'd appreciate and take much better care of it than I ever would." Memory brought the paper closer as she began to slowly scan over it.

"Honestly? Yes."

"Seeing as you say we treat people according to how we see ourselves, I'm sure you'll appreciate my wanting to read this agreement thoroughly before signing it."

"Fine. But I would like to make one request, if I may," Montgomery said.

She laid the paper down on her lap and stared at him. "And that would be?"

"That we keep this between the two of us. I'd prefer you not mention any of this to Aunt Sarah or anyone else for that matter."

Memory looked hard at him. "Why . . ." She nodded, then smiled. "Of course."

Chapter 16

*And the mean man shall be brought
down, and the mighty man shall be
humbled, and the eyes of the lofty
shall be humbled. . . .*

Isaiah 5:15

Reverend Marshall Walker walked into his old friend's
hospital room. Occasional whirling, hissing, sucking, and pumping sounds from the various medical machines filled the air. Poppa Knight's wife had called
him Saturday morning at her husband's request. She'd
also informed Reverend Walker that Poppa Knight's im-
minent departure was at hand. For whatever reason,
Reverend Walker didn't come Saturday. It was now Tuesday.

"Hey, Poppa Knight, can you hear me?" Reverend
Walker said in his slightly bass voice. "It's me—Marshall." He was standing next to the bed. Poppa Knight
had been in a coma since Saturday afternoon and was
now on a ventilator.

"If only you had come Saturday when I called," Mrs.
Knight said. "I told you how dire things were. If
you'd have made it before Saturday afternoon, you
might have—"

"I'm sorry. You know I wanted to, Sister Knight. It just
couldn't be helped," Reverend Walker said. "Duties.
You understand?" His face softened as he looked at
her.

In truth, he could have come Saturday. *But then, who would have been in charge of the ministers' meeting?* There was much to discuss—namely, his upcoming pastor's appreciation. In a few weeks, top folks would be coming into town from all around the country. He didn't really need the other ministers' input. Although secretly, he did enjoy watching the awe shown whenever he mentioned certain bigwigs' names he knew personally and those taking part in his celebration. If anyone would understand why he couldn't make it Saturday, he knew Poppa Knight would. Sundays were always full with two worship services and afternoon preaching engagements. Mondays were his off-days. So Tuesday was really the first day he could come. How was he supposed to know before he could get there Poppa Knight would slip into a coma? After he heard about it, he knew Poppa Knight wouldn't know he was there no matter what day he came now.

The light-skinned, medium-size-framed Mrs. Knight excused herself and left the room to give the two of them some alone-time together.

"Well, old friend, it looks like you're trying to give up on us," Reverend Walker said to Poppa Knight. "Believe me, I understand. I suppose this just got to be too much for you. We've seen a lot in life, that's for sure. But don't you worry. . . . I promise, I plan to preach a heart-wrenching, powerful sermon at your funeral—one folks won't soon forget. I owe you that much. You absolutely deserve it. Not that I'm trying to hurry you along or anything. You know I have nothing but love for you. Together, we've been through much, my friend—you and I. So much that even today, you're the only person on earth who holds my deepest, darkest secret . . . our secret, really. That alone proves how close we are and have remained." He slowly lowered himself into the chair next to Poppa Knight's bed and leaned in closer, placing his hand on the rail of the bed as he continued.

"I suppose when you do leave us, you'll be taking all those secrets with you. I'm going to miss you, there's no question about that. You've been a good friend and a loyal confidant. Although I admit you did change somewhat on me this past year. You even went as far as visiting Pastor Landris's church, more than once from what I hear. But I'm not mad at you. Oh, no. And don't you worry about good old Pastor Landris, either. I'm going to make sure he's well taken care of after you're gone."

He looked up and watched as Mrs. Knight dragged herself back into the room. "It's hard seeing him like this," Reverend Walker said to her. He stood up and wiped away a nonexistent tear.

"Yes. The doctor feels we should take him off life support. At this point, I'm just not sure what I should do." She forced a smile. "What if he really could get better later? What if I tell them to do it, but if I'd merely waited another day or another week . . . ?"

Reverend Walker went to her. "Sister Knight, there are times when we need to learn to just let go and let God. The way I see it is, if God wants our dear brother to remain with us, He'll keep him here long after that man-made machine is turned off." He pointed at the ventilator. "If God wants him to come on home to glory to be with Him, then who are we to stand in God's way?"

Mrs. Knight broke down and began to cry. "I know what you're saying is right. But it's so hard. In spite of our ups and downs, Paul and I had a pretty good marriage. Not perfect by any stretch of the imagination. But for the most part, it worked for us. We loved each other. And this past year, oh"—she clapped her hands and shook her head as she blushed—"has been positively wonderful! Even with him being sick and all, it's been almost like I was married to a totally different man." She yanked out four paper tissues.

Reverend Walker embraced her. "I must apologize. I was so busy; I wasn't there much for either of you. I'm sure this *has* been a challenging time for you both."

She looked up at him, wiped her tears with the fistful of tissues, and smiled as she nodded. "Yes, it has. I know how busy life can be and especially life in the ministry. But others have filled in where you couldn't. His friends have visited regularly, doing whatever they could here and there . . . giving words of encouragement just when we needed a word the most. Theodore, and especially . . . especially Reverend Grant."

Reverend Walker nodded. "Reverend Simpson certainly is a good man," he said, commenting on Reverend Theodore Simpson only. Reverend Grant had become distant with him lately. He was changing . . . like Poppa Knight had. So Reverend Walker wasn't sure what was going on with him, nor did he care to talk about Perry Grant right now. He continued to console Mrs. Knight.

"And then there's Pastor Landris. He has been a true godsend," she said. "I truly, truly thank God for him."

Reverend Walker pushed her away gently and looked at her. "Pastor Landris?"

"Yes," she said, dabbing at her eyes with her tissue as though that would stop the flow. "In fact, he came by early Saturday morning and again Saturday afternoon after Paul went into this coma." She looked down and smiled at her husband. "That morning, Paul asked him to preach his funeral."

Reverend Walker fought to maintain his composure. "He did? Well, now, you do know Poppa Knight has always said if he ever went before me, he wanted me to preach his funeral. You don't really believe you can take seriously what he said on Saturday . . . seeing that

he was most likely too heavily medicated to even know
what he was saying, do you?"

"He was pretty lucid. That's why I suppose he wanted
to see you on Saturday. He wanted to say his good-byes
himself and make sure some of his last wishes were
known. Maybe he wanted to relay to you his desire regarding his funeral and Pastor Landris. I can't honestly
say what all he wanted; he didn't tell me before he
lapsed into this coma."

Reverend Walker pulled her back close to him again.
"Well, let's not talk on such things right now. I believe
Poppa Knight's going to pull through, and all this talk
about a funeral will be for nothing. At least for now,
anyway. We all have to leave here someday; this is not
our home. We're just pilgrims traveling through this
unfriendly land. But we know that God is still in the
healing business. Who's to say what our Father in Heaven
is up to when it comes to our brother in the Lord?" He
released her and planted a kiss on her cheek as he patted her on the back.

He then looked at his Rolex watch so that there
would be no mistaking he was checking it. "Look at
the time. So much to do. I really must be going now.
You, of all people, know that a pastor's work is never
done." He had a look of true sincerity. "Are you going
to be all right here alone?"

She took a deep breath as she nodded. "I'm not alone.
There are others here with me in the waiting room."
She exhaled as she carefully and tenderly took hold of
her husband's limp hand and placed it against the side
of her face.

Reverend Walker hugged her once more, then started
out of the room. Right before he completely walked out,
he turned around and looked back at his long time
friend . . . one more time, and nodded.

Chapter 17

*Until I come and take you away to a
land like your own land, a land of corn
and wine, a land of bread and vineyards.*

Isaiah 36:17

Memory came back after having met with Montgomery Powell the Second. Sarah had given her a
key so she could come and go as she pleased. She'd
been there a week now. Theresa had gone home Saturday, shortly after noon when Maurice came back and
got her and the children. Lena and Richard were still
there. Other than "Hello" and "Good night," Lena and
Theresa had barely exchanged twenty words with
Memory after that first day.

Lena knew how much Sarah wanted everyone to get
along and become a true family. She only wished she
could trust Memory's motives enough to do that. She and
Memory hadn't had a real chance to sit down alone together and talk. Memory had told Sarah earlier that day
that she was going out to see a little more of Asheville.
The last time Memory was in Asheville, she'd been in
her midteens.

Lena looked out the window when Memory was
leaving that afternoon and saw her get into a black Lincoln Town Car. Curious, she watched as it drove away.
Lena couldn't help but wonder who Memory could
possibly know well enough that they would send a car

for her. That same car brought her home a few hours later.

"When you get time, I'd like to talk with you," Lena said as soon as Memory stepped foot back into the house.

Holding tight her purse's strap, Memory said, "I have some time right now."

"Can we go up to my room? I have something I need to show you," Lena said.

They went to the bedroom Lena and Richard stayed in whenever they visited.

Lena closed the door and motioned for Memory to have a seat on the couch.

"Lena," Memory said as she sat down while reaching into her tourist-bag-size purse. "I have something I want to give you first before we begin." She pulled out a black velvet box and held it out to her daughter.

"What is it?"

"Take it and see for yourself," Memory said. Noting Lena's hesitation she said, "Please" in a not-so-pleading voice.

Lena took the box and opened it as Memory had instructed. She looked at Memory as her knees began to buckle, causing her to sit beside her. "The Alexandrite necklace. But I thought : . . Didn't you sell this for a reward? How did you get it back?"

Memory released a sigh. "Lena. I made a mistake, and that mistake cost me dearly. It cost me the love and trust of my family. You and Theresa mean so much to me—you have no idea how much. Yet both of you have barely been able to force yourselves to look at me except with a look of contempt and disdain this whole week we've been here."

Lena shook her head reflectively as she took out the necklace and touched it lovingly and gently with her fingers. So many memories came flooding back as she gazed down at this spectacular piece of jewelry. Tears welled up in her eyes—she couldn't help but think of Big Mama and those last days spent together. "I'm sorry. I'm confused. Does this mean you really *didn't* sell it?" She buttoned her lips tight, then relaxed them.

"Can we not talk about that part of our past right now? I admit I was wrong, and I'm apologizing. I never should have taken that necklace the way I did. But I'm trying to make things right. I'm asking you to forgive me. Please." Her eyes were now pleading.

Lena looked at her. Again, she shook her head as she slowly held the necklace out to Memory. "Here you go."

"What? You don't want it? You can't find it in your heart to forgive me? What?"

Lena began a nervous laugh. "No. That's not it at all. This necklace has always belonged to you. I didn't know that when Big Mama told me to keep it safe. But I've learned this much to be a fact after all that's transpired." She grabbed Memory's hand; holding it, she let the necklace drop. It appeared as though it was being poured into Memory's palm.

Memory put the necklace back in its box and back in her purse. "Okay, I'm lost now. If you didn't want the necklace, then what has all this silent treatment been about?"

"You don't get it. It's been about love and trust and the breaking of that love and trust. I opened up my heart to you, and again you stomped on it like it was nothing. Only it wasn't just *my* heart you trashed this last time around. When you left in 2001, you trampled Theresa's heart as well. Let's move on." Lena stood, walked over to the dresser, and opened the bottom drawer. Taking out a wooden box, she walked back with it.

Instantly, Memory recognized it. "That's the box the Alexandrite necklace was in when that woman, Grace, gave it to Mama . . . to Mamie," Memory said, stuttering slightly as she hurriedly spoke. "But it was empty when I found it, and I threw it away. I distinctively remember throwing it away. How did you happen to find it?"

Lena stood next to Memory. "It's not exactly the same box. There were three of these made. Big Mama had one—that's the box that held the necklace and other things given to her by Grace. Sarah had one she gave to a woman named Pearl Black for safekeeping here in Asheville right before she was sent away all those many years ago. And then . . . there was this one. The one Grace left to me and you in her will."

Memory took the exquisite box and examined it more closely. "I love the workmanship."

"Your father made it. Your biological father, that is," Lena said as she continued to stand there. "A man named Ransom Perdue."

Memory's face suddenly drained of all color and expression as she looked at Lena. "My father?" She tried to compose herself. "Ransom Perdue? I hadn't even thought about that. I've only known Willie B. as being my father. I'm sorry, but I need a moment to digest this. That kind of caught me off guard." She stood up, purse on her shoulder, and held the box against her chest. Pacing, she mindlessly ran her hand over the box.

"Memory, Grace left that box with instructions for you and me to open it together. She also left a video she recorded."

Memory turned and shot her an evil look. "I've been here for a week. Why are you just now telling me this?" She backed away from Lena until she bumped into the bed and could go no farther. "Have you seen what's inside this box already?" she asked.

Lena shook her head. "No, I haven't. And the reason I'm just now telling you this . . . Quite honestly, I'm

aware of how much Sarah loves you. But you have hurt
and disappointed so many people so many times, Memory, I found it difficult to even be in the same room
with you. I've tried hard to understand how or why you
do the things that you do. And do you know what's so
bad? It doesn't seem to bother you. It's whatever serves
you at the time. It's never the other way around."

Memory looked at her. "Lena, when I took that necklace, believe me, it bothered me. And do you know
why? Because of you and Theresa. For the first time in
a long time, I actually felt like I had and was part of a
real family. But after I did that, I knew that was the end
of all of that. I knew neither of you would ever forgive
me. And judging from the look on your face even after
everything now, I see I was right."

"I just don't understand why you do what you do."

Memory sat down on the bed. She set the box down
next to her. "The thought of all that money made me
greedy to the point where I didn't care about anybody
else other than myself. That's why I came to Atlanta in
the first place. But something changed while I was there.
I changed. And if only you knew how horrible I felt
leaving Theresa the way I did that day, that horrible day
that only seemed to have gotten worse as the day went
along. And then knowing that I had a brand-new great-
grandbaby that I'd likely never be able to see or hold . . .
Oh, that tore me up something awful inside."

"I'm sorry. But I still don't understand why you did it."

"Sometimes we get ourselves into things pride won't
let us walk away from. I never knew how much I was
going to love you or Theresa . . . or that baby even, which,
incidentally, I only got to see this past week. But I'd already made a deal with the devil, so to speak, and there
was no way of getting out of it. I'm trying to prove to
everybody that I *have* changed. This necklace"—she

took the necklace out of her purse and out of the box—
"should say how much." Memory sighed. "So . . . what
do we do about *this* box?"

"We break the seal. We take this special key"—Lena
poured an unusual-looking key out of a small manila
envelope and held it up, then went and sat on the bed
next to Memory—"and we open it. We go wherever the
contents of that box happen to take us."

Memory set the necklace on the bed, picked up the
box, and started to break the seal, when she stopped.
She handed the box to Lena. "Why don't *you* do the
honor?"

Lena took the box and looked at Memory. This was
the first time in all of her life she could ever remember
her mother putting someone else before herself. She
looked at Memory, nodded, then smiled.

Lena broke the wax seal off the box. She placed the
key inside the lock and turned it. Slowly opening the
lid, she and Memory began exchanging looks between
them.

The door to the bedroom flew open. "I'm sorry," Gayle
said, practically out of breath. "But you need to come
quick! It's Ms. Fleming. Something's wrong. She's asking for you both."

Lena closed the lid quickly and set the box down on
the bed right next to the necklace. "What's wrong with
her?"

"Her breathing's not stable. Her blood pressure has
shot up. I called her doctor, and he said we had to get
her to the hospital as quickly as possible. The ambulance is already on its way, but Ms. Fleming insists you
both need to come right now," Gayle said.

Lena and Memory were already out of the door
while Gayle was still speaking.

"Grandmother, what's wrong?" Lena asked as she

hastily took hold of her grandmother's now cool and clammy hand.

Sarah looked at Lena and frowned. "Memory? Where's my Memory?"

Memory stepped over and up where she could be seen better. "I'm right here."

Sarah smiled, reached her other hand over to Memory, and closed her eyes. "That's good. That's good." She fought to speak and breathe. "You're both here . . . together. That's good. . . ." She suddenly became quiet as she appeared to merely drift off to sleep.

Chapter 18

Sapphire had spoken with Dr. Holden and had become concerned when she learned that Charity had taken the notebook and left the safety of Dr. Holden's office to read what was inside it.

"Why did you just let her leave?" Sapphire respectfully asked Dr. Holden over the phone.

"Now, you know I can't force anyone to stay here, no more than I could have forced her to read it while she was in my presence, nor taken it back when she refused to read it while she was here," Dr. Holden said. "Besides, I didn't see anything, at least from what I read, that would be too much for her to handle."

"Well, I've been calling her for the past hour, and she's not answering either her home or her cell phone. I'm going over to her house to make sure she's all right."

Standing outside Charity's house, Sapphire rang the doorbell. No answer. She knocked. She called from her cell phone. She called out "Hello" as she knocked. But no matter which route she took, there was no answer. Pressing the doorbell repeatedly, Sapphire prayed Charity would come to the door and relieve her increasing concern. Beginning the cycle again, she rang the doorbell, called from her phone, called out to "Anyone in there," and knocked. For whatever reason, there was no answer.

Sapphire knocked on the door a few more times. After ten minutes of no response, she walked around the house and peeped through any of the windows she was able to see into. The house was eerily quiet, but she knew that didn't mean Charity wasn't in there.

Knowing it was past his work time, Sapphire called Dr. Holden on his cell phone.

"Dr. Holden, I'm at Charity's house, and she's not answering the door, either." Sapphire pressed the doorbell while speaking as though she were trying to show him.

"Sounds to me like she's just not home."

"Yes. Or maybe she read the notebook and everything came flooding back to her. Who can say what might have happened?"

"I'm telling you, I didn't see anything in there that would send Charity over the edge. Sapphire, you know if I had, I wouldn't have given it to her the way that I did."

"But you did say it shed at least *some* light on what may have happened."

"A hint. But in my opinion, it wasn't some conclusive, damaging revelation."

"Respectfully, Dr. Holden, but you know what may not be damaging for one can be devastating for another," Sapphire said. "What if there was coded information in it that holds the key to some unwritten message only Charity could decipher?"

"I believe Charity has made tremendous progress these past months. So even if that's the case, I trust that she'll come through this just fine," Dr. Holden said.

"I pray that's so." Sapphire looked at her watch. She had asked Pastor Landris earlier if it was okay for her to visit Johnnie Mae. He thought seeing Sapphire would be good for her. "I'm going now. I want to stop by and see Johnnie Mae before it gets late."

"I thought they asked people not to visit her right now," Dr. Holden said.

"I cleared it with Pastor Landris. Besides, I wasn't planning on staying long."

"Please give her all of our best."

"I will."

"And Sapphire?"

"Yes?"

"Don't worry about Charity. She's a lot stronger than you give her credit for."

"Yeah. Well, I'm going to leave a note on her door to let her know I was here."

Sapphire went to the hospital and located Johnnie Mae's room. She stopped as soon as she stepped inside. "Charity?" she said with a smile and a huge sigh of relief.

Charity smiled back. "Hi, Sapphire."

"Well, hello there, Sapphire," Johnnie Mae said with a grin. "Now, how awesome is this? Two of my favorite people here at the same time."

Sapphire walked over and kissed Johnnie Mae on the cheek. "How are you?"

Johnnie Mae nodded as she quickly glanced at her stomach. "We're doing okay."

Sapphire sat down in the other chair in the room. "I just left your house," Sapphire said, addressing her attention to Charity.

"My house?" Charity asked. "What were you doing at my house?"

"Checking up on you. . . . Making sure you're okay."

Charity smiled. "As you can tell, I'm fine."

Sapphire nodded. "So I see."

Johnnie Mae quickly picked up on some tension in the room. She wasn't sure where it was coming from or why, but it was definitely thick enough to dip a spoon in.

A nurse came in, pushing a small cart. "I don't mean to put you two out, but I have a few things I need to do. It shouldn't take but ten or fifteen minutes," she said.

"Why don't you both go down to the cafeteria and get a cup of coffee or a bite to eat? By the time you get back, I'm sure we'll be done," Johnnie Mae said, looking from Sapphire to Charity as she spoke.

"I realize we're supposed to be staying out of the way," Charity said. "Besides, I've been here once already today. Why don't I just come back another time?"

"Now you're going to make me feel bad," Johnnie Mae said. "I really want to see you both; I love the company. Go get something or do something and come back in about fifteen minutes." She lowered her head, raised it, wrinkled her nose, then said, "Please."

Sapphire looked at Johnnie Mae, then Charity. "You know, I think that's a great idea. I haven't eaten anything since lunch, and this will give you and me some time to talk, Charity. You can catch me up on what's going on with you these days."

"See now, this is going to work out for everybody," Johnnie Mae said. "The nurse can do what she needs, you two can visit with each other for a little bit, then the both of you can come back and visit with me a while longer."

Sapphire and Charity left the room and caught the elevator to the cafeteria. Getting something to eat, they exchanged looks as they set their trays down on the table.

Sapphire began. "Johnnie Mae must have somehow known we needed to talk."

"So it appears," Charity said. "Would you say grace?"

She bowed her head, as did Sapphire, who prayed a short prayer of thanks for the food they were about to receive. "Okay," Charity said as she picked up a chunk of chicken salad with her fork, "what exactly do you feel we need to talk about?"

Sapphire concentrated her full attention on Charity's face as she tried to read her. "I know we had a session last week, but how are you? I mean *today*, how are you?"

"I'm doing very well. My life feels normal for a change, and I like it. There haven't been any blackouts or unaccounted-for time as far as I can tell. It seems there's only me and my life to deal with these days. That was our goal when we began, right?"

"The goal was to get your personalities integrated . . . to make you whole again. But also to ensure you stay all right. Listen, Charity, Dr. Holden told me about the notebook. He said he gave it to you today during your session. Have you read it yet?"

Charity looked down as she began to play with her food. "No."

Sapphire used a quiet, nonthreatening voice. "May I ask you why not?"

Charity looked up at her. Sapphire's eyes were piercing, but in a good way. She felt like Sapphire honestly cared. "I'm afraid of what it might unleash. Sapphire, I'm doing really well now. We thought I needed to face what happened all those years ago in order for me to reach a good place. Well, we can see I'm there already without it. What if the words in that notebook send me back to a divided place again? What if I can't handle it the way you and Dr. Holden believe I can?"

"But you need to face it, Charity. That's how strong-holds are brought down." Sapphire leaned in closer. "Why didn't you read it while you were in Dr. Holden's office?"

"Because then I would have *had* to read it. He would

have sat there waiting for me to do it, saying things to urge me to do it, and I wasn't ready." She took a sip of her cola. "I just wasn't ready. To be honest, I'm not sure when or even *if* I'll ever be ready. Maybe it's best we leave the past in the past. Besides, if Faith wrote it, maybe she was merely setting me up so she could do her worst damage and rid herself of me once and for all."

"The Faith personality knows you have support now." Sapphire sat back. "I think she may have written that because she knew you were stronger, and that she truly wasn't needed, separately from you, anymore. She wanted to leave you with the truth so you could be whole again. Faith is still inside of you. . . . She's a part of the real you—the strong part you've always possessed."

Charity bit down on her bottom lip, then placed her hand over her mouth to keep from crying.

Sapphire leaned in again and touched the back of Charity's left hand that now rested on the table. "Charity, what are you thinking right now? What's getting you so upset? Dr. Holden would never have given you that notebook if he thought it would damage the progress you've made. This much I'm certain of. Dr. Holden's one of the best."

"But what if you and Dr. Holden are wrong? What if those words mean something to me that you or he has no way of knowing? Do I really want to take that chance? Do *you* want to, after all the work and efforts you've put into helping me finally get to this great place in my life? You, wrestling with the conflict-of-interest question when it came to Faith being part of me and whether or not you should even treat me?"

Sapphire fell back against her chair as though she were letting go of something she'd been tightly holding on to. "Why didn't you just read it with him there with you?"

Charity speared a grape tomato with her fork and stuck it in her mouth. Chewing it up and swallowing it, she said, "Because I don't know if I ever really want to know the truth. Whatever it was, it can't be good. It caused me to develop split personalities."

Sapphire reached over and touched the back of Charity's hand that held her fork. "Charity, you were a child then. A child. You're not a child anymore. What you might not have been able to handle then, you're a different person now." She removed her hand. "Would you like for me to read it, or at least be there with you when you do?"

Charity's body visibly relaxed; she looked up and smiled. "Yes. I really would like you to be there."

"Okay," Sapphire said as she released a quiet sigh. "When would you like to do that? We can go to your house, my place, or to my office—wherever you feel more comfortable. Whenever and whatever you feel will work best for you."

"I have the notebook in my car. Can we go to my house after we finish visiting with Johnnie Mae? That's if you don't already have plans."

Sapphire smiled. "Sure." Sapphire could see the tenseness come back in Charity's face. "Relax. . . . Everything's going to be all right. You and I, with the help of the Lord, are going to get through this together."

Charity forced a smile in return. She nodded. "Yeah," she said, trying to maintain a smile that, despite her best efforts, continued to fall. "Yeah."

Chapter 19

*Now will I sing to my well-beloved a
song of my beloved touching his vineyard. My well-beloved hath a vineyard
in a very fruitful hill. . . .*

Isaiah 5:1

Pastor Landris had just finished powering down his
computer. Johnnie Mae was in the hospital, and he
was doing his best to effectively juggle church work,
home life, and family obligations while making sure he
spent as much time with her as possible. His main pri-
ority was to keep his wife calm during this touchy and
stressful time. Dr. Baker had laid the entire situation
out to him. She'd held nothing back. They were main-
taining close checks on both Johnnie Mae and the
baby. So far, things appeared to be stabilizing.

Brent Underwood had become Pastor Landris's trusted
right-hand man. Angela Gabriel was Johnnie Mae's executive assistant for the things dealing with her books
and speaking engagements and her work at church.
Brent and Angela became engaged on Valentine's Day,
with the wedding, to be held at the church, set for mid-
October. They'd secured a new golf-course clubhouse
facility called Ross Bridge for the reception. Angel, as
most called her, had been extremely busy managing and
rearranging Johnnie Mae's calendar as needed, while
continuing to work diligently on her own wedding plans.

Pastor Landris looked up as Brent rapped his knuckle
on his opened door.

"You're getting ready to go?" Brent asked, seeing Pastor Landris shutting down and putting things away for the day. He stepped inside, closing the door behind him.

"Yeah."

Dressed in a white shirt that didn't require a tie in order for him to look as though he was dressed up, Brent was a businessman from his heart. "May I speak with you a minute before you go?" Brent asked. "I promise I'll be brief."

"Sure, Brent. No problem." Pastor Landris pointed at the chair in front of his mahogany desk and sat down.

Brent sat and began to smile. Pastor Landris smiled back as he patiently waited. He had a feeling, from the grin plastered on Brent's face, where this conversation was most likely headed.

"You know I love Angel, right?"

"Yeah, I kind of picked up on that." Pastor Landris continued to return Brent's smile. "Your being engaged and set to be married soon was a dead giveaway," Pastor Landris said seriously but jokingly.

"Well, we're running into a small problem. Let me see. How do I say this?" He darted his head in and out a few times as he made various facial expressions.

"Why not just come right out and say it?" Pastor Landris said, smiling.

"Yeah. Well . . . you see . . . things have been getting a bit intense with us here lately—Angel and I." He looked at Pastor Landris, trying to gauge his reaction. "I'm talking sexually. . . . I don't mean sexually, but I mean when we're together. It's like sparks and electricity and sweating, with increased heart rates, which is not good with that much electricity flying about. Angel walks in a room, and I light up like a Christmas tree. I mean, literally. I can't help it. I find myself smiling just thinking about her."

"Oh, you mean like now?"

Brent started laughing and shaking his head. "Yeah, like now. It's hard to keep my mind on anything because it somehow manages to wander back to thoughts of her. I don't know what happened. I've been with other women, but I've never felt anywhere *near* anything like this with anyone else before. I'm Brent Underwood. And it's not lust."

"So, are you two still . . . ?"

Brent sat up straight and quickly dropped his smile. "Oh, we're still keeping things holy. But Pastor Landris, I have to be honest with you—it's hard. I never knew anything could be so hard. Maybe it's because I've never made a true commitment like this with a woman *and* with God. I suppose what I'm trying to say is, Pastor Landris, I don't think Angel and I can make it to October fifteenth."

Pastor Landris tried to maintain a straight face. "What if you two spent less time alone together until then? You know, only do things with other people. Talk on the phone instead of in person, those sorts of things."

"Pastor Landris, I sit in my office working hard, and all day long, I'm thinking about her. I walk around with this silly grin on my face throughout the day. No matter who I'm talking to, somehow, my thoughts end up drifting to thoughts of Angel. Sitting here . . . right now . . . talking to you, my pastor, who I know has plenty of troubles of your own, and the thought of her is right here with us. I want to be with Angel now. Four months feels like an eternity to me. Sure, my head knows I can hold out until then, but my heart has gone off on a tangent all its own."

Pastor Landris nodded. "I feel you. Believe me, I feel you. And don't think for a minute that I'm so religious I don't understand what you're saying. Tell me. How does Angela feel about this?"

"The same way I do. We can be sitting innocently on the opposite ends of the couch watching a television program together, and it's there. Just last night, she was handing me the remote control, my hand touched hers, and she pulled back like I had burnt her or something. The next thing I know, she was on her feet saying 'You have to go!' and she put me out of her apartment. We can't even kiss anymore, quite frankly, because we're afraid where that may lead us. I'm just being honest with you."

Pastor Landris sat back and started swiveling his chair. "If you two can manage to keep focused and keep yourselves until October, I assure you, you're going to have some kind of a special honeymoon."

Brent stood to his feet. "That's the problem. Angel and I talked extensively on the phone last night and earlier today at lunch, and we both decided we can't wait. We were wondering if it's possible for you to marry us in the next two weeks." He stuck his hand in his pocket. "I know you have a lot going on. I promise you, she and I discussed this from all angles. We really don't want to get married in the courthouse—that's just too impersonal. I know we could ask another minister to perform the ceremony, but . . ."

Pastor Landris stood and walked in front of Brent. "There's nothing that would bring me more joy than to marry the two of you. But are you sure about this? You guys were planning a pretty elaborate wedding ceremony."

"Here's what we were thinking. We could have a secret ceremony, just a few people knowing about it. That way we'd be legally married and fully permitted to be a married couple in every sense of the word. We could still have the ceremony in October, which would be for everybody else's benefit," Brent said. "I don't want to take Angel's dream wedding away from her. I know how much it means to her. She's so sentimental about everything. But Pastor Landris, the truth of the matter is, we can't wait to become one. There's no need in us trying to fool ourselves and continuing to play with fire."

"If you want to have a private ceremony, we can do that. I admire you both for your resolve to keep yourselves pure until marriage. Many couples would have just acted on their feelings, with *only* four months left to go." He gently slapped Brent on his back. "But I'm proud of you both." He smiled. "It takes a *real* man, a *real* woman, to stand like you two are choosing to do. *Anybody* can cave in."

"So, if you can look at your calendar and see what will work for you, we'd like to have it on a Friday or Saturday, if that's possible. I know you have your hands full already."

"What about a Sunday evening?" Pastor Landris asked.

"That would be fine. I just thought you might not want to do it on a Sunday. That's why I didn't suggest it."

Pastor Landris hunched his shoulders. "A Sunday evening is fine with me. Just let me know what date and time you and Angela desire, and we'll go from there." He walked back around to his desk and wrote himself a note.

"I'm going to let you finish up so you can get on out of here." Brent reached his hand across the desk to shake Pastor Landris's hand. "Sorry for holding you. Thanks again for hearing me out."

Pastor Landris pumped his hand once with a firm handshake then sandwiched his hand with his other hand prior to releasing it. "No problem. It's been my pleasure. As I said, you're a good man, Brent Underwood. And I'm proud to know you."

Brent shook his head and smiled. He looked like a little boy who had just been commended for having

118 *Vanessa Davis Griggs*

helped a person in need cross the street. "It's funny. You often tell me how proud you are of me. You rarely ever hear that come from one man to another. I've certainly never heard it from my own father."

"That's a 'man thing' we need to get out of," Pastor Landris said as he went and took his suit coat off the back of the closet door in his office and put it on. "It's particularly important we as men tell our children how we feel—both sons and daughters. Let your father know what you need from him. Help him to help you become the man God is calling the men of your generation—the Joshua generation, the *'Well able to take the land'* generation—to step up and be. He just may not know hearing something like that is important to you. Tell him how you feel." Pastor Landris placed his hand on Brent's shoulder and shook him gently. "Communication is the key to *any* successful relationship—both the vertical and the horizontal ones. Remember that."

Brent nodded and smiled as he turned and walked away. He placed his hand on the door handle, then turned back to Pastor Landris. "Yeah," he said, smiling even more. He pointed his index finger at Pastor Landris to show his appreciation once again, then left.

Chapter 20

*And even to your old age I am He; and
even to hoar hairs will I carry you: I
have made, and I will bear; even I will
carry, and will deliver you.*

Isaiah 46:4

S arah opened her eyes and looked up.
Memory smiled at her. "Welcome back," she said.

Sarah turned to survey her surroundings. "What happened? Where am I?"

"You're in the hospital," Memory said. "Lena's here."
Lena moved closer to the forefront, where it would be
easier for Sarah to see her.

"How are you feeling?" Lena asked as she took hold
of Sarah's hand.

Sarah shook her head. "I was at home. What happened?"

"You had a slight stroke, but the doctor says you're
doing much better," Lena said.

Sarah slowly raised her left hand and, just as slowly,
let it back down.

"It didn't appear to have caused any major damage,"
Memory said, realizing that must be what she was
looking to see. "At least, not from what they can tell so
far."

"When can I go home?" Sarah asked Memory.

"They want to keep you here for a few days—mainly,
to check you out some more and for observation purposes. Just making sure you're really okay."

Sarah looked at Lena. "I feel just fine. I'd like to go home now. I really don't care to be here. Didn't y'all tell them I have my own nurse at home? Gayle? Where's Gayle? She can monitor me from my house." She looked around the hospital room slowly. "I just don't want to be here."

Lena brushed back the stray graying hair that had made its way out of the pulled-up bun Sarah was wearing. "Gayle's talking with your doctor now. You'll be able to go home soon. Everybody just wants to be sure you're okay. This is for your own good."

Sarah turned her focus more toward Memory. "Please get me out of here. I don't want to be here. I've lost too much time being confined as it is already. Always for my own good. I feel fine, truly I do. Will you please tell them I'd prefer being at home?" The more she spoke, the more agitated she was becoming. She reached out her hand to Memory.

Memory took her hand. "We'll see what we can do. But we want you to be okay first and foremost. A few days in here won't be that bad. And Lena and I will be here with you every step of the way." She looked at Lena and smiled. "Won't we?"

Sarah squeezed Memory's hand. "You promise?"

Memory smiled. "I promise." She looked at Lena again. "Don't we?"

Lena smiled down at Sarah. "You know we're not going to leave you here all alone. You don't ever have to worry about being alone again. We promise. One of us will be somewhere close by as long as you're here."

Sarah smiled, then closed her eyes. "Never alone," she started mumbling again and again. "Jesus promised never to leave me," she said, then quietly started drifting off to sleep again. "Never to leave me alone . . ."

Lena and Memory walked out of the room. "Richard will be here shortly. He was going to take us back to the house, but one of us should be here when she wakes up again," Lena said.

"I was thinking the same thing. Why don't you go back to the house tonight, and I'll stay. Then I'll go in the morning while you stay," Memory said.

"Are you sure? I know you're probably tired now, too. You were out earlier visiting the city before this happened. I don't mind if you go home while I stay."

"I'll be fine. I'll just make myself comfortable in that reclining chair. . . . Stretch it out—you know the routine. When I get tired enough, I'll simply close my eyes and catch me some shut-eye. I've learned how to pretty much sleep anywhere with no problems."

"Okay, I'll go home and do what I need to, get some rest, and be back here first thing in the morning." Just then, Lena spotted Richard and a middle-aged white woman walking toward them. "Here's Richard now," she said.

When Richard and the woman reached Memory and Lena, Richard hugged Lena.

"How is she?" he asked.

"She was awake and talking earlier. She's asleep right now." Lena looked at the woman, impeccably dressed in a flower-print, form-fitting dress, standing beside Richard. "I'm Lena Jordan—Richard's wife . . . Sarah's granddaughter. And you are?"

"Oh, I'm sorry. This is Polly . . ." Richard looked at her for help in recalling her last name.

"Swindle. *Mrs.* Polly Swindle. I'm a good friend of Sarah's." She shook Lena's hand, then Memory's. Her speech was proper, clearly London English mixed with a kiss of some Southern influence.

Lena smiled slightly. "Oh, yes. Polly. My grandmother has mentioned you quite often. Thank you for looking in on her the way that you do."

"Oh, I adore Sarah Fleming."

Lena turned to Memory. "And this is my mother—Memory."

"So this is Memory," Polly said. "I finally get to meet you. Sarah has waited so long for this, and when she told me you were here, I wanted to come over right then and there to give you a great big Asheville, North Carolina, welcome-home hug."

"So why didn't you?" Memory asked with a smile.

Lena gave Memory a "behave yourself" look.

Polly continued without missing a beat. "Sarah asked me to give you some time alone. So you could get better acquainted. I believe she was planning on a dinner party or something of the sort so we could all meet. And now, this happened. . . ." She looked toward the door where Sarah was. "Tell me. Is she going to be all right?"

"She's holding her own," Memory said. "You know with her age and all, it complicates things a little more. We're hoping to be able to take her home in a day or two, though."

Polly clapped her hands. "That is *great* news!"

"So, Polly, how is it you happen to be here with Richard?" Memory asked, her face not showing any hint of friendliness.

Polly looked at Richard as though she thought he would tell how they ended up together. When he didn't offer the explanation, Polly smiled and turned to Memory and Lena. "I just happened by the house. Quite frankly, even though Sarah had asked me to give you all some time, I just *had* to come by to see how she was doing. I don't know if you're aware of this"—she looked from Memory to Lena—"but I generally stop by every Saturday morning to chat with Sarah. Of course, last week she called because she was expecting you, Memory. Then she learned you weren't coming, but she left me a message that Lena and Richard were here so there was no need for me to come by as I normally do. When I did speak with her, she told me you had indeed made it and that you all were getting to know one another famously. I didn't come this morning out of respect for her previous request. But I suppose we must have some sort of connection, because for some reason I felt compelled to come by tonight, wishes or not. That's when I learned what had happened."

"Polly was there when you and I were on the phone," Richard said to Lena. "It was just when I would have been trying to figure out how to find the hospital. I would have had to call one of my golfing buddies—"

"And that's when I volunteered to bring him myself. I know how difficult it can be for folks from out of town to find certain places and the like. Since I was coming here anyway, it didn't make sense for us to drive separate vehicles. Plus, this way was easier on him."

"Well, we thank you for that," Lena said. "Memory's going to stay here with Grandmother tonight while I go home and rest up. Then I'll come back and relieve her in the morning."

"I'm going to peep in on her. If she's awake, I'll speak for a few minutes just to let her know I was here," Polly said. "I imagine you all must be exhausted and anxious to get home. I won't be long."

"Take your time," Memory said as she watched Polly sashay inside.

After she was in Sarah's room, Lena turned to Memory. "Well, now, she seems nice enough."

"Yes, she does," Richard said, nodding his head in agreement.

Memory stared at the door without making a comment one way or the other. "Uh-huh," she finally said as she continued to stare at the closed door. "Yeah. Right."

Chapter 21

Say ye to the righteous, that it shall be well with Him: for they shall eat the fruit of their doings.

Isaiah 3:10

Driving her own car, Sapphire followed Charity home. After they were inside and sitting on the couch in the den, Charity reached in her purse and pulled out the stenographer's notebook. She stared at it. Holding her head up, she looked at Sapphire.

"Will you read it first, and if you believe, as Dr. Holden did, that I'll be all right when I read it, then I will." Charity held the notebook out to Sapphire.

"Sure," Sapphire said as she reached over and took it out of Charity's hand. Sapphire opened it up and instantly saw all the doodling and scribbles.

"You have to go more toward the back to find where actual words are written," Charity said. "At least, that's what Dr. Holden told me."

Sapphire turned a lot of pages before reaching a page that had readable writing. After she read it, she held her breath for a few seconds, then exhaled slowly as she looked over at Charity. "I'm not going to lie to you. There may be a few troubling things here; I can't know for certain. But I do agree with Dr. Holden. I don't believe it will hurt the progress you've made. And there's no denying you have made tremendous progress."

"I guess you're right if you call Hope and Faith leaving me as separate personalities progress. I just know I don't ever want to revert back to where I was before. It's been nice living life without having to wonder what might have taken place during missing clumps of time. That's all gone now. Or at least it seems that way."

Sapphire moved a little closer to Charity. She handed her the opened notebook. "I'm here, and however you deal with this when you read it, I promise I'll be right here for as long as you need me to help you work through this." ·

Charity glanced at Sapphire. "Well, here goes nothing."

She began to read. As she turned the pages, tears began to flow down her face. Sapphire looked for some tissue. She got up in search of the bathroom. When she returned, she handed Charity a box of pink tissues. Charity pulled out a few and began gently dabbing her tears as she looked at Sapphire.

"It was my fault," Charity said, almost whispering it. "It was all my fault."

"What was?" Sapphire asked. *What am I missing?* She'd read what was there.

Motherphelia was outside working in her flower garden. Outside of family, flowers and working in her garden was her only other passion. She'd come into the house when Charity ran outside to get her. Motherphelia had thrown down her hoe and came rushing in. She'd heard the urgency in Charity's voice. Yelling at Mr. Lucious, she told him to leave. Demanded he leave. Everyone called the elderly man Mr. Lucious, including Motherphelia. Mother begged Motherphelia not to do it . . . to give him just one more chance. Where would he go? He had no place else; he had no one but us. Still, Motherphelia did it. She

*told him he had to go, and he would—one way or
another. "No more chances. Three strikes and
you're out!" she said. "The nerve of you! I want
you out of this house now!"*

*Mr. Lucious stumbled as he made his way to the
door. Then he stopped. Turning around, he raised
his shirt and pulled out a gun tucked in the band
of his pants. He threatened everybody, talking all
out of his head. But Motherphelia meant business. She didn't back down. Coming closer, she
told him to leave before he'd really be sorry. "And
don't you ever step foot back inside this house
again! I mean it, Lucious," she said.*

After that day, he never did.

*Motherphelia loved him, that much I'm sure.
Who could resist his smile and infectious laugh?
But nothing could rival with her love for Charity.
And that day, she proved there was nothing she
wouldn't do when it came to her greatest love—
Charity.*

"Charity, is there something you're remembering
that's not written there?" Sapphire swiftly kneeled down
on the floor in front of Charity and grabbed both of her
hands in hers. "Charity, talk to me. Do you recall what
happened that day?"

Charity slowly began to nod. "The gun. I'd forgotten
about the gun. Mr. Lucious pulled it out and started waving it around, pointing it at everyone. He was so drunk.
He shouldn't have been drinking. Mother told him as
much. Motherphelia claimed that demon juice made a
perfectly good man smack crazy. He wasn't supposed
to drink at all—that was the agreement. He didn't mean
to. I guess he just couldn't help himself."

"Charity, who was Mr. Lucious?"

"Mother and Motherphelia called him Mr. Lucious,

with the exception of that day Motherphelia lost it and merely called him Lucious. That's what they taught me to call him. Oh God!" Charity began to cry out as she bent forward and gently rocked. "Please help me. I can't do this. I can't handle this. Faith can. I thought I could, but I can't."

"Charity, stay with me now. We're getting there. I want you to take a deep breath and tell me what you re- member that's not written here." She continued holding on to one of Charity's hands as she raised the notebook up with her other one. "What's not in here?"

Charity pulled her hand out of Sapphire's and fell back against the couch as she continued to cry. "Mr. Lucious had visited before in the past. But he showed up at our door one day, and against Motherphelia's objection, Mother allowed him to move into a makeshift bedroom. He'd lived there for months now, but on this day, he got real drunk. 'Drunker than a skunk,' Motherphelia said. The agreement was, he could stay as long as he didn't drink. He was normally quiet and reserved, but alcohol seemed to unleash demons in him."

Charity sat up straight. "I would overhear my mother remind him of that when she smelled liquor on his breath. Whispering it at times . . . taking him off to a private area to talk, she'd tell him he had to stop before he got caught. Mother tried her best to keep it hidden from Motherphelia. She made him drink lots of coffee and use mouthwash to mask the smell. Still, I'd see him, several times, sneak swallows from a bottle he kept under the couch that remained full no matter how much he drained it. The way that bottle kept mysteriously refill- ing itself made me believe it was a magic bottle or something."

Charity slowly closed her eyes, then opened them. "But Mr. Lucious was so nice to me, even when he drank. He would tickle me or do something to make me laugh. Every day, without fail, he played this one record he absolutely loved. 'The Dock of the Bay,' by Otis Redding. And every day, he would give me either a silver- or half-dollar. When my mother discovered he was secretly giving me money, she told me those coins might be worth a lot later, so I should give them to her for safekeeping."

"Charity, why was he giving you money every day?"

Charity looked at her and started shaking her head as the tears rolled down her face. She bowed her head, and the tears began to fall into her lap, plummeting on her folded hands like drops of rain hitting dirt-dry ground before finally being soaked up.

"Charity . . . Did Mr. Lucious sexually molest you?" She waited a few seconds. "Charity, talk to me. Did Mr. Lucious molest you? Look at me. Charity, look at me."

Charity forced herself to look at Sapphire.

Sapphire spoke deliberately and forcefully. "Did Mr. Lucious sexually molest you?"

"No. He did not," Charity said as she began to make successive heaving sounds.

"Then I don't understand. What happened that affected you the way it did? What happened that caused you to need separate personalities? What created Faith and Hope?"

Charity began to cry out loud. "Don't you get it, Sapphire? I loved Mr. Lucious. I . . . loved him! Mr. Lucious was Motherphelia's husband—my father's father. Mr. Lucious was my grandfather, and I *adored* him! Motherphelia never would have come in the house right then had I not gone outside and gotten her. My mother told me to go to my room and play. But instead, I ran as fast as I could and got her. I made her come inside. Had I not, then maybe, just maybe, nobody would have gotten hurt and things would be different today."

She looked at Sapphire as she tilted her head. "You see? It was my fault. All of it. A chain of horrible events happened because of things I did. Me."

Sapphire sat on the couch and put her arm around Charity to stop her now-incessant shaking. "You're doing fine, Charity. It's okay. I'm here." Sapphire looked toward Heaven. "God, please help her," she whispered. "Please, Jesus. We need You."

Sapphire was painfully aware that this was surely only the beginning of even more revelations to come.

Chapter 22

For thus saith the Lord, Ye have sold
yourselves for nought; and ye shall be
redeemed without money.

Isaiah 52:3

"Charity, take your time and tell me everything you remember. It's going to be okay. You're doing fine," Sapphire said.

Charity stood and started pacing around the room. "From all I can recall, I'd never met my grandfather before that year when I was seven. That's when he started coming to the house. I gathered he'd left my grandmother a few years into their marriage. But after this tall, white-haired man showed up, my world as I'd known it flipped. Up was down, and down was up. Motherphelia wasn't her usual jovial self. In the beginning, the two of them argued violently, so naturally I didn't care for him much. Before he came, I'd never even heard Motherphelia raise her voice, let alone lose her temper. She was mild-mannered . . . queenly. After he moved in, there was Motherphelia singing, dancing, smiling, and cooking for him like they'd never exchanged a cross word between them."

Charity looked at the palm of her hand as though it was her first time ever seeing it. She went and sat back down. "When he wasn't drinking, he was all you'd imagine a grandfather to be. He'd let me climb up in his lap, and he would make up some silly song while bouncing me on his knee. He loved to tickle me, although Moth-erphelia didn't like him doing that. In fact, if she saw him starting up, she'd shut him down. There were times when he would drink, and you could smell it on his breath. If Motherphelia felt he'd taken only a few swigs, and I was anywhere in the vicinity, she would make me go to my room. I was sent to my room a lot following his arrival. When she'd give the okay for me to come back out, he'd either be gone or locked away in his room."

Sapphire sat quietly, patiently allowing Charity to tell her story at her own pace. Occasionally, she'd nod or smile, but she kept her eyes completely fixed on Char-ity.

"Then there was that fateful day—the day he got so drunk, he continued to drink right there in the den without even bothering to hide it. He patted his leg, his signal for me to come and sit in his lap. Trying not to be disrespectful or rude, I shook my head. He got up and started to chase after me. When he caught me, he commenced with his normal tickling ritual. I don't know if he did it on purpose or if it was because he was drunk, but he put his hand in the wrong place a few times. My mother came over and began talking nice to him. Smacking his lips, he looked at her the way he looked at smothered pork chops. He turned on 'The Dock of the Bay,' grinned, then tried dancing with her."

Charity rubbed her forehead a few times. "My mother was trying to keep things hushed. Telling him he needed to 'Go sleep it off' before Motherphelia came in and caught him. At one point, he pushed her up against the wall and started trying to kiss her as he groped her. Re-maining calm, my mother told him he didn't really want to do that. That he would be put out of the house for sure if he didn't stop all his drunkard nonsense. But he kept on." Hands in a prayerlike position, Charity pressed them up against her lips.

"I then heard the trembling . . . the fear in her voice. That's when I ran outside to get Motherphelia despite my mother's demand that I go to my room now. Motherphelia would make him stop. She was working in her flower garden, flowery garden gloves on, a garden hoe in hand. I told Motherphelia that Mr. Lucious was hurting my mother. As soon as she heard, she threw down that hoe and made her way to the house, peeling off her gloves as she hurried inside. I now fully understand how she must have felt walking inside and finding her husband all over my mother. He was so drunk, it looked like he'd fallen asleep standing there against her. My mother was struggling to push him off of her, but he was too large. Motherphelia, who was nearly as big, yanked him by his shirt and flung him off, causing him to stumble and fall. He laughed. That's when she told him he had to leave. She didn't put up with his mess when they were together years ago, and no matter how much she still loved him, she wasn't about to put up with it now. And she did love him; you could see it in her eyes. Sober, he was charming and irresistible. Mother pleaded with Motherphelia not to put him out on the streets again. He wasn't well. He was too old to be out there fending alone. 'Phelia, regardless, he's still family,' Mother said."

Charity stood. She took her hands and pulled her hair back taut, then let it go. "My mother assured my grandmother that he would quit drinking. Now that he was seeing the consequences of his actions, he would surely straighten up this time. 'Just give him one more chance,' Mother begged. Motherphelia said it wasn't so much his drinking she couldn't stomach, but who he became when he drank. She called it a stronghold and told my grandfather he'd have to find Jesus to be delivered. He laughed and said if Jesus was lost, how was

He possibly going to be able to help him even if he did find Him?

"Well, that infuriated Motherphelia. She yelled for him to get out. He told her he needed to get a few of his things . . . that he'd come back later for the rest. Walking to his room, he came back in minutes, empty handed. He walked to the front door, then turned around. That's when he pulled out the gun and started waving it and pointing it in a drunken stupor. Motherphelia looked at me and softly told me to go to my room. For some reason, I just stood there like she hadn't said a word to me. Motherphelia and Mr. Lucious continued. He grabbed me, and that was it." Charity began to sob out loud.

"He placed the side of the gun against my face. I should have gone to my room like Motherphelia told me, but I hadn't. I just *had* to see what was going on. I wanted to tell him good-bye. He'd given me half-dollars and silver dollars. He'd played endlessly with me during those six months he'd been there. Truthfully, I didn't want him to leave. I didn't. My daddy was gone, and he'd made me feel like I was a little princess or someone equally as special." Charity grabbed more tissues and gently dabbed at her tears.

"What happened next, Charity?" Sapphire stood and touched Charity's hand. No more just her therapist, she was now a caring friend.

"He staggered as he held his arm around my neck, warning us not to do anything stupid. He said he didn't have anywhere else to go, and he had no plans to leave anytime soon. My mother started crying, but Motherphelia kept her cool. She continued talking to him while calmly telling him to let me go. She reached out for me. He started to push me forward, then quickly snatched me back. I don't know why, but that's when I decided to fight him—a seven-year-old attempting to fight a grown man. I wanted him to let me go. Mother-phelia yelled for me to stop and to just be still, but I was determined to get away. I bit his hand. He yelled out as he released his grip. I ran in the direction of Motherphelia. He cursed, and the next thing I knew Motherphelia was shoving me hard to the floor just as I heard a firecracker-like noise. Motherphelia fell." Charity let out a pained cry. "I thought she'd slipped when she shoved me. But, she was so still . . . lying there . . . her hand pressed against her stomach. She wasn't moving."

Sapphire hugged her. "You're doing great, Charity. It's okay. It's okay."

Charity gently pushed her away. "No, it's not! It's not okay! There was blood . . . soaking through her top. Don't you see, Sapphire? Motherphelia got shot because of me!" Charity wiped her nose. "Me! I flipped when I saw the blood. Mother screamed out her name. Motherphelia tried to move. She started mumbling that everything was going to be all right. My grandfather must have sobered up enough to realize what had just happened, because he dropped the gun and rushed over to her. 'Phil,' he said, short for Ophelia. 'I'm sorry.' Then he panicked. It appeared he was debating whether or not he should try and pick her up. 'Get away from her,' I yelled. 'Leave her alone!' Motherphelia tried to take control of the situation, but she was so weak." Charity paused and stared into space.

"I saw him glance over at the gun," Charity said, continuing. "I wasn't sure what he was planning to do next. He must have seen me look at it. Something suddenly rose up in me. We raced for it. I got there first. I was only trying to protect Motherphelia. There was a struggle as he tried to wrestle it away from me. I really was no match for him, even in his drunken state. The gun fired. My mother screamed. He fell to the floor."

Charity shook her head. "I made my way back to

Motherphelia. That's when she made me promise I wouldn't tell a soul what happened. It would be our secret until she told me otherwise. She was going to fix everything, but she needed me to be a big girl and do exactly as I was told. I was to go to my room and not come out until my mother came and got me. But I refused to leave her side. Later, I heard sirens and then a loud pounding on our front door. Someone identified himself as the police and demanded that we open up. 'Go now,' she whispered. 'Quickly.' I froze. 'Now!' she yelled, still barely above a whisper. 'And don't forget, not a word to anyone.' She smiled, then looked at my mother, who then grabbed my hand and dragged me to my room. I was crying more than ever now. I didn't want to leave Motherphelia there like that. She needed me. My mother shook me and told me to stop it and to be quiet. For Motherphelia, I did as I was told."

Sapphire held Charity in her arms. There were no more tears now. It was as though Charity had successfully depleted her reservoir.

Sapphire moved strands of hair out of Charity's face and brushed them back in place. She looked in Charity's eyes. "It was an accident, Charity. An accident."

Charity shook her head. "Yeah, an accident. Only, he died, Sapphire. My grandfather died because of me. And I never told a soul what happened that day. I've never talked about it with anyone, including my mother. I suppose, in part, because I didn't remember. Faith and Hope made certain of that. And that secret became the tri-fold cord that bound us together."

Sapphire pulled Charity down on the couch by her shoulders as she herself sat down. "Charity, what happened with your grandmother?"

Charity's eyes began to glaze over. "They took her to the hospital. Not long after that, Mother told me she'd died." Charity looked intensely at Sapphire as her lips began to quiver. "I never got to see her again. They didn't even let me go to her funeral. Motherphelia went to be with Jesus. She left me, and it was all my doing."

"Charity, you rarely talk about your mother. What happened with her?"

Charity shook her head slowly. "After my grandmother died, my mother became what people in the neighborhood called 'a certified alcoholic.' Ironic, huh? But I suppose, just as I had done, she found her own way to forget. And I don't have to tell you this, but life as we'd known it was never the same again."

Chapter 23

"How are you feeling now?" Sapphire asked Charity.

"Drained, but okay. I just wish I could understand how I could have blocked something like this completely out of my mind all these years. It makes no sense."

"To your mind it made sense. May I make a suggestion?"

"By all means," Charity said.

"Don't dwell on it now. What's important is that you *have* remembered and that you're coping wonderfully, from everything I'm seeing now, anyway," Sapphire said.

"Sapphire, why do you think my mother allowed me to go all of these years and never talked about this with me? I was a child. I needed her."

Sapphire took her by both hands. "Your mother probably never knew how much it affected you. She may not have realized anything was even wrong with you. And since you never mentioned what happened, she likely concluded you were fine and it was best not to stir up the bees, so to speak. Plus, it sounds to me like she started self-medicating with alcohol. I'm curious, though. When she found out about your Dissociative Identity Disorder diagnosis this year and that you were being treated, what did she say?"

Charity stood and rubbed her hands slowly together. "To be honest, I haven't told her about my disorder and what's going on with me. I figured she had her hands full without all of my burdens. She drinks excessively, and she's married to this man who, I'm convinced, beats her, although she works hard to hide it. When I relocated to Birmingham back in 2001, I was looking for a fresh start. I tried to get her to come with me, but my mother is never going to leave New Orleans. It's her home. It's all she's ever known, and she's not the type to move out of her comfort zone."

Sapphire nodded. "Which is why she stays with someone who abuses her. Though painful, it's familiar to her. In her mind, at least she feels she knows what to expect."

"Yeah. She gets drunk, passes out, and claims she doesn't remember much of what happened before or after that. Me, I developed Dissociative Identity Disorder, a.k.a. multiple personalities, with my manifested personalities being Faith and Hope. I allowed them to deal with things I didn't want to deal with. But honestly, I didn't want to dump my troubles on my mother. That's why she didn't come when I was in that facility. She knew I was having some problems and was getting help, but she didn't know the severity of what was going on. I suppose it's about time I come clean and tell her everything."

Subtly, Sapphire glanced down at her watch. It had been almost three hours since she'd first arrived. "How do you think you'll tell her?"

Charity pursed her lips, then bit down on her bottom lip. "I'm not sure. But I know I need to go home and talk to her face to face. Maybe discussing what came about that day will release her from her own torture as well. I would also like to find out what occurred after the police came inside the house, and what they were told took place, as well as what happened with Motherphelia. I don't know any of these things."

"Since no one seems to have been charged," Sapphire said, "it was likely ruled either self-defense or an accidental shooting."

"Well, I think I'll be visiting New Orleans in August. My mother usually takes her vacation then. I can go spend the week with her since I can't get her to come visit me," Charity said. "She and I can catch up, and maybe I can do a little investigation into the parts of this story I don't know, now that I recall what actually took place." Charity looked at the digital clock on the mantel. "My goodness, look at the time. Sapphire, you've gone above and beyond the call of duty. My bill this time is going to be a whopper."

Sapphire grabbed her purse and stood up. "I do have to go. But we've accomplished so much tonight, thanks in part to Faith and that message she wrote. Faith must have known what would click for you. Now valleys in your life have been exalted. Mountains and hills have been made low."

Charity smiled. "And the crooked places have been made straight. Or at least, we're working on them."

Sapphire walked to the door. She stopped and turned around. "I would like to know what exactly it was that made things click for you."

"The gun, which I'd forgotten about, and recalling 'Mr. Lucious' in the context of how things were. . . . How much Motherphelia loved him. That last paragraph Faith wrote, for some reason, brought back a flood of memories I'd gone to much trouble to forget."

Motherphelia loved him, that much I'm sure.
Who could resist his smile and infectious laugh?
But nothing could rival with her love for Charity.

And that day, she proved there was nothing she wouldn't do when it came to her greatest love—Charity.

A little after Sapphire left, Charity picked up the phone and dialed.

"Hello," a woman's voice on the other end said.

"Mother, it's me—Charity."

"Charity, baby! It's been a while since I've heard from you. I'm so happy you called."

Charity was relieved her mother sounded sober. "Mother, there are some things I believe you and I need to talk about. I'd like to come home when you take vacation if you don't have any major plans. I really need to see you. I want to talk to you about *that* day."

"What day, baby?"

"That day Motherphelia and Mr. Lucious, my grandfather, got shot and died."

There was suddenly an eerie silence.

"Mother, I remember everything. Everything. And you and I need to talk. There are things that have happened over these years . . . things I'm positive you can't possibly know concerning me. Things I've dealt with because of what took place that day."

Charity could hear her mother as she began to cry. "You remember? Everything? You remember *everything*, Charity? All of it?"

"Yes, everything—all of it. Everything except what transpired after you took me to my room."

Her mother seemed to quickly compose herself. Her voice became strong and commanding. "I tell you what. You come home to New Orleans the last week in August. Come, and I'll tell you whatever you want to know. It's past time we finally lay this to rest. I think Motherphelia would want that. Yeah, I *know* she'd want this now."

Chapter 24

*And the Lord said unto Satan, Hast
thou considered My servant Job, that
there is none like him in the earth, a
perfect and an upright man, one that
feareth God, and escheweth evil?*

Job 1:8

It was Tuesday, and Johnnie Mae had been in the hospital for a little over a week now. Charity had visited her at the hospital several times. On her last visit, she told Johnnie Mae all she'd learned about what had caused her to split into multiple personalities. Johnnie Mae was both enthralled and amazed at how the mind could find a way to protect a person the way it had done with Charity. She hated what Charity had gone through, but it was evident by her bubbly attitude, coupled with her now-more-balanced personality, that she was going to be all right. Johnnie Mae could see traits of Hope and Faith alongside the Charity she had known and grown to love dearly over these past months. With God's touch, Charity was completely being made whole.

Landris was in his office at church. He made it a point to go by the hospital and see Johnnie Mae in the morning hours before he went in to work. In the afternoon, he would pick up Princess Rose from the summer day-camp program she was attending and take her with him to see her mother. He'd been off all day on Monday, so he was able to spend more time with both Johnnie Mae and Princess Rose. Tuesdays, no matter what was going on, were always hectic for him, but this Tuesday had been unusually so.

"Pastor Landris, Angel Gabriel is here to see you," his executive assistant announced over the intercom.

"Thanks, Sherry. Please send her in." Landris hit several keys on his computer just as Angel walked in.

"Thank you, Pastor Landris, for seeing me at the last minute. I know how super busy you are and that you're trying to get out of here so you can get to the hospital."

Landris pointed to the burgundy leather chair as he smiled. "Have a seat. It's fine. All a part of the life I've chosen. You said it was important."

"It is. I'll get right to it." She opened up a red folder. "You know I'm handling all of Johnnie Mae's personal, book-related, and church business for her while she's out. Well, several things have surfaced that need to be addressed immediately, but I realized I probably shouldn't show them to Johnnie Mae at this time. Especially since the whole idea is to keep her as stress-free as possible while she's in the hospital."

"And please know I appreciate everything that you're doing toward that end."

Angel pulled out a letter. "This was delivered today." She handed it to Landris. "It's from a lawyer. It appears Johnnie Mae's mother has rescinded the power of attorney from Johnnie Mae and granted it to Johnnie Mae's oldest sister, Rachel."

Landris read the letter, then released it. It floated like a feather, then dropped like a rock to his desk. "I don't believe it," he said, shaking his head while twisting his mouth.

"Those were my sentiments as well."

Landris picked up the letter and leaned back then forward as he bit down on his bottom lip. "The nerve of them to claim Johnnie Mae is not in a position to carry out her duties in executing their mother's affairs while she's in a delicate state herself." He shook the letter. "Johnnie Mae doesn't need to have to deal with something like this. Rachel knows she's in no position to fight her; she's fighting for our baby. That's why Rachel chose now to do it. I *knew* she was being too nice. It figures she was up to something."

"It is disheartening when family members do things like this."

"Well, don't you worry. I'll handle this one." He put the letter back down on his desk.

Angel sat back in her chair. "But if her mother's condition *is* getting worse—"

"Her condition doesn't appear to be any worse now than it was six months ago. In fact, her medication seems to have stabilized her. Rachel just believes this is an ideal time to take over. She's counting on Johnnie Mae not being able to fight her, that's all."

"At this stage, would Johnnie Mae's mother even be considered competent enough, by the legal system, to sign a legally binding document to change anything?"

"I'll admit Mrs. Gates has stretches where her mind is present and very lucid. It's possible she was fully aware of what she was doing when she signed this. Then again, it's also possible Rachel took advantage of her during one of her confused states. I'm going to speak with my sister-in-law myself, although I don't know what good it will do."

"Well, while you're talking to her about that, you may want to discuss this document with her as well." She handed him a thick packet of stapled pages. "Rachel is also having the house changed out of her mother's name into her own."

Landris took it and started reading. He couldn't do anything except shake his head and laugh out of frustration. "I *do* not believe this. Yet, there it is . . . POA, Rachel Turner. And according to this, with the exception of Johnnie Mae and their baby brother, Christian, who remain to agree not to contest it, all of the other siblings have signed off on it," Landris said. He threw the packet on top of the other paper. "Goodness. What next?"

Angel pulled out yet another piece of paper with an envelope clipped to its back. "Well, I hate being the bearer of more bad news, but Johnnie Mae received this certified letter from Jean Cannon, one of Princess Rose's aunts on her father's side." Angel handed him the letter. "She says she's called and left several messages for Johnnie Mae to call her. Since Johnnie Mae hasn't done so as yet, she's sending that certified."

"Jean wants Princess Rose to come and stay with her while Johnnie Mae is in the hospital," Landris said without bothering to read what the letter said. "I haven't even mentioned her calls to Johnnie Mae. Johnnie Mae will never go for that. There's no way she wants Princess Rose all the way up in Chicago while she's here in the hospital. No way. I told Jean that when she and I spoke last week. I thought that was the end of it."

"According to that"—she nodded toward the letter—"it's not. She obviously has a problem with you keeping her niece. She believes Princess Rose should be with family. And since no one in her family is presently in a position to take Princess Rose for the weeks or months that may be needed while Johnnie Mae is in the hospital, she feels the only option is for Princess Rose to come to Chicago and stay with her."

Landris looked at the letter and began to read it. When he finished, he tossed it on top of the ever-increasing stack. "I'm not going to lay this on Johnnie Mae. I'm not. So I'll call Jean and talk to her again. Princess Rose is fine where she is. She's happy in her own home. Princess Rose doesn't even know this aunt, and it's not because Johnnie Mae hasn't tried to get them to spend time with her. But after Solomon died and she married me, his entire family cut off communication with both Johnnie Mae and Princess Rose. Of course she would choose *now* to want Princess Rose to visit her. But I can't do something like that to Johnnie Mae. It's just not a good time. Jean *must* know this."

Angel placed the empty folder on the corner of the desk and sat up straight. "What if you ask Johnnie Mae . . . just to be sure? She really might not mind her staying with this aunt while she concentrates on her health and the health of this baby," Angel said.

"When Princess Rose walks in that hospital room, Johnnie Mae's face literally lights up. I know her. If I tell her what Jean wants, it'll cause nothing but more stress. She'll be trying to figure out if that would be the best thing to do, knowing that Princess Rose may be distressed about going, knowing that she doesn't want Princess Rose to go or to feel abandoned during all of this. Things are hard enough right now on both of them as it is. Besides, Princess Rose has Johnnie Mae's family around. And she's used to them."

"Still, why not let Johnnie Mae know what's going on and see what she thinks about it? Then you'll know how she'd like you to proceed. Johnnie Mae is strong."

He hunched his shoulders. "I just wish I knew what Jean's *really* up to."

"Well, on a more positive note, Johnnie Mae has gotten another stack of mail from fans of her books. The word must be circulating that she's in the hospital. I literally have a bucket full of cards, letters, and e-mails to carry to her. Johnnie Mae insists I bring them to her even though she's supposed to be resting. I see how much they cheer her up. There are definitely a slew of folks who care about your wife, no denying that."

"Yeah, I know. We've had to funnel many of the flow-ers she's been receiving out of her room. It was so many, the nurses said they were sucking up all the oxygen." He chuckled. "I thought they were joking; I quickly learned they weren't. Now when she receives flowers and fruit baskets, she takes off the card to see who sent them, then gets a nurse to carry them to some elderly or other patient who may not have received much, if anything, in the way of gifts or visitors. It works out all around."

Angel retrieved the folder off the corner of the desk and stood up. "Do you want to keep all of those?" she asked, pointing to the papers on his desk.

"Yeah, I'll handle them. And thanks for screening things and not just passing them on to Johnnie Mae. I'll have to pray about these," he said, placing his hand on top of the stack. "Johnnie Mae has a right to know what's going on, but I don't want to do anything that will upset her or put her or our baby at more risk right now. I just don't."

"I understand. I only wish those folks did," she said, pointing once again to the stack. She placed the papers back inside the folder. "Changing the subject, Brent and I want to thank you again for agreeing to perform our marriage ceremony and keeping it quiet. I sort of felt bad even asking you, with all that you have going on these days."

"Like I told Brent, it will be my pleasure. Truthfully, I admire the two of you for taking a vow to keep yourselves until marriage. And when you saw you possibly weren't going to be able to honor that commitment, instead of giving in to the temptation, you decided to take steps to still do things God's way. Now, that's real integrity there."

"Even if it means having a secret ceremony," Angel said, nodding, "before the big one?" She smiled. "Brent is *so* sweet. This was his idea. He knows how much work I've put into planning our wedding. And having a reception at Ross Bridge is neither easy nor cheap. We have already invited a lot of people, and they're so excited about attending our wedding. We didn't want to cancel the whole thing and end up disappointing everybody."

"Oh, I understand," Landris said. "You don't have to explain things. Believe me, it's an honor to do this. You and Brent are special to both me and Johnnie Mae. I just hate that Johnnie Mae won't be able to attend the actual ceremony. But she will be able to come to the ceremony in October, along with our *new* baby." Saying that caused him to grin.

Angel said good-bye and left. Landris opened up the folder, picked up the papers, and scanned each piece again. Picking up the phone, he touch-toned a phone number.

"Jean? This is Pastor Landris. If you have a few minutes, I'd like to talk to you about this letter you sent certified to Johnnie Mae. You and I spoke briefly last week, but perhaps I failed to make clear the situation we're dealing with down here."

"Pastor Landris, you've stated your case perfectly. Nevertheless, our family would prefer our late brother's daughter be with someone in *his* family, since it appears Johnnie Mae won't be capable of taking care of her for a while."

"I assure you, Princess Rose is being well taken care of, even with Johnnie Mae in the hospital. I take her to see her mother every day, and both of them look forward to that. As I told you before, Johnnie Mae doesn't need stress right now. She's in a rather fragile state at a critical point in her pregnancy." He sighed audibly. "May I be frank with you?"

"By all means," Jean said.

"I really would prefer not to dump any of this in Johnnie Mae's lap right now. I understand you'd like to see your niece, and I'm sure once we're past this crucial point and the baby is here, something can be arranged." He picked up his Mont Blanc pen and began to twirl it between his fingers like it was a miniature baton. "You understand?"

"Well, Pastor Landris. Let me be frank with you. I have another sister who is not as nice or considerate as I am attempting to be. She lives there in Birmingham, and she doesn't have a problem with going to that hospital and laying it all out on the table for Johnnie Mae. Honestly, this sister can't take care of Princess Rose, which is why I stepped up. But Pastor Landris, this is our niece we're talking about—my brother's only child. Frankly, she's not your biological daughter. And although I'm sure you're a decent man, none of us are comfortable knowing our brother's child is being left totally alone in a house with just you, while Johnnie Mae is in the hospital for who knows how long."

Landris had a scowl on his face. "Excuse me, but what exactly are you trying to imply?"

"I'm not trying to imply anything. All I'm saying is Johnnie Mae could be in the hospital for—what? Another two . . . three months? We don't want any mess. Our family just believes it will be best for all concerned if Princess Rose is staying with someone else other than alone with a man who is not her real father but merely a stepfather."

"Step or not, I *am* a real father to her. So are you saying that if one of Johnnie Mae's sisters took Princess Rose while she's in the hospital, you'd not be pursuing this?"

"I don't know if we can trust that, either. Let me level with you. Even though I have the means to take Princess Rose, I'm really not that excited about having to care for a child, any child, at this point in my life. I have a very active career and social life. But someone

has to protect that child. It looks like I'll have to sacrifice and be the one."

She paused and then continued. "Now, either you can
let Johnnie Mae know what I'm proposing, at a great
sacrifice to myself, mind you, or we'll figure out another way to let her know. And Pastor Landris, I assure
you we're not trying to add stress to anyone, but our
family is willing to take this as far as we have to. If you
think about it, this could actually be a blessing in disguise. If I have Princess Rose, then that gives you more
time to concentrate on your wife and the baby you both
are fighting so desperately for. So my deal to you is
this. I'll give you until tomorrow evening to get back
with me with your and Johnnie Mae's decision. After
that, I take the next step. Good-bye." She hung up.

Landris stared at the phone, then hung it up. Closing
his eyes, he began to pray.

Chapter 25

*While he was yet speaking, there came
also another, and said, The fire of God
is fallen from heaven, and hath burned
up the sheep, and the servants, and
consumed them; and I only am escaped alone to tell thee.*

Job 1:16

"Pastor Landris," Sherry said as she stuck her head into his office. "I have a surprise for you." She opened the mahogany wooden door wide.

A golden-haired woman dressed in a royal blue pantsuit waltzed in. "Well, hello there, darling."

"Mom, what are you doing here?" Landris asked. He stood and hurried to greet her.

"I came to see about you . . . all of you," Virginia LeBoeuf said. She hugged her son tight as he kissed her cheek. "How is Johnnie Mae?" she asked. "And the baby?"

"So far, so good. Our confession is all is well. But why didn't you tell me you were flying in today? I could have picked you up from the airport."

She waved him away with her hand and gracefully sat in the chair that faced his desk. "Nonsense. You didn't need to. You have enough on your plate as it is."

He sat in the chair next to her. "How did you get here? Did Thomas bring you?"

She cocked her head and raised an eyebrow. Patting his hand, she smiled. "No, Thomas didn't bring me. But I did stop by to see him at the halfway house on my

way here. I can only assume, with all that's going on
with you, you haven't seen him lately."

"No, I haven't seen him in a couple of weeks. But I
did call him just yesterday. It was a brief conversation.
I quickly picked up that he wasn't in the mood to talk.
Or maybe it would be more accurate to say he wasn't in
the mood to talk to me. So what prompted you to make
that statement? Am I missing something?"

She set her Louis Vuitton purse on his desk. "Your
brother has completely quit taking his medication."

"What makes you think that?"

"A mother knows. Besides, I asked him point-blank,
and he admitted it. He claims he's doing so much better
now, he feels it's unnecessary for him to keep having to
take it. I tried to explain to him that his medicine is not
a cure by any means, but a tool to help him manage his
bipolar disorder." She placed her hand on her chest as
she let out a deep sigh. "Well, you of all people know
how unreasonably hardheaded your brother can be when
he's normal. Unfortunately, all of us also know how
bad things can get with him when he's not taking that
medication." She started glancing around his office.

"What are you looking for?" Landris asked. "What
do you need?"

"Some water. You used to keep a pitcher of water in
here. Talking about medicine made me remember I need
to take my *own*. Can you get me some water, please?"

"Sure," he said as he went to the mini-refrigerator,
grabbed a bottle of water, then handed it to her. "What's
your doctor saying these days?" He knew this was a
touchy subject with her, one—over the past months—
she generally found a way to skirt around.

"Oh, you know them—forever wanting to do this test
or another. I suppose that's why people call what they
do 'a practice.'" She twisted the cap off the medicine

bottle first and shook two round blue pills into her hand, then twisted the top off the bottled water. Carefully placing one pill in her mouth, she took a swallow of water, snapped her head back, then repeated the process. "I *despise* having to take pills," she said as she screwed the childproof cap back on the medicine bottle and put it back in her purse. "That's probably where your brother gets it from."

Landris continued eyeing her without saying a word.

"What?" she said after a minute of him staring silently at her. "You don't like my new golden hair color?" She began to pat her hair. "What?!" she snapped.

"Mom, are you even supposed to be here right now?"

She set her purse back on the corner of his desk. "Well, I'm here, aren't I? So I guess that means I'm *supposed* to be here."

"That doesn't answer my question. But allow me to rephrase. Does your doctor know you're here, and did he say it was okay for you to come?"

She smiled and touched his hand. "I don't need a doctor's permission to come see about my children. I'm sure you understand that, especially now that you have Princess Rose in your life. And you're *really* going to appreciate it once this new baby gets here." She took another sip of water. "What time are you going to the hospital to see Johnnie Mae today?" she asked, attempting to change the subject.

He looked at his watch as he walked back behind his desk and sat down. "I usually have to pick up Princess Rose from summer day-camp by five. I'll take you to the house and get you settled in. By the way, where is your luggage?"

"Oh, Sherry has it out there with her. Some nice-looking gentleman was kind enough to bring them in for me. It's only two pieces. I'm only staying a few days."

He smiled. "Traveling light this trip, huh?"

She gave him one of her infamous "behave your-self" looks.

"Sorry," he said, laughing. "It was a joke, Mom. A joke."

Landris hurried to finish up despite his mother's in-sistence she was fine and he could take his time. Legs stretched out, head laid back on the arm of the couch, Virginia had made herself comfortable with her pledge to him that if something important came up he needed to handle in private, she would step out swiftly so as not to hinder him.

Landris was working away when out of nowhere she suddenly said, "The doctor says I need to have triple-bypass heart surgery."

Landris stopped and glanced over at her with a puz-zled look. "What?" He began to frown even more. "When? I mean, when does he want you to have it?"

"As soon as possible," she said, sitting up completely and setting the *Oprah Magazine* she was reading down on the coffee table. "'Yesterday' was his exact word."

"Then why are you here, Mom?"

She moved closer to the edge of the couch. "Be-cause you and Thomas need me."

"But Mom . . ."

She smiled. "Continue what you were doing. You need to get finished. I don't want you getting behind because of me. Everything's going to be all right."

"Mom—"

"George Edward Landris," she said with a look only a mother can give her child, "we walk by faith and not by sight! The just shall live by faith. I'll tolerate no negativity or undue concern, especially not from you. We will keep our eyes on Jesus, the author and the fin-isher of our faith. I've prayed about this already. And I refuse to live my life in fear. I just won't do it. Not ever again. Not now that I know the truth. What's that scripture that speaks on fear?"

Landris picked up a tattered and worn handwritten index card from off his desk and walked it over to her. He handed it to his mother, and as she read it silently, he began to quote it out loud. "Second Timothy, first and seven. 'For God hath not given us the spirit of fear; but of power, and of love, and of a sound mind.'"

She smiled as she looked from the card to her son. "Yes." She nodded. "But if you'll permit me, I'd prefer to say it this way. God has given us the Spirit of Power, the Spirit of Love, and the Spirit of a Sound Mind. And no matter what happens to us in *this* life, we win. The children of the Most High God, whose salvation has been secured through Jesus Christ—in the end, no matter what—we still win." She pressed the card against her heart and closed her eyes as she lifted her face toward Heaven and smiled.

Chapter 26

*While he was yet speaking, there came
also another, and said, The Chaldeans
made out three bands, and fell upon
the camels, and have carried them
away, yea, and slain the servants with
the edge of the sword; and I only am
escaped alone to tell thee.*

Job 1:17

Sherry knocked on the door and came inside after
Pastor Landris said, "Come in."

"I'm sorry to interrupt again, Pastor Landris"—
Sherry nodded to both Landris and his mother—"but
Mrs. Knight is on the phone. She sounds really upset
and said she would only be a minute."

Landris told her it was fine; he would get it. Sherry
left.

"Excuse me, Mom, while I take this," Landris said.

"Do you need me to step out?" she asked as she
quickly scooted forward on the couch to get up to leave.

"No," he said, raising his hand for her to stay where
she was. "You're okay."

Landris picked up the phone and, after a few minutes of conversation, softly placed it back in its cradle.

"Bad news?" his mother asked as she looked intensely at his face.

"Reverend Knight just died. His wife is having a
hard time, even though everyone—including her—was
expecting it to happen at any time."

"I'm sorry. I know you two had become close, especially during this past year. Death is never easy on
those left behind, even though we know—as sure as we

live—it's coming to each of us. If the rapture doesn't take us first, death is the corridor we all must go through. But for those of us in Christ, Jesus is our door. I'll pray for the family's loss."

"Yes, it's natural we miss our loved ones physically. But in loving memory, they forever remain in our hearts. I often think of my sister, killed in that church parking lot by that speeding driver when she was only twelve, and my father, who died shortly after her. I know and can now rejoice that—at least for those who die in Christ— to be absent from the body is to be present with the Lord. Our loss is their gain. That's why I'm so committed to what I do. I pray that none should perish . . . that all would come to accept Jesus as their Savior and be saved. That's the reason it's important I preach the Word in season and out—that Jesus died on the cross and God raised Him from the dead." Landris turned the pages of the calendar he kept on his desk in spite of all the electronic gadgets that duplicated the schedules of his time and quickly wrote on one of those pages.

"Mrs. Knight wants to have his funeral this Saturday at twelve o'clock," he said. "There's just so much going on in my life." He shook his head. "I tell you what."

"I'm certain she'll understand your not being able to make it," Virginia said.

"A few weeks ago, Reverend Knight asked me to preach his funeral. It was one of the last requests he asked of me before he went into a coma. That's what his wife was calling to find out—whether I was in a position to preach his eulogy still. I told her I would do it, so I'll just have to find a way to manage. I'm not confessing this, but honestly, it feels like before I get past one thing good, here comes something else."

"You know what the French say: *c'est la vie*—that's life," his mother said.

He looked at his mother, then at the digital clock on

his desk. "I know you're ready to get to the house and get out of your traveling clothes. I'm going to send Sherry a note to put the funeral on my main calendar, finish up a few more things, and then we can go." He turned back to his computer.

After about ten minutes of tapping keys, he put away the things that were on his desk and stood up. "All done," he said. "Now let's go get Princess Rose." He went and got his suit coat and quickly put it on. "We'll go to the house, and if you feel up to going to the hospital today, we can all visit Johnnie Mae. I know she's going to be surprised to see you." Towering over her by about eight inches, he hugged his mother again, this time longer than usual. "I'm so glad you're here, Mom," he said. "I really am."

She looked up at him and smiled. "Me, too." She nodded. "Me, too. What was that song Bob Marley used to sing?" She began singing the words, "Everything's going to be all right." She smiled again. "God said He would never leave us nor forsake us. Because He tells us that, we can rest in the fact that everything really *is* going to be all right."

"No matter what we may be going through, God knows, and He promised He'd be right there with us through it all," Landris said, walking beside her, his arm around her shoulders. "*Through* it all. I know God is going to bring us through. And we can count on what God promises us because He is not a man that He should lie."

Virginia smiled. "God knows, and He cares. It's like I've heard you say so many times since you made Jesus the Lord of your life. It's good to be saved."

"Oh, I know that's right!" Landris said as he opened the door. "It *is* good to be saved!"

Chapter 27

*While he was yet speaking, there came
also another, and said, Thy sons and
thy daughters were eating and drinking
wine in their eldest brother's house. . . .*

Job 1:18

Landris, his mother, and Princess Rose went in the house. Preparing to go see Johnnie Mae, Virginia and Princess Rose were upstairs changing. Virginia had bought Princess Rose a sundress identical to the one she was changing into. Landris had just come from carrying his mother's luggage upstairs to her room, when the phone rang.

"George, thank goodness I found you," Thomas said. "I called the church and they said you'd left already. I tried calling your cell phone, but you must have been out of range or something, because it went straight to your voice mail."

"Hey, man. Mom tells me you're not taking your medicine. Is that true?"

"Aw, man, she told you that? You know how Mom can be."

"So are you taking your medicine or not?" Landris untied his baby blue necktie and slid it from around his neck. "You promised you were going to do right."

"See, that's why I'm calling. Mom must have also told someone here I wasn't taking my medicine. The director said she was going to call you to come talk to me and her," Thomas said. "You know how they are with their rules. Dotting every i; crossing every t. I told her she didn't have to call, that you were already planning to come by."

"Well, I was getting ready to go to the hospital to see Johnnie Mae right now. Can it wait until tomorrow morning?"

Thomas sighed. "I suppose it could, but they're claiming I'm not acting rational. She insists she has to see you today, if it's at all possible. If you ask me, I'd say they all just need to get a life. George, those pills were starting to do things to me I didn't like." He lowered his voice. "And between me, you, and the couch, I believe these folks are really out to get me. I don't trust anything they give me these days to eat or drink. That's why I have my own stash here in my room. I think they're trying to slip me something."

Landris looked at his watch as his mother walked into the room with Princess Rose's hand gently tucked inside of hers. Landris couldn't help but admire how cute they looked dressed alike. "Thomas, no one's out to get you. You were doing so well. They were about to sign off on your release. Why would you just stop taking your medicine?"

"Because I saw a commercial on TV about the drug I happen to be taking, and the lawyers were saying if you've taken this medicine that you may have a case against the makers of it. I believe the pharmaceutical companies are just using us as guinea pigs. You remember the Tuskegee experiment, don't you? Well, I refuse to let these folks continue experimenting on me and messing me up. Fixing one thing but making something else go wrong. Then you need to take another pill just to fix the new problem you didn't have prior to your being treated for the previous thing. Something's wrong with that! Can you just please come by and tell this lady you and I talked, and you agree I don't need to take this medicine anymore? Better yet, why don't I just check out and come help you out?"

Landris looked at his mother and stepdaughter and smiled. "Thomas, look. I'll be by there to see you before we go to the hospital. But I can't stay long, now." He was trying to cover, not wanting his mother to suspect anything major was going on. He'd visit Thomas and see for himself how he was really doing, then proceed from there.

Arriving at the facility, he talked to the director briefly, then went to Thomas's room. Landris could tell immediately there was a problem. Thomas wasn't in bad shape, but it was obvious 'he was spiraling headfirst in that direction. His eyes showed signs of little sleep. He couldn't manage to be still for more than a few minutes at a time. As soon as they came inside, he had jumped up and poured them a glass of apple cider, even though Landris told him they weren't staying long and didn't want anything to drink.

"Thomas, listen to me," Landris said. "I know you think you're fine, but, man, you're not. You need to start back taking your medicine. All right?"

Thomas looked at his mother, then Princess Rose. "Hey there, little beauty," he said to Princess Rose. "Uncle Thomas has something for you." He walked over to the cabinet and took out a bag of Gummi Bears. Walking back, he held out the bag to her. "I know you love these. It's okay. You can take it. I bought the whole bag for you."

Princess Rose looked at Landris, who nodded it was okay. She reached up slowly and took it. "Thank you," she whispered, then grinned—her two bottom teeth visibly missing.

"I know that's your favorite kind of candy," Thomas said. He briskly brushed his face as though he were trying to brush crumbs or something from around his mouth. "I bought those just for you. I know you've been having a hard time with your mother being in the hospital and all. Uncle Thomas just wants you to know he's thinking about you."

Landris looked at his watch. It was six-thirty. He needed to hurry if he wanted to visit with Johnnie Mae for any real amount of time. *Where does time go?* he wondered.

"Thomas, you're in this facility so you can be on your own while still being monitored and treated medically," Landris said. "And you were doing great while you were taking your medicine. You were starting to act more like your normal self again."

"Man, I'm still cool. See, the way I figure it is the medicine has fixed the problem, so there's no reason to keep taking it. I believe I'm healed, in the name of Jesus"—he raised his hands in praise—"so I'm acting like I believe. Isn't that what you preach all the time? That we should act like we believe the Word of God is true?"

Landris glanced over at his mother, who had a look of pain on her face as she watched her oldest son. "What I preach, when it comes to areas like this, is that God also gave us sense, and He still intends for us to use wisdom. I'm not going to tell you that God can't completely heal you from your disorder, Thomas. But in your case, until it's fully manifested, you need to continue taking your medicine."

"But see now, even the logic behind *that* statement is whack. How are we going to ever know that I'm healed if I keep taking the medicine? See, the only way for us to know that I'm healed is for me to stop taking the medication for sight. You get it?"

"Thomas, stop talking foolishness," his mother said. "Your brother teaches that healing can, in some cases, be assisted through doctors. The word 'doctor' means healer. Your doctor prescribed medication that has helped you tremendously. I told you earlier today it's not a cure, but it helps you manage your thoughts and actions better."

"So are you saying that God can't heal me from this?" Thomas asked Landris, seemingly ignoring his mother's statements. He cocked his head to the side. "Are you saying that I shouldn't stand in faith because it's not possible for God to be able to do something like this for me? Are you saying my situation is too *hard*, even for God?"

"No, Thomas. I'm not saying God can't heal you," Landris said.

"Then what are you saying? That God *can* heal me, but He really can't, or should we say *won't*, because you don't think I have enough faith?"

Landris ran his hand over his face. "It's not that." He let out a sigh. "Thomas, please . . . just take your medicine. Okay? Because if you don't take it, you're just going to continue deteriorating and end up right back where you started from, if not worse."

"See, now that's not the kind of faith or support I need," Thomas said. He picked up the untouched glasses of cider and began pouring them back into the bottle. "I'm here believing God for my healing, and you're here speaking all this negative junk! It's like you're a hypocrite or something. You preach one thing, but obviously you don't really believe it." He looked at Landris as he screwed the top back on the bottle. "So, do you believe in healing or don't you?" He stopped what he was doing completely and waited.

"Yes, Thomas. I believe in healing."

"Then why can't you believe with me for mine?!" His voice cracked as he spoke.

"Thomas!" Virginia stood up and walked over to him. "Thomas, baby. Look at me." She reached up and touched his face with both hands. "Look . . . at . . . me." He looked at her. "You need to take your medicine," she said lovingly. "Do you know what a blessing from God it is to even have medication that can help you?" She went over to her purse and took out her bottle of blue pills. "Do you see these? Well, I've had to take them every day for a few months now," she said, shaking the bottle in his face. "And if I hadn't, I can't promise you I'd be standing here even now. If I can take my medicine while believing God for *my* total healing, then what is the problem with you doing the same?"

"Mom, it's different in your case."

She frowned. "How so? What if I was going around spouting off the same thing you're doing? I could decide against taking my medicine, but my not taking it means my heart might stop. What would *you* be telling *me*? What would you be saying to me?"

Thomas shook his head. "Mom, I'm telling you your situation is different. You don't need to be playing with your life that way."

Virginia touched his hand. "And you don't need to be playing with your life this way, either. Do you know how bad you can get if you don't take your medicine? Do you? We've seen it, Thomas. And believe me, it's not a pretty sight. You're putting your life in danger. Your judgment is off. You don't see it, but we do. Can you just trust me and your brother along with the people here? Trust that we see what you don't? Baby, you can't see right now that you're really not doing as well as you think without your medicine."

Landris stood. "Thomas, please. I have a lot happening now. I don't want you back in bad shape, because then I'll have to be worried about you, too."

"Where is your medicine?" Virginia asked.

Thomas let his head drop in defeat. "All right. All right. I'll take it."

"Then go get it right now and take it while I'm here," Virginia said. "I want to see you take it. And I want to see the medicine bottle for myself so I can be certain it's really your pill and not just an aspirin or something." She crossed her arms and waited.

Thomas got his medicine and gave it to his mother, who examined it then shook a pill into his hand. He took it, opening his mouth wide to show her it was indeed gone.

Landris's cell phone began to ring. He looked at the caller ID. "Pastor Landris."

"Pastor Landris, this is Dr. Baker. We need you to get to the hospital right away. Right away. I'm here already. We'll talk as soon as you get here. Just please hurry."

Chapter 28

And the Lord said unto Satan, Behold, all that he hath is in thy power; only upon himself put not forth thine hand. So Satan went forth from the presence of the Lord.

Job 1:12

Princess Rose and Landris's mother went with him to the hospital. As soon as Landris arrived, he stopped by the nurses' station and had Dr. Baker paged. She came quickly and led him off to another area to speak privately.

Virginia and Princess Rose went in the waiting room and sat down. Virginia could see the sadness on Princess Rose's face. She called her over to her and let her climb up on her lap. "I imagine it's been hard having your mommy away, huh?" Virginia said as she looked at Princess Rose and smiled.

Princess Rose nodded, then relaxed into Virginia's loving embrace.

"Well, I'm here. And you know we all love you, right? All of us."

"Yes," Princess Rose said as she blinked several times. "But I miss my grandma, too. I'm talking about my mommy's mama."

"Oh, so you haven't seen your grandma lately?"

"I saw her a little before Mommy went in the hospital. But I haven't seen her since then. Am I still going to get to see Mommy today like Daddy Landris said I would?"

Virginia hugged her. "Honestly, honey, I'm not sure right now. But I think so." She looked away then ran her hand slowly over Princess Rose's hair. "Oh, look," she said, pointing to the now-open door. "There's Daddy Landris."

Princess Rose jumped down and ran into Landris's open arms. He picked her up and swung her gently while hugging her tight. Virginia stood up as he came closer to her. She didn't say anything but tried to gauge his facial and body expressions to get some insight into what might be happening. His uptight demeanor told her things must be pretty intense.

"Sweetheart, I'm sure you're hungry. How about you and Nana go down to the cafeteria, and you can get whatever you want to eat." He set her back down on the floor.

"Hamburger and French fries?" Princess Rose asked with a grin.

"Whatever you want," Landris said, grinning back.

"Are you coming too?" Princess Rose asked Landris as she twisted back and forth.

"No. I need to see about Mommy and the new baby."

"Is the new baby here already?" Princess Rose asked as she smiled and began to jump up and down.

"Not yet." Landris looked at his mother, his eyes pleading for a little assistance.

"Come on, Princess Rose," Virginia said, reaching down and taking her hand. "Let's go see what they have in the cafeteria. I'll even break down and have dessert with you. Your choice."

They walked out of the waiting room together. Virginia and Princess Rose headed for the elevator—Princess Rose skipping the whole way. Landris watched them get on the elevator, then started toward Johnnie Mae's room.

He knocked on the door, then stuck his head inside.

Johnnie Mae was sitting up, the television was off, and she was twiddling her thumbs.

"Hey," he said as he walked in. He leaned down and kissed her softly on her lips.

"You've spoken with Dr. Baker?" Johnnie Mae asked as she stared at him.

"Yeah. She called and told me I needed to hurry. J. M., listen," he said, calling her by the name, years ago, she once had insisted everyone call her. Now, he used it only during very special times.

She turned her head away. "I don't want to hear it, Landris."

"Johnnie Mae, you have to let them take the baby now."

She looked at him. "It's too early. Just a few days longer and at least I would be seven months then. A few more days, and the baby's chances of survival will increase drastically."

"Johnnie Mae, you don't have a few more days. According to Dr. Baker, you really don't have a few more hours. Dr. Baker insists she has to take the baby now."

Johnnie Mae reached out for Landris. He held her close. "Landris, please don't do this. Please. Let's just pray. Okay? Right now . . . me and you. We just need to pray, that's all. The prayers of the righteous availeth much." She began to cry. "Please, Landris. We can't do this now."

He held her even tighter. "Johnnie Mae, I *have* been praying. Constantly, I've been praying. We've all been praying. And I believe God has answered us. The baby has a great chance of being all right at this stage. Dr. Baker is an outstanding physician. The neonatal unit will be there ready and waiting. These days, premature babies grow up perfectly fine without any lasting effects or problems. It's almost becoming routine."

Johnnie Mae pulled away from him. "But Landris, I

feel like I'm going to be all right. Honest, I do. In my heart . . . down in my spirit, I feel it. We don't have to put the baby through this. Why won't you trust me on this? I'm going to be fine." Her eyes were pleading with him. "Give our baby a little longer. Help give our baby a fighting chance."

He smiled at her. "Baby, I trust you, but I'm not willing to take this chance with your life in the balance. Dr. Baker is going to perform a C-section on you. She's getting things prepared as we speak."

"You told her it was okay to do it?" She had a frown on her face now.

"Yes."

"Why, Landris? Why? Why would you do that before you came and talked with me about it first? I told her I didn't want to do that. This is still my body. I should be the one who ultimately gets to decide."

He tried to take her hand; she quickly moved it away. "I can't believe you told her she could do it. I told you what I wanted when I first came here. I told you from the start. You could have at least come in and talked to me about it before you told her it was okay." She reached over and quickly took his hand in hers. "Go find her and tell her you've changed your mind. Tell her you and I talked . . . that we prayed about it and that we've decided we're going to totally trust God with this."

He kissed her. "Johnnie Mae, I trust God more than anyone will ever know. And I trust that God is going to bring both you and our baby through this. Johnnie Mae, I know Dr. Baker told you everything. That even taking the baby now, we still have a fight for your life on our hands. You'd better believe I'm praying right this second like you'll never know. I don't need you mad with me or upset with me about this decision. I'm not the enemy."

He released a long sigh. "I'm here for you, Johnnie Mae. And I don't ever want you to doubt my love for you. You're going to have the C-section. Then you, me, Princess Rose, and this new baby are going to go on and live our lives to the fullest. When this is all said and done, we're going to have a testimony like nobody's business and be able to tell people just how God brought us through."

She held onto his hand even tighter now. "Where is Princess Rose?"

"With my mother."

"Virginia's here?" she asked with a lift in her voice. "Did you know she was coming?"

"No. She surprised me. We were on our way here to see you when Thomas called, so we stopped by to see him." Landris didn't want her to know that there was a problem with Thomas, so he left that part out. "Thomas gave Princess Rose a bag of Gummi Bears. While we were at his place, Dr. Baker called and said I needed to get here in a hurry. Mom and Princess Rose went to the cafeteria so you and I could talk alone."

Johnnie Mae began to smile nervously. "I'm really not being fair, am I?"

"Honestly, you're just doing what you think is right. Johnnie Mae, I have to believe our baby is going to be all right even being born this early. Dr. Baker explained everything to me—the best- and worst-case scenario for both you and the baby. So I know that if you don't have the baby within the next few hours, there's a good chance you're not going to make it through tomorrow. I'm not going to sugarcoat this situation at this point. And that possibility, Johnnie Mae, is not fair to Princess Rose . . . or to this baby or . . ." His voice started to trail off. He wiped one of his eyes.

She touched his face as she tilted her head. "Or to you," she whispered, finishing a statement she knew he probably wouldn't. "I'm not being fair to you, either."

He looked at her. "I love you, Johnnie Mae. I want to

spend the rest of my life with you. A long, healthy life.
I want your children to know and hear you, and not hear
about you from other people. Both children. And personally, Johnnie Mae, I'm not willing to put your life on
the line when there's another way we can do this that
can possibly save both you and the baby. I prayed about
this before I ever opened my mouth to tell Dr. Baker it
was all right to do it. It's still all in God's hands."

"Landris, I know. I know this has to be hard on you,
too. I just can't help but wonder, by doing this now, does
this mean we don't trust that God will take care of it?"

"Johnnie Mae, I believe this is God's way of taking
care of it. God still has to guide Dr. Baker and that
medical team's hands. We're not doubting God any less
going this route. In fact, I believe we have to trust Him
that much more. We must trust God to go in that operating room and do what man has no control over. We
still have to have faith—the working kind of faith . . .
unwavering faith."

Johnnie Mae smiled and caressed his face. "Are you
going to be there with me?"

He hugged her. "We're one. That means where one
goes, the other must follow. We're in this together. Yes,
I'm going to be right there by your side, holding your
hand."

"Is it possible for me to see Princess Rose before I
do this?"

He smiled and stood up straight. "Sure. I'll go get her."

"Landris . . . will you call my mother for me? I can't
talk to her right now." Her voice was breaking up as she
spoke. "Will you call her for me, and if it seems like she's
okay, and if she feels up to it, will you see if someone
will bring her here for me?" She glanced down at her
now-clasped hands.

"Of course. I'll call her," he said, then pulled out his
cell phone and pressed the number to speed-dial.

Chapter 29

For He put on righteousness as a breastplate, and a helmet of salvation upon His head; and He put on the garments of vengeance for clothing, and was clad with zeal as a cloak.

Isaiah 59:17

Sarah was now resting at home. She'd stayed in the hospital for two days. Memory and Lena had stayed with her during those days. Sometimes taking turns, sometimes there at the same time.

"You know what I'd like for us to do," Sarah said to Memory and Lena. "I'd like to celebrate Christmas . . . here . . . together."

Lena smiled. "I'm sure we can do that. Christmas is some six months away. We can have a grand Christmas celebration."

"Sounds like a lot of fun to me," Memory said.

Sarah began to shake her head. "No, I don't mean wait until December. I mean, I want to celebrate Christmas now."

"Now? But it's June," Memory said.

"I know it's June," Sarah said with a sheepish grin. "But who says we can only celebrate Christmas in December? What about we celebrate it this month? Lena, didn't you and Richard get married in June?"

Lena nodded. "Yeah. Both Theresa and I will be celebrating our anniversary on June twenty-second."

"Then would you like to have a Christmas-like celebration on your anniversary, or would it be best not to mix them?" Sarah asked as she brushed a strand of hair out of her face.

"I think it would be best not to mix them," Memory said, although the question wasn't addressed to her. "Lena and Theresa may want to spend that special time with their husbands," she quickly added.

"Oh dear," Sarah said. "I suppose that is selfish of me to wish to impose on their anniversary date with my own desire."

"No, I think it's a great idea. I can run it by Richard to be sure it's okay with him, and, of course, Theresa and Maurice, since we're looking for this to be a family affair. But if you want to have Christmas in June, and you'd like to include our anniversary, it's fine with me," Lena said.

Memory got up and looked at the calendar pinned on Sarah's bedroom wall. "Did you know June twenty-fifth is a Saturday?"

"Really?" Sarah said. "Well, that would be even better! We would be celebrating Christmas exactly six months ahead of time if we go with that date. Let's do it then. Let's shoot to celebrate our own special Christmas celebration June twenty-fifth."

Lena took Sarah's hand and patted it. "If that's what you want, Grandmother."

"I'll let Minnie know so she can get the place changed around. Oh, and can one of you call Polly and ask her to get in touch with the people she usually gets to come in and decorate the house for Christmas for me? Polly's number is in my address book in this nightstand drawer." She patted the nightstand, then clapped her hands as she began to laugh. "Oh, I just believe this is going to be the best Christmas ever! Ever!"

Memory smiled at Sarah. "I can't wait," she said.

When Memory and Lena left Sarah's room, they stopped when they were farther down the hallway.

"What do you really think?" Memory asked Lena. "Why do you think she wants to do this now?"

"I don't know."

"Do you think she's getting ready to leave us or something?" Memory asked.

Lena looked at her mother and shook her head. "Honestly, I don't know. But if this is what she wants to do, there's no downside to doing it. I say, let's do all we can to make this the best Christmas celebration ever."

Chapter 30

And the loftiness of man shall be bowed down, and the haughtiness of men shall be made low: and the Lord alone shall be exalted in that day.

Isaiah 2:17

"Richard, what did you do with that box?" Lena asked.

"What box?"

She pushed both fists into her waistline. "The Wings of Grace box. You know, it was on the bed. I left it on the bed when all the commotion was going on to get Sarah to the hospital a few days ago. When I came home, it was gone. I figured you put it up."

He shook his head. "It wasn't me. I haven't seen it since you showed it to me that one time. I didn't even know you brought it here with you."

"Are you *sure* you didn't move it? It was right there on the bed."

"Lena, I might be getting old, but I'd remember if I'd seen that box and put it somewhere."

Lena looked in the drawer where she had originally placed it, then other drawers throughout the bedroom. She looked in the closet and under the bed.

"Are you sure you had it in here last?" Richard asked as he began searching the uncluttered room.

Lena stopped and stared at him. "I'm sure. It was right there on that bed. Memory and I were in here talking. In fact . . ." She suddenly stopped talking, went to the bed, dropped to her knees once more, and began looking under the bed.

"Why are you looking under the bed again?" Richard asked. "It's not that small of a box you wouldn't have seen it the first time you looked."

She stood up. "I was looking for the Alexandrite necklace," she said.

"The Alexandrite necklace? Okay, now I'm really confused."

"The Alexandrite necklace." Lena walked over to him. "Memory gave it back to me. The same day I showed her the Wings of Grace box. Gayle came in while we were talking and told us Sarah was sick and needed us to come quickly. Memory and I jumped up and left everything right where it was. The Alexandrite necklace . . . the box . . ."

"All right, come sit down," Richard said, grabbing her by the hand and pulling her down on the bed with him. "Now, did you come back here after you left to go see about Sarah? You know, to get your purse when you got ready to go to the hospital that night?"

Lena thought for a second. "I didn't need a purse because we rode to the hospital with Gayle. I had about thirty dollars in my pocket from when you gave me back my change after you went to the store for me," Lena said, "so I didn't have to come in here."

"All right. So you didn't come back in the room at all after you left until . . ."

"Until you and I came home later that night." Lena began to shake her head slowly. "When we got home, it was late. I was tired, and I pretty much crashed. I didn't think about them because I guess I thought you had put them away or something." She shrugged her shoulders, then shook her head even more. "I don't believe this. I just don't believe it. She did it to me again."

"Who did what to you again?"

"Memory. If you didn't move the box and the necklace, then that can only mean she must have sneaked back in here at some point and took them both."

"But when would Memory have had a chance to do that? If you both were in here together, you both went to see about Sarah, you went to the hospital together, and you came home before she did that night," Richard said, "when could she have done it?"

Lena turned more to face him. "I don't know when she did it. Maybe while I was watching them put Sarah in the ambulance. I can't remember if Memory was there with me during those fifteen to twenty minutes or not."

He took her hand and held it. "Tell me what you were saying about the necklace."

Lena started talking, moving her hand up and down as she spoke. "Memory and I came in here to talk. I was going to tell her about the box her grandmother, Grace, left for us to open together—that third Wings of Grace box. But before I could do that, Memory pulled out the Alexandrite necklace and handed it to me."

"But how? I thought she turned that necklace in for the million-dollar reward."

"I don't know how she did it, and I didn't get a chance to find out. All I know is that she said she wanted to give it back to me," Lena said. "She claimed she wanted to make things right between us. All of us. I gave it back to her. She laid it on the bed."

"If that's the case, then why would *she* take it? Lena, that doesn't make sense."

Lena had a smirk on her face. "Because she's trying to convince me she has changed when she really hasn't, that's why. And to think I almost believed her, too."

"Lena, listen. I don't think you should jump to any immediate conclusions about Memory, the necklace, or that box. I'm sure there's some kind of a logical explanation."

"Like?"

"Like maybe someone else saw them and put them up for you. But you should ask Memory before you get all worked up about it. She may have just put them up to keep them safe, and in the commotion—like you forgot—maybe she forgot to tell you."

Lena stood and started toward the door.

"Where are you going?" Richard asked.

"To ask her. I'm going to settle this once and for all."

Lena went to Memory's closed door. Standing and about to knock, she could hear Memory talking to someone. Detecting only one voice, she concluded Memory was on the phone. She started to walk away, when suddenly she stopped in her tracks.

"Sam, I told you. I'm sorry I just got a chance to call. It's been crazy around here. But guess what? I got it back," Memory said in a slightly muffled but audible voice. "It took some doing, but I got the Alexandrite necklace back. More than that: an early July ninth birthday present to *me*. Only thing is, I think I may be in a slight pickle. You know, a bit of a jam. All right, in plain English . . . in trouble."

Having heard enough, Lena turned around and rushed back to her room.

"That was quick," Richard said. "What happened? Was she busy? Not there?"

Lena fell into his arms. "Just hold me, please. Hold me, okay?"

"What happened? Did you get to talk to Memory and ask if she took them?"

Lena pulled herself away from his embrace. "I didn't have to. I was standing outside her door about to knock. I heard her on the phone. She was telling someone named Sam that she'd gotten the necklace back." Lena laid her head back on Richard's shoulder. "If she took the necklace, Richard, then she took the box as well."

Richard rubbed her back as she cried. "I'm sorry, Lena girl. I'm *so* sorry."

Chapter 31

So shall they fear the name of the Lord from the west, and His glory from the rising of the sun. When the enemy shall come in like a flood, the Spirit of the Lord shall lift up a standard against him.

Isaiah 59:19

"Lena, would you like to tell me what's bothering you?" Sarah asked as she sat propped up in her bed.

"Nothing," Lena said.

"Listen, dear. I've been around a long while. I can tell when someone has something on their mind. Now, if you just don't want to share it with me, that's one thing. But to tell me it's nothing is just not true, and you and I both know that."

Lena forced a smile. "I really don't want to talk about it."

"Well, all right then. But if you're worried about me, I'm feeling so much better. It was a blessing having you and Memory here with me throughout this ordeal." Sarah pushed her body up to sit more erect. "Every time I opened my eyes in that hospital room, one or both of you were there. I had to remind myself it was real . . . that I wasn't dreaming."

Lena leaned over and patted her on her hand. "I'm glad, Grandmother."

Sarah looked toward the window. "It's a beautiful day today. I'd really love to go outside." She turned back and smiled at Lena. "Do you think we could all eat out on the terrace for lunch today? Just us girls—me, you, and Memory. I'm not trying to cut Richard out, I'd just like it to be only us three."

"If you want to do that, I don't see why we can't. The doctor said that the more you get up and move around, the better it will be for you." Lena stood up. "And you know Richard practically lives on the golf course these days, so he's already up and gone. But I'll let Monica know," she said, referring to the cook. "Is there anything special you'd like her to fix for lunch?"

Sarah shook her head. "No. But before you leave, sit back down and let's talk."

Lena came back and sat down.

Sarah reached over and grabbed her hand once more. "Lena, I know you and Memory have had your seasons of being angry."

Lena tried, but couldn't help it. She turned away just from the mention of Memory's name.

"Lena, look at me. I don't know what has happened recently, but you can't keep letting things fester between you and your mother." She patted Lena's hand twice, then released it. "A few days ago you and Memory seemed to be really connecting. What has happened, seemingly in one day, that changed things?"

Lena stood up again. She didn't want to be close enough for Sarah to look in her eyes. "Nothing, Grandmother. Now, I really need to go let Memory and Monica know about our lunch plans. I'll ask Monica to fix some of your favorite dishes."

"Lena, I love you," Sarah said as she stared at her. "But I love Memory, too. Yes, she's done some pretty horrible things. Yes, she's disappointed a lot of people. Yes, she's hurt people I care deeply about. But Lena, in loving Memory I have to let all those things go. In loving Memory, I have to learn to forgive. In loving Memory, I have to give her a chance to prove that she's really changed, and I have to do that without holding back any of myself or my heart. If I don't, I may miss out on things and moments I can never get back." Sarah reached her hand out to Lena. "I've missed too much already. I don't want to live out the remainder of whatever time I have distrusting or guarding my heart. Because in doing that, I limit the joy I could experience. I want to feel it all. And if that means having to take the good with the bad, then so be it. If in loving Memory it means I may be hurt, then I'll just have to take that chance."

Lena squeezed her hand. "I'm glad you can do that," Lena said.

"Talk to her," Sarah said sternly. "Tell her what you think. Tell her how you feel. Give her a chance. Fight for what's right. We must stop letting the devil win."

"Has Memory said something to you?" Lena asked out of curiosity.

"No. But I can feel the difference in you both. I asked her about you last night, and she became instantly sad. Her whole countenance changed. When I asked her what had happened between you two, she told me she didn't know . . . that you had abruptly shut down on her, and she was at a loss as to what had occurred to cause it."

"Is that what she told you?"

"Lena, I don't believe she's the same woman anymore that *you* believe her to be."

Lena took her hand back. "How do you know that, Grandmother? You've only known her for less than two weeks. You don't know how manipulative she can be. You don't know how she can make you think she really cares about you only to stab you in the back when you least expect it." Lena saw the shocked look come over Sarah's face. "I'm sorry. I'm sorry. I don't mean to upset you. You don't need this now. I apologize."

"It's okay. I'm strong enough to hear this. But will you trust me on this? At least tell Memory what's bothering you in regards to her. You may discover this is all some big misunderstanding. If you talk about it, you won't lose precious time that honestly can never be gotten back. Confrontation is not always a bad thing. I learned that when I had to go against Montgomery and the others to take back what was rightfully mine. It would have been easy to just walk away. Sometimes we have to meet a thing head-on."

Lena leaned down and kissed Sarah on the cheek. "I hear you."

Sarah grabbed Lena's wrist and held her before she could stand back up straight. "Do more than just hear me. I want the two of you to resolve whatever is going on between you. If you can't do it for yourselves, then please, can you do it for me?" She released her grip.

Lena stood up and straightened her top by pulling it down. She nodded.

"Oh, and Lena? Just in case you're wondering, I had this same conversation with Memory a little while ago. Sometimes you have to wash off all the junk to see the true treasures in life. I don't know what happened, but I know you need to put whatever it is out there and get to the bottom of it so you can experience all God has for you. Deal with it before it ferments that much more."

Lena leaned down and kissed her again. "For you, Grandmother, I'll do it."

"Not just for me; do it for yourself as well. Do it for your own child and for her children." Sarah nodded, then looked back toward the sunlight that streamed like a beam through her window. "What a beautiful day, Lord. You've given me one more day. This *is* the day that the Lord has made, and I *will* rejoice and be glad in it. I will! Thank You, Lord. I thank You for one more day."

Chapter 32

Thy sun shall no more go down; neither shall thy moon withdraw itself: for the Lord shall be thine everlasting light, and the days of thy mourning shall be ended.

Isaiah 60:20

"All right, Lena. Let's talk," Memory said as soon as Lena entered the kitchen.

"I need to tell Monica—"

"That Sarah wants to have lunch out on the terrace," Memory said, completing the sentence for her. "I've already told her. So . . ." She held her hand out toward the terrace. "Shall we go talk?"

"Sure," Lena said with an attitude that showed in her body language.

Lena stepped out the door first and sat down at the patio table. Memory sat directly across from her.

"So tell me—what did I do?" Memory asked.

Lena let out a small huff. "Like you don't know."

"Lena, I don't know. We seemed to have been making progress that evening we were talking in your room. We pulled together to take care of Sarah while she was in the hospital. When Sarah came home, you were fine. Then, in the last twenty-four hours or so, it's like someone left the freezer door wide open, and it's causing a deep freeze to go throughout the entire house."

Lena shook her head. "Just stop. Why don't you just stop?" She looked at Memory, her eyes visibly sad.

"Stop what?" Memory asked, clearly annoyed. "Stop

trying to make up for my past mistakes? Stop trying to do the right thing by you and by Sarah and Theresa if I get the chance? Stop what?"

"Stop lying. Stop pretending that you care about other people when you don't," Lena said in a controlled but stern voice. "The only one you really care about is yourself."

"Lena, what are you talking about? Why don't you just come out and say what you have to say and quit leaving breadcrumb trails, expecting me to follow you? Just say it and get it over with."

Lena sat back in the chair and made a long sucking sound with her teeth, then buttoned up her lips before relaxing them. "Okay. Let's play another game. Let's play Tell the Truth No Matter What for a change."

"Fine. If it will help you get past whatever this is you're going through at the moment, then bring it on," Memory said.

Lena sat forward. "This is how we're going to do this. We'll tell the truth no matter what the truth really is, and no matter whose feelings may get hurt in the process. It's just you and me. All right?"

"Go ahead. Ask away," Memory said as she leaned in toward Lena.

"Did you or did you not take the Wings of Grace box?" Lena asked.

Memory began to laugh. "Oh, so it's that again. Yes, Lena. I took it. You know I took it."

Lena looked a little shocked. "You took it, and you're admitting it?"

"Yes, I took it," Memory said. "That's old news. So you're telling me that you've been walking around mad all day yesterday because of something I took back when you were young? Something you didn't even know existed until you were older?"

Lena sat back against the chair. "Okay." She nodded

her head swiftly. "Okay. Okay, so now you're back to playing games again."

"You asked me if I took that box. I'm telling you the truth. Yes, I took it."

"I'm talking about the box that was in my room the other day. You remember . . . the one Grace left in her will for me and you to open together. We were in my room when Gayle came in, and I left it on the bed. *That* Wings of Grace box."

Memory folded her hands together. "I didn't take that box, Lena."

Lena began to smile a phony smile. "Of course you didn't."

"Lena." Memory leaned in closer. "I'm telling you the truth. I didn't take that box. Look into my eyes, Lena. I promise you, I didn't take it."

Lena looked at her. "What about the Alexandrite necklace? It just so happens to be missing as well. I suppose you're telling me you didn't take it back, either?"

Memory reached over and grabbed both of Lena's hands. "Lena, why would I give that necklace back to you, then turn around and take it? That makes no sense."

Lena removed her hands from Memory's. "I don't know. That's what frustrates me about you. I never know why you do anything. All I know is it hurts like you'll never, ever understand." Lena stood and walked to the limestone banister. "I want you to really love me. I've always wanted you to want me." She turned and looked at Memory as tears ran down her face. "But you never seemed able to. And every time I decide to give you one more chance, it's obvious you don't really care. Because you manage to stomp on my heart all over again like it's some kind of a sport to you."

Memory stood up and went to her daughter. "Lena, I am sorry for all the hurt I've caused you. I sincerely am. I thought giving you back that necklace would make up things to you . . . that it would let you know how much I really do love you . . . how sincere I really am about us being closer."

Lena began to cry. "Then why take it back like that? I said you could keep it."

Memory pulled her close and held her tight. "I'm sorry I hurt you. I'm sorry you don't feel you can trust me. But Lena, I've been on the up-and-up with you since I've been here. I didn't take them. I'm trying to make amends here. Lord knows, I'm trying. I really am."

"And why is that?" Lena asked, pulling away from her mother's embrace. "Why now? Is it because you see a bigger payday with Sarah? Are you just biding your time, trying to pretend to be a changed woman who loves the Lord now, all of a sudden?"

"Don't discount my love for God. He changed me, Lena. Whether you believe that or not, that's the truth. The old Memory would definitely be looking at all of this trying to see how she could score big and get out fast. But God took out that old, stony heart"—she put her hand over her heart area—"and gave me a brand-new, clean heart. And now, I just want to serve Him and do right by people."

Lena walked back over to the table and stood by the chair she had just occupied. "Memory, if you've changed, then what about that phone conversation you had the other night?"

"What phone conversation?" Memory walked over toward the table. "Oh, you heard me talking on the phone? So what are you doing? Spying on me now?"

Lena sat down and folded her arms across her chest. "I heard you the other night on the phone, but I wasn't spying on you. I was coming to ask if you might have put the Wings of Grace box up along with the neck-lace. I was looking for them, thinking originally that

Richard had put them up during all the commotion with Grandmother going to the hospital. Night before last, I asked him. He didn't move them, so we thought you might have put them up . . . you know, for safekeeping."

"So you came to my room and heard me on the phone?" Memory asked as she sat down.

"Yes." Lena started rocking her body a little. "You were talking to someone named Sam."

Memory tilted her head slightly. "So, what all did you hear me say to Sam?"

"Why don't you tell me what you said? That way I can see how truthful, how much on the up-and-up, you really are these days," Lena said.

"Okay, Lena. I'm going to tell you everything. I'm going to tell you about Sam and about Montgomery Powell the Second—"

"Montgomery Powell the Second? You know Montgomery?"

"Yes. I met him that Saturday when I told you I was going out to visit Asheville. You remember, the night I came home and gave you back the Alexandrite necklace."

Monica came outside with a tray. "I thought you two might like some fresh lemonade," she said, setting the tray with a glass pitcher and two glasses filled with crushed ice on the table.

After Monica left, Lena poured Memory a glass of lemonade, then herself. Taking a sip, Lena set her glass down. "All right. I'm all ears," Lena said as she sat back, relaxed.

Chapter 33

Truth shall spring out of the earth; and righteousness shall look down from heaven.

Psalms 85:11

"First off, when you came to my room the other night and heard me on the phone, I was indeed talking to Sam," Memory said.

"And I suppose Sam is another one of your con-artist buddies like that phony lawyer friend you had come to Theresa's house that day," Lena said with a slight smirk.

"Sam is my closest and dearest friend. Her name is Samantha McCoy, and she really has been the only person who's tried to show me the error of my ways." Memory took a drink of her lemonade. She held the glass up in the air and looked at it. "Ahhhh! Now that's *real* lemonade," she said, then set the glass back down.

"So I guess I'm supposed to believe Sam is a woman?"

Memory hunched her shoulders. "I'm not trying to make you believe anything. You say you want the whole truth. I said I'd tell you the truth. You'll either believe what I'm saying or you won't, but it's not going to be on me. Anyway, Sam was like me at one time—always trying to find a way to get over on somebody. Actually, we viewed it more like trying to figure out a way to get ahead."

"Okay, let's say Sam really is a woman named Samantha. What were you talking about the other night?"

Memory looked down, then back up. "I was telling Sam that I'd managed to get the Alexandrite necklace back."

Lena started nodding her head and smiling in a sarcastic way. "Exactly. At least you're telling the truth about that."

Memory leaned in. "I was telling her I'd gotten the necklace back from the person who had ended up with it . . . after I took it out of the safe-deposit box and turned it over to Christopher Harris, a.k.a. Christopher Phelps of Phelps & Phelps."

"So you're admitting you did steal the necklace?"

"Lena, you already know that. I was wrong, and right after I did it and found myself sitting there waiting for Christopher to pick me up, I wanted so badly to turn around and somehow put everything back the way it was. But I couldn't," Memory said. "I'd already deceived Theresa, and she was on her way to the hospital to have my great-granddaughter. Christopher picked me up shortly after Richard dropped me off at the bus stop."

"You still could have taken the necklace back and returned it to the safe-deposit box," Lena said as she exchanged looks with her mother. "We could have gotten past all of this."

"Oh, yeah. I can see *that* working out. Anyway, it was too late to turn back. Christopher took the necklace and put it up for safekeeping while he made arrangements to get the reward money for it." She took another swallow of lemonade. "We were supposed to split the million dollars sixty-forty, my favor. Instead, that snake decided to double-cross me." She looked up and smiled. "I suppose you can say the con got conned."

"So you're telling me you didn't get anything from the necklace?"

"Oh, Christopher was not heartless. He came by and left twenty thousand dollars for me with Samantha.

That's how she and I ended up close. Sam is diabetic, and she's lost both her legs because of it. She was living in a ground-level apartment. Christopher and I had an apartment two floors above hers. We would see Sam on occasion and speak. After Christopher turned in the necklace, he told me we would have to wait a few days for them to verify that the necklace was genuine and not just some fake."

"And you believed him," Lena said.

"Why wouldn't I? That was a million dollars they were giving up. Everybody knows they weren't going to give up that much money without checking out the merchandise first. Christopher was the one who knew the guy who was paying the reward." Memory let out a hard sigh.

"Anyway, Christopher left and never came back. I was worried something bad had happened to him. One day I was on my way out a few weeks after not hearing from him. Sam stopped me. She didn't know my phone number, and she couldn't get up the stairs to come find me. That's when she gave me a package she said Christopher had left with her to give to me. She didn't understand why he didn't just bring it up to me himself. I opened it, and there was cash money inside with a note thanking me for everything."

"Wow," Lena said.

"Sam saw me break down. She opened up her door for me to come in. We talked, and I told her everything. I don't know why it's easier sometimes to tell a stranger things like that, but it was for me. That's when Sam explained to me the truth regarding the law of sowing and reaping." Memory primped her lips in a snooty way, then laughed.

"Oh, I'm sure you wanted to hear that," Lena said sarcastically. She drank the last of her lemonade. Reaching over and picking up the pitcher, she offered Memory a refill. Memory held her glass up as Lena poured.

"Actually, Sam was just what I needed at the time," Memory said as Lena filled her glass. "I didn't need to stay in an apartment under my own name, so I took her up on her offer to move in with her. She needed someone there to help out, and I needed to keep a low profile until I was sure things had blown over." Memory swirled the liquid in her glass slightly before putting the glass up to her lips and taking a sip. "To be honest, I was also hoping Christopher might have a change of heart and come back for me. I knew if he did, he would come to Sam's apartment to see if she knew where I was."

"Did he ever come back?" Lena asked.

"Nope. But a lot of other people started showing up asking for me," Memory said. "Sam was great, never letting anyone know my whereabouts, even after I left her place. We've always kept in touch. She got saved and started telling me how she was praying for me. I'd go back and stay with her on occasion, but it seemed best for me to keep moving since I couldn't seem to shake those private detectives that had nothing better to do, it seemed, than track me down."

"So how did you get the Alexandrite necklace back?" Lena asked.

"I believe it was the summer of 2002 that I received a letter at Sam's place. It was from some man in Asheville, North Carolina, who said he was sure he had something I'd like to have back. His name was Montgomery Powell the Second, which meant nothing to me except possibly some clever trick to smoke me out."

"Montgomery, the one you went to see the Saturday Grandmother got sick?"

Memory nodded, using her whole body in a rocking motion. "Yes. Anyway, until Johnnie Mae Landris told me the truth about my real mother a few weeks ago, none of this had made sense or, truthfully, any difference. When Johnnie Mae told me everything, including the fact that Sarah was in Asheville, I started to call Sarah that night. But I just couldn't manage to bring myself to hear the truth, at least not then." Memory laughed. "It's funny. It was like as long as I didn't come face to face with it, it was merely a thought . . . a remote possibility . . . words spoken by some woman I barely knew, who could be wrong. I knew I had become a different person, but what if this knowledge sent me back to being the person I thought I'd buried when I gave my life to Christ?"

"So you're sincere about the Lord?" Lena asked with a quizzical look. "It's not just a con you're using to get over?"

"Lena, it's the most incredible feeling and experience I've ever had," Memory said, touching Lena's arm. "It's hard to describe, but to actually put someone else first, instead of yourself, that's just something I can't honestly say I'd ever done before in my entire life. Not until Jesus came into my heart. He changed me."

"So you didn't want to see Sarah that day Johnnie Mae told you everything because you were afraid you really hadn't changed?"

"I suppose I was afraid I might hurt her the way I had hurt you and Theresa," Memory said, removing her hand from Lena's arm. "I didn't want to take the chance of finding out that maybe I really *hadn't* changed. That the old Memory was just waiting for the chance to rise up . . . to be resurrected. My intentions had been to leave the Landrises' house and disappear quietly into the night."

"What made you change your mind?"

"Sam did," Memory said with a nod. "That's what . . . or should we say who. I called Sam, and she prayed with me that night. She told me she'd seen a change in me, and that the right thing for me to do was go and meet my mother. Also, that if I ever got the chance to make things right with you and Theresa, I should do it . . . *whatever* I had to do to make it right. So I called the number Johnnie Mae gave me for Sarah, told the person who answered the phone that I had a special delivery for Sarah Fleming, but I couldn't make out the address as written and needed to verify it. Whoever answered the phone gave me the address. I got on a bus, and here I am."

Lena stared deep into her eyes as Memory held her head up high. "You're telling the truth," Lena said.

"Yes."

Lena released a sigh. "So tell me. How does Montgomery fit in all of this?"

Memory raised an eyebrow and smiled. "Are you sure you want to hear this part right now?"

Lena looked at her watch. It was nearing noontime. Sarah would be down shortly. She nodded. "Yes. I want to know everything. But it will be lunchtime in about twenty minutes," Lena said. "So you need to hurry up."

Chapter 34

*Fill their faces with shame; that they
may seek Thy name, O Lord.*

Psalm 83:16

"As I was saying, Montgomery sent certified letters
to Sam's place for me. Samantha signed for them
because she didn't know whether or not they were
something important since no one, other than possibly
Christopher, would know I was there unless I had told
them." Memory sat back against the chair.

"So it appears Montgomery not only knew *who* you
were but *where* you were," Lena said. "And how long
ago did you say this was?"

Memory frowned and twisted her mouth as she bit
down on her thumbnail. "The first letter came about
three years ago, around June of 2002." She began to nod.
"A couple more letters came over the years."

"Grandmother began searching for you October of
2001, as soon as she learned you were still alive. So
Montgomery must have learned of your whereabouts
some months after that." Lena shook her head. "But
why? Why would he want to make contact with you?
What is he up to?"

"I take it Montgomery must really be bad news?"
Memory popped her lips and scrunched her mouth as
she spoke.

"Yeah. I've had a taste firsthand. He's definitely someone to steer clear of."

"Then what I've done may not have been a good thing," Memory said. She leaned her head back and exhaled loudly. Sitting up straight, she began to shake her head once more.

Lena leaned her body in closer. "What did you do?"

"I was the one who called Montgomery. It was a few days after I arrived. If you recall, you and Theresa weren't too happy to see me when I showed up in your lives again. I was curious as to how he might possibly fit in this ever-evolving puzzle. For some strange reason, I'd kept his three letters in my pocketbook. I knew he lived here in Asheville. I'd been mysteriously summoned back to Asheville after having left here when I was fourteen. So I decided to give him a call and see what he had to say. He turned out to be quite a little charmer over the phone, and, surprisingly, he seemed genuinely excited to hear from me."

Memory sat back against the chair and situated her body more comfortably as she continued. "I didn't want him able to see where I was calling from in case he had caller ID. I have a calling card I generally use for long-distance calls, so I decided to use it to call him, even though I knew it was a local call. We talked, and eventually I admitted to him I was in the city. He insisted that we meet, again enticing me by saying he had something he was certain I wanted back while being adamant that he couldn't tell me anything more than that over the phone. He also informed me that he knew I was here at Sarah's house. That kind of bothered me a little."

"That is interesting."

"He didn't want me to mention anything to anyone here about him or the call. If I did, he said he would somehow know, and that the sweet deal he was planning for me would immediately be taken off the table before I ever even got to know what it was."

Lena crossed her legs at her ankles. "Oh, yeah . . . a real charmer, that Montgomery Powell the Second. So you felt safe enough to go off alone and meet with a stranger, in reality, without letting anyone know?"

Memory smiled. "Lena, you know I haven't lived a charmed life all these years. I've hung out with some rough folks, to put it mildly. I learned a long time ago how to take care of myself."

"But you're older now. It was dangerous when you were young, but even more dangerous now that you're almost seventy," Lena said, crossing her arms.

"I know. That's why I told Sam everything. I gave her the phone number here and told her that if I didn't call her back before the night was over, she was to call you and tell you everything she knew about Montgomery and my seeing him. In all that happened Saturday night, I almost forgot to call her and let her know I had made it back okay. I ended up having to call her from the hospital. We spoke long enough for me to let her know I was all right, with a promise that I'd call her again later when I could talk."

Lena unfolded her arms and looked toward the doorway. "Grandmother likely will be down soon."

"I know; I'll hurry." Memory took a deep breath and released it. "Montgomery had the Alexandrite necklace."

"What?" Lena said, shocked.

"And somehow, he knew that you and Theresa were upset with me about my having taken it. He said he wanted to give it back to me—"

Lena started shaking her head. "He wanted to *give* it back? The man paid two million dollars to get it, and you're telling me he was going to just give it back to you out of the goodness of his heart?" She shook her

head even faster and turned up her nose as though she
had suddenly caught whiff of something that had been
dead and hidden away for weeks. "I don't think so."

"He mentioned he'd paid two million dollars for that
necklace," Memory said, still showing her shock. "Two
million dollars."

"Yes. And according to Pastor Landris who knows
all about this, your *boyfriend* got one million of those
dollars, minus your twenty thousand. Frankly, I don't
have time to tell everything I know right now," Lena said.
She started rotating her index finger in a circular motion, indicating to Memory she needed to finish up her
story. "Please hurry."

"I asked him how he knew Sarah, and he told me
about his father being Sarah's half-brother," Memory
said.

"Yeah, I know all about that. Get back to you, him,
and the necklace."

"As you already know now, Montgomery ended up
giving it to me."

"For what reason? What did you have to give him or
promise him in return in order for you to get the necklace? That's what I want to know."

Memory stood up and walked over to the door and
looked inside. It was quiet, but she could smell the various cooking aromas that were slipping through the
cracks, making their way outside to the terrace from
the kitchen.

Lena got up, walked over to the door, and practically
dragged Memory away from it. "Tell me what you did
in order to get the Alexandrite necklace."

Memory walked away from Lena over to the limestone banister and looked out at the rolling blue hills.
"I don't believe I did this."

Lena came over and stood next to her. "What . . .
did . . . you . . . do?"

Memory looked at her. "I signed a document stating that I would sell him this house, at a fair and marketable price, of course, should I be the one to inherit it upon my mother's death. That's what."

Lena stared at her. "How could you?" Lena started walking away.

Memory ran and grabbed her arm. "Lena, I did it because I love my family. I love you, and I love Theresa, and I love my great-grandbabies. I wanted to make things right with us. I figured if I had the necklace and gave it back, you and Theresa might forgive me for having taken it in the first place. You might have thought I'd kept it all this time. You know—no harm, no foul."

Lena wriggled her arm out of Memory's grip. "But how could you agree to sell this house like that? I thought you said you'd changed? You haven't changed! This is exactly what you did when I was sixteen years old. You took the house that Big Mama left me, and you sold it without any regard for anyone else other than yourself. It was about what you wanted. It's always about you . . . always what's best for you." Lena stared at her, then plodded away. She turned and looked at her before opening the door. "How could you do that to your own mother?" she asked. "How could you?"

Memory walked swiftly to catch up with her. "Lena," she yelled. "Lena!"

Lena opened the door and went inside the house, quickly making her way up the stairs to her room. Closing her door, she locked it, then fell to her knees as she began to quietly cry.

Chapter 35

Thus saith the Lord, thy Redeemer, the Holy One of Israel; I am the Lord thy God which teacheth thee to profit, which leadeth thee by the way that thou shouldest go.

Isaiah 48:17

Lena sat on her bed. Looking at her watch and seeing it was close to noon, she got up and wiped the tears from her eyes and face with a wet washcloth. Knowing she had to pull herself together, she went to Sarah's room with a big smile on her face. Sarah was holding onto Gayle's arm with one hand while holding a walking cane with the other.

"Grandmother, are you ready for lunch?" Lena asked cheerfully.

"I absolutely am," Sarah said. She walked up to Lena and looked into her eyes. Lena looked away. "Is Memory already downstairs?"

Lena nodded. "Yes, she's on the terrace waiting."

"Good," Sarah said as she removed her arm from Gayle's arm and wrapped it around Lena's. "Thanks, Gayle. Lena will see me downstairs. You can run on and take care of that errand you said you needed to handle."

Gayle nodded. "Thank you. I'll be back in a few hours. Y'all have fun, now."

As Sarah and Lena slowly made their way down the stairs, Sarah stopped on the landing area before starting down the last set of stairs. "Give me a second,"

Sarah said. "This is more than a notion. Definitely a lot more work than I first thought," she said.

"It's fine. Take your time. We don't have any reason to rush."

Sarah stood there. "So . . . did you and Memory talk?"

Lena nodded.

"Is that why you're upset?" Sarah asked, looking up at Lena from her slightly bent position. "Did things not go well with you two?"

Lena looked at her and smiled. "It went okay. We didn't get to finish our conversation, but we covered a lot of ground."

Sarah grabbed Lena's arm tighter. "Well, I won't pressure you about it. If you want to talk, I hope you know I'm here."

"I know," Lena said as she started moving along with Sarah's pace.

They stepped out on the terrace, and Sarah immediately shielded her eyes with her hand. "What a *lovely* day!" Sarah said, grinning.

Memory got up and met Sarah and Lena. She helped Sarah to the chair underneath the oversized patio umbrella. "You look so pretty in your flowery dress," Memory said as she held on to Sarah, who was lowering her body slowly into the chair.

"I've always loved flowers. Chocolate and flowers. I thought I'd brighten my day even more by wearing this dress."

Lena and Memory sat down. Monica rolled out the serving table and began setting the table. It didn't take her long to finish. "If you need anything else, let me know," Monica said.

"Food fit for queens," Sarah said as she lifted the sterling-silver domes and began putting various items on her plate. "This looks more like a Sunday dinner than a Thursday lunch on the terrace. Will you look a' here.

There are collard greens with okra, grilled chicken, and squash casserole. Oh, I simply love Monica's squash casserole! Nobody can touch Monica's squash casserole. As an old friend of mine in Selma, Alabama, Ms. Azile, used to say when we ate something that was absolutely delicious, 'That woman know she can put her foot in it.'"

"We told her to fix all your favorites," Lena said, smiling.

"So I see," Sarah said. She looked at Memory. "Will you please say grace?"

Memory looked at Lena, then Sarah. "Of course." They bowed their heads as Memory prayed a short prayer. "Amen," she said.

They began eating in silence except for occasional comments about a certain dish.

Sarah set her fork down. "Okay, so who wants to tell me what's going on here?" She looked from Lena to Memory. "Memory? Lena?"

"Nothing, Grandmother. Just enjoying the food and the company," Lena said.

Sarah looked at Memory again. "Will *someone* please tell me the truth for a change and stop all of this foolishness of trying to protect me?"

Memory looked at Lena. "It's all my fault," she said to Sarah. "I'm ruining your beautiful day. Lena's upset with me, and, truthfully, she has every reason and right to be."

"Don't do it," Lena said to Memory. "I'm not upset. I just have a lot on my mind. Richard's becoming quite a little golfer these days. I was thinking he would be bored, and it looks like he's more active here than when he's at home." Lena put a forkful of food in her mouth. "You're right, Grandmother. This squash casserole is divine! Monica definitely put her foot in this. Don't you think so?" Lena asked, now addressing Memory.

"Yes," Memory said, taking a bite of squash casserole. "It's delicious."

Sarah didn't say a word. She just sat there and watched as Lena continued on with a few minutes more of frivolous chitchat about nothing really.

"Lena, I should have brought my straw hat down with me," Sarah said. "Would you be a dear and run up to my room and get it?"

Lena smiled as she looked at Sarah, then Memory.

"I'll get it for you," Memory said, pushing her chair back as she started to stand.

"If you don't mind, I'd like Lena to get it for me," Sarah said, touching Memory's hand. She looked at Lena. "She's the youngest between us. That's if you don't mind?"

Lena smiled and got up. "Of course I don't mind." She wiped her mouth and placed the crisp, white linen napkin down next to her plate. "I'll be right back."

"It's in the chifforobe," Sarah yelled as Lena opened the French door.

After Lena left, Sarah dabbed her mouth, being extra careful not to wipe off her ruby red lipstick she'd so artfully put on. She set her full attention to Memory. "Now, would you like to tell me what's going on?"

Memory wiped her mouth and took a few swallows of lemonade. "Nothing," she finally said.

"Memory, please don't insult my intelligence or my sanity. Something is going on, and I want to know what it is." Sarah stopped eating and folded her arms across her chest.

Memory looked up at the sky, then at Sarah as she let out a loud sigh. "Okay. Okay. I'll tell you. For one thing, I met with Montgomery Powell this past Saturday. It was the same day you got sick. The day you went to the hospital."

Sarah nodded. "Is that all?"

Memory shook her head. "I got the Alexandrite necklace back. The one I'm sure you're aware that I took from Lena and Theresa a few years back."

Sarah nodded again slowly. "Let me know when you're finished," Sarah said.

Memory sat back against her chair. "I gave Lena the necklace. She gave it back. Lena showed me the Wings of Grace box your mother left for me and her to open together." Memory cocked her head to the side. "We left them on Lena's bed, and now both the box and the necklace have mysteriously disappeared out of her room."

"Would you care to tell me how you managed to get that necklace back?"

"I made a deal with Montgomery. He had it." Memory stopped and readjusted her body in the chair. "I signed an agreement that says if I should inherit this house, I'll sell it to him."

Sarah nodded, her demeanor remaining the same. "So, I see."

"Now that the necklace and the box are both missing, Lena thinks I'm probably behind their disappearance." Memory waited for Sarah to say something. "But I didn't take them."

Sarah picked up her knife and fork, cut off a piece of her grilled chicken, placed it in her mouth, and proceeded to chew slowly.

Lena walked back outside, handed Sarah the hat, and sat down. "It wasn't in the chifforobe," Lena said. "It was in your closet, on the top shelf."

"Oh, I suppose someone must have moved it then." Sarah ate one of the peas in a pod.

Lena looked at Sarah, trying to figure out what may have happened while she was gone.

Sarah pointed her fork at Lena's plate. "You need to eat, dear."

Lena smiled at Sarah, then looked over at Memory,

whose demeanor had completely changed since she'd gone to get Sarah's hat.

Memory looked back at Lena. "I told her everything," Memory finally said to Lena.

Lena narrowed her eyes somewhat, her eyebrows furrowing as she frowned. "Told her what?"

"I told her about Montgomery and our meeting, about the necklace, and how the necklace and the box are both missing now," Memory said.

"Why?"

"Because I asked her to," Sarah said. "And I needed to know." Sarah ate some more of the squash casserole. "Let me ask you something. The Wings of Grace box— did you get a chance to see what was inside of it before it went missing?"

"No," Memory said. "Gayle came to Lena's room just after we unlocked it."

"And I never opened it before that day, so I don't know what was in there," Lena said.

Sarah set her fork down in her plate. "Lena, you believe Memory took the box and the necklace, correct?"

Lena tried to smile and play it off. "Why are you ruining this perfect day with talk about things like this, Grandmother?"

"Because something is going on here, and we need to get to the bottom of it. I believe it's Hosea four-six that says, 'My people are destroyed for lack of knowledge.' I don't care for our family to be destroyed. I've waited too long to get here, and I don't intend to tiptoe around issues any longer because no one wishes to upset the apple cart. Let's get to it so we can figure out what's going on and know exactly what we're dealing with here. Knowledge is always power. Always. I will not allow our family to be destroyed. So let's do what needs to be done, however painful it might be."

"Do you think I took that box and the necklace?" Memory asked Lena.

Lena looked at Sarah. Sarah's look was stern.

"I think it's a strong possibility you may have," Lena said. "You went to see Montgomery, and you weren't planning on ever telling us that. Do you have any idea the agonies and heartaches those people have put Grandmother through all these years, going all the way back to his father and uncle?"

"I really don't," Memory said. "All I know is he had the necklace, and I felt that getting it back was one way I might have a chance of you and Theresa not being angry with me anymore."

Sarah touched Lena's arm. "What Montgomery and my half-brothers did is my battle." She looked at Memory. "They were the reason I was locked away all those years from my home until Johnnie Mae Taylor, now Landris, with the help of the Lord, aided me to set things straight. Montgomery lived here in this house until I had him removed in October of 2001. So, please, tell me everything you know about him wanting this house."

"He wants to buy it from me should I inherit it from you. But I didn't believe you were really intending to leave me the house, so I didn't see any harm in signing that paper he had me sign in order for me to get the necklace back."

Sarah nodded. "Well, he is correct regarding my intentions for this house. My will does state you'll inherit this place upon my death."

"How did he know that?" Lena asked.

"Obviously, someone is leaking my confidential information to him," Sarah said.

"Do you think it's your lawyer?" Memory asked.

"No. My lawyer, Lance Seymour, is a trusted and loyal friend. He wouldn't do something like that."

"What about someone in his office? Maybe Montgomery has someone on his payroll in there or paid them for your information," Memory said.

"The Wings of Grace box and the necklace," Sarah began. "Tell me from the start what happened there."

"I gave Lena the necklace. She took out the Wings of Grace box. We broke the seal and unlocked it with its special key," Memory said, looking at Lena for agreement.

"Then Gayle came in and told us you were sick and needed us. We got up and left everything on my bed," Lena said. "I came home later that night from the hospital and, honestly, I wasn't thinking about the box, the necklace, or anything else except getting some rest. I suppose I thought Richard had put them away when he came home. I asked him about them the day before yesterday, and he said he hadn't seen them at all."

"So naturally she thought I took them," Memory said. "With my track record, I can't say I blame her. But I promise you both, it wasn't me."

"Lena, do you believe Memory now?" Sarah asked.

Lena looked at Memory. "It's like I want to. But Memory and I have a history. I just don't know. I can't think of anyone else who may have moved them or would have taken them except her. Not in that time frame. The timing is suspicious."

"Well, I don't think Memory took them," Sarah said. "There's something else going on around here, and I think we need to put our heads together and get to the bottom of it. We must pull together, because the Bible tells us that a house divided cannot stand."

"But Grandmother, how can you be so sure it wasn't Memory who took it?" Lena asked as she looked at Sarah intensely. "I've seen what she's capable of doing."

Sarah looked at Memory. "I know because somehow a mother knows when her children are lying. They may not

always want to admit that they know . . . but they know."
She took a deep breath and released it. "So let's see what
we can figure out."

"You need to change your will and leave this house
to Lena or Theresa," Memory said. "Anybody except
me. I may have signed that paper, but I'll not be a part
of Montgomery's plans to hurt you. I won't."

Sarah placed her hand on Memory's. "You let me
take care of this my way. I may be old, but I still have
my wits about me. I still have a few tricks up my sleeve.
There's more than one way to crack open an egg. We
need to find that Wings of Grace box, though. I have a
feeling my mother had something important in there.
That's why she wanted the two of you to open it together."

"But what if whoever has the box has already removed its contents?" Memory asked.

"We'll just have to pray that's not the case. Let's not
think negatively." Sarah reached over and took Lena's
hand, then grabbed hold of Memory's hand. "Let's pray."

"Yes," Lena said. "The Bible says one can put a thousand angels to flight, and two can put ten thousand. There
are three of us here. Ecclesiastes says that a three-corded
strand is not easily broken. We *must* stand strong."

"Lena and Memory, I want you to take one another's
hand," Sarah said as she bowed her head. "Dear Father
in Heaven," Sarah began. "We come to You asking for
guidance and Your help. Please Jesus, order our steps
in the way we should go. Keep us strong as a family that
we may be pleasing in Your sight. Heal any hurt that
still lingers among us. Remove all fear and replace it
with love. For we know that love covers a multitude of
faults . . . a multitude of sins. Father, we acknowledge
that we have all sinned and come short of Your glory.
Forgive us. Heal us. Direct us. These things we ask in
the name of Jesus, Amen."

"Amen," Lena and Memory said in unison. Memory squeezed Lena's hand. Lena squeezed back.

"Let's do this," Memory said. "Let's find out what's going on around this place."

Sarah smiled. "I don't know where Monica is with our dessert. Could you go tell Monica we're about ready for dessert now?" Sarah asked Lena.

Lena got up and went inside.

"Thank you," Memory said to her mother.

"For what?"

"For loving me," Memory said.

Sarah nodded. "I can't help it. It's as natural to me as breathing. Don't you worry now; we're going to fix this. And you and Lena . . . in the end, you're both going to be all right. I feel it in my heart."

"I hope so."

"Hope is always a good start, but don't ever stop with hope. Always . . . always move on to faith. And not just any kind of faith, I mean the working, love kind of faith."

Chapter 36

*For since the beginning of the world
men have not heard, nor perceived by
the ear, neither hath the eye seen, O
God, beside Thee, what He hath prepared for him that waiteth for Him.*

Isaiah 64:4

When Gayle returned from her errand, Sarah was
in the foyer about to go back upstairs to lie down.

"How was lunch, Miss Fleming?" Gayle asked as
she closed the front door.

"Divine," Sarah said. "Monica outdid herself. Then
we had this rich chocolate cake for dessert. You know,
I've *always* been partial to chocolate."

"Yes, you've told me. And I told you that you need
to be careful that you don't indulge too excessively, especially when it comes to sweets."

Sarah waved her hand. "I'll be ninety years old on
October first. I think I'm allowed *some* indulgence at
my age. I don't want to get to Heaven and wish I'd
eaten just one more slice of chocolate cake that I happened to have turned down because somebody felt it
was bad for my health." Sarah looked at Lena. "Gayle
can take me up from here."

Lena started to protest, then decided against it. She
nodded and went back in the kitchen to find Memory,
who had insisted on helping Monica clear the dishes.

Memory was, in reality, working to find out what
Monica knew about the missing items from Lena's
room. She'd remembered that Monica was still at the

house when Gayle came in the room to let them know Sarah was ill. The best way to determine who might have taken the things was by hard questioning and the process of elimination.

When Lena walked in, Monica was closing the dishwasher and turning it on. The quiet rumblings of the dishpan-hand-saving appliance began.

Monica smiled at Lena, appearing almost relieved to see her walk in. She finished wiping off the kitchen countertop. "That's pretty near all I can tell you," Monica said to Memory in her own brand of Southern drawl. "I'm sorry I can't be more help."

"What you told me was good," Memory said. She stood up. "I suppose I'll get out of your way," she said as she walked past Lena and nodded that she was finished with Monica.

"Is there any more lemonade left?" Lena asked.

"Yes," Monica said. "In fact, I just finished making a fresh batch and put it in the refrigerator. It's not cold yet, though."

Lena walked over, opened the cabinet, and took down a glass. She pushed the empty glass against the button that produced crushed ice. Opening the refrigerator door, she grabbed the gallon glass pitcher of lemonade by its handle and poured—turning the pitcher sideways when her glass was half full to ensure a slice or two of lemon would flow into her glass. Taking a sip, she let out a deliberate sigh to indicate her satisfaction.

"I tell you, Monica. You make the best lemonade," Lena said. "Not too sweet, not too tart. It's always just right."

"You sound like Goldilocks in *Goldilocks and the Three Bears*," Monica said with a chuckle. "Just right." She mocked the way Goldilocks said it in the story.

"I want to thank you for that fabulous lunch. It was perfect. Absolutely perfect!"

Monica rinsed out the dishrag, folded, and draped it across the divider in the sink for later use. "I'm just glad to have Miss Fleming home safe. She really gave us a scare."

"I suppose I'll go see what I can get done," Lena said as she made a show of leaving.

"Lena?" Monica called out to stop her from leaving just yet.

Lena stopped and turned back toward her. "Yes?"

"Memory was asking about some things that were in your room that appear to have come up missing. I just want to let you know, I had nothing to do with it. I would never do anything like that. I told that to Memory, but if you don't mind me saying this, and I know I don't know her all that well, but you can't always tell what Memory's up to or thinking," Monica said. "She's not the most tactful. With her, what comes up usually comes out. No sugar or artificial sweetener added."

"I know." Lena took another sip of lemonade. "So, what did you tell her?"

"Just that about ten minutes after y'all left for the hospital, I locked up and left."

"And no one came by before you left?"

Monica shook her head. "Not while I was still here. And I didn't go upstairs."

Lena smiled and nodded. "Thanks. And for the record, I didn't think you did it. The best I would have hoped for with you is that you moved them, you know, put them up for me, and just maybe forgot to mention it with all that's been going on around here."

"Miss Fleming's been too good to me. I would never do anything to cause her or anyone in her family discomfort or stress. And I don't steal. I just don't do that."

Lena went to Memory's bedroom. When she walked in, she sat in the wingback chair. They exchanged looks.

"I believe we can eliminate Monica from our list of suspects," Memory said.

Lena sat back in the chair and relaxed. "Yeah, she told me what you were talking about before I walked in."

"I'm *pretty* sure it wasn't her," Memory said. "Monica's too much of a scaredy-cat. If she'd done it, I believe she would've broken down or confessed when I questioned her. So let's go back over everything." Memory crossed her legs as she sat. "We were in your room. We'd broken the seal and unlocked the box. Gayle rushed in and said Sarah needed us. We got up to go see about her. Did Gayle come to Sarah's room with us?"

"Honestly I don't remember. I just remember running to Grandmother's room."

"I don't remember, either," Memory said. "Did you come back to your room after you went in to see Sarah?"

"No. I had money on me, so I didn't need my purse." Lena brushed a speck off the chair's arm. "Gayle drove us to the hospital in her car, so I didn't need anything else."

"Okay, so let's scratch Monica's name off with a tiny question mark beside it. I mean, she could be lying, but my gut feeling says she's not. And Richard said he didn't move them?"

"No, Richard didn't see them, and he came home after we'd gone to the hospital."

"So it looks like whatever happened, happened between the timeline of you and I leaving the room and before Richard came home from playing golf." Memory stood up.

"Where are you going?" Lena asked.

"To talk to Gayle. I'd like to know what she knows, if anything, about this."

Lena got up. "You don't really think she moved them, do you?"

"Somebody took those things. And I want to know who and what we're dealing with here," Memory said. "One way or the other, we're getting to the bottom of this!"

Chapter 37

*Blow the trumpet in Zion, sanctify a
fast, call a solemn assembly. . . .*

Joel 2:15

Landris pushed open the door and held it for Johnnie
Mae's mother as she walked into the hospital room.

"Mama," Johnnie Mae said, holding out her arms to
her mother. Mrs. Gates hurriedly went and embraced
her middle child.

"Hey, baby," Mrs. Gates said. She rubbed Johnnie
Mae's hair as she stood above her. "I hear you're not
doing so good right now. Well, it's going to be all right.
God is still on the throne."

Johnnie Mae looked up at her mother. "You know
me?"

"Now, what kind of a crazy question is that? Of
course I know you," Mrs. Gates said. "You're my baby
girl—Johnnie Mae."

Johnnie Mae looked down at her hands. "They have
to take the baby early."

"Yes. Landris told me." She glanced over at him.
"But I don't want you to worry none. Just keep on
trusting and believing God. He hasn't failed us yet, has
He?"

Johnnie Mae couldn't help but smile. Her mother
was her normal self again, at least for now. That in itself was a miracle and even that much more special,

since it was happening during a time when she really needed her.

Two nurses came in. "We're ready to take you in," one of the nurses said to Johnnie Mae.

Mrs. Gates took Johnnie Mae's hand and squeezed it. "It's going to be okay. Jesus will be there with you. And I'm going to be in the waiting room, waiting on you when you come out—you and my brand-new grand-baby." She squeezed Johnnie Mae's hand again, leaned down, and softly planted a kiss on Johnnie Mae's fore-head. Nodding her approval, she stepped back to allow Landris an opportunity to get to her.

Landris came and took Johnnie Mae's hand. "Your sisters are here, and Donald. They're all in the waiting room with my mother and Princess Rose."

"Thank you for bringing Princess Rose in to see me so quickly. Your mom and Princess Rose looked so cute dressed alike. Princess Rose is being such a big girl." Johnnie Mae smiled nervously. "You're going in there with me, right?" she asked.

"Of course."

She looked at her mother. "Mama, you know you can come in with us if you like. They'll let you come in," Johnnie Mae said, looking at the nurses for their con-currence.

"Oh, no, baby. I'm going to let you and Pastor Lan-dris have this special moment to yourselves. But rest assured, I'll be out here praying, waiting, and cheering you two—well, actually, three—on. You can count on that." She came back over and patted Johnnie Mae's hand. "I'm going to go now. Okay?" She leaned down and gave Johnnie Mae another kiss on her forehead, this time allowing her lips to linger. She brushed her hair with her hand one more time. "Stay strong," she said as she walked to the door, then left.

Johnnie Mae grinned before letting out a joyful laugh.

"She's doing so well today," she said. "Thank God." She looked up. "Thank You, Lord."

"Yes, she is," Landris said.

He stepped back as the nurses got Johnnie Mae ready. As they began wheeling her out of the room, she reached her hand out for his. She could see from the look on his face, although he was working hard to hide it, he was concerned. She watched his face and could see his lips were moving ever so slightly. She knew at that moment he was praying. She closed her eyes as she too said a prayer for herself and their baby. And she said a special prayer for Landris, her husband, who was standing by her side.

"You know we're going to be all right," Johnnie Mae whispered to Landris as he stood next to her in his blue hospital cap and gown in the operating room, waiting as various hospital personnel were doing the things that needed to be done.

"I know," Landris said as he smiled. "I know."

Chapter 38

This people have I formed for Myself;
they shall show forth My praise.

Isaiah 43:21

Johnnie Mae was in the operating room having a C-section while various members of her family congregated in the waiting room. An hour and a half had passed, and they hadn't heard anything.

Donald glanced at his watch. "How long does something like this usually take?" he asked, never one good at waiting.

"I thought they would have been out by now, too," Marie said.

Rachel, who had stood minutes earlier and was pacing somewhat while wringing her hands, said, "Unless there were complications."

"Let's try not to think negatively," Landris's mother said. "We must continue believing that everything is fine."

Mrs. Gates hugged Princess Rose, who was sitting on her lap, then reached over and patted Virginia's hand. "Thank you. You took the words right out of my mouth."

Rachel sat back down. "Well, you'd think somebody would have come out here and told us *something* by now. Something. But I suppose no news is good news."

"You know what we need to do?" Marie asked. "Pray. We need to pray."

Rachel looked at her. "Well, what exactly do you think we've been doing all this time?"

"No, I mean pray as a family," Marie said. "As a whole. We need to touch and agree as we pray together."

Rachel looked around at other people sitting in the area. "I don't believe any of these people here care to hear us pray out loud," she said.

"Excuse me," Marie said to the other four people in the waiting room. "Would y'all mind if we prayed in here?"

The man sitting at the far end shook his head. Two women sitting next to each other on the right-hand side smiled and said they didn't mind.

Marie looked at the woman nearest them. The red-headed woman smiled. "I'd really rather not hear your prayers myself. But I think they have a conference room you can go in if you really want to pray in that manner."

Donald looked at the woman. "So you're telling me this is a free country, but if I want to pray, I can't pray unless you say it's okay?"

"Donald, don't," Marie said as she got up and walked over to him. She knew her brother. "It's okay. We can go to the conference room. Really, it's not that big of a deal."

"No, I want to pray right here," Donald said, getting to his feet.

"Donald, it's not like you're such a religious person that you need to make a scene about this," Marie said. "It's okay. We'll go find a conference room and pray."

"I don't want to go find a conference room to pray. I want to pray right here, right now, right where I am. And if that bothers anybody in here, then they can just close their ears or leave," Donald said as he stood flat-footed in a stance of pure defiance.

"Listen, you asked if I mind if you prayed out loud

in here," the woman said. "I told you I did. Personally, I don't think your right to pray trumps my right not to hear you pray," she said.

"Well, quite frankly, I don't think your right to *not* hear me pray trumps my right to pray if I want to talk to *my* God. This is America. We have certain guaranteed rights, certain freedoms here. A few things like freedom of religion and freedom of speech."

The woman shifted her body. "But you don't have the right to infringe upon my rights."

"I'm not infringing. You still have the right to remain silent and/or the right to leave," Donald said.

"Donald!" Mrs. Gates said. "Don't be rude."

Donald turned and looked at his mother. "Mama, I'm not being rude. All I want is to be able to praise God for the work I know He's doing in there with my sister and her baby. I want to pray and ask God for His help, His mercy, and His grace. God created us for His glory. He created us to praise Him. You told us that. Since we were little, you've told us not to be ashamed of God, no matter where we may find ourselves. God made a way for me to be able to pray and get my prayers heard, through Jesus, *whenever* and *wherever* I need to. And right now, I feel we need to pray. My sister is in there fighting for her life. Her *life!* Her baby is fighting for its life. We don't have time to be playing around, looking for some conference room just because somebody doesn't want to hear us pray. None of us objected when she was gossiping, talking all loud on her cell phone essentially about nothing! We sat here and had to hear that mess, whether we wanted to hear it or not. She didn't stop and ask if we minded her talking to them. At some point, followers of Jesus are going to have to take a stand and quit letting people continue to push us out."

Donald then bowed his head and began to pray. "Our Father, which art in Heaven. Lord, I know it's been some time since You've heard from me. But Lord, my sister has been a faithful servant. Not perfect by any means, but faithful. And she needs You now."

As Donald prayed, the rest of his family stood, grabbed a family member's hand, and formed a circle. "Lord, I ask You to please place Your arms of protection around her and that little baby. Give them strength. Heal them, right now I pray, Father. Whatever they need right now, Lord, You know. And You're able to do it. Touch them right now. Give us strength, Lord. Have mercy on all of us. Forgive us of our sins. Please hear our cry. Johnnie Mae and I may have had our differences, but I don't want to lose my sister." Donald's voice began to crack and break up. Unable to continue, he stopped speaking.

"Lord, we thank You that You hear us always," Marie said as she picked up where Donald left off when he no longer could go on. "We thank You that You're the ultimate doctor. That You can do what man can't do. That You can go where man can't go. Father, give George . . . Pastor Landris strength, that he may be able to stand—come what may. Help, Lord. Move, Lord. Heal, Lord. Touch, Lord. These and other blessings we ask in Jesus' name. Amen."

When Donald opened his eyes, he saw that the man and the two other women were standing with them. But the woman who hadn't wanted to hear them pray had left.

A few minutes later, Landris opened the door and walked in. He wasn't grinning from ear to ear the way a new and excited father would normally be doing at this time.

"What's wrong?" his mother asked as she rushed to him. "What happened?"

"It's not good," Rachel began to say out loud as she shook her head. "I can tell by the look on his face. It's not good."

Virginia hugged her son as he sat in a chair. "The baby?" she asked.

A momentary smile crossed his face. "A boy," Landris said before he began shaking his head. "He's so small. A fighter for sure, though. But Johnnie Mae . . ." He started to choke up.

"What's wrong with Johnnie Mae?" Mrs. Gates asked as she stepped to him.

Landris looked up at her with tears in his eyes. "She's in SICU," he said. "She's not doing well at all. Dr. Baker says she's extremely critical. She can't promise anything at this juncture. There's nothing more they can do for her. Everything is in God's hands now. Dr. Baker says the next twenty-four hours will really be crucial." He shook his head some more, then allowed his mother to hold his head against her shoulder.

"Is Johnnie Mae conscious?" Rachel asked, her voice trembling as she spoke.

He sat up and shook his head. "No. She didn't even get to see the baby. He's so tiny—three pounds and two ounces. They took him to the neonatal intensive care unit. He's struggling to breathe. They have him hooked up to all these tubes and wires. They say it's not looking good for him, either." Landris sat back against the chair. "I did get to touch him. For one minute, I touched him. For one glorious minute, I held my hand on his tiny body, and I prayed like nobody's business. He was so perfect, this tiny little being—my son. I have a son." He beamed with pride, then a shadow of sadness came. "Johnnie Mae didn't get to see him. Things went haywire. They put me out of the operating room as they worked frantically on her." He looked toward Heaven. "God, she has to pull through. She has to. I realize You're sovereign. But God, please. I know that You didn't bring us this far to leave us."

Chapter 39

Behold, ye trust in lying words, that cannot profit.

Jeremiah 7:8

Montgomery Powell the Second sat in the darkened room with a brandy glass in his hand.

A high-pitched voice broke into the quietness. "My goodness, Montgomery. Why on earth are you sitting here in the dark like this?" The woman turned on a floor lamp.

"Polly Swindle, must you *always* make an entrance when you come into a room?"

"Of course I must always make an entrance. Now, what was so important that you felt you had to summon me here like you did?"

He set the glass on the coffee table. "The box."

"The box?" she asked as she slowly lowered her thin frame down onto the other end of the sofa on which Montgomery was sitting. "What box, Monty?"

"The so-called Wings of Grace box. My sources tell me that you may be in possession of it, as well as a certain Alexandrite necklace."

"Your sources, huh? Well, dearest Montgomery, maybe you should get yourself some new sources." Polly stood up and adjusted her tight-fitting houndstooth crop jacket, then smoothed down the front of her matching A-line skirt.

"Polly, don't play with me. I want the box and everything that was inside of it. As for the Alexandrite necklace, I may allow you to keep that as your reward, provided whatever is inside that box is worth it to me, of course. Now sit down."

She looked at him.

"I said, sit down!"

She quickly sat. "I'm telling you, Monty, it wasn't me."

"Okay, let's start over," Montgomery said. He stood and poured some brandy into another glass. "The box is missing. Lena and Memory are desperately trying to find out what happened to both it *and* the necklace. I know this because I hear that, earlier today, they were questioning the staff at my aunt's home." He handed Polly the glass.

Polly took the brandy, swirled it, sniffed it, then took a polite sip. "Fine as always," she said before setting the glass down on the coffee table. "So you say they're questioning everyone? Have they figured out what might have happened to the things?"

He sat back down. "No. And since I specifically planted you in my aunt's life to find out whatever I needed to know, when I need to know it, then *you*, my dear, need to tell me *something*." Montgomery crossed his legs and began to swing the top one.

Polly picked up her glass, held it up to her face, and swirled it again. "Sarah went to the hospital on Saturday night," Polly said, then took another sip of brandy. "Gayle called me and told me that when they were waiting for the ambulance to arrive. I went to the house and ended up driving Lena's husband to the hospital to meet up with the rest of them. I then brought Lena and her husband back home late that night, and now I'm hearing from you that things are missing from the house. The way you're behaving, they must be quite important—the necklace, I know. But the box sounds like it is as well."

"So what are you telling me?"

"That I don't know anything more than you obviously do," Polly said as she took yet another sip from her glass.

"Pauline," he said, invoking her birth name. "Are you telling me the truth here?"

"Monty, you know me. We've known each other for almost half a decade now. Have I ever lied to you?"

Montgomery stood up. "Well, somebody has to know something." He walked to the window with its drawn, red velvety draperies. "Then who do *you* suspect took them?"

Polly sipped more of her brandy. "You've talked to Gayle, you say?"

"Yes."

"And I gather she told you she didn't take them?"

"That's what she told me when she came by earlier today." He turned and walked back to the sofa. Picking up his brandy glass, he drained it dry, then set it back down.

"And you believe her?"

"I believe her about as much as I believe you," Montgomery said, narrowing his eyes as he gazed at her before he began scanning her body slowly from head to toe.

Polly leaned in seductively, set her empty glass on the table, and smiled. "It sounds to me, Monty, you have serious trust issues. Perhaps you should consider some form of therapy. I know a wonderful doctor, if you're interested."

"Oh, I'm sure you do." He walked over to her and pulled her up to a standing position. "Did you take that necklace and that box?" he asked.

Polly winced. "Montgomery, stop it. You're hurting me."

He pressed in harder. "Did you . . . take . . . those things?"

She tried to pull herself out of his grip. "Stop it! I told you, you're hurting me."

He shook her. "One more time, Polly," he said. "Did you take the Alexandrite necklace and that Wings of Grace box out of Sarah's house?"

"No, I did not take the Alexandrite necklace or the Wings of Grace box *out* of her house! Now let go of me!" Tears made a pool in her eyes as she stared back into his.

Montgomery released her and began to pat and smooth down her shoulders. "Sorry about that. I really didn't mean to hurt you. I spoke with Gayle on her cell before you arrived. When she was here earlier, it was before I knew those things were missing. She said she didn't take them. You say you didn't. What are you two doing there if you can't handle simple tasks?" He went and poured himself some more brandy.

Polly sat down on the sofa and gathered herself. "Okay, I can understand you being upset. But Gayle had plenty of opportunity to get those things for you. She's right there in the house. They trust her explicitly. And she was there on Saturday night when those things went missing. It seems to me, she would be the most likely candidate."

Montgomery stopped and stared at her. "Who said the things went missing Saturday night?"

Polly picked up her clearly empty glass and attempted to drain what amounted to only a drop of brandy.

Montgomery walked over with the decanter and poured a little more brandy in her glass. He put the crystal top back on the decanter. "How did you know those things went missing Saturday?" he asked in a slightly different way this time.

She drank the brandy in two gulps and smiled. "I don't know when they went missing," she said. "I just assumed it was Saturday. It would have been a perfect time with so much happening." She held her glass out to him for a refill. He obliged. "The issue isn't *when* it happened, but who could have taken them. You seem pretty sure Gayle didn't do it. Maybe it was Sarah's cook, Monica, or perhaps the housecleaner, Minnie. Truthfully, I wouldn't put it past that so-called daughter of Sarah's—Memory. We know she stole that necklace once. From her own daughter and granddaughter no less."

"But that just makes no sense. Why steal a necklace you already have in your possession?"

Polly laughed. "Monty, don't you see, darling? You have to think like a criminal. It's the perfect crime with the ideal cover. You take the necklace yourself, act like it was stolen, then sell it. If I were you, I'd have my people check out all the pawn shops and antique jewelry sellers around town." Polly took another sip. "Unless evidence shows up that someone else really might have taken those things, I'd put my money on Memory."

Polly's cell phone began to sing a ringtone by Sting. Looking at the number on the caller ID, she smiled. "It looks like Sarah is calling even as we speak. Excuse me while I take this." Polly answered it, talked for a few minutes, then clicked the phone off. She grinned. "Speak of the devil, and he'll usually appear. That was Memory. Seems Sarah wants to celebrate Christmas early this year. They want me to get my décor people to come to her house and set up Christmas decorations befitting a celebration to top all celebrations. Sarah's planning to have Christmas in June—the twenty-fifth to be exact."

Montgomery snickered. "Christmas in June? Sounds to me like Auntie Sarah may be feeling she doesn't have long for this world. This is perfect! And just think—this will give you even more of a chance to see what else you can find out as you help them plan." He began to rub his hands together. "Now, how marvelous is all of this?" He smiled. "After all these years, things are finally beginning to fall into place. Finally!"

Chapter 40

Hast thou not known? Hast thou not heard, that the everlasting God, the Lord, the Creator of the ends of the earth, fainteth not, neither is weary? There is no searching of His understanding.

Isaiah 40:28

Angel and Brent located Pastor Landris in the hospital waiting room near SICU. Three days had passed since Johnnie Mae had delivered her baby, and she still had not regained consciousness.

"Pastor Landris, you need to get some rest," Angel said after they'd gotten all the pleasantries out of the way and talked general stuff for a few minutes. "Brent and I will stay here until you come back while you go home and get some real rest."

"I'm fine. I want to be here when Johnnie Mae wakes up," Landris said.

Angel quickly glanced at Brent, his cue to feel free to jump right in.

"Listen, Pastor Landris," Brent said, "we're a little concerned about you as well as your health. Your mother is especially concerned. She told Angel you've only gone home to change your clothes, then you're right back here. That's not good, and you know it."

"God is sustaining me. He's renewing me. I'm okay. And I am getting *some* rest."

"Where? In a chair in this room?" Angel asked. "Pastor Landris, we're not saying you shouldn't be here at all. You just need to take better care of yourself, that's all," she said. "You just *have* to."

Landris put his hand in his pants pocket. "My wife is in a coma," he said. "My son is fighting for his life. They need me. They need to know I'm close by. *I* need to be here for them for *me*."

"But you can't possibly keep this pace up," Brent said. "You're not God, who neither slumbers nor sleeps, nor does He have a need to."

"I know I'm not God," Landris said, frowning at Brent as he took his hand out of his pocket.

Angel stepped a little closer to Brent as she sheepishly looked up at Landris. "Brent didn't intend it the way you're taking it. That's why you need to go home and get some rest. And I mean some good uninterrupted sleep, not just a quick power nap. A person can become edgy when he or she hasn't gotten enough rest. Lack of sleep affects the brain. . . . It affects the way we function. Please, Pastor Landris, all we're asking you to do is to go home and get some rest. That's all. Then you can come back renewed, refreshed, and ready to go another round or two, if you have to."

Landris smiled. "I keep telling you I'm fine. But I appreciate you two for caring about me and my well-being. Johnnie Mae is going to come out of this coma any minute now. I know she is. And I plan on being close by when she does. After this is all over, I can catch all the *z*'s I want. God is *absolutely* sustaining me through this. All of this is merely a trying of my faith. Like a stress test, only we can call it a faith-endurance test."

Angel glanced at Brent before casting her attention back to Landris. "Mrs. Knight called the church yesterday evening. Sherry was out of the office, so they transferred the call to me," Angel said. "She'd heard what was going on, and she asked me to tell you that she's praying for you, Johnnie Mae, and the baby. Also, she'll see you on Saturday."

Landris pressed his hands to his head. "Oh my goodness. Today is Friday, isn't it? Her husband's funeral is tomorrow."

"Yes. That's another reason she called," Angel said. "In light of everything, she wanted you to know that she understands if you're not able to preach Reverend Knight's eulogy."

"But I promised him. I assured her I would do it," Landris said as he glanced at the clock on the wall. The next official visiting time for SICU patients would be in ten minutes. "Please call her and let her know that I will be there as planned."

"Pastor Landris, no disrespect, but we can't even get you to leave here to go home to get some rest. Now, if you won't leave to rest, what makes you think you're going to want to leave tomorrow to preach a funeral?" Brent asked. "And better still, how effective do you really think you're going to be if you're trying to preach, dead on your feet from a lack of real sleep?"

Landris looked at Brent. "I promised Reverend Knight and his wife I would do it, and I intend to keep that promise. The same way I promised the two of you I would perform your marriage ceremony this Sunday. And yes, I plan on keeping my promise on that, too."

Angel looked down at her freshly pedicured sandaled feet, then back up at Landris. "You're not going to perform our ceremony," she said in a low but strong voice.

Landris frowned. "I'm not? And why?" he asked.

"Because there's too much going on in your life at the moment," Brent said.

"So, what are you planning on doing then?" Landris asked. "Who are you going to get to perform your ceremony in my place?"

Brent took Angel by the hand. "Right now, Pastor Landris, Angel and I have decided to focus on what we can do to help you, your family, and the ministry we have committed to."

Landris began to sway slightly, not believing how wonderful they really were. "I appreciate that, but I told you before that I'm fine. I realize there are things that require my attention, and I plan on taking care of them. However, I still maintain that my wife is going to wake up any minute now, and things will be back to normal before we know it. Well, as much as normal can be for us, now that we have a brand-new baby."

"We believe that, too," Angel said, smiling to let him know she was being sincere. "But Brent and I feel there's too much going on for us to only be concerned about ourselves and our own needs. Therefore, we've made the decision to wait until October fifteenth, just as we'd originally planned to do anyway, to get married. In the meantime, we'll be centering a good portion of our attention and energy on what we can do to help you, the church ministry, and Johnnie Mae. I mean, the mail I pick up daily at the post office for you guys is almost an all-day job to go through at this point. And I don't mind."

Landris bowed his head and shook it slowly and reverently. "Thank you," he said. When he looked back up at them, tears filled his eyes. He blinked to force the impending tears back. "Thank you for caring so much. I truly thank God for you . . . both of you. But are you positive about waiting?"

Brent looked lovingly at Angel and smiled. "We're positive. This decision will cause us to have to make a few adjustments in our personal lives, though. But we decided that if we add more of what you normally do to our own duties, we'll be much too busy to even *think* about each other, let alone spend a lot of tempting alone-time together."

"Johnnie Mae really is going to wake up any minute, you know?" Landris said. He was mostly trying to get them not to worry too much.

Angel smiled again. "And when she does, and she goes home, knowing you the way we do, you're still going to be spending a lot of time here," Angel said. "At least you will be until your son is finally released to go home. You'll be right here watching him grow bigger and stronger by the minute."

Landris nodded. He looked at Angel first, then Brent. "You feel I'm not being realistic about this, don't you? You can tell me the truth."

"No, sir," Brent said. "I think you're showing us, by example, the meaning of true faith. You believe, and you're acting like you believe. You want to be here when Johnnie Mae wakes up. You want to be the one who tells her about her new son. Personally, I appreciate you for demonstrating what strong faith looks like. I only pray I will be like that with our family, if and when the time comes," he said, looking adoringly at Angel.

"As you've taught us, there is walking in the flesh, then there's walking in the Spirit," Angel said. "Brent and I know we can choose to either walk in our flesh at this point or walk in the Spirit when it comes to how we feel and act during the times and occasions we're with each other."

"We're choosing, on purpose, to continue to walk in the Spirit," Brent said. "Will that take much prayer?" He laughed. "Oh yes! But people are dealing with a lot these days. If the worst problem Angel and I have right now is that we love each other so much we almost can't stand it, then I think we're doing pretty well here, and we shouldn't complain. With constant prayer, and a determination to keep our eyes on Jesus, I believe our present situation is something we can manage, at least for the next four months."

"Trust me—a man with a ton of experience, especially lately—in certain situations, four months can feel like it's a lifetime. We can still have the ceremony Sunday, now," Landris said. "My being here doesn't mean I'm wholly neglecting my obligations or duties. I'm handling responsibilities and all prior commitments. In fact, there's a nice little chapel here. We can go to it right now, and y'all can tie the knot today if you want. I just know and feel in my heart that by Sunday Johnnie Mae will be up and doing so much better, she'll most likely be figuring out ways to get me to take her to see our son every opportunity she gets. I'm sure she won't mind me missing in action for a little while to perform a marriage ceremony—your marriage ceremony, at that."

Brent smiled. "I know. And should we see we can't handle this like we thought, then we definitely know how to find you. As you can see, we did it today. Besides, how long can it take to say a few vows anyway?"

"I'm serious, Brent . . . Angela," Landris said, calling Angel by the name he usually called her, "you let me know now. And if I need to work a marriage ceremony into my schedule, then I'll do just that."

Landris's cell phone began to vibrate. He pulled his phone out of his pocket and looked at the screen. "Pastor Landris," he said hurriedly. "Yes, Dr. Baker. No, actually, I'm here in the SICU waiting room. Yes, of course. I'll be right there." Pastor Landris clicked off the phone. "That was Johnnie Mae's doctor. She needs to see me right away." He then dashed quickly out of the waiting room.

Chapter 41

S arah was feeling much better. She was excited about the planned, untraditional Christmas in June. There wasn't a lot of time left to shop before the twenty-fifth arrived. The decorators had done a fantastic job, virtually transforming the mansion into a Christmas winter wonderland. Polly had been to Sarah's house many times, ensuring that things were being handled properly and to her friend's satisfaction. Only after the live fourteen-foot Christmas tree donned presents underneath it was Polly able to get Sarah to talk about anything other than the upcoming celebration.

"So tell me, Sarah," Polly said as they sat leisurely in the parlor admiring the beautifully decorated tree, "what prompted you to want to do this? I mean, what urgency caused you to want to celebrate Christmas in the month of June?"

"I just thought it'd be a grand idea," Sarah said. "This will be my first Christmas with my daughter—my entire family, all together, celebrating it for the first time ever."

"Is that all? There's no other reason you're doing this in June?"

"None, except I just couldn't bear having to wait until

December for Christmas to arrive. It was entirely too
far away for me. Besides, this gives me yet another opportunity to spend some quality fun time with my child,
grandchild, great-grandchild, and great-great-grand-
children. That's never a bad thing." Sarah smiled just
thinking about them.

"Oh, Polly," Sarah bubbled over with renewed excitement, "I am so blessed! I can't explain how wonderful this feels right now. You of all people know how
long I've prayed for this to happen. And now it has. My
daughter is here with me! We *could* wait until December to celebrate Christmas, but why must we, if we
don't have to? Why must we *have* to have specially designated days to spend special moments with the ones
we love? Why wait until Mother's Day to let a mother
know she is appreciated? I say do it now! Why should
Valentine's Day be the day dedicated to show love?
What's wrong with now?" Sarah nodded. "I wanted to
celebrate Christmas now, so that's what we're going to
do. Where in the rule book does it say we *must* wait
until December to do it?"

"Nowhere, I suppose. But it is quite out of the ordinary," Polly said in her usual prim and proper way.
"*Quite.*"

Sarah picked up her teacup and its matching saucer
and sipped her green tea. "I'm certain you've figured
out by now that *I'm* out of the ordinary. I'll turn ninety
years old on October first. Do you have any idea how
many people never make it to that age? I've missed
seventy Christmases with my daughter—seventy. I know
in some folks' eyes, Memory and I may be a tad bit too
old to be excited about Christmas. But I've learned to
take what I can, when I can, and go with it. We must
take the lemons we're given in life and make a to-die-
for lemon meringue pie. Christmas is supposed to be
about celebrating the greatest gift we, as a people, were

ever given. A gift that began our salvation—Jesus' birth. Traditionally when we celebrate Christmas, we give gifts to others. Well, who says we can't celebrate Jesus' birth in June? In fact, what's wrong with Christmas everyday?"

Polly's eyes widened from sheer disbelief. "I certainly *hope* you're not intending on leaving that tree up all year around," she said. "Besides being sociably unacceptable, I hear it's bad luck if a Christmas tree is left up until New Year's day, let alone afterward."

"Forget the tree, okay? And forget superstitions. Anyway, a Christmas tree has nothing to do with Christ, not really."

"People say it represents the hanging of Jesus on the tree," Polly said.

"We won't bother going into a discussion about how pagan practices got mixed in with Christian values, all right? Let's just keep our eyes focused on the fact that, number one, Jesus *was* born; number two, He died on the cross; number three, and most importantly, on the third day He rose; and four, He now sits at the right hand of the Father, making intercessions on our behalf." Sarah blotted her forehead and face with her white handkerchief, then leaned her head back as she gently blotted her neck.

"Are you still hot?" Polly asked, fanning Sarah slightly using her hand.

"Warm, but I'll be all right. It's just part of aging. You'll see as you grow older."

"Sarah, I heard some rumblings around the house about some items they say came up missing a few weeks back," Polly said, trying to work this topic into the conversation.

Sarah sat comfortably and relaxed. "Oh? Now, where did you hear that from?"

Polly stood up and walked over to the tree. "I don't

wish to say," she said. "I don't want to get anyone in trouble. But they say it was a necklace and some sort of special wings box?" Polly looked at Sarah for a response. Sarah remained silent.

Polly moved an angel ornament from one spot to another. She then strolled casually back over to the sofa and stood. "So, did you ever find the items, or do you at least have an idea as to who might have taken them?" Polly continued her probe.

Sarah fanned herself with her handkerchief. "I'm sorry, Polly, but could you go and see what's taking Monica so long to bring out our tray of snacks? She knows I need to eat on a regular schedule."

Polly looked at Sarah and nodded. "Sure. I'll be right back."

When Polly returned, Sarah was still being mesmerized by the beautiful tree.

"That decorating crew did a lovely job, lovely," Sarah said, looking all around.

Polly looked around the entire room as well. "They certainly did. It feels just like Christmas in here. Although I'm not sure I'm in full agreement with you having the fireplace lit at the same time the air conditioner is going full blast. That fire may be what's causing you to be so warm. That and the hot tea you keep consuming."

Sarah laughed. "Oh, I only had them light the fireplace to set the atmosphere. I wanted you to experience the full effect of what it will truly be like the day we celebrate Christmas come June twenty-fifth. And tea contains antioxidants, great healthwise."

Polly sat down next to Sarah. "Sarah, has the doctor told you something that you haven't shared with the rest of us? You know you can always talk to me. So has he?"

Sarah smiled. "You mean besides the fact that I'm

not as young as I used to be? And my best days are most likely behind me?" Sarah sat back, becoming more relaxed.

"Yes, something like that. I'm trying to figure out why you decided it was imperative that you celebrate Christmas right now . . . in June."

Sarah released a sigh. "Polly, the truth is, none of us know how long we have on this earth. I pray I celebrate many, many Christmases . . . many holidays, and, honestly, just plain old regular days with my family . . . with all of you, really. But I also don't want any of us wishing we'd done something that we could have done and didn't." She reached over and patted Polly on her hand. "I want to live the remainder of my life, however long that may be, without any regrets. Do you understand what I'm saying?"

Polly looked at Sarah. She appeared different. There was a glow about her quite unlike anything Polly had ever seen in all her time knowing her. "Sarah, you've always been good to me," Polly said. "And truthfully, you've been a loyal friend. When we first met at church some three years ago, I had no idea how deeply I would come to care for you. You've always treated me like family. Sarah, there's something I need to tell you."

"Sorry, Miss Fleming," Monica said as she brought in a tray of food and set it down on the coffee table. "I apologize for being a bit tardy with your snacks. Alfred, the gardener, cut himself and needed some assistance getting cleaned up. I know how you feel about people who aren't supposed to be inside here roaming free in your house. I had to accompany him to the washroom and wait until he was finished so I could see him out." Monica situated things as needed, which included setting up a tray next to Sarah so she wouldn't have to reach too far to get her food.

"It was a pretty nasty cut," Monica said, continuing

with her story. "I would have gotten Minnie to do it, knowing that you were waiting on this, but she was upstairs working somewhere. Honestly, I didn't think it would take him that long, but as I said, it was pretty nasty, and it took some time to get him fixed back up good."

"Oh dear. So is he all right now?" Sarah asked. "I declare, it seems like every other day that man has something happen to him where he needs some reason to come inside. Just last week, I was sitting outside, getting a little vitamin D via the sun, when I saw him sneak around and go through the kitchen door. I don't think he knew I was out there or that I saw him doing that."

"Oh, that," Monica said. "Well, you see, ma'am, that was kind of my doing. I'd offered him a plate of food. Not one of your good plates, mind you—but the carry-out plates we keep handy for company who want to take food home. Alfred had been so helpful with getting things ready for the people who decorated for Christmas, finding that tree and all. I just wanted to do something special for him. I hope you don't mind."

Sarah continued putting various snacks on her plate. "Of course I don't mind. There's plenty of food here, and if someone doesn't eat it, it's just going to go to waste and end up thrown out anyway." Sarah stopped and shook her head. "I didn't mean to imply that that was the only reason it's okay. We always have more than enough food around here to share, and then some."

"You don't have to explain to me, Miss Fleming," Monica said as she stepped back even farther out of the way. "I understand *exactly* what you mean. You're generous to the bone, with a heart of gold, so no one would ever misunderstand your intentions."

Sarah wanted to put Monica back at ease. "The decorators did a fabulous job with this house for Christmas, don't you think, Monica?"

Monica's eyes lit up. "Oh, Miss Fleming, I was just telling Alfred that very same thing. I had said in the past that it seemed the stores were starting earlier and earlier putting up Christmas decorations. Then you upped and beat them all by doing this in June. Truthfully, I wasn't quite sure how it would feel around here. Some folk might call this crazy, but being here, especially with your whole family expecting to be present, I know it's going to be a special time indeed. And to top it off, you're hiring a caterer so even *I* get to enjoy the festivities, just like I'm part of the family. I got to tell you, that there for me is priceless, Miss Fleming. Priceless, I tell you. I declare, you're the best!"

Polly began to overtly fidget. Monica caught her rolling her eyes a few times.

"Oh, I'm sorry," Monica said. "I'm standing here gabbing away like you two invited me to socialize or something. I didn't mean to hold you up from conversating," Monica said, practically inventing a word. "Conversating"—definition: *talking.*

"You're fine, Monica," Sarah said. "We're just sitting here chewing the fat"—her word for talking—"in awe of this magnificent Christmas tree and other fine decorations."

"Well, if you two need anything else, just yell," Monica said. "I'll be in the kitchen getting dinner ready. I think you're going to like what I'm fixing, Miss Fleming. It's something new, but it involves some of your favorite food items." Monica then left.

Polly couldn't help but notice how content Sarah seemed lately. "Now," she said, but first, clearing her throat, "what were we talking about before we were interrupted?" She was making a big show of how she couldn't recall, when she could. "That's right!" She daintily clapped her hands. "You were about to tell me whether or not you ever found out what happened to the items that were missing. It's my understanding there was some kind of a special box, possibly with important items inside, and a necklace."

"You keep bringing that up," Sarah said. "And you keep saying you heard it from someone here at my house. I'd like to know who you heard it from." Sarah stopped and looked at Polly.

"Now, I told you, Sarah, I don't want to get anyone in any trouble."

"I can assure you, no one here is going to get in trouble," Sarah said, slightly smiling. "So tell me. Where did you hear that those items were missing?" Sarah stopped smiling, her look now somber. "I want to know when, where, and how. And Polly, I want to know now." She sat calmly, sipped some more of her green tea, and waited.

Chapter 42

Then Job arose, and rent his mantle, and shaved his head, and fell down upon the ground, and worshiped.

Job 1:20

Landris walked out of the conference room after speaking with Dr. Baker. Johnnie Mae's vitals were not good at all. Dr. Baker wanted to prepare Landris for the worst. She believed, at this point, it was going to take a miracle for Johnnie Mae to pull through. She told Landris he needed to go home and possibly get some things in order, just in case. When Landris refused to accept her report, she told him to at least go home and get some rest so he'd be refreshed for whatever was to come.

"I insist, Pastor Landris," Dr. Baker said. "You need to get some rest. There's nothing your being here all hours of the day and night can do right now. Go home, get some rest, and come back later. I've given strict instructions that should your wife as much as twitch, the attending nurse is to call both you and me. You'll have time to get here if she wakes up."

"*When* she wakes up," Landris said, correcting her.

Dr. Baker looked at him. "Pastor Landris, you know I believe in God. I *know* God can heal—I've seen it happen. I've also seen people who believed in God with all their hearts, only to find out God's answer was no. Things don't always work out the way we pray and believe it will. It's a part of the circle of life, and the reason there are counselors and support groups for family members to talk to before and afterward. I can call someone who's been through this before to come speak with you, if you like."

"Dr. Baker, my Bible tells me that God's answers are 'yes' and 'amen.' My Bible explains that faith is the substance of things hoped for, the evidence of things not seen. The Word of God is all the counsel and speaking to that I need right now," Landris said. "Listen, I appreciate what you're trying to do here. But I'm not going to allow the devil to sow even one seed of doubt into my mind or find a way to manage to sneak a word of doubt into my confession. The devil *is* defeated. He has no power. Jesus stripped him when He conquered death, hell, and the grave, declaring He had all power. Jesus gave that power to those who confess Him. The Bible states that life and death are in the power of the tongue. Therefore, I'll only say what the Word of God says. I'll only speak life."

"Pastor Landris, you know I respect you *and* your ministry," Dr. Baker said. "But I am a doctor who promised I'd always be up front with my patients and with their families. I'm only telling you the facts about what's happening as I see and have them before me right now."

"And I respect that," Landris said. "But thanks be to God that the facts are not always the truth. The facts may be, from a medical standpoint, my wife is not doing well. But the truth is, by Jesus' stripes, my wife is healed. I don't know how God is going to do what He's going to do, but as long as I have breath in me, I'm going to believe and speak the Word of the Lord. I thank God, who always causes us to triumph."

"I've told you, from a faith standpoint, I'm right there with you," Dr. Baker said. "But medically speaking, I have to say it doesn't look good. It doesn't look good at all. This will definitely be an uphill battle we're fighting."

Landris looked at her. He could see in her eyes, the windows to her soul, she really was pulling for them. "I tell you what, Dr. Baker. I'm going to go home. And I'm going to get before the Lord. I'm going to remind Him of His Word, just like God instructs us to do. Not because He's forgotten, but because He needs to know that *I* know what His Word says. That *I* know when I speak His Word, His Word won't return unto Him void. That *I* understand His Word will accomplish that which He has sent it to accomplish."

Dr. Baker nodded. "Pastor Landris, I pray you're right. But if things don't turn out the way you believe, we both know that God is still on the throne. We also recognize that, on this earth, it really does rain on the just and the unjust."

"I'll continue praying for you, Dr. Baker. All I can tell you is, stand and see the salvation of the Lord. I don't know why my family is going through this. But I know, in the end, this will be used for God's glory. Satan may have meant it for bad, but God is going to use it for good. God will be glorified, regardless of what happens. Now, if it's all right with you, I'd like to go in and see my wife," Landris said.

Dr. Baker took him in to see Johnnie Mae. He prayed for her, laying his hands on her as he prayed fervently. "The prayers of the righteous, avails much," he said softly as he walked out of her room. "The prayers of the righteous, avails much."

Landris then went to see his son. Early on, the staff had told him that parents of babies in NICU were permitted to visit their children at any time, and that a nurse would be with them always. When he arrived at NICU, his baby's doctor was there and wanted to speak privately with him. He informed Landris that his son had suffered a minor setback. They were doing what they could for him. He just wasn't sure whether or not the baby was strong enough to fight his way through this last bout of respiratory complications.

"Of course, had he stayed in his mother's womb even a few days longer, his chances of survival would be much higher," the doctor said. "Right now, we're still looking at a sixty-percent probability that he'll make it. The mortality rate of premature babies has improved much over the past twenty years. It's amazing really," the graying doctor, who looked to be in his early fifties, said. "Modern technology and new medical techniques, the things we now know that weren't known in past years, all of these things are contributing to higher survival rates for preemies," the doctor said. "Just know we're doing everything we can. I'm just not sure whether or not all we can do will be enough to pull your son through. I'm not saying this to be heartless or cruel, but I do like parents of our premature babies to be armed with the facts throughout the process."

The day his son was born, Landris was told that even if his baby did make it, it was possible he might have lasting complications into adulthood. When they'd finished their report to Landris on that first day, Landris had merely responded to them by saying, "Do what you have to do and what you can do, but just know, I speak life over my child, in the name of Jesus, I speak life. And not just life, but life more abundantly. God *can* and *is* able to do what you can't. This I *do* know."

All the doctors associated with his baby's care had tried, both in the beginning and unsuccessfully, to get Landris to see things from a more realistic standpoint. He was told it was great to have faith, but he also needed to deal with reality.

"I hear what you're saying," Landris had said to the

doctor that day. "And no disrespect to you, but I'm going to stand on God's Word. What you're saying to me about my son is not God's best for him. God desires us to have His best, and I declare and decree the Word of the Lord right now over my son. He's healed and he's whole. He *will* live and not die."

"We understand how you feel, Mr. Landris," the baby's attending pediatrician had said. "But we live in a real world, with real issues. At some point, you're going to have to face what *is* and not how you *wish* things to be."

"I beg to differ, Doctor. But at some point, every knee *will* bow, and every tongue *will* confess, that Jesus is Lord. Right now, I'm confessing He is Lord over premature complications. He's Lord over premature death. And I mean that to apply to my wife, whom you have nothing to do with, and my son, who has been placed, at least for a season, in your and this hospital staff's care. Still, my God holds you and the people here, including my son, in His hands. I won't speak anything that doesn't line up with God's Word. I refuse to destroy my son's chances with my mouth."

Now, here Landris was, once again, being given one negative report after another; first, from his wife's doctor, then his baby's. He left the hospital and went home. Princess Rose, who was playing a card-matching game with Landris's mother, ran and greeted him as soon as he walked in the den. "I *miss* you!" Princess Rose said, hugging him tight.

Landris spent time with them, then went upstairs. Closing the bathroom door, he kneeled down in front of the vanity and began to pray like he'd never prayed before.

"I'm not going to ask You why we're going through this, Lord," Landris said. "I'm not. I have to trust You. I don't care what those doctors say. I trust You no matter what problems continue to rear their ugly heads. I pray for all who have been trying to come against us. Forgive them, Lord. I pray for the misguided souls who think they're doing right, when clearly they're marching down the wrong path. Lord, my wife and child are fighting for their lives right now. I don't know anything else to say other than what You've instructed me, in Your Word, to say. I don't know any other way, except Your way. Lord, I've done what You told us we should do during situations like these. I'm leaning completely on You. Please, Jesus, I need You now more than ever. I can't do anything without You. I need You. . . . We need You. Please, hear my cry. These things I pray in Jesus' name, Amen."

Landris stood up. He started unbuttoning his shirt. Frustrated, coupled with exhaustion, he ended up ripping off two buttons when he couldn't get the buttons through the tight buttonholes. He took the shirt off, then placed a towel around his neck and shoulders. Searching for scissors usually kept inside one of the drawers in the bathroom, he found them and stood squarely in front of the vanity mirror. Lifting one strand of dreadlocks, he took the scissors and cut it. He then cut another, and another, until he'd cut off all of his dreadlocks. Landris then walked out of the bathroom to his closet, took a black shirt off the hanger, and put it on. He went downstairs, got into his car without even telling his mother he was gone, and drove off.

"Whoa, man, what happened to you?" his barber, who'd helped him maintain his dreadlocks since he moved back to Birmingham, asked when he walked through the door.

"Reggie," Landris said calmly as he sat in the chair, "shave it off."

Reggie jerked back. "Say what? Look, man, I heard about what's going on with your wife and son. I'm sorry. I know you're under a lot of pressure. I don't think you may be thinking clearly. Maybe you should go home and get a little rest," Reggie said.

"I'm fine, Reggie. Now, please . . . shave it off," Landris said.

Chapter 43

Whereas ye know not what shall be on the morrow. For what is your life? It is even a vapor, that appeareth for a little time, and then vanisheth away.

James 4:14

"What did you do?" Virginia asked her son when Landris walked back in the house. "George, honey, come and sit down."

"Mom, I'm okay," Landris said.

His mother stared at his head as she walked toward him. "I don't think that you are. I think you really need to go upstairs and lie down."

"I told you, I'm okay."

Virginia spoke slowly. "No, George . . . I don't think you are okay. Do you realize you've shaved your head? All of your hair is gone, George. You're . . . bald."

Landris smiled as he rubbed his shaven head, then laughed out loud. "Yeah. Gone. I know."

"So do you want to tell me what made you do that?" Virginia asked, as though she didn't want to talk too fast or too loudly for fear that that might be the thing to send him completely over the edge.

"You know, it's not because I thought my dreads were wrong or against God in any way. There are plenty who have been trying to get me to cut my dreadlocks because they thought it was wrong, or they disagreed with them being on a preacher more than anything." He opened the refrigerator door and grabbed a bottle of water. "But I was praying earlier about everything that's been happening these days."

"I know. I know. It's been hard on everybody," Virginia said, paying close attention to his face to see whether or not she could detect what was really going on with him. "That's what I mean. This is a lot for anyone to handle. Even the strongest person would find something like this difficult to bear."

"Mom, listen to me. I'm fine. I've prayed about what's going on. Now I'm standing on God's Word and His promises. That's all I can do. I didn't shave my head to move God or to make a point or a statement. I didn't shave my head because I felt like I was in sin or in error and that doing this would make things right with God so He could move on my behalf. That's not how God operates. God doesn't look at the outward appearance of man. He looks at our hearts. I shaved my head because I felt the need to take off some dead weight. My hair felt as though it was carrying around in it so much stuff. It's hard to explain, but as soon as I started cutting my dreads off, all of a sudden I started feeling lighter. With each lock I cut, it was as though the things of the past were being cut away as well." Landris ran his hand over his clean-shaven head again.

"Reggie, my barber, cleaned it up for me. So today I start anew," Landris said. "Whatever happened yesterday is gone. Just like my hair—it's gone, all gone."

Virginia began to nod. "I think I understand what you're saying. But you still need to get some rest. When Johnnie Mae wakes up, as soon as she looks at you, she's going to think *you're* the one who needs to be hospitalized. And when the two of you bring that newborn home, believe me, you're going to wish you'd gotten all the sleep you could have."

Landris laughed then kissed his mother on the cheek. "Thanks, Mom. Has anyone told you lately that you're the best?"

"Not in the past"—she looked at her watch—"twenty-four hours. Oh, and before I forget"—she walked over to the counter and tore a sheet of paper out of a pad—"you got three messages while you were out trying to be like Mike."

"Like Mike?"

"Yeah. Michael Jordan. You know, the baldhead thing you've got going there? Which, by the way, let me be the first to tell you, isn't for everyone. Take it from a mother who cares, you need to let at least some of your hair grow back, and I mean quick." Virginia handed him the paper with the three messages on it as she rubbed his head.

Landris looked at the names and numbers. One was from Minister Maxwell, one of the preachers who was taking over things for Landris while he was out of pocket caring for his family; one was from Mrs. Knight; and the last one was from Reverend Walker. Out of all the names listed, Landris was most surprised to see Reverend Walker's. He'd never really talked with him before. In fact, the closest he'd gotten to the man was when Thomas was about to marry Faith, and he and Johnnie Mae had sat outside in the church's parking lot, waiting for his mother to return.

"Did Reverend Walker say anything?" Landris asked with a quizzical look.

"Just that it was urgent he speak to you today." Virginia slid an oblong glass dish into the oven, then wiped her hands with a paper towel. "I'm making Princess Rose macaroni and cheese. She said that's what she wanted for supper tonight. That poor child is missing her mother like crazy." Virginia threw the paper towel in the trash can. "But if you ask me, that Reverend Walker person needs some lessons in manners. Maybe he thought I was your maid or something. But even if that were the case, he needs to learn how to talk to people and not talk down to them. I guess I shouldn't expect any more out of him. At Thomas's wedding, he was planning to keep going forward with the wedding ceremony even though I was stretched out on a church bench." She giggled.

Gathering grapes, Bartlett pears, plums, strawberries, and a handful of blueberries out of the refrigerator into a colander, she walked over to the sink. Running water over them, Virginia transferred the fruit to a bowl. "I'm going down to the game room to play with Princess Rose. But between you and me, the child is driving me crazy with that song, 'Unwritten.' I mean, I like it and all, but she wants to play it over and over again."

Landris laughed as she left. He went and got the cordless phone, then sat down in the den next to the kitchen. Landris decided to call Minister Maxwell first. Minister Maxwell just wanted to check in with him and be sure there wasn't anything he needed from either him or anyone at the church. He brought him up to speed on matters he felt Landris needed to know, without burdening him with the things he didn't. Landris then called Mrs. Knight back. The person who answered said she was gone and wouldn't be back until sometime after seven.

Looking at the third message, Landris dialed the number. He couldn't even *begin* to fathom what Reverend Walker might possibly want with him.

Landris waited for someone to pick up.

"Hello," a deep male voice said.

"This is Pastor Landris calling for Reverend Walker."

"Pastor Landris, thank you for returning my call so quickly. How is your family? Your wife and your new son, specifically?" he asked.

Landris hesitated for a second. He couldn't say they were fine, because, from a realistic standpoint, they were both in critical condition. He didn't know how much Reverend Walker knew already, and for whatever reason, he really didn't want to go into lengthy details regarding the situation. "We believe all is well," Landris said.

"God is able," Reverend Walker said. "And we know that He won't put any more on us than we can bear, that's for sure. If God has brought you to it, somehow He'll bring you through it. That's not a cliché for me. It's a certified fact."

"Absolutely," Landris said as he stood up and began to pace near the fireplace. "I must say, I was surprised to have a message from you. So, to what do I owe the pleasure?" Landris said, deciding to get right to the point.

"Oh, of course. How inconsiderate of me. I know you have a lot going on, with your wife in such bad shape at the moment, and your new baby barely hanging on, a son, right? Have you named him yet?"

"No, we haven't named him as yet. I'm waiting on my wife so we can do that together," Landris said, picking up his bottle of water and taking a swallow from it.

"You probably should go on and do that. Give the baby a name," Reverend Walker said. "I'm sure you want to name him George Jr. or the Second. It's a joy when you produce boys, because you know you have someone to carry on the family name. I have five boys myself—three by my first wife and two by my second. The wife I have now can't seem to birth anything *but* girls, so I now have two little girls. It's okay, though. I have sons to carry on the name, so there's no real pressure on me at this point in my life. I can enjoy my little girls the way a doting father is supposed to. Now, Landris is a pretty unusual name. I know your mother has to be proud that at least one of her children has finally given her her first biological grandchild. Your mother was the one who answered the phone when I called earlier, right? I'm sure she's proud. With Thomas and his condition, I doubt he'll ever have children. How *is* your brother, by the way?"

Landris paused and counted to ten. "Much better, thank you."

"That's good to hear. I really like Thomas. I'm glad he's getting some help. I felt something wasn't right with him when he was here with us, but I try living my life without judging people, at least too harshly, anyway. I'm sure you understand that."

"Listen, Reverend Walker. I can't talk long. I've been at the hospital the past three days and only came home to get a little rest before I go back," Landris said.

"I'm so sorry. Of course. Here I am just going on and on. But I did call for a reason, other than to check on you and your family, of course." Reverend Walker cleared his throat. "I know you're supposed to be preaching Reverend Knight's funeral tomorrow."

"Yes."

"Well, there appears to be a change of plans. I'm sorry, I guess Joyce must not have had a chance to speak with you yet."

"You mean, Mrs. Knight?"

"Yes, Joyce Knight, Poppa Knight's lovely wife. Well, actually his widow now. Anyway, she and I spoke extensively last night, and she now wants *me* to preach Reverend Knight's funeral."

"I don't understand. Reverend Knight asked me, and the last time I spoke with Mrs. Knight, she still wanted me to honor his wishes and do it. So what changed?"

"Pastor Landris, your wife and child are in the hospital fighting for their lives. You don't need this kind of distraction. If I know you the way I *think* I do, it's probably next to impossible to get you to leave that hospital. What if your wife is still in that coma tomorrow? Do you honestly believe you can preach a funeral decently? Poppa Knight has been a great friend to too many people. He deserves the best send-off we can give him, and I intend on doing just that. I'm not implying you won't do a great job, because from what little I've heard of you, they say you're an outstanding teacher of the Word."

Landris began to laugh with disbelief as he sat down, shaking his head.

"Listen, Pastor Landris. Poppa Knight and I were close—closer than most brothers, if you want to get technical. If I may be transparent with you, it's going to be hard, even for me, to stand up there and preach over my dear friend's remains. But I also know I can do all things through Christ, who will give me the strength I need to do it."

"I believe He'll give me strength as well."

"I know that, Pastor Landris. And quite frankly, this is not a contest between you and me. The reality is, your family needs you. There's no reason for you to be worrying about preaching a funeral just because you gave your word to a dying man before you knew what was coming your way. None of us knows what tomorrow will bring. This little time we're here on this earth is like a vapor. One minute you see it, and before you can explain what you saw, it's gone—just like that. That's why, in the book of James, somewhere around the fourth chapter, it tells us we ought to say, 'If the Lord will, we shall live, and do this, or that.' You had no way of knowing this trouble was headed your way. You made a promise you fully intended to keep. God knows your heart. But you need to put your energies toward those who are still on this side of the earth."

"Is that what you told, Mrs. Knight? That she was

being unfair by trying to hold me to a promise I made, that I fully intended to honor?" Landris asked.

"I told Joyce that Poppa Knight was wrong to have asked you in the first place when he'd said I would be doing this if it came to him departing before me. You didn't know him like I knew him. He and I had history together. Lots of it. You knew him when he was a mere shell of his previous robust stature. Now, please don't take this the wrong way, but, Pastor Landris, you cannot do what I'm going to be able to do tomorrow. You just can't. And frankly, your preaching style is not what the people who knew him best are accustomed to. You don't bring enough fire with it, at least not enough for most of our taste."

"Listen," Landris said, "I have a call in to Mrs. Knight already. She called and left me a message earlier. Until I've spoken to her and she tells me otherwise, or unless the Lord says differently, I plan to be standing, at noon come tomorrow, doing what I was asked to do."

"Pastor Landris, I'm going to let you go and get some rest. Clearly, you need some sleep. But allow me to give you a bit of advice before I hang up. You don't *really* want me as an enemy. Trust me, you don't."

"Is that supposed to be a threat?"

"Oh, no. I don't make threats. I make promises. And I promise you, you might want to rethink any idea you may have about crossing me. Greater men than you have tried and failed. But listen, I didn't call you to get into all of this. I'm sure you and I will have our day to really talk. You speak with Joyce. She knows the deal. You see, Poppa Knight is no longer around to flex his muscles against me. People seem to have been under the mistaken impression that I was afraid of him, like he had something on me."

"So did he?"

Reverend Walker laughed. "That's a good one. I respected him, but let's just say that whatever Paul 'Poppa' Knight *may* or may *not* have had on me is safe and securely with him at this point in time. After I say this, I'm really going to let you go. But I once heard someone wisely declare that the only way to keep a secret between three people, is if two of them are dead. I'm not trying to be cold or insensitive, but they also say 'dead men tell no tales.' So whatever Poppa Knight might have known, he kept it to himself all these years, and it looks like he took all of that with him. Now, you take care, and you take care of that family of yours. I'll say a little prayer for all of you. Have a good night," Reverend Walker said, then hung up.

Pastor Landris looked at the phone that now buzzed with only a dial-tone. His mind immediately went to the *Private and Personal* envelope Reverend Knight had given him over a year ago. The envelope he'd been told to keep in a safe place and to open only should Reverend Walker attempt to come against him.

As much as Pastor Landris wanted to open that envelope right now, he knew this was not enough to warrant him learning something, he suspected, ultimately, could have dire consequences for a fellow brethren in the Word.

Chapter 44

The grass withereth, the flower fadeth:
but the word of our God shall stand
forever.

Isaiah 40:8

L andris spoke with Mrs. Knight over the phone after
he woke up from about four hours of sleep. She
confirmed what Reverend Walker had said to him earlier.

"Mrs. Knight, I need to ask you something, and I
want you to be honest with me."

"Sure, Pastor Landris. What is it?" Mrs. Knight said.

"Is this what you want to do? Would you prefer that
Reverend Walker deliver the eulogy for Reverend
Knight's funeral instead of me?"

"Honestly, I was in total agreement with what Paul
wanted," Mrs. Knight said. "His funeral at the church
he'd worked so hard to build, and you preaching his eulogy."

"Then why are you changing things now?"

Mrs. Knight let out a sigh. "Marshall presented a lot
of good arguments for why I should allow him to preach
it—a few of which I agree with. Truthfully, you really *do*
have your hands full with your own family troubles and
heartaches. And it *is* wrong of me to insist you do this
when there are obviously plenty of others willing and
quite capable of carrying on," she said.

"Is that the only reason you're changing it? I really

want to do this, and it's not a problem for me. I've gotten a little rest; I'm ready for another round."

"Pastor Landris, Marshall is not one who is used to being trumped by anyone. It doesn't matter whether it's me, you, or someone else, no one will get in his way. This is not the first time he's reminded me of his position and power. I admit, it's been a long while. When Paul first heard how Marshall was trying to boss and push me around early on in our marriage, he had a nice little *'chat'* with him, as Paul put it. I don't know what all my husband said to him, but whatever it was toned him down in ways I never could have imagined. Every now and then, he would try something again, and Paul would shut him down quickly. I suppose Marshall feels free now to go after any- and everybody he wants, with Paul no longer here to stop him. I don't know."

"Are you telling me Reverend Walker is forcing you to do this?" Landris waited for her answer; she didn't say anything. He then heard sniffling, and he knew she was now crying. "Mrs. Knight, are you all right?"

"Pastor Landris, I don't want any trouble. I just can't handle it on top of everything else I'm dealing with. Please, let it go, okay? You *do* need to concentrate on your own family. In fact, I feel bad taking time away from you right now. Why don't you just focus on your problems and leave me to deal with mine."

"Mrs. Knight, I appreciate you for caring about me and my family. But I also want you to know that I promised Reverend Knight I would look after you for him. If Reverend Walker is trying to intimidate you or is threatening you in any way, I want to know about it. He has no right to do anything like that to you. And I won't stand for it."

"Pastor Landris, what can you do? Marshall Walker is an influential, powerful man of God with a bully pulpit, even more so now that my Paul is gone. That's why it's best you and I just let sleeping dogs lie."

Landris thought again of the envelope. He didn't appreciate Reverend Walker seemingly bullying a woman, an elderly woman at that, who'd just lost her husband.

"Pastor Landris, I'm going to go now. If you find you can come to the funeral tomorrow, I'll be happy to see you. But if your family needs you, then you spend the time with them and don't you feel bad about missing Paul's funeral. I know that's what Paul would have said to you. It's what he would have wanted. You were there for him when he was alive. That's what counts in life. We'll leave Reverend Walker in God's hands. The Lord says vengeance belongs to Him. Marshall's manhandling doesn't bother me. If he wants to preach Paul's eulogy that badly, then he can. And please know that you and your family are definitely in my prayers. God will get the glory in all of this. I know that in my heart. I feel it in my spirit. So don't you get discouraged. God has your back."

"And my front, and my side, my top, and my bottom, too," Landris said. "Mrs. Knight, will you promise me one thing?"

"What's that?"

"If Reverend Walker tries to push you around again, will you let me know?"

She laughed. "You sounded just like Paul when you said that."

"Promise me that you'll let me know," Landris said again.

"If I feel like I really need you when it comes to Marshall, I promise I'll let you know. But in truth, after this funeral is over, I'll probably never have a reason to talk *with* or *to* Marshall again. When your wife wakes up, you tell her what a blessed woman she is. You're a good man, Pastor Landris. And I and my family are proud to know you."

When Landris hung up, he went to the safe in his bedroom and tapped in the four-digit security code. Opening the safe, he moved items around until he found the envelope Reverend Knight had given him. He pulled it out, opened it, and looked inside to see what it contained. Sitting down on the sofa in his room, he examined everything closely.

After he finished, he put everything back in the envelope and clamped it back shut. "Lord, now that's definitely some deep stuff there. I don't know when, if, or how I'm supposed to use a thing like this. I'm really going to need Your guidance on this."

The phone rang. "I got it," he yelled loud enough for his mother to be able to hear him. "Hello," he said.

"Pastor Landris, my name is Nurse Wren, and I'm calling from the hospital. The doctor asked me to call you. We need you to get here as quickly as you can."

"Is this about my wife? Has she awakened?" Landris asked.

"Sir, all I know is that Dr. Freeman asked me to call you and tell you he needed you to come to the hospital as soon as you can. He'll speak with you when you get here."

"Dr. Freeman? But that's not any doctor I'm familiar with. Is this about my son?"

"Sir, just come to NICU and ask any nurse at the desk to page Dr. Freeman upon your arrival. He'll talk with you then."

Landris got off the phone, told his mother he was going back to the hospital without mentioning the call he'd just received, and began to pray as he hurriedly got in his car. "Heavenly Father, I don't know what's going on, but You know. I'm still standing on Your Word, Lord. I'm not going to allow anything to move me off Your

Word. I thank You, in advance, Lord, that my wife is healed. I thank You that my son is healed. You are worthy to be praised. No matter what happens, Lord, I will praise You. I have nowhere else to go *but* You. No one else to turn to *except* You. Please don't ever leave me. Be with me, Lord Jesus. Continue to cover me, I pray."

Chapter 45

S arah continued to wait for Polly to speak. Polly fid-
dled with her hair, then her hands for several minutes. Sarah sat patiently. Polly then glanced down at
her watch.

"Will you look at the time?" Polly said, grabbing her
purse as she stood up. "I almost forgot; I have an appointment today. I'm supposed to see my therapist at
three."

"Sit down," Sarah said sternly, but nicely. "We both
know you don't have anywhere you need to be right
this minute. Now, Polly, I want to know how you knew
about the missing Wings of Grace box and the Alexandrite necklace. And please don't insult my intelligence
again by trying to get me to believe that someone here
told you and you can't tell me because you think you'll
get them in trouble."

"What are you trying to imply?" Polly asked.

"Sit, and I'll tell you what I've learned over this past
week."

Polly nervously sat down.

Sarah picked up a petite spinach quiche and bit it.
She set the rest back on her plate. "Would you care to
tell me how well you know my nephew, Montgomery?"

"Montgomery?"

"Yeah. You know, Montgomery Powell the Second."

"I've met him a few times at various social functions around town. But I don't know if I can answer how well we know each other. That's a relatively broad question."

Sarah began to nod her head slowly. "All right, then. If you like, you can go on to your appointment. There's no real reason for you and I to waste each other's time any longer."

Polly stood up as she watched Sarah. Sarah picked up the rest of her quiche and ate it.

"Sarah," Polly began, "I don't know what you *think* you know, but I believe someone has misinformed you."

"No, Polly. I think someone has misinformed *you.* But if you want to play this little game, then you go right ahead. I just thought the right thing to do was to give you a fair chance to tell your side. However, I can't make you tell the truth if you're bent on keeping up your little charade." Sarah picked up a slice of cucumber and bit it.

"Seriously, Sarah, I don't have a clue what you could be referring to. I mean, I've seen Montgomery. Our paths have crossed. In fact, I admit, I've been to his house a few times, mostly to discuss things regarding you. Truth be told, I didn't appreciate some of the things he's done to you, and I wanted him to know where I stood on the matter."

"Okay, Polly." Sarah picked up another cucumber slice and ate it. "I'll have a check cut tomorrow and put in the mail to you for the work you've done toward this Christmas celebration."

"But I'm not finished," Polly said. "We still have to come up with the menu to give to the caterer we're bringing in. You were going to get that to me by the end of this week, remember?"

"Oh, you're finished." Sarah picked up a broccoli floret, stuck it in her vegetable dip, and ate it. "Trust me, you're finished," she said.

Polly walked closer to Sarah and sat back down next to her. "I don't understand." A worried look came over her face. She covered her mouth. "Okay. Okay. Let's talk about this now. I don't know what all you want to know."

"I want to know why you took those items. I want to know where they are. Then you might want to explain to me how you could come in here, pretend to be my friend, then stab me and my family in the back the way you've done."

"That's not what happened, Sarah. I truly do care about you. I do!"

Sarah wiped her hands on her napkin. "Then *why* did you take those things?"

Polly smiled nervously. "I don't have those things."

"I know," Sarah said.

"Then why are you questioning me?" Polly was starting to break down, shaking slightly. "Why are you acting like this?"

Sarah stood up. "I have such a time with the circulation in my legs these days," she said. "I find when I move around, it really does help." She walked over to the Christmas tree, with the assistance of her walking cane, and gazed up at it. Turning around, she made her way to a straight-back chair and sat down diagonally across from Polly. "Why don't you tell me what really happened that day, dear? Come on, the truth."

"You mean Saturday?" Polly swallowed hard. "The day they say those things likely went missing? Well, let's see. I came by here after Gayle called me and told me you'd been rushed to the hospital. When I arrived, no one was here. Everybody was gone. The house was completely empty."

"That's when you decided to use the key I gave you to get in the house in case something ever happened to me and you had a need to get in? The truth, Polly."

Polly smiled while rocking a little. She nodded. "Yes. But I didn't come in looking for anything in particular. Montgomery had asked me to find out whatever I could on Memory and Lena. What better time to snoop than when I was sure the house was completely empty? But I wasn't planning on giving him anything that would really hurt either of them. Just find enough to make him feel he could continue to trust me."

Polly looked at Sarah, trying to deduce what Sarah was probably thinking now. "I searched the room where Memory was staying," Polly said, continuing with the story. "There really wasn't anything of importance in her room. Then I went to Lena's room, and jackpot! Right there on the bed was a beautiful handcrafted box with the key in the lock. I went over, was about to open the box to see what was inside it, when the necklace laying beside it suddenly caught my eye. I picked it up, not knowing at the time that it was the infamous Alexandrite necklace. I mean, how would I know that? It was my understanding from you that it was missing—taken some years back by Memory from Lena, which had precipitated their falling out." Polly reached down and picked up the glass of iced tea Monica had brought in for her and wet her throat with several swallows.

"Before I got a chance to look in the box," Polly said, setting the glass back down, "I heard someone open the front door and close it."

"Lena's husband, Richard," Sarah said.

"Yes, it was Richard, although I didn't know that at the time. Of course, the last thing I needed was to get caught upstairs snooping with everyone gone. I knew I had to act fast, so I grabbed the box, stuck the necklace inside of it, and as quickly and as quietly as I possibly could, I scurried out of the room. At first, I wasn't sure which way to go. Then it hit me—your room."

Sarah looked puzzled. "My room?"

"Yes, your room. You weren't there, but if I was discovered, I could easily play off my being in there. After all, you'd given me a key to your house. You obviously trusted me and would trust me to get something out of your room if it was needed. You'd gone to the hospital, so I could have easily and plausibly been looking for something for you. I could use our relationship and closeness as a cover if I had to."

"And no one would have been the wiser," Sarah said, shaking her head.

"Exactly." Polly drank some more tea, then politely cleared her voice. "I stayed in your room and waited to see if whoever had come in was planning to come upstairs. When I heard the heavy footsteps on the staircase, I knew I couldn't be caught with that box and necklace still in my possession. So I looked for a good place to hide it until I could come back and retrieve it later." Polly looked at Sarah as she moistened her lips.

"What happened after that?"

"I cracked the door, peeped out of it, and saw it was Richard. He was going into the room I'd just left. I then remembered my car was parked out front, and he most likely saw it when he came home. As soon as he closed the bedroom door, I attempted to sneak down the stairs. Just as I reached the top step, he came back out. I turned in a hurry and pretended I had just made it to the top step and was slightly out of breath. He spoke, and I played it off like I had come in the house a few minutes before him, that I'd been downstairs looking to see if Monica was still around when I heard someone go up the stairs. Thinking it was Gayle, Lena, Memory, or Monica, I'd come up to see."

"Knowing you, you probably then made him believe you were relieved when you saw a man coming out of the door, and it was him instead of some intruder."

"You know me. I was about to tell him they had taken you to the hospital when Lena called. I could tell she was trying to tell him how to get to the hospital."

"And that's when you, being the Good Samaritan that you are, volunteered to drive him to the hospital, further covering you and your actions," Sarah said.

"That's not totally true. I volunteered because I was planning to come to the hospital and check on you anyway," Polly said. "So we left here in my car and went to the hospital to see about you." Polly pressed her lips tightly together, then relaxed them. "I'm sorry, Sarah," she said. "I really am."

Sarah nodded. "Uh-huh. Now, tell me how Montgomery fits into all of this."

Polly stood up and paced back and forth as she spoke. "Montgomery came to me back in 2001, when you first had him thrown out of this house. Naturally, he was furious with you and everything else that had transpired. He didn't have an avenue inside here to see what was going on—"

"So he got you to befriend me."

"Originally, that was my purpose. He asked me to see if I could use some of my Southern charm I was known for and become part of your close inner circle." Polly walked back over to Sarah and kneeled down in front of her. "But I genuinely did grow to care about you, Sarah. True, it may have begun with him putting me up to it, but you're a remarkable woman I've come to adore over the years. I see you as a true friend."

Sarah smiled and shook her head. "Unbelievable," she said. "Unbelievable."

"Sarah, I haven't been supplying Montgomery with

much information lately. In fact, he's upset with me right now. He knows the Wings of Grace box is missing, as well as that necklace. But I wasn't the one who told him that. You have to believe me. Someone else on your staff must have leaked that information to him. The part about me having heard it from someone on your staff was true, indirectly anyway. Someone told Montgomery, who told me. But Sarah, Montgomery desperately wants that box, even more than he wants the necklace." Polly sat down on the floor in front of Sarah, which, for an always-prissy Polly, spoke volumes. She took Sarah's hand. "Please forgive me. I've wanted to tell you about this for so long. I just never knew how."

"Of course you did," Sarah said, patting Polly's hand once.

Polly looked up at Sarah with sad eyes. "Tell me, if you will, how did you figure this out?"

"Oh, I didn't," Sarah said.

Polly pulled back. "You didn't?" She got up off the floor, confused now.

"No," Sarah said. "I didn't."

"Then who did?"

"Well, you see, we've been racking our brains about what could have happened. Memory and Lena questioned everyone here but got nowhere. Then today, I started thinking. You were the only one we hadn't questioned, although I really couldn't see how you would have been able to pull anything like that off, if you had. Then I thought about something Richard said about you bringing him to the hospital. He couldn't believe he didn't notice your car outside when he came home from playing golf. But it had to be there, since you were here in the house already. He said you'd come in right before him, but he couldn't understand how you got up the stairs so fast without him hearing you. You're not the quietest, when you walk up steps." Sarah squeezed the arms of the chair.

"I knew I had given you a key to get in," Sarah continued. "But honestly, until just now, I really didn't know you'd done it."

Polly laughed as she began to shake her head. "Wow, you're good."

Sarah looked up at Polly. "Thank you. Now, where are the box and the necklace?"

Polly turned her back to Sarah. "Montgomery asked that same thing last week." She turned around and faced Sarah. "They're upstairs in your room . . . under your bed."

"Is that why you were trying so hard this past week to get in my room? You wanted to get the box and the necklace back," Sarah said in deep thought. "When you brought that empty cardboard box with tissue paper in it to my room the other day and sat it on the floor next to my bed, you intended to get the Wings of Grace box from under my bed and put it in there so you could sneak it out of my room undetected, didn't you?"

Polly flopped down on the sofa. "Yes. You see, after I brought Lena and Richard home from the hospital that night, it dawned on me that the house wouldn't be empty anymore, and I wouldn't be able to get the box out of your room. I needed to get it."

"And what were you planning on doing with the box and the necklace when you got them?" Sarah asked.

"Honestly, Sarah"—Polly smiled—"I really don't know. But Montgomery really wants that box, along with all that it contained inside. So much so, he offered to give me the Alexandrite necklace as a reward for the box, should I happen to get it to him."

"So this past week, your being here on the pretense of helping, while constantly being under foot, was merely a guise . . . a ploy to gain access to my room?" Sarah asked. "And for whom? Montgomery, the man who continued to perpetrate what his father and uncle began some seventy years ago? I shared my heart with you, Polly. You know how hard all of this has been on me just over the years we've known each other." Sarah shook her head slowly. "How could you? How?" She held out her hand. "My key, please."

"I'm sorry, Sarah." Polly opened her purse, took Sarah's house key off her key ring, and placed it in Sarah's hand. "I never used that key to take anything from you."

"Until now." Sarah closed her hand. "I'm sorry as well," Sarah said. "I'll have a check mailed to you tomorrow for services rendered for the Christmas celebration."

"You don't owe me anything. Really you don't. But now that you know everything, can we start over? I'd still like to be friends," Polly said, lowering her head.

"You know, if you hurry, you can probably make that three o'clock appointment you said you had," Sarah said. "Good-bye, Polly." Sarah looked away.

"Sarah, at least say that you forgive me. Please. I need to know you forgive me."

Sarah looked at her. "I forgive you, Polly. Mostly for me . . . but I forgive you."

"Mostly for you? I'm sorry, but I don't understand what you mean by that."

"I forgive you for me," Sarah said. "See, forgiveness is as much for the one who was wronged as it is for the one who did the wrong. I've lost too much in life already to waste time holding on to anything toxic. I forgive you, Polly, because I refuse to allow the negative that comes with unforgiveness to rob me of anything more in my life."

Polly leaned down, tears flowing, and hugged Sarah.

"Thank you," she said. She started to leave. "And for the record, I don't have a three o'clock appointment today."

Sarah smiled as she slowly rose to her feet. "And for the record, I know that. Good-bye, Polly. I do wish you well. Now, please . . . allow me to see you to the door."

Chapter 46

To appoint unto them that mourn in Zion, to give unto them beauty for ashes, the oil of joy for mourning, the garment of praise for the spirit of heaviness; that they might be called trees of righteousness, the planting of the Lord, that He might be glorified.

Isaiah 61:3

When Memory and Lena returned from Christmas shopping later that evening, they were shocked to see Sarah still sitting in the parlor with the Christmas tree. But even more shocking was what was on the coffee table in front of her.

"The Wings of Grace box?" Lena said. "Where did you find it? Who had it?" she asked.

Sarah took the Alexandrite necklace and held it out. "I'm not sure who this goes to now," she said.

Lena and Memory both came closer. Lena looked at Memory. "That's yours," Lena said of the necklace.

"But I gave it back to you," Memory said.

"I know, but I want you to have it. It should have been in your possession to begin with. Grace left it for you, so it belongs to you."

"Then it's mine to give to whomever I want," Memory said, "and I want you to have it. You can give it back to Theresa again, if you like."

"Will somebody just take it?" Sarah said, in a scolding-type voice.

Memory and Lena exchanged looks and laughed. Memory came and got it, then promptly handed it to

Lena. "Please. If you really want to make me happy, you'll take this."

Lena acquiesced and took it.

"Put it on so I can see how it looks on you," Memory said. Lena put it on and stood back, playfully striking poses. "Beautiful," Memory said.

Lena looked at the box. "Grandmother, you haven't said where you found them."

Sarah smiled. "Don't worry about that. I told you both that I still had a few tricks left up my sleeve."

"Have you looked in the box yet?" Lena asked.

Sarah shook her head. "Except to take the necklace out, no, I didn't. For whatever reason, my mother chose to leave the two of you this to view together. I'm a bit tired now. It's been a long and trying day, to say the least. I think it's past time that I go up to my room and retire for the evening."

"I'll help you," Lena said as she started toward Sarah.

"Are you ready to go up now, Miss Fleming?" Gayle asked as she seemingly appeared out of nowhere.

Sarah looked in her direction. "Gayle, dear, as always, your timing is impeccable." Sarah began to stand up. Gayle came over and helped her up the rest of the way. "I think I might be starting to get rusty. That's what happens when you sit for a while." She looked at Memory then Lena as she took a few baby steps forward to get her joints working again. "Let this be a lesson to you all. You need to always keep moving if you don't want to rust up."

Memory laughed. "All right. We'll keep that in mind."

Memory and Lena sat there with the box beside them on the sofa. They quietly waited until they were certain Gayle and Sarah were completely upstairs and they'd heard Sarah's door close.

"Where do you suppose this box came from?" Lena

asked. "I mean, it's been missing now for well over a week. Then, out of nowhere, it suddenly reappears."

"I don't know, but I'm curious as well where she found it. Even more importantly, why wouldn't she tell us any more than she did?"

"Well, the key is still here in the keyhole, just like we left it," Lena said as she examined the box. "Do you think anyone, besides Grandmother taking the necklace out, has been inside of it since we last had it?"

"Who knows? But it appears someone would have had to, since we certainly didn't put the Alexandrite necklace inside of it when we had it. Someone had to open it up to put the necklace in it. And since Sarah's not talking, we may never find out who took it. But I sure would like to know."

Lena ran her hand over the box again. "I just love these boxes," she said. "Shall we?"

"Well, you can have the box when we're finished," Memory said. "It's only fair, especially since I was the one who threw the first one I ever came across in the trash."

"Yeah, but I hear your father made this box with his own two hands. This may be the closest thing you ever come to having something his hands actually touched."

"All the more reason you should keep it. Haven't you figured out yet that I'm not at all the sentimental type?" Memory said. "Now, shall we open this up and check out what's inside before something else happens and stops us again?"

Lena raised the top. The signature carved wings were on the underside of the top. Lena traced the details of the fine craftsmanship with her index finger. "This is so beautiful," she said.

"Yeah, looks like my dad was really talented when it came to stuff like this."

Lena began taking some things out of the box: vari-

ous papers, a couple of rather unique brooches, two exquisite rings. She then came across a certificate of birth.
"Now, this is strange. It's not exactly a birth certificate,
but it appears to be something a midwife would give
for a child's birth."

"Who is it for?" Memory asked, leaning over to get
a better look at it.

Lena handed the frail piece of paper to Memory.
"See for yourself."

When Memory looked at it, she saw the child's
name, Ransom Powell, although the name Powell had a
single line through it, and written above it was the name
Perdue. "It looks like my father's birth certificate. But
why would his birth certificate be in a box Grace,
Sarah's mother, would have? And why would Grace
leave it for us to find?"

"I don't know," Lena said.

"The mother's name is scratched out, but it looks like
it was someone named Adele Powell," Memory said,
holding the paper up close to her eyes so she could get
a better look at it. "The father's name is totally scratched
out. I can't make out what it was."

"Let me see that again. My glasses are much better
than yours," Lena said, holding out her hand. She looked
at it. "I can't make it out, either. But why would your
father's last name have Powell, then be changed to Perdue? That makes no sense at all."

"I know. Let's see if anything else is in here that might
explain things a little better," Memory said. They went
through the rest of the things. Other than more jewelry
and lots of papers that didn't mean a whole lot to them,
there was nothing to help them.

"Well, this other stuff I understand being in here,"
Lena said. "But I'm lost when it comes to that paper with
your father's name on it. There's nothing in here, from
what I can see, that explains why Grace felt it neces-

sary to include your father's official birth record in a box left to us. Unless, of course, she merely wanted you to have your father's legal birth record . . . as a keepsake. You know what? We might be too old to do this."

"Didn't you say Grace left a videotape and a journal or something like that along with this box?"

"The tape," Lena said in a tone that clearly indicated Memory was absolutely correct. "I hope I brought it with me." Lena got up and headed out of the parlor to go to her room. "I was in such a hurry to pack and get here. I pray I remembered to bring it, although, if I did, I don't remember exactly where I may have put it when I unpacked."

"I pray you brought it," Memory said as she sat holding the box and the birth record while waiting for Lena to go upstairs to her room and look for the tape.

"Got it," Lena said, triumphantly holding the tape in the air when she came back.

"Now, we need to find a videocassette player in this house," Memory said. "There's definitely not one in here," she said, looking around the room that didn't even have a television.

"Grandmother had one put in the playroom for the children to watch when they come over."

"Let's go," Memory said, hopping up on her feet. "Maybe Grace will open our eyes and tell us something more on the videotape."

They went to the playroom, popped in the videotape, and began watching it.

"I sort of remember her. She was regal-like back then, too," Memory said, seeing the elderly woman on the screen. "She didn't smile much, except on the occasions when she was talking directly to me. Now I know why. I was her granddaughter."

They listened as Grace spoke about various things concerning why she had done what she did, and how much she truly loved Memory in spite of sending her away with Mamie Patterson. How she wished things could have been different. Then they heard it, what they were looking for.

"You may be wondering why Ransom Perdue's birth record is in that box," Grace said. "And why I left that for you two, as opposed to my daughter. Pearl Black, an old friend of the family, brought that to me before she died. I wish she'd given it to me decades ago. Had she, then things for my daughter might have been vastly different. You see, Ransom was born to a woman named Adele Powell. Adele was married to a man named Winston Powell. Adele, incidentally, is the woman my husband was married to prior to me. Adele died right after giving birth to Victor Fleming Jr. Like Pearl, Pearl's mother was a respected midwife. Pearl's mother was there when Adele gave birth to Ransom. The problem was, Adele was a white woman married to a white man. Or so everybody thought. Keep in mind this was in the early nineteen hundreds. Adele was, in actuality, a black woman who had apparently passed for white. She'd married a white man named Winston, and, from what I hear, she'd tried everything to keep from ever having a child with him, claiming she didn't want children. Of course, we now know that her fear really was of having a baby that might come out looking black. Disastrous, when you happen to be married to a racist." Grace took a deep breath and released it.

"Nevertheless, she did get pregnant. And according to Pearl, when it was time for her to have the baby, she made her way to Pearl's mother on some pretense that she was out and about when she went into labor. There is much dispute of that being true. The belief is that she purposely sought out Pearl's mother just in case the baby did come out clearly a black child. Her husband would have most certainly accused her of being with a black man. He never might have guessed it was due to the blood that ran through her veins." Grace took a few seconds to readjust her body before continuing.

"The baby was born. Pearl's mother gave the baby to her and proceeded to fill out the proper paperwork on the newborn as was required by the state. Adele looked at her baby closely, thought the baby had a slight color to him, and asked Pearl's mother honestly what she thought. Pearl's mother concurred that her baby would most certainly darken in a few weeks. He was already dark around the top of his ears. She was told there would be no way of hiding his true color."

Grace uncrossed her legs as she relaxed a little more. "Adele decided to confide in Pearl's mother and asked her if she could possibly find her baby a good home, as there was no way she could take a black child back to her husband's house. No way. From my understanding, especially back during that time, black people were known to take in children that relatives and neighbors didn't want to raise or couldn't take care of. Pearl's mother took the baby and gave him to a friend of hers. People didn't show birth certificates like we do today, so no one ever knew the truth. Ironically, Ransom Perdue grew up being the best of friends with Pearl. Of course, Pearl didn't find out any of this until years after Ransom disappeared. Pearl was a wealth of folks' secrets. Things her mother told her and things she learned first-hand—untold history and knowledge she told me she's written down and documented. Who knows where those documents are, now that she's gone?"

Grace leaned forward. She seemed tired and out of breath now. "I'm going to end this here. But I needed you to know the truth. Montgomery Powell the Second's grandmother was a black woman. Everybody knows how he feels about black people. It wouldn't be impossible to prove this fact about Montgomery's heritage, if needed. Had I been in possession of this information when my stepson, Heath, was alive, I would have used it to get Sarah out of those horrible places and back home where she belonged.

"Sadly, it's too late for me to do anything with it. But Montgomery is as bad as his father was. Should you need leverage on him, I wouldn't hesitate to use this information. And not to sound like I'm chewing bitter grapes, but I don't know if we can really be sure that Adele's son, Heath, was truly even Victor Senior's child. After all, she *was* still married to Winston Powell when she conceived him. Do with this information as you deem necessary, if it's not already too late, and help bring my daughter home where she belongs. Sarah deserves better than she's gotten in life. It's too late for me now. I'm one hundred and two years old now. My time on this earth is at hand. I couldn't save my child, not like I wanted to. I pray, between you two, you can do a better job than I."

The tape went blank.

"Oh my," Lena said. "This is huge."

"I don't get it," Memory said. "This is 2005. Nobody cares about stuff like this anymore. The one-drop rule is a thing of the past. And everybody knows there were some light-skinned black folk who passed for white. I could have passed if I'd ever wanted to. So Montgomery Heath Powell Sr. had a black mother. So what? I had a white mother. So what?"

"You don't understand. For Montgomery Powell the Second, it really is a big deal," Lena said. "You see, the first time I ever met Montgomery, he was acting like the biggest racist. You should have heard him. It was scary, really. He called us all kinds of names. Then Grandmother made a reference to him possibly being a descendant of black people. I don't know if she knew that for a fact or whether she was just bluffing to get him to back down, but it did cause him to get off-balance. Grandmother held up an envelope. She told him she had proof. After everything was over, I questioned her about it. She gave the envelope to me and said that if knowing made that much of a difference to me, I could open the envelope and see for myself what it contained."

"So what did you do with the envelope?" Memory asked.

"I burned it."

"You did what?"

"I burned it," Lena said as she shrugged her shoulders. "I realized it really didn't matter to me. But now this. . . . This is some pretty substantial evidence here."

"So what do we do with it?" Memory asked.

"Grace left this for me and you," Lena said. "It's obvious she still didn't know where her daughter was. I suppose Grace was hoping we might somehow be able to use it to help get Sarah back home where she had failed all of those years."

"I wish Grace had found us. Then we could have all worked together to find Sarah before Grace died. She didn't get to see her daughter for years. It's a generational curse."

"A curse we're breaking now. But Grace likely felt if she wasn't able to help her daughter with all her power and resources, we wouldn't have been able to do much. But why not use this on Montgomery while she was still alive?" Lena asked. "If it could be effective against him, why not use it herself instead of leaving it for us? I don't get it."

"Maybe she did," Memory said. "It's obvious she didn't get this until she was too old and ill to fight anymore. Then you have to know who you can trust, because in the wrong hands, this evidence could have been totally destroyed."

"I do know, before we found Grandmother, Montgomery seemed to have been making plans for *her* to die. I'm not saying he was going to kill her or anything, but he claimed she was ill and near death. I'm sure he was scheming to legally obtain this house. The copy of the deed to this house that was inside the box," Lena said, "wasn't that in Grandmother's name?"

"I believe it was."

Lena pressed the eject button, took out the videotape, and turned off the VCR. "I think we need to talk to Grandmother. It's high time we stop this playing around and start pulling together." They started walking out.

Memory stopped at the doorway. "After you," she said, playfully bowing while allowing Lena to walk past her.

"Thank you, Mother," Lena said.

Memory stood still. She couldn't help but get emotional. After all, this was the first time, since Lena was around six years old, that she'd called her mother.

Chapter 47

*Then shalt thou delight thyself in the
Lord; and I will cause thee to ride upon
the high places of the earth, and feed
thee with the heritage of Jacob thy father: for the mouth of the Lord hath
spoken it.*

Isaiah 58:14

Landris waited for Dr. Freeman at the nurses' station.

"Mr. Landris," a short man with dark brown hair said
as he extended his hand to greet him. "I'm Dr. Freeman.
Thank you for getting here so quickly."

"Tell me what's going on. I just checked on my son,
and he's not in there."

"I'm sorry, Mr. Landris. Did the person who called
not tell you *anything*?" Dr. Freeman's beeper went off.
His glasses sat close to the end of his nose as he read it.

"No," Landris said. "She just said I needed to get
here right away, and you would tell me everything."

"I'm so sorry, Mr. Landris. If you don't mind, can
you walk with me?" he said as he started down the hall.
"Your son was still having major problems with his
breathing. We had what we call an endotracheal tube,
ET for short, in his windpipe. This was getting air and
oxygen to his lungs at a regulated rate, but something
started happening and—"

"Dr. Freeman, is my son okay?" Landris asked in a
tone demanding an answer.

"Your son is fine—for now, anyway. I believe we were

able to stabilize him. I sent him down for a few tests. That's why he wasn't in there when you looked in on him."

Landris let out a sigh of relief. "Thank You, Lord," he said, looking upward and lifting his hands in a form of praise.

"I'm sorry if we worried you. I don't like saying this sort of stuff over the phone, because I understand how anxious parents already are. Sometimes things get lost in the translation, and it can create a nightmare of a problem for both the doctor and parents."

"I'd like to see my son. When will he be back? I want to be sure he's okay."

Dr. Freeman nodded. "That was the CNS beeping me to let me know she was on her way back with him now."

Landris had become quite familiar with various medical terms. He knew that CNS stood for clinical nurse specialist. He waited outside NICU for his son's return. When they brought him back, Landris spent thirty minutes with him. Glancing at the clock on the wall, he saw it was seven fifty-five. Eight o'clock was the last official visiting hour of the day for SICU patients. He left his son's side to go be with his wife.

"Johnnie Mae, you need to wake up," he said, letting the rail down, making it easier for him to hold her hand. "We have this beautiful son, and he wants to meet you. He's small, but he's so beautiful. I can't explain how it feels when I look at him. Oh, I know, I'm not supposed to call a boy beautiful. Okay, handsome. He's so handsome. How about that? But he needs you right now. Princess Rose needs you. We all need you.

"Your mother's memory has reverted back. That happened shortly after the baby was born. She did get to see him, and she knew he was your new baby. She also knew you weren't doing well. Something, huh? How she could be so much like her normal self one day, then back to not knowing who anyone is the next. She likes my mother a lot, though. Princess Rose was so happy to be able to spend some time with her, I can't even begin to tell you. Your mother still talks and plays with her, even when she can't remember who she is. I can see it bothers Princess Rose when your mother doesn't recall things. I've had to stop Princess Rose a few times from getting frustrated about it. It's hard to explain something like Alzheimer's to a child. In truth, it's hard for grown folks to understand.

"My mother's been a little tired. She tries to hide it from me, but I can tell. I know it has to do with her heart. That's why she only comes to the hospital once a day. I don't think she's even supposed to be in Alabama, but she had to come see about us. Her doctor wants to perform triple-bypass surgery on her. And Thomas had quit taking his medicine. I didn't tell you before because I didn't want you worrying about it. You were dealing with enough already. I think we convinced him to start back taking his pills. I don't know. I suppose we'll find out soon enough. I wish I knew how to get him to see he can't be playing around with his medication like that. Every time I turn on the news lately, somebody with bipolar disorder is getting killed because they're either not on medication and should be or they were on it and decided to stop taking it. The people who encounter them didn't know why they were acting the way they were and felt threatened. I've got to get through to him that this bipolar disorder is nothing to play Russian roulette with.

"He accuses me of preaching faith and healing but not really believing in it. I don't know, maybe I'm wrong to think medical and Godly healing *can* go hand in hand when needed. Maybe if I had enough faith, you'd be awake by now. Maybe if I had enough faith, our son wouldn't be struggling for his next breath now. They took him for some tests today. He seems okay. I just spent the past half hour with him. Guess what? He grabbed my finger. Well, maybe not *really* grabbed it, more like brushed it when he moved, but it was like he was letting me know that he's determined to hold on. Oh, you're going to be so proud when you wake up and see him. I know you are. He's a fighter, all right. Why won't you open your eyes, Johnnie Mae? I know you can hear me. I know you can." He laid his head down next to her hand, then raised it back up.

"Mrs. Knight is letting Reverend Walker preach Reverend Knight's funeral. I probably wouldn't have minded so much except I believe he bullied her into it. He all but threatened me. I don't know what I've done to make that man have it out for me. Reverend Knight warned me to watch out for him. In fact, he gave me something as leverage against him, should I ever need it. I hadn't planned on ever opening that envelope, but I have to tell you, I did look at it. Reverend Knight was right. If what's in that envelope was ever to come out . . . well, I don't know if the statute of limitations has run out for him to serve jail time for it, but Reverend Walker could definitely be ruined. Then again, in this day and age, who can say how people will really react?

"You're probably wondering what he could have done that could be so bad. How about he raped his twelve-year-old cousin when he was sixteen? Just the thought of that makes me mad. And would you believe he got away with it, too? According to the papers Reverend Knight gave me, when Marshall Walker and Paul Knight were teenagers, supposedly as a prank, they decided to rob Marshall's uncle, who owned one of those mom and pop stores. The family lived above the store. Marshall's young cousin was minding the store that day. I guess Marshall decided, since she was there alone and the opportunity was presenting itself, he'd also take her upstairs and have his way with her as a bonus to the robbery. They'd worn ladies' stockings over their faces as masks when they went in, so his cousin didn't know who he was. Not at first, anyway.

"According to the file, Paul Knight thought Marshall's taking her upstairs was part of the prank. After all, they weren't planning on keeping the money. That's what Marshall had told him prior to them doing it. Marshall just wanted to teach his stingy uncle a lesson. Of course, that wasn't at all what happened. After the incident, the police were called in. Both Marshall and Paul were placed temporarily in juvenile detention while things were being sorted out. A few months following the incident, the store/house burned to the ground. Marshall's uncle and his cousin both perished in the fire, which was ruled accidental due to faulty wiring. Because Marshall Walker and Paul Knight were juveniles at the time of the *alleged* incident, that incidentally was dismissed without prejudice, their records were sealed. Paul Knight kept all of this documented information along with other collaborating and pretty damaging evidence. Information he left to me.

"But enough about that. I'm sure you don't want to hear about all of this junk happening out here in this crazy world we live in. Johnnie Mae, I need you to come out of this. Who else on earth will I have to share my deepest thoughts with? I need you. I love you dearly. I tried to show you how much I loved you before any of this ever happened. But they say you never really know just how much you love a person until that person's no longer around. At least when you or I go out of town, we can pick up the phone and talk. How do I reach you now? So please, Johnnie Mae. Please. Open your eyes. For me, for Princess Rose, for your mother, for our son fighting to make it. He's waiting on a name, and I refuse to name him without you. I have faith you're going to pull through this. So open your eyes. Do you hear me, J. M.? Please . . . open your eyes."

Chapter 48

> They shall not labor in vain, nor bring
> forth for trouble; for they are the seed
> of the blessed of the Lord, and their
> offspring with them.
>
> Isaiah 65:23

Lena knocked on the door. "Grandmother, it's me and Memory. Is it okay if we come in?"

"Just a minute," Sarah yelled back. Sarah looked at Gayle. "Not a word to either of them about Montgomery or Polly," she whispered as she leaned forward.

"You know you can trust me," Gayle said in a low tone while continuing to fluff the two pillows she normally placed behind Sarah's back when propping her up. "Are you certain you feel okay? You look a bit flushed. You've been quite a busy little bee today."

"Yes, I feel okay." Sarah yawned as she lay back now. "Maybe I *am* a tad bit sleepy."

"Well, I'll check your blood pressure again as soon as Memory and Lena leave," Gayle said as she finished getting Sarah situated comfortably again. "Then I want you to rest."

"Thanks, Gayle."

Gayle opened the door, letting Memory and Lena in as she headed out.

"Are you gone?" Lena asked Gayle as they literally passed each other in the doorway. "We didn't mean to run you off or anything."

"Oh, you're not running me off. I have a few things

that require my attention," Gayle said as she flashed a
smile at Lena. "I'll be back in a little while, Miss Fleming."

Sarah nodded. "I'll be all right."

Gayle left. Memory moved the chair next to the nightstand over to Sarah's bed. Lena went and got the chair
usually kept folded in the corner and placed it next to
Memory so Sarah could easily see them both at the
same time.

"Grandmother, we just went through the Wings of
Grace box," Lena said, deciding to get straight to the
point. "We then watched the videotape your mother made
and left for us, preferably to view together if it was at
all possible. Those were her instructions."

"That's right, there *was* a videotape," Sarah said. "I
forgot you told me that. I'm sure had she suspected it
would be almost four years before that happened, she
may not have placed that restriction on it. But knowing
my mother, that was her way of ensuring you would
find Memory, if you two weren't already in some type
of contact." Sarah lay back, relaxing more into the pillow. "Was there anything interesting in the box or on
the tape? That's if you can share that information with
me. I don't wish to pry into something that may be
none of my business, so feel free to tell me if I am."

"Yes, there was something. In fact, there was something of interest to you, I believe," Memory said. "It
has to do with Ransom Perdue."

"Ransom Perdue was your father," Sarah said, looking directly at Memory. "I told you about him. Is there
something I don't know? Did my mother say what happened to him after he left and never returned?"

"No," Memory said. "But there was something in
the box and on the tape that I don't think you knew. We
have reason to believe that Ransom Perdue was possibly your stepbrother."

Sarah pressed her body harder into the pillows, as though she needed to be braced. "What? Oh, that's just hogwash!"

Lena looked at Memory, not believing Memory had put it in those terms and blurted it out like that. Although when Lena actually thought about it, that's precisely what it boiled down to. "What she meant to say is, from what appears to be an official record of Ransom's birth, his mother was actually Adele Powell."

"Adele Powell? She was my half-brothers', Heath and Victor Junior's, mother."

"Yes. Adele, your father's wife before he married your mother," Memory said.

"But that can't be," Sarah said. "Ransom was a black man. What are you saying?"

Lena recounted for Sarah everything they'd learned concerning Ransom, his mother, Adele, Pearl's mother's delivery of Ransom, and her secretly finding him a home.

Sarah shook her head. "I'm sure Ransom probably didn't know the truth. That is so sad, so sad. Deception; it's a curse, I tell you. That's what it is—a curse."

"It sounds like Ransom was Adele Powell's son, so that could *technically* make Ransom your stepbrother, although I wouldn't have put it the way Memory did," Lena said, throwing Memory a look of slight reprimand. "I am curious, though," Lena continued, turning her attention back to Sarah. "This has to do with Montgomery the Second. You insinuated on that day we first met that he may have had some black in his blood. Did you know his mother was a black woman passing for a white when you said that?"

Sarah laughed, placing her hand over her heart. "Heavens no," she said.

"Then you were bluffing when you said that to him?" Lena asked.

"I would have made a great poker player, don't you think?" Sarah asked.

"And the envelope you gave me?" Lena asked, referring to the envelope Sarah had held in her hand during her standoff with Montgomery . . . refusing to fold back in October of 2001.

"Oddly enough, I'd picked up that envelope only minutes before I made my way out the door when Johnnie Mae and all y'all came here," Sarah said. "I'd scribbled a note to tell Johnnie Mae what was really going on—the fact that I really was being held against my will. My intent was to slip that envelope to her if anything happened and she was forced to leave me here again."

"So had I opened that envelope instead of burning it . . . ?"

"You burnt it? I never knew that." Sarah laughed. "If you had opened it instead of burning it, you would have found my plea for help. But it worked, didn't it? It flustered Montgomery." Sarah began to chuckle. "And I thought for sure Johnnie Mae's husband was about to give Montgomery a real . . . what do the young folks call it?" She started snapping her fingers to try and help her recall the words. "What do they call it?"

"A beat down," Memory said, familiar with the terminology.

"That's it, a beat down!" Sarah said, continuing to laugh at the thought of it.

"Do you think Montgomery has any idea his grandmother was black?" Memory asked Sarah.

"Probably not," Sarah said. "But Montgomery is the kind who would hate something like that even being out there remotely as a topic of discussion." Sarah coughed a few times. "I believe my nephew is as protective of his so-called pristine reputation as his father was. There's no way Montgomery's white buddies will allow a black man to remain in their exclusive club. I don't care how white he may look on the outside." Sarah began to cough again. She covered her mouth with her hand.

"Are you okay?" Lena asked, getting up quickly and pouring some water, then handing it to her.

Sarah took a few sips. "I'm fine. I suppose I *am* tired, though. I think I'd like to take a little nap. Could you ask Gayle to come up when you go down?" Sarah asked.

"Sure," Lena said, taking the hint that Sarah was ready for them to leave now. She looked over at Memory, who remained sitting. "We're going to go and let you get some rest," Lena said, heading for the door. She was hoping Memory would get the hint this time. Memory continued to sit there. "Oh, Grandmother, before I forget to tell you. Theresa called. They decided they want to celebrate their anniversary on Wednesday, so they're not planning to drive up until Thursday for the celebration on Saturday."

"They should come on up on Tuesday," Sarah said. "They could go out together up here. I could watch the children for them while they're gone. Then they wouldn't have to bother with hiring a babysitter, and *I* would get yet more time to spend with my darling little great-great-grands. Why don't you call Theresa back and tell her that for me?" Sarah took another sip of water, then set the glass on her nightstand.

"That would be too much on you," Lena said. "Those little *darlings*, as you call them, can be a little *handful*. Trust me."

"Personally, I think it's a great idea. I'll be here," Memory said. "Between the two of us, four while Gayle and Monica are still around, we can certainly handle a couple of kids. That way you and Richard could also spend a night out on the town."

"That does sound tempting," Lena said. "It would give

us all a little more time to spend together. And that's always a good thing in my book. Are you two sure about this?" Lena looked from Memory to Sarah for confirmation.

"Absolutely. Call her and see what she says." Sarah closed her eyes. "It will be a joy having my family all here again, under the same roof, this time without any tension or any animosity. My child, grandchild, great-grandchild, and my great-great-grandchildren, five generations, all here together. It will be just as it says in the Bible. They won't labor in vain nor bring forth for trouble because they are the seed of the blessed of the Lord. Yes, I am indeed blessed." Sarah continued talking as her speaking became more and more sluggish, almost as though she was talking in her sleep. "I've got to get someone to talk to the caterer for our Christmas celebration. I'm sure Gayle will help me. I can always count on Gayle. Yeah, I trust Gayle. She's always said . . . I can . . . trust . . . her."

Sarah stopped talking altogether. She'd drifted completely off to sleep. Lena beckoned to Memory for her to get up and leave with her. They stepped out the door and closed it quietly.

"What was she talking about a caterer?" Memory asked when they reached the end of the hall. "Polly's taking care of all of that for her."

"Who knows?" Lena said. "I wouldn't put much stock into what she was mumbling then. She most likely was tired and just talking in her sleep."

"Maybe," Memory said. "Maybe."

Chapter 49

*For since the beginning of the world
men have not heard, nor perceived by
the ear, neither hath the eye seen, O
God, beside Thee, what He hath prepared for him that waiteth for Him.*

Isaiah 64:4

Landris sat in Johnnie Mae's room. It had been four
weeks since she'd had her baby. A baby whose weight
was now miraculously up to four pounds and three
ounces, but who still didn't have a name donning his
incubator-crib other than "Boy Landris." Landris was
back at church, preaching on Sundays and doing limited other duties throughout the week. His mother was
at his house, helping him take care of Princess Rose,
although he'd told her many times she really needed to
go home and see her doctor about her heart or at least
see a doctor in Birmingham just to make sure she was
still doing okay. His mother's presence there seemed
enough to satisfy Johnnie Mae's sister-in-law's quest to
try and get temporary custody of Princess Rose or
cause trouble.

Taking a cue from her son, who was speaking healing scriptures over his wife and child and playing healing tapes in Johnnie Mae's room while he wasn't there,
Virginia started listening to tapes on healing. Landris
had said this was spiritual warfare, and it was imperative that they fight this war with the right tools. Thomas
was out of the halfway-house medical facility, and while
he was continuing to grow stronger, fighting to get dis-

ability benefits, and find his own place, George had told him he could stay at their house.

Dr. Baker had consulted with other doctors. Landris was told that none of them agreed Johnnie Mae should be kept on life support any longer. After all, it had been a month now. As much as Landris might not want to face the fact, Johnnie Mae appeared all but gone. The majority agreed, with the exception of Dr. Baker and one other colleague, that if Johnnie Mae didn't regain consciousness within the next day, two at the most, realistically, the machine should be disconnected. Certain organs would likely start shutting down soon anyway. There was still the possibility of brain damage, although nothing indicated for sure that that had occurred. They couldn't know for sure *until* she regained consciousness, and it didn't look as though that was going to happen.

Landris listened as doctor after doctor tried to convince him that his wife could likely be in this state for as long as the machines were hooked up to her—months, even years. It was important that he face that fact and make peace with letting *her* go in peace. Turning off the life-support machine wasn't necessarily a death sentence. It was possible she might begin breathing again on her own. It might even jumpstart her system back to recovery. "There are many documented cases where this very thing has happened," one doctor explained.

However, Landris set his face like a flint. There was nothing else to be said if it was contrary to God's Word, as far as he was concerned.

His hair was already growing back. He kept it cut low to his head, definitely a different look on him. He'd been led by the Spirit of God to do a fast—no food or juices, only water to keep him hydrated—while praying for seven days.

The following day, after having heard all the doctor's recommendations, Landris walked in to visit Johnnie Mae on what was the final day of his seven-day fast. Her private room was filled with Rachel and her family, along with Johnnie Mae's mother, who, to Landris, clearly looked as though she didn't have a clue why she'd been dragged in there.

"What's going on?" Landris asked Rachel.

Fighting back her tears, Rachel said, "We came to say our good-byes."

"Good-bye?" Landris asked in sheer astonishment. "Good-bye? Good-bye to whom?"

"I was here yesterday when one of the doctors was here. I asked him point-blank, and he told me the truth, George. They want to take Johnnie Mae off life support tomorrow. I'm sure your insurance provider has long been in agreement with that." Rachel stared hard at him. "You knew about this, and you weren't even planning on saying anything to us? That's low, George Landris. That's low. We deserve to know what's going on. Marie and Donald came by earlier. My brother Christian and his family are planning on being here later this evening. It takes about three hours for him to drive up from Columbus, Georgia. You should have told us what was going on. Johnnie Mae is our sister, my mother's daughter." Rachel started crying. "No matter what *you* believe, we have a right to know the truth."

Mrs. Gates came and patted Rachel on her back. "There, there," she said. "Don't cry. I'm sure whatever it is can't be all *that* bad. It's going to all work out, you just wait and see."

"Listen, Rachel," Landris said, keeping his voice low and even, "we can't go giving up now. We have to believe the Word of the Lord. With long life, God will satisfy her. She will live and not die. That's all God's Word."

"Stop it!" Rachel said. "Just stop it!" She pressed her hands over her ears. "I'm so sick and tired of all you super-religious folks burying your heads in the sand about what God *will* and *won't* do!" She removed her hands from her ears.

"The Bible also says it rains on the just and the unjust," Rachel said. "Plenty of people have prayed for loved ones to live and not die, and do you know what happened to a good number of them?" Rachel stepped away from her mother and children and walked closer to Landris, who was close to the bathroom door. "They died anyway! You've given this your best shot, George. I give you that much. I know Johnnie Mae would be *very* proud of how vigilant you've been throughout all of this." She sighed. "But it's time for you to face some cold, hard facts here. She's gone, George. I wish it was different, but this is real life. And none of us are getting out of here alive. We're all going to die someday. Now is Johnnie Mae's time. We need to say our good-byes, remember the good times and the joys we've shared, and let her go on in peace."

"Rachel, let's not do this in front of Johnnie Mae."

"She can't hear anything, George. She can't hear us! She's all but gone, and you're forcing her to linger here because you don't want to face that truth. If God wanted things to be different, He could have kept her from going through this in the first place. All your praying and believing didn't keep her from getting toxemia. All your praying and believing didn't keep that baby in NICU from being born prematurely. If God loves you so much, then why not just keep you from even having to go through any of this at all? If God cared anything about all of your praying and believing, why hasn't He woken Johnnie Mae up? According to you, God can do anything but fail."

"Excuse me," Mrs. Gates said, "but, little lady, I wouldn't go there if I was you. You don't want to mess with God like that. Trust me, you don't."

"Rachel, I said I don't want to do this in front of Johnnie Mae." Landris spoke through clenched teeth, keeping his voice low. "She *is* going to live and not die! Do you hear me?"

"Says who?" Rachel said.

"Says the scripture I'm standing on."

She laughed cynically as she shook her head. She then spoke softly. "Look at our mother, George." She pointed at Mrs. Gates, who had returned to look out of the window. "Do you know what we've been confessing and believing about her? That she would be healed from this memory robber. That she would return to her old self again. That this is just some mistake, something that can easily be fixed. Look at her!" Rachel said, continuing to point to her mother. "She doesn't even know that's her daughter lying there. But I brought her anyway, and do you know why? Because I felt she needed and had a *right* to be able to say good-bye to her own child—a child she doesn't even remember giving birth to!"

Landris grabbed Rachel by the arm and started pulling her out of the room.

"Let go of me!" she yelled. "Let go! Have you lost your cotton-picking mind? You can't be grabbing on folks like that."

"Stop this!" Landris said after he pulled her outside the room and closed the door.

Rachel snatched her arm out of his grip. "Let me go!" She stood against the wall.

"I'm sorry. I didn't mean to manhandle you. Rachel, look, I know you're upset. But you can't do stuff like that in front of Johnnie Mae *or* your mother." He shook his head. "You can't let your frustrations and your hurt spill out and over to affect others the way you just did in there."

Rachel started crying. Landris gave her a handkerchief and hugged her. "I'm sorry," she said. "I know. I'm just so *mad* right now, I don't know what to do! Why doesn't God hear us? Why does He allow things like this to happen to good people? My sister is a good person. My mother is a good person. My daughter is still on drugs, and I've prayed . . . Lord knows, I've prayed for her. She seems worse off now than before I took the children. I thought at some point she'd hit rock bottom and get some help. I've all but lost her. I'm trying to come to terms with that. My mother, who has served the Lord faithfully, faithfully, do you hear me? Now look what's happened to her. Do you have any idea what it really feels like to have your own mother look at you and ask you who you are or talk to you like you're some stranger she just met on the street? Saying things like she just said to me in there? Then after you tell her who you are she looks at you like *you're* the one who's lost *your* mind? Do you have any idea, George? Do you?"

He stepped back. "I have an idea what it feels like to have the woman you promised to love, honor, and cherish, until death do you part, be lying in a hospital bed with doctors and all their fancy degrees telling you there's no more hope left while you stand in faith, against all hope. I have an idea what it feels like to have your only son be born prematurely with doctors telling you it's a good chance he's not going to make it. And every day, they act like it's a miracle he's still here on *that* day, but they're not sure he'll make it to the next. I know what it feels like to have your brother deal with a mental disorder while accusing you of not having enough faith that God will heal him as he takes himself off his mind-regulating medication, and you're not sure you can get through to him that he can't start playing around with something like that. I know what it feels like to have your own mother being told she needs triple-bypass heart surgery, but she seems determined to put it off while telling you she plans to stand by your side for as long as you need her as you go through some of the darkest hours of your life. While deep in your mind and heart, you're concerned about her heart possibly giving out before she's either healed or had the necessary surgery." He wiped his face with one hand.

"I know what it feels like, Rachel, to pray and expect God to move, only to be told things are still the same, if not worse, the following day. But you have to stand in faith and trust God, because honestly, who else do we have to turn to?" Landris said. "I stretch my hands to God daily. I don't know or have any other help *except* Him. Sure, any of us can throw a temper tantrum like Job did after our interludes of what seem to be unrelenting troubles. The time when Job told God he regretted ever being born.

"We can be upset with God the way the prophet Jeremiah was, despite the fact that God had told him in advance what he could expect to happen. We can refuse to go or do what God has instructed us, the way Jonah did. But trust me. God has a way of getting our attention. Even the apostle Paul experienced some of the same feelings we do. And Jesus, the Son of the living God, prayed and asked God to remove this bitter cup from Him, only to concede seconds later, 'But not my will, but thine be done.' Jesus was on the cross, and during His darkest hour, when it seemed God had turned away from Him completely, Jesus prayed and asked God why had He forsaken Him."

Landris reached out and touched Rachel on her hand. "I know you love your sister. I know you do. I even know that you're mad at God right now for what feels like Him turning a deaf ear to our prayers for her, mine included. But you have to know that God is still in control. He's sovereign, which means He reigns. He has not left us. He didn't leave Jesus, who, by all accounts, appeared defeated when they took Him down from the cross and placed Him in a tomb. It doesn't get any more over than that, but look what God did. Rachel, I don't know how God is going to do what He's going to do. But regardless of *what* happens, God will still get the glory out of it. I refuse to allow Satan to steal God's praises due to Him."

"What are you going to do if Johnnie Mae dies? And there's a great possibility that's about to happen," Rachel said as she wiped her tears with the handkerchief Landris had given her earlier. "God may decide not to save her. What are you going to do then? Will you still be spouting off all this religious stuff? Or will you question your own faith? Will you believe it was your fault because you really didn't have enough faith to move God? Or will you conclude that God really didn't care, and even though He could have raised her up, He chose not to?"

"I'm going to stand, Rachel. That's all God told me to do—stand. In spite of what happens in my life, I'm going to stand and trust God, because God *is* God."

"That's easy to say right now. Johnnie Mae is technically still here with us. I don't think that's what you'll be saying tomorrow or whenever they finally turn that life-giving machine off and her breathing ceases." Rachel dabbed at her now-closed eyes as she continued with sporadic sniffles.

"Let me tell you something," Landris said in voice that emanated peace. "I believe *right now*, when it matters. Faith is now. And that machine in there is not the life giver—God is. I can believe my wife is healed because when Jesus was being beaten, the stripes He endured were *for* our healing. The Bible says, by His stripes we *were* healed. Not that we're going to be—we were. Johnnie Mae is not the sick trying to get healed; she *was* healed by Jesus' stripes over two thousand years ago. It's already done. Now . . . I'm going back in there and lay hands on her and pray and speak the Word only and believe. I believe my wife *will* recover, do you hear me? I know it. And how do I know? By faith. My faith is all the evidence I have to show you, but I believe it's already done. Therefore, I will act like I believe. And if that means putting all the negative people who are hindering God's Word from going forth in that room out, including you and the doctors if I'm forced to, then I'll have all of you put out."

"What?" Rachel asked, jerking back in disbelief as she placed her hand on her hip.

"You heard me. I didn't stutter when I said it. I don't care if they intend to turn the machines off tomorrow or the next day. Right now is an opportunity for God's power to be shown in action. We talk a good talk. But God is looking for faithwalkers. When Jesus went in to heal Jairus's daughter, they laughed Him to scorn. And the Bible says that Jesus put them out. As a follower of Jesus, if I find I have to, I'll start putting folks out or bar them from going in if I feel they're a hindrance for God's healing power to go forth."

Rachel started laughing. "You see, now I know you done lost your mind! That's what happens with you Jesus folks. George, that was Jesus that did that. I know Jesus, and, Pastor Landris, you're no Jesus. These doctors will get a court order on you if they have to. You know they will. That's what that doctor told me yesterday. They will get a court order to have the machines turned off if they feel they need to."

"Rachel, I'm not trying to argue with you right now. And as for that doctor and getting a court order, the Word of God says that no weapon formed against me shall prosper. The point is, Jesus did great works. He said we would do greater works than He did. I believe that, and I intend to operate in it."

"And you're going to look foolish doing it, too."

"Then so be it!" Landris started walking back toward the door. He turned around. "From now on, when you come through this door, you should consider this the no-doubter zone. In other words, if you can't leave your doubts on this side of the door, then don't bother bringing them in there with you."

"You're really crazy, do you know that?" She stepped closer to him.

"So I'm crazy, huh? I've lost my mind? Okay, so we've all but lost Johnnie Mae already, in your eyesight. So tell me, sister-in-law, what do I have to lose if this doesn't work?"

Rachel grabbed him by his upper arm. "George, why don't you go in there and prove *everybody* wrong! Oh, I pray that you do. I pray that God not only hears you, but that He answers your prayer. For my sister's sake, for the sake of all those who want to believe that God not only *can* but *will* move in a mighty way. Go on, George. Prove to *everybody* who may have ever doubted God that we *were* and *are* wrong!"

Landris nodded and smiled at her as he placed a hand on her shoulder and patted it. "So . . . are you coming back in?"

"Sorry, George, I'm going to wait on this side. From what I've been told, beyond that door is the no-doubter zone. But if you don't mind, will you please tell my children and grandchildren to come on out so we can go home, and to bring my mother out with them? And George, when Johnnie Mae awakes, give her a kiss for me, will you?" She nodded, then covered her mouth with her hand as she held in her cry.

Chapter 50

It was seven PM, and Landris was alone with Johnnie Mae. He quietly played some of her favorite old-time gospel and contemporary gospel songs while reading scriptures to her from the books of Proverbs, Psalms, and Isaiah. He played a CD he'd recorded on healing and the power of what Jesus has already done for those who believe. Landris took his wife's lifeless hand and prayed with her as fervently and passionately as if she'd been awake and was participating in the prayer with him. He was determined he would continue this vigil through the night. An RN came in from time to time to check on Johnnie Mae.

As the RN was getting ready to leave the room, a little after ten o'clock, she touched Landris on his shoulder. "Pastor Landris, I've never been one to go to church much. But if you don't mind me saying, there's something special about the way you worship and praise God even in the midst of your trials and tribulations that makes me want to know more about Him. Whatever you have, I sure would like some of it."

"God is a person, not an it," Landris said with kind correction. "And He is *truly* worthy to be praised," he said. "When things are going great for us, we should praise Him. When things aren't going so great, we still should praise Him, with our eyes fixed on what He's *going* to do to turn things around. I'm not moved by what I see. For in the natural right now, I'm being told that it looks like there's little hope. I live by faith—faith in who God is and not merely in what He can do. If God never does another thing for me, if God never answers another prayer request, I will still praise Him just for who He is. God is worthy to be praised. Therefore, I praise Him when I'm up, and I praise Him when I'm down."

"You've been told by the doctors that your wife is not doing well," the nurse said, "yet there is such a peace about you. That's the kind of peace I'd like to have. You possess a joy that seems to exude from you . . . like you're expecting something good to happen any minute. I want that kind of joy in my life."

Landris continued to hold Johnnie Mae's hand as he stood and faced the nurse. "Serving the true and living God will have that kind of effect on you. He'll give you a peace that truly does surpass all understanding. I can't explain to you why I'm able to stand in the midst of the storms of life and be at peace, except to tell you that having Jesus onboard makes all the difference in the world. There's something about knowing Jesus is on-board that allows you to sleep like a baby even when the ship is being tossed and driven. When God gives you joy, it's an unspeakable joy, the kind the world can't give and the world has no power to take away—a joy that becomes strength in weakness." He smiled briefly. "I have a question for you. Are you saved?"

She gave him a quick grin. "No, I'm not. I've seen too much hypocrisy in so-called Christians. It's a huge turnoff. I decided a long time ago if that's how being a Christian is, then I didn't care to have any part of it."

"Listen to me. You can't allow other folks to keep you

from receiving salvation. When you face Judgment Day—and you will someday—you're going to have to stand for yourself. You'll be asked why you should be allowed into Heaven. How will you answer that question? Are you going to say you chose not to accept Jesus as your Savior because of how other people, who said they were Christians, acted?" Landris shook his head again. "I'm sorry, but that excuse is not going to fly in Heaven."

"Then what do I say? That none of the Christians I knew and met during my lifetime ever bothered to stop and minister to me? That they saw I wasn't living right but felt it wasn't their job or place to at least tell me about Jesus and His plan for salvation? Pastor Landris, there are plenty of nurses here who profess to be Christians. They make a huge show, carrying and reading their Bibles. But not one of them has ever taken the time to talk to me about Jesus. They talk about their family, their problems—large and small, as though there is no hope. They talk *a lot* about other folks. But not one has bothered to ask me if I'm saved or talk to me about becoming saved the way you are doing now. It's like Jesus is a sort of symbol they use to show how great *they* are, instead of a testament to how great He is. But the way you've been these few times I've seen you since your wife was moved to this floor makes me desperately want what you have. So please tell me, Pastor Landris, what must I do to be saved?"

Landris gently released Johnnie Mae's hand, careful to place it lovingly next to her side. He glanced quickly at the nurse's badge to make sure he had her name correctly. "Jackie," he said, "the Bible says we were all sinners, born into sin because of what the first man, Adam, did. Because of sin, we were separated from God our Father. The Bible declares that the wages of sin is death. But Jesus, God's only begotten Son, the second man, Adam, voluntarily came down to earth to die on the cross to pay for our sins. Mine, yours, my wife's, the world's ... He died for all our sins. Essentially, Jesus was crucified in our place. Jesus went to hell in our place. And on the third day, God raised Jesus up from the dead. Now, by faith, do you believe this?"

Jackie was crying now. She nodded as she spoke. "Yes," she said. "I believe that."

Landris took her by both hands. "Then I want you to repeat after me. Lord, I'm a sinner. Please come into my heart."

Jackie repeated the words as instructed.

"I confess with my mouth the Lord Jesus Christ. And I believe in my heart that God has raised Him from the dead."

Jackie said those words as she kneeled down on the floor and began to cry even more. She began to thank God for His mercy and His grace as she continued to weep.

"The Bible tells us that if we confess with our mouth the Lord Jesus Christ and believe in our hearts that God has raised Him from the dead we shall be saved. You're saved now because you believe in Jesus and what He did to save you from sin. You're now an heir and a joint-heir with Jesus Christ, my new sister in Christ, and legally part of God's royal family. Jackie, let me be the first to welcome you to the family of God. God is worthy to be praised." Landris released her hands and began giving God a wave offering.

"Thank You, Jesus," Jackie said, crying as she looked upward with her arms extended high. "Thank You for dying for my sins. Oh Lord, I've done so much wrong, but You loved me. Before I ever knew You, You loved me. Thank You for saving me."

"Thank You, Lord," Landris said, praising God along with her. "Oh, we thank You, Lord. I know You and all the Heavenly hosts are rejoicing right now as one more

soul has been added to the church—not a building, but
the body of Christ. Lord, we thank You for this sister.
Touch her right now, in Jesus' name. You know what she's
in need of. Pour out a special blessing upon her. Release Your anointing on us. Lord, You're awesome. In
the midst of everything that's going on, even now, I feel
Your presence in this place. I feel You moving right now.
Move, Lord! Heal, Lord! Show Yourself strong, Lord! I
bind the works of the devil, right now in Jesus' name. I
loose Your angels to perform the Word that You have sent.
I speak life! I thank You for healing right now. Thank
You, Lord." Landris paced near the bed. "Thank You,
Lord. Yes, we praise You. Yes, Lord. Yes, Lord. My soul
says yes!"

Landris started jumping up and down. He was trying to keep it quiet since he didn't want to disturb other
patients. But it was hard for him to hold his peace.
Jackie was jumping up and down, too, praising God.
Landris walked over and took Johnnie Mae's hand as
he continued his prayer. "Johnnie Mae is already healed,
Lord. My wife . . . my helpmeet, bone of my bone and
flesh of my flesh . . . by Your stripes, she's already
healed, in Jesus' name. In Jesus' name. Now, let Your
Word be true and anything that man has declared that
is contrary to Your Word, let it fall right now, Lord."

"I feel Your presence," Jackie said, obviously amazed.
"He's real. God is real," she said. "I've never felt anything like this before in all of my life." She began waving her hands in the air. "Thank You, Jesus! Thank You
for saving me. Little old me! Thank You for loving me
so much that You laid Your life down for me! For me.
No one has ever loved me like that. I thank You for the
work You're doing in this room right now."

Landris kneeled down beside the bed as he continued to hold onto Johnnie Mae's hand. "Lord, Your Word
says we will be able to lay hands on the sick, and they

will recover. Your Word says, when we pray, we should believe that we have received. *When* we pray, that's what Your Word declares. I have prayed, I've delighted myself in You, regardless of what things have looked like. I now believe I *have* received the desires of my heart! I thank You. Thank You, Jesus."

Suddenly, Landris felt a slight squeeze to his hand. He stopped, wondering if it had just been his mind playing tricks on him or merely some type of involuntary movement. He stood and stared at Johnnie Mae, trying to see if what he thought had actually occurred, in fact had. "Look. Did you see that?" Landris asked Jackie. He leaned closer. "Johnnie Mae, open your eyes," he said. "Johnnie Mae, I need you to open your eyes. Come on now. In the name of Jesus, I command you to open your eyes!"

Landris could see it. As he stood there watching her, Johnnie Mae looked like she was definitely struggling to open her eyes.

"We need a doctor here," Landris said, controlling his tone so as not to be too loud, as he glanced at Jackie, who was already on her way out the door. Quickly, his attention returned to Johnnie Mae's face. "Come on, baby. Come on. You can do this. I'm right here. Come on, now. Open your eyes."

Johnnie Mae squeezed his hand a little again. Then, just as a butterfly's wings flutter before the butterfly takes flight and flies away, Johnnie Mae opened her eyes. She looked at him and struggled to reach up, as though she was trying to touch his face. Then, there it was: a tiny smile crossed her face for her beloved.

"Landris," she mouthed his name.

Chapter 51

Even every one that is called by My
name: for I have created him for My
glory, I have formed him; yea, I have
made him.

Isaiah 43:7

Johnnie Mae recovered rapidly following that fateful, faith-full night. It was amazing to all just how quickly. To take some of the miracle buzz making its rounds throughout the hospital away, a few of the doctors who'd declared hope was all but gone reported that it wasn't at all uncommon for someone to come out of coma, even years later, to a full recovery. Johnnie Mae had no damage whatsoever to any part of her body. Her heart was good, her brain was fine, and she hadn't suffered a stroke, which had been a major concern. The next day, she was moved to a different floor.

A nurse stuck her head inside the door of Johnnie Mae's room. "We have a surprise for you," she said as the door opened wider. And there, in a special incubator crib, was Johnnie Mae and Landris's baby boy. Landris, who had opened the door for them, came in behind them.

Seeing her son, Johnnie Mae placed her hands over her mouth and began to cry.

"Oh, please don't cry," the nurse said. "This little fellow has waited a long time, a whole month, to meet you. We even put him in a special little doodad," she said, referring to his blue hooded outfit, "especially for this first meeting."

The nurse gave Johnnie Mae something to sanitize her hands. Then she carefully took the baby out. "Mommy, he's doing so good," the nurse said. "From what I hear from Daddy, the doctors say if the two of you continue improving like you're doing, you both may be going home close to the same time." She placed the baby in Johnnie Mae's awaiting arms.

"Only one thing," the nurse continued as she released him into Johnnie Mae's care, "I believe he *might* be getting a small complex. See, all the other babies have names, and, as you can tell, his placard still says 'Boy Landris.' Now, Mommy, I've been told we've been waiting on you to give this little jewel a name." She looked at Landris and grinned.

Johnnie Mae couldn't take her eyes off her son. "He's beautiful! Oh, Landris, look at him. Isn't he beautiful?"

"Oh, you should have seen him before we started him on that workout routine," Landris said. "The doctors and nurses had their routine for him to do, and I had mine."

"Workout routine?" Johnnie Mae asked, looking to Landris for a better explanation.

"Yeah, workout routine," Landris said. "His faith workouts. He and I have been lifting the Word of God, getting all fit and in shape, like nobody's business. Go ahead—ask him about a scripture. Any scripture. He can probably tell you chapter and verse for some of them." Landris grinned. Seeing his wife and baby son in tandem, he thought how perfect they looked together. He took out his cell phone and, using the camera feature, quickly snapped their picture.

"Landris, don't be doing that," Johnnie Mae said, smoothing down her hair with her hand. "I know I look a hot mess . . . like death warmed-over right now. My hair grew out, while you—on the other hand—went and cut yours completely off. I still can't believe you did that." She looked at his low-cut hairstyle and smiled. "But I like it."

"What did you just say?" the nurse asked Johnnie Mae. "A hot mess? Death warmed-over? I've heard a lot in my day, but I can't say I've ever quite heard it put like *that* before. And if you ask me, I don't see anything wrong with either of your hair. But then again, I'm a red-headed white woman who has trouble deciding whether to part or not to part my hair, and if so, which side, so what do I know?"

"Johnnie Mae, you look beautiful," Landris said, handing his phone to the nurse. "Will you do us the honors of taking our very first family photo, please?" He stepped over next to Johnnie Mae and placed his face against hers. "Say cheese, baby Landris," Landris said.

"Isaiah," Johnnie Mae said.

Landris turned to her. "What?" he said, just as the camera snapped.

"Oh, you moved," the nurse said to Landris. "Now we'll have to take it again." She held the camera up once more. "Okay, ready this time? On the count of three. One, two, three." She snapped it again, then looked at the screen. "Oh, that's a good one!"

"Isaiah," Johnnie Mae said, looking from her son's face to her husband's. "I'd like to name him Isaiah." She then directed her attention exclusively to Landris. "Will you be terribly disappointed . . . I mean, if he's not a junior or the second?"

"Honestly, I'm just grateful to God that Isaiah is finally in his mother's arms."

The nurse handed Landris his phone. She pulled a clipboardlike holder from below the portable crib. "Middle name?" she asked. "Little Isaiah here needs a middle name. If you'll give that to me, then we can finish this form for his birth certificate, you two can sign it, and we can get this baby filed with the State of Alabama and make his name official."

Johnnie Mae looked up at Landris. "Do you have any preferences for a middle name? Any ideas?"

Landris looked at her, then the baby. "You and I were tossing around a few names at one time, remember? I just don't know."

"Well, you can think about it and let us know later," the nurse said. "Someone from the business office usually gets this information. They asked me because they knew I was coming in. Someone can come back and get his middle name later."

"How about Barron Edward?" Landris asked.

"What are you saying? You don't like the name Isaiah?" Johnnie Mae asked.

"No. I mean, no, that's not what I'm saying. Isaiah is a great name. In fact, I've been studying the book of Isaiah these past few weeks. I read passages to you while you were in that coma. What I mean is . . . let's name him Isaiah Barron Edward Landris."

"Four names?" Johnnie Mae said. "Can we do that on a birth certificate?" She looked to the nurse for an answer.

"Sure," the nurse said, looking at the form. "There's nothing that says you can't."

"Isaiah Barron Edward Landris," Johnnie Mae said, repeating it several times. "Oh, I love that! It's so strong." She touched her baby's tiny arm. "What do you think, Isaiah?"

"Well, not that I count, but I love it, too," the nurse said as she wrote it down and handed the board to Landris. "If you two will look that over, be sure everything's correct, then sign it, you'll be all done with giving this precious, precious baby a name that I'm sure all the other babies will be envious of when he returns." She smiled. "Now, don't you go in there telling the other babies I said that, either," she said to Isaiah as she winked. She went over to the wall and pressed the bottle to apply sanitizer to her hands.

"Okay, I have to get little Isaiah back to his temporary place of residence," the nurse said, reaching out for him and taking him out of a reluctant Johnnie Mae's arms. "He's still lifting his weights, as Daddy put it, so he can continue growing better and bigger and stronger. Aren't you, little fellow?" the nurse said in a baby-friendly voice to Isaiah. "We don't want to tire him out too much, especially on his first official day out to see you, now, do we?" she said, again saying that last part using a baby-friendly voice.

Landris and Johnnie Mae signed the form as the nurse carefully placed Isaiah back inside his portable crib. Landris handed the clipboard, with the signed paper, back to the nurse.

"When can I see him again?" Johnnie Mae asked.

"Don't worry," Landris said, "I'll take you in to see him whenever you want. Just as long as you promise me you won't try and overdo things. You're still recovering, you know?"

The nurse pushed Isaiah's crib to the door. "Tell Mommy and Daddy bye-bye," the nurse said as she stood waving. "Say 'Bye-bye, Mommy. . . . Bye-bye, Daddy. I'll see you later,'" she said, mimicking the way Isaiah would probably say it if he could talk.

"See you later, Isaiah," Johnnie Mae said as she blew him butterfly kisses. "Bye-bye. . . . Mommy loves you. Bye." She waved until he was gone. She looked at Landris, rubbed his hair on one side of his head, lovingly caressed his face, then began to cry.

He held her in his arms. "I know, baby. I love you," he said. "Truly, I do."

Chapter 52

Declaring the end from the beginning, and from ancient times the things that are not yet done, saying, My counsel shall stand, and I will do all My pleasure. . . .

Isaiah 46:10

It was the last day of August 2005, and Gayle stood before those in attendance at the reading of Sarah Elaine Fleming's last will and testament to say a few words.

"Miss Fleming asked me, a few months after I came to work for her, if I would consider being the executor of her will," Gayle began. "I told her that I knew nothing about doing anything like that. She assured me that her lawyer"—she nodded to acknowledge Lance Seymour—"would handle all relevant details, and all I would need do was to carry out certain wishes and duties associated with it as requested or required."

Gayle took two steps to her right. "I, like all of you here today, will truly miss Sarah Fleming. Miss Fleming was more than someone I took care of medically, more like a beloved family matriarch than an employer. One of the most joyous occasions I've ever been blessed to have been a part of was this past June when we came together and celebrated Christmas in what some would call out-of-season. As those of us who attended know, it was very much *in* season and very much on time. Who knew that would be her last Christmas celebration? It was indeed Miss Fleming making her exit on her own terms. She almost reached her ninetieth birthday, but that was not to be. She taught us to live in the now and to celebrate each moment as though it were our last. In truth, none of us really know when our last day will be." Gayle nodded as she pursed her lips.

"Most of her wishes are self-explanatory," Gayle said. "I'm sure with some things, you may have questions about why things were done the way they were, or what she may have intended. I'll do my best to answer any questions I'm asked, as best I can. But I can only relay to you what she told me. That being said, I'll turn the actual reading of the will back into the capable hands of her lawyer and good friend, Mr. Lance Seymour."

After the reading was over, Memory sat there utterly stunned. Gayle had been correct about most things not needing to be explained. But there were a few things, not actually regarding the will, she wanted to know for herself.

Memory pulled Gayle off to the side. "May we talk?" she asked.

Gayle smiled. "Sure. Let's go find a room where we can have some privacy."

They went down the hall of Mr. Seymour's place, a once-quaint house now converted into an office building, and found a small room with a couch. Gayle closed the door once they were inside, and they sat down.

Memory bit down on her bottom lip, then pressed her lips together. "My mother was more than generous to me in her will. Frankly, I'm still taken aback by the vastness of her wealth. She was quite charitable to many. Having known her, even for just that short time, I learned the type of person she was. She was truly a remarkable and caring person. I am curious, though, as to how you managed to be chosen as the executor of her will. Listen, I don't know how to say it except to just say it," Memory said.

Memory folded her hands, then placed them in her lap. "Gayle, something, quite frankly, isn't adding up for me about you. You see, twice, once before the Christmas celebration, and then again just before my mother died, I heard you on the phone talking to Montgomery. I know it was him because I overheard you address him by his name both times. I had fully intended to talk with you about that, after the celebration was over, but I wanted to put some distance between such a joyous occasion, and what I knew could potentially turn into an all-out war in the house if things went badly."

Memory looked down at her hands, then back up. "She and I were in her room talking. We were eating chocolate cake. You of all people knew how much she loved chocolate. We were really bonding, having a great time together. She was laughing, then suddenly she got quiet. I thought she'd fallen asleep. Just that fast, she was gone."

Gayle looked at Memory. She tilted her head to the side. "You really *do* favor her. . . . Your mother. You favor her a lot. Especially your eyes. You have her eyes." Gayle smiled. "Memory, there's something I want to tell you. Your mother asked me not to let you or Lena know this originally, but a few days before the Christmas celebration, she said it was okay to tell you anything I felt I needed to. Sarah knew I had talked to Montgomery those days and all the other times before that. In fact, my talking and dealing with him was all her idea."

Memory chuckled. "Gayle, now I *was* born during the day, but let me assure you, it wasn't yesterday. You're going to have to do a lot better than that to pull one over on an old pro like me. Now, it's my understanding that Montgomery, as well as his father before him, did a lot of damage to my mother's life. It was because of their actions that we were both robbed of precious time together. So why would my mother have you talking to the likes of Montgomery at all?"

"It's true, Montgomery did do a lot of damage. Which is why, when I came to work for Sarah, she devised a plan for us to ensure he would never get a foothold or gain that much power over her, her children, or her children's children ever again. Those were her exact words."

"How do I know that you weren't just playing her?" Memory asked. "What if you merely took advantage of an elderly woman like so many others have done in the past? Look, I've done my share of getting-close-and-doing-people-in in my lifetime. I know how this works. This would have been a sweet gig for you—money, power, and wealth, all rolled up into one."

"Memory, your mother trusted me. She trusted me with her life. What you don't know is that the legendary Pearl Black was my grandmother. Her last name was Williams after she married, but most folk still called her Pearl Black. Before my grandmother died, she told me the story of Sarah and her child—that would be you. She'd heard from a woman named Johnnie Mae Landris—I know you're familiar with her—that your mother was possibly still alive. She knew for a fact that unless you'd died after you were with the Pattersons, you were still alive. She told me if there was ever a time where I found I could make things right for Sarah Fleming, she wanted me to do it. I made her a promise that I would. In fact, my grandmother made me promise her two things on that day. So when Sarah needed a home-nurse, I applied for the job. Her lawyer, Mr. Seymour, didn't play when it came to Miss Fleming, especially in the early days when everyone was looking for Montgomery to retaliate in some way. Mr. Seymour and his people did all kinds of background checks on me, both officially and unofficially."

"I'm sorry, but I'm not familiar with Pearl Black. . . ." Memory paused. "Wait a minute. Pearl Black, that was the woman Grace spoke about on the videotape—you mean, that Pearl Black?"

Lena opened the door and stuck her head inside. "I'm sorry. I don't mean to interrupt, but we were worried about you," she said to Memory. "I really wasn't trying to eavesdrop, but did I just hear y'all saying something about Pearl Black?"

"Yes, I just told Memory that Pearl Black was actually my grandmother," Gayle said.

Lena looked shocked. "Pearl Black was your grandmother?"

"Yes. Please come in and sit while I finish the story," Gayle said. "This will save me from having to repeat it to you later, Lena." Gayle scooted over so there would be room for Lena to sit next to Memory.

"As I was telling Memory, Pearl Black was my grandmother," Gayle said, continuing. "I came to work for Miss Fleming at the end of October 2001. And yes, Miss Fleming told me everything, so I know you're familiar with Pearl Black, as well as her significance to your family," Gayle said, addressing Lena at this time.

"I was up front with Miss Fleming from the start about who I was," Gayle said. "Still, Mr. Seymour checked me, and my story about who I was, out thoroughly. As I was just telling Memory, when it came to Miss Fleming, Lance Seymour was always superprotective. I told Miss Fleming all that my grandmother, Pearl, had told me before she died." Gayle then repeated all she'd said that Lena had previously missed.

"Miss Fleming decided to keep who I was a secret from everyone, including her family," Gayle said. "When a man like Montgomery Powell the Second is involved, you can never be too careful."

"I'm sitting here wondering why Grandmother never

told us any of this," Lena said. "She knew I was familiar with Pearl Black. In all these years, she could have
mentioned *something* to *me. Something.*"

"I can't answer that question, but when Montgomery
learned I was employed as Miss Fleming's personal private home-nurse," Gayle said, "as expected, he wasted no
time in contacting me and making me a lucrative offer.
I listened to what he had to say, then told Miss Fleming
everything. She was the one who came up with the plan."

"What plan?" Memory asked.

"That I would keep my identity from everyone including her family and close friends, that I would keep
a low profile so as not to draw attention to myself, and
that I would not only *talk* to Montgomery but agree to
cooperate with him as much as possible. I would essentially be like a double agent."

"So Montgomery wanted you to spy on Grandmother?" Lena asked.

"Yes. He wanted to know everything he could about
her intentions, who she talked with, who she visited,
who visited her, who she trusted—"

"Who was in her will when it came to her house,"
Memory said.

"Exactly. Things like that." Gayle stood up and began
pacing as she spoke. "Miss Fleming always told me
what to tell him. I quickly gained his trust as a reliable
informant, just as she'd planned. Even at almost ninety,
Miss Fleming was truly a sharp lady, sharper than most
that are a third her age."

"So you were the one who told Montgomery about
the problems between me, Lena, and Theresa?" Memory asked.

"Yes. I told him about your having taken the Alexandrite necklace from them, which, as it turns out, was like
he'd hit the jackpot. He had the necklace, which neither

of us knew at the time. He was ecstatic, thinking things were finally 'falling into place perfectly,' as he put it."

" 'Falling into place' because he had been the one to pay the reward for the Alexandrite necklace that caused me to go searching for Lena in order to get it back in the first place," Memory said.

"Yes. But that wasn't part of the plan," Gayle said. "He'd gotten the necklace back before things turned around so badly for him when Miss Fleming returned to the Fleming mansion and took possession of it. Originally, he wanted the necklace because it was part of the family's legacy . . . a family heirloom."

"A family heirloom he obviously didn't have a problem letting go of when it suited his needs," Memory said, referring to how he was willing to trade the necklace for her promise to sell him the house.

"Knowing that the necklace had caused such a rift in your relationship with your child and grandchild fit right into his new plan," Gayle said, standing in front of them. "I'm not implying, by any means, that he shared his thoughts and plans with me. But when things are going well for Montgomery, there's a certain gleam in his eyes, and he *loves* to brag."

"But why would you tell him we were having problems?" Lena asked. "Didn't you know he would use it to try and destroy us if he could?"

Gayle looked more at Lena as she answered her. "My instructions from Miss Fleming were to do whatever it took to make him believe I was on his side. As long as Montgomery trusted me, he would be satisfied with coming to me for information he needed inside the house. That always provided Miss Fleming with a heads-up. I had no way of knowing he had that necklace in his possession to be able to use against you. I could never have guessed that."

"So you were the one who took the necklace and the Wings of Grace box out of Lena's room that night?" Memory asked, sitting back against the couch.

Gayle shook her head. "No, it wasn't me."

"Then who was it, and how did Grandmother get it back?" Lena asked.

"It was her friend Polly. We had suspected Polly might be playing both sides, but we weren't positive how much she was, if she was. Miss Fleming never told me this, but I believe Polly purposely sought her out to befriend her. Although I will say that after Polly spent time with Miss Fleming and got to really know her, she genuinely did care about her. I'm certain that couldn't have done anything except complicate whatever deal she may have had with Montgomery."

"That makes no sense," Memory said. "I don't understand. How could Polly have gotten the necklace and the box? She wasn't anywhere around when it came up missing."

"Polly had a key to the house. Miss Fleming trusted her that much, in spite of her suspicions about her and her loyalty. Miss Fleming learned from Mr. Seymour's people that Polly knew Montgomery well. They happened to roll in the same circles. When Miss Fleming got sick that Saturday and was taken to the hospital, I called Polly to let her know. From what Miss Fleming told me after she learned the truth, Polly came in right before your husband"—Gayle looked at Lena—"came in from playing golf. She saw the necklace and the box on the bed, when she heard someone enter the house. She took the necklace, put it in the box, and left your bedroom. She went to Miss Fleming's bedroom, feeling she'd have an easier time explaining being in there if she got caught."

"I still don't understand. Did she take the box and necklace home? Did she give it to Montgomery?" Memory asked. "What did she do?"

"Fortunately for y'all, she hid it under Miss Fleming's bed with plans to get it later," Gayle said. "And that's where I found them. Actually, it was Miss Fleming who figured all this out and told me where to find them."

"So why didn't she tell us?" Lena asked. "She knew we were trying to find out who took those things. We even questioned you, Gayle."

"Miss Fleming believed deep down Polly was still a good woman. Polly had made a mistake by getting in bed with Montgomery, and I mean that both figuratively and literally. But Miss Fleming cared very much for her. Polly and Miss Fleming had shared lots of great and memorable times together. She was never one to just throw love she had for a person away merely because things had gone badly."

"So that's why she left that brooch to Polly in her will?" Lena said, happy that some things were starting to make a little more sense. "Grandmother took the brooch out and showed it to me right before the Christmas celebration. She told me how much Polly adored it, and just how much it was worth," Lena said. "She was planning on giving it to Polly as a present during our Christmas in June festivity. A festivity Polly was noticeably absent from. Now we know why."

Lance Seymour knocked, then opened the door when he was told to come in. "We were wondering where y'all went. You gals all right in here?" he asked with his deep, pure, unadulterated Southern drawl.

Gayle smiled. "Yes, we're fine."

Lena stood up. "I need to go find Theresa and Richard. I'm sure they're probably wondering if I got lost when I came looking for you. It's getting late. I know everyone's ready to get on home."

Memory nodded as she slowly stood up. Lance and Lena left together. Memory and Gayle stayed behind a few minutes longer.

"I want to thank you for all you did for my mother," Memory said.

"Memory, your mother was truly one in a million," Gayle said. "She loved you more than you'll ever know. I'm going to miss her—truly, I am. But she certainly surprised me leaving me that one hundred thousand dollars in her will. I had no idea she was doing anything like that. No idea. This shows how much executors really know."

"Yes, she was a special woman. I only wish I'd gotten to spend more time with her. That's the tragedy of all of this. But I do love how she put the house in a trust for Theresa's children. Now, that was a real classy move." Memory laughed. "Especially in light of Montgomery's plans to try and get that house. Checkmate!" Memory shook her head as she smiled, looked down, then back up. "So, what are your plans now?"

Gayle shrugged. "I told you earlier how I'd promised my grandmother two things. One, if I ever got the chance to do right by Sarah Fleming, I would. Well, I've accomplished that. Seeing all of you together is such a fantastic feeling. The other thing my grandmother asked me to do was to see if I could locate her oldest daughter, Arletha. I doubt she's still living, but I promised my grandmother I would at least find out what happened to her."

Memory laughed. "That's funny. I met a woman named Arletha a few months back. Arletha Brown is her name. Maybe this woman is the person you're looking for. Arletha is not a common name at all. This woman I met lives in Birmingham, Alabama."

"Interesting. I have a second cousin who moved to Birmingham a few years back. Her name is Angela Gabriel. We call her Angel. She's a member of Pastor Landris's church. You wouldn't happen to know her, would you?"

"No, I can't say our paths have ever crossed," Memory said.

"Angel's mother was Rebecca. She died when Angel was about five years old. My grandmother, Pearl Black, was the one who raised her. Arletha happens to be Rebecca's mother. Until just before my grandmother died, no one—including my grandmother—hardly ever spoke of Arletha or mentioned her name. My grandmother is the reason I ended up moving to Asheville. I came to see her before she died. After she passed away, Angel wanted to pursue a job opportunity in Birmingham. Grandmother's house would have been sitting there empty unless the family decided to rent it out. The thought of strangers in her house; not taking care of it . . . I just couldn't see that. So I bought my grandmother's house and moved in. I'm pretty sure the woman you met can't be my great-aunt," Gayle said as she glanced at her watch, then started for the door. "That would just be *too* easy. Nothing's ever *that* easy."

She and Memory walked out of the door. "Honestly," Gayle said, "I doubt Arletha is even still alive. According to my grandmother, she's been gone for almost fifty years now, by last count. And she never came home to see Grandmother in all of those years. Not once. I can't imagine—I don't care what might have happened—a daughter not *ever* going home to see her mother. Not ever? I do know there was a huge falling out that occurred between them. All Grandmother said was that her daughter was prostituting her body and being loose throughout the neighborhood. She wasn't about to have any daughter of hers acting like a tramp. Not while she was alive and breathing and could do something about it. She told me she even went as far as to disown her. So Arletha left one day, without a word, a good-bye, or anything else. Grandmother said she never heard from her again. She most likely married,

so her last name would be different, which always makes
a search that much more difficult."

"Well, like I said, Arletha is not a common name.
There's no harm in checking out this woman I met. But
there's no way the person you just described could be
this lady. I rented a room from her for a few weeks. She
is super-religious and very judgmental, especially of
sinners. But I'll be happy to give you her phone number and address. If it's not her, at least you can scratch
her name off your list."

"That sounds great," Gayle said. "Give me her information, and I'll check her out. My cousin, Angel, the
one I was just telling you about, is getting married October fifteenth in what my mother claims will be the
wedding to top all weddings, at least for our family.
I'm going, so I'll be in Birmingham in a few months.
Maybe I'll call this woman and see where it leads, although I'm not going to get my hopes up. Still, I promised my grandmother I would try. That's all I can do."

"Maybe you can get your cousin to do some legwork
for you since she lives in Birmingham. She could go
check out Arletha Brown for you."

"My grandmother specifically asked me not to tell
Angel anything unless or until I find Arletha." They
reached the lobby area and could see the rest of the
family was there waiting for Memory.

Gayle stopped walking so their conversation could
remain out of earshot. "As I said, my grandmother or
others in the family never spoke of Arletha, so Angel is
limited in what she knows. If I bring this up without
having found Arletha, it will just open up a can of
worms none of us need or want right now. I suppose
that's why Grandmother asked me to do this instead of
involving Angel. Between me and you . . . my grandmother always favored Angel over all her children,
grandchildren, and great-grandchildren. I'm not jeal-

ous, though. There's always seemingly a favored one in every family. My grandmother was extremely protective of Angel when she was alive. They were close."

"I understand," Memory said, looking in her pocketbook for a pen and a piece of paper to write down Arletha's phone number and address. She handed the information to Gayle. "In a way, I kind of hope this is what you're looking for. Although I'm not sure that after you meet the Arletha I knew whether you'll believe it to be a blessing or a curse. But at least if this turns out to be her, you would have kept yet another promise to your grandmother."

Gayle took the paper, looked at it, and carefully placed it in the side pocket of her purse.

"If you'll permit me," Memory said, "I'd like to give you a word of advice. This comes from personal experience. I believe it's always better to learn from someone else's bad experiences as opposed to having to always learn from your own. Secrets like these always have a way of coming back to haunt folks. Secrets can rob, and secrets can destroy. If I were you, I'd tell Angel what's going on, even if you never find her grandmother." Memory changed her purse to hang from her other shoulder.

"Personally," Memory continued, "I believe your cousin has a right to know. If I could go back and do things over in my life, there are so many things I would do differently. One thing, I never would have left Mamie Patterson's house the way I did. And I wouldn't have ever taken that necklace from Lena and Theresa. Then I may have learned about Sarah that much earlier, and who knows how much more time she and I might have had together. If only things had been done differently. But you can't go back and change things. So take heed to the counsel of one who knows from firsthand experience. It will be better, for all around, to be up front now. Allow my life to serve you in making a better choice as you proceed."

"I'll take those words under advisement," Gayle said. She and Memory hugged. Then Gayle walked over to the others and said her good-byes to them.

Gayle's job was done. It was now time for her to move on to other things.

Chapter 53

Wherefore comfort one another with these words.

1 Thessalonians 4:18

"In loving memory, the Harris family," the tall, lanky woman said, standing before an overflowing congregation, reading a pledge given, in lieu of flowers, of one thousand dollars toward a newly established scholarship created to bless deserving young people.

Because of her death, people were praying mightily for Pastor Landris. Many speculated as to how he could possibly preach a funeral for one so close and dear to his heart. They'd heard the explanation of why he said he *had* to do it. "It's what she would have wanted," he had said. He was laying aside his own grief and pressing toward the mark of a higher calling in Christ Jesus, just as he'd been anointed and appointed by God to do.

Still, there were plenty that doubted he'd be able to do this without breaking down.

A collective stillness swept over the congregation when he rose to speak. The white casket below was a blanket of beautiful white roses. Landris had truly spared no expense when it came to her. There was nothing more he could do to show his love for her on this side. This time of speaking would be to comfort and minister to those grieving the loss of a loved one or those who would lose a loved one in the future. He needed to tell those who might not know Jesus Christ all about His mercy that endures forever. He wanted to tell them what Jesus has already done to ensure the salvation of those who choose to accept Him as their Lord and Savior.

Landris would never be able to fully explain to anyone exactly why things had happened the way that they had. Yes, she *was* doing well. She had been through a lot, but she had also made it through. In truth, no one expected her to die—not now, anyway. Not when everything was going so wonderfully in her life. It had truly come as a shock.

Isaiah Barron Edward Landris had come home to a grand homecoming. Landris could be thankful and comforted in knowing that she'd at least gotten to spend time with Isaiah before she died. There were still many who questioned why God would allow this to happen. But Landris refused to be dragged into that conversation or speculation. He thanked God for the time she *did* have and for the precious moments she'd gotten to spend with her family prior to this tragedy happening. Landris thanked God for how He had allowed her to see and hold Isaiah. He thanked God for the memories he would forever cherish in his heart of her. Memories he would share with his son one day. Pictures that would forever be embedded, in loving memory, inside of him of her holding Isaiah in her arms . . . flooding his little face with kisses while proudly beaming.

Instead, Landris directed others to begin looking at what they have to be thankful for instead of always focusing on what's lost or what will never be experienced.

"Regardless of what happens," Landris had said, "God is *still* God, and He's *still* worthy to be praised."

He stood before a packed building—a magnificent edifice she'd reverently sat in, in awe of God's power, the day they had officially moved in it as a congregation—now to preach her funeral. There were so many who had come to show their love, support, respect, and to say good-bye. For a brief moment, his eyes rested on Princess Rose as she sat next to Johnnie Mae's mother and his heart couldn't help but go out to her.

"If you will, please open your Bibles to First Thessalonians chapter four, beginning at verse thirteen," Landris said, then waited as the congregation complied. "I want you all to understand that, although we *will* miss her"—he paused, composed himself, and nodded—"and I personally will miss her greatly, this is not a sad occasion. This is a celebration of the life of one who was loved and, to some, adored. This is a celebration for one who has gone home to be with the Lord. We know this is not our home. We didn't come here to stay. We're merely strangers passing through for a few seasons. And although she may have moved out of this earthly vessel, she's not really gone; she simply changed her address. As the apostle Paul so aptly declared, to be absent from the body is to be present with the Lord. She's with the Lord now. In truth, she's in a much better place than even we who remain are, because she *is* with the Lord."

Landris looked down at his Bible. "First Thessalonians four-thirteen says, 'But I would not have you to be ignorant, brethren, concerning them which are asleep, that ye sorrow not, even as others which have no hope.' Now, if I didn't read anything more, that Word right there should minister to someone. Our loved ones, who were in the Lord and have gone on, are not dead; they're merely asleep. 'For if we believe that Jesus died and rose again, even so them also which sleep in Jesus will God bring with Him.' Is anybody really seeing what's here? This scripture specifically addresses those who are saved, with salvation being the confession of sins and the belief that Jesus died and rose again. They are the ones who sleep in Jesus—those who are saved. This scripture

assures us that God will bring those who are asleep in
Jesus with Him. Oh, somebody ought to give God some
praise right about now," Landris said.

"Glory! Hallelujah!" people began to cry out along
with other words of praise.

"That's right," Landris said. "This is something to
be excited about. Verse fifteen goes on to say, 'For this
we say unto you by the word of the Lord, that we which
are alive and remain unto the coming of the Lord shall
not prevent them which are asleep.' Verse sixteen, 'For
the Lord himself shall descend from heaven with a
shout—'"

"Glory! Hallelujah! Thank You, Jesus," the people
said, interrupting him with shouts of praise.

Landris continued. " 'For the Lord Himself shall descend from heaven with a shout, with the voice of the
archangel, and with the trump of God: and the dead in
Christ shall rise first: Then we which are alive and remain shall be caught up together . . .' " He emphasized
the words "caught up" and paused as he raised his fist
in the air, fighting hard not to cry. "If we're not asleep,
so to speak, and we're here when Jesus comes back,
we're going to be *caught up* together with them"—he
looked back down at the scripture, blinking back the
tears that tried to blur his vision, and continued reading—" 'in the clouds, to meet the Lord in the air: and
so shall we ever be with the Lord.'" Landris couldn't
hold back. He began jumping up and down. He praised
God like he had never praised Him before. He couldn't
stop the tears that now freely flowed down his face.
"God is good!" he shouted. "God is good! I don't care
what's going on in your life, God is *still* good, and He is
worthy to be praised! She was saved, and now she's with
the Lord! I'm saved! Jesus saved me! Oh, it's *good* to be
saved! This is not the end here! When we come to this

place in life, this is not the end! God is so good! This is *not* the end of the story!"

The entire congregation was now on its feet, shouting and praising God. They shouted for at least ten minutes.

"If you're here today and you're not saved, or you've backslidden and you want to be restored . . . if you want to get back right with God, then will you come today and give your heart . . . give your life to Jesus? The Bible tells us that Jesus left the riches of Heaven and came down to earth. He walked on this earth, showing us how to live, move, and have our being. He was nailed to a cross, not for anything He'd done. He was crucified for our sins. Our sins. Jesus paid the price for you to have salvation. Freely He has given, freely you can receive. Don't allow the payment Jesus paid for your sins to be in vain. But to receive it, you must come to Him."

Landris stepped up to the edge of the stage. "Whosoever will, won't you come? My intent is not to cause an emotional decision about something this important during a time like this. But I have to put the information out there and give an invitation to come to Jesus because it *is* that important. I want you to meet me in Heaven.

"So every time I get the opportunity, I want to share the message of Jesus so someone who may not know Jesus will be able to hear about Him and accept Him. I'd really love to see everyone here at the gathering that will be in Heaven. And what a day that's going to be. I care about your salvation. God cares, and He doesn't want anyone to perish. There's no reason to. Jesus went to prepare a place for us. And they tell me that the wicked shall cease from troubling there. They say the weary will be at rest. Me, I just want to see Jesus. I want to see Him, face to face. And I won't waste time telling Him what folks did to me down here. He knows, He knows. I just want to walk and talk with Him in Heaven. I want to be in His presence. Do you want to ensure that your name is written in the Book of Life? Then come." Landris spread out his arms as he'd done so many times before.

And people did come. The ushers had them line up in the aisles. After those who were interested were in lines, they were led off to a prayer room to receive salvation or pray for restoration as needed.

The choir began to sing "When We All Get to Heaven."

Landris stepped down and walked over to the casket. "I love you," he whispered, as he kissed two fingers and touched the casket. "See you in Heaven," he said.

The pallbearers came forward to carry the casket out. Landris went to the front row where his family was and hugged his brother, Thomas.

"That was beautiful, George." Thomas gave Landris a long, brotherly embrace. "I don't know how you were able to do that. I know I couldn't have done it. But you did a wonderful job. I know she's looking down, and she is *so* proud of you. I just know that she is."

Landris nodded. He was so full now, he couldn't say anything. He left Thomas and walked over to get the baby. "Come on, Isaiah," he said. "Daddy's got you. Just like God has us safely in His arms, Daddy has you safely in his."

"You did good," Johnnie Mae said as she touched his arm once he had the baby securely on his shoulder. "I know God is pleased. You did what He's called you to do, in season and out of season. Many lives have been changed today. I am so proud of you right now. I know your mother is proud."

Johnnie Mae thought back on all that had happened over the past few months. She'd had a son prematurely. They both had almost died. But against all the odds,

God had brought them through. What a testimony they had to share with the world. Still, she thought of those who had died: Reverend Knight, Sarah Fleming, and now Landris and Thomas's mother, Virginia LeBoeuf. Three people she'd known personally, all within months of each other. She'd often heard her mother say that death seemed to always come in threes. She'd never really taken that statement much to heart. Nonetheless, there was no denying that three people she knew had transitioned. And because they were saved, she could rejoice knowing that they were now . . . present with the Lord.

Landris couldn't help but think about how his mother had come to Birmingham some three months ago expressly to support her family. He thought about how she'd been there when he and Johnnie Mae had needed her the most. How she'd taken care of Princess Rose and was right there when a healthy Isaiah Barron Edward Landris was finally released to come home. *What a day of rejoicing that day was!*

His mother had stayed a month longer, simply because she couldn't pull herself away from her grandchild when he came home. In fact, she was looking for a house to purchase. She was planning to move to Birmingham. She'd assured Landris she would be spoiling Isaiah; she'd already begun making good on her promise.

Then she went back to her own house, opting to have her bypass surgery there if it was still even needed. Landris and Thomas both insisted she could have the surgery in Birmingham, where all of her family already was. Everybody knew that UAB Hospital was world-renown for just that type of surgery. But she opted to go home anyway. She wanted to use the doctor she'd started out with when her heart problem first emerged. All of her records were there. It would just be easier, with less complications, to go home, and if the surgery was still needed, to have it there. Her doctor said she should have the surgery.

So Landris and Johnnie Mae packed up the family, including Thomas, and they went to be there for her the way she'd been there for them. She kept insisting she'd be fine. She had lots of friends and some family around who would gladly come by, check on her, and take care of her if she needed them to. She didn't want them leaving their home to come be with her, not now, not after all they'd been through. "Isaiah just got home. You guys have been through a lot. Spend this time with each other. I'll be back to Birmingham before you know it," Virginia had said.

But Landris wasn't hearing it, and neither was Johnnie Mae. Virginia had been there for them; now it was their turn to be there for her.

Virginia's doctor advised her she should have the surgery even though there were some noticeable improvements in her heart condition. So she consented to the surgery. She went into the operating room and suffered a heart attack during surgery. The doctors tried desperately, thirty minutes or so, to revive her. It was to no avail.

She died on the table.

Johnnie Mae put her arm around Landris as they walked behind the casket and behind Minister Maxwell, who led the recessional out of the church.

When they were about to get into the car to go to the cemetery, Landris leaned over and whispered, "I love you, Johnnie Mae. I really do."

She looked at him, took her thumb, wiped away the tears that rolled down his face, and, with a smile, she said, "I know." She wiped his tears once more, then wiped her own, and said, "I know."

Here's an excerpt from *The Truth Is the Light* . . .

Chapter 1

*The stone which the builders refused
is become the head stone of the corner.*
—Psalms 118:22

"Crown me!" said the ninety-nine-year-old, dark-chocolate-skinned man, who didn't look a day over seventy. He sat back against the flowery-cushioned chair and folded his arms, all while displaying a playful grin.

"Crown you?" said a thirty-five-year-old with matching skin tone, who resembled a slimmed-down teddy bear. Shaking his head, he mirrored the old man's grin. "*Crown* you?"

"That's what I said. So quit stalling and get to crowning me."

The younger man first started to chuckle before it turned into a refrained laugh. "Gramps, I've told you twice already: we're playing chess, not checkers. The rules are different. There's no crowning a piece when it reaches the other side, not in chess."

"You say that there is my queen, right?" Gramps touched the game piece that represented his queen.

"Yes."

"Well, if there's a queen, then there's *got* to be a king with some real power a lot closer and, frankly, better than this joker here." He touched his king. "So quit bumping your gums and crown me so I can get some real help in protecting my queen." Gramps nodded as he grinned at his favorite grandson, proudly displaying his new set of dentures.

Clarence Walker couldn't do anything but smile and shake his head in both amusement and adoration. "I've told you. Because there's already a king on the board"— he pointed to the king—"we don't crown in chess. Just admit it. You don't really want to learn how to play chess, do you? That's why you're acting this way."

"I tried to tell you from the git-go that I'm a checkers man and strictly a checkers man. When you get my age, it's hard for an old dog to learn new tricks. I know how to fetch. I know how to roll over and even play dead. But all this fancy stuff like walking on your hind legs and twirling around . . . Well, you can take that to some young pup eager to learn. Teach the young pups this stuff. With checkers, I move, I jump, and I get crowned when I reach the other side. Just like Heaven." He pointed his index finger and circled it around the board. "I get enough kings, I set you up, trap you, wipe the board with you, and like normal—game over." Gramps stroked his trimmed white beard.

Gramps was now on a roll. "All this having to remember pawns, knights, rooks, and bishops, which direction each moves in, how many spaces they can move when they move . . . I ain't got time for all of that. Then to have a king that's less powerful than his queen? Check and checkmate? Nope, I can't get with that. You know what your problem is, don't you? You don't like me whuppin' up on you like I normally do. You're trying to find somethin' that'll confuse old Gramps. Now is that check or checkmate?"

"No, Gramps. I'm merely trying to help keep you sharp. That's all. Studies show that when you do something new and different, it exercises your brain. You *do* know that your brain is a muscle, so it needs working out just like the rest of your body does."

"Humph!" Gramps said. "If I was any sharper, merely passing by me too closely would cut you." Gramps sensed his grandson had something more on his mind he wanted to talk about other than chess. Gramps leaned forward and placed his elbows on the table as he put his clasped hands underneath his chin. "Okay, so what's going on with you?"

Clarence sat back and became more serious. "Gramps, I'm getting baptized this coming Sunday night. I gave my life to Christ . . . for real this time. It wasn't just going forward to shake a preacher's hand like when I was twelve and my daddy made me do it to get it over with. Do you think you'd care to come and see me be baptized on Sunday?"

A smile crept over the old man's face as he leaned back against his seat. "So you done finally seen the light, huh?"

"Yeah, Gramps. I've finally seen the light. And I'm not running from the Lord anymore. Something happened to me on Sunday. I can't explain everything about it. But I know that the same man that walked into that building is not the same man that walked out. Something changed on the inside of me; it was an inside job. *I* see a difference."

The old man nodded. "Oh, you preaching to the choir now. I understand exactly how you feel. I ran from the Lord for a long time myself, both physically and figuratively." Gramps readjusted his slender body more comfortably. "I know your mama is happy about all of this. My baby girl has been doing some kind of praying for you, yes she has. And knowing your daddy like I do, I'm sure he acted like the father of the biblical Prodigal Son who finally returned home after wallowing for a time in a pigsty."

"Mom is *too* excited. She kept grabbing my face and pressing it in like she used to when I was a little boy. Like she wanted to be certain that I was really real—that it was actually me she was talking to and not some dream or figment of her imagination. Now Dad, on the other hand, probably would have been happy had I done this at *his* church."

Gramps leaned in. "Hold up there, whippersnapper. You mean to tell me you were somewhere else when this miraculous conversion occurred? You telling me this didn't take place at your daddy's church?"

"No, Gramps. It didn't happen at my daddy's church."

"Well, look out below! I'm sure *that* went over like a boulder falling off a tall building in New York City during lunchtime."

"You know my daddy."

"Yeah. Me, of all people, knows your daddy. Not one of my favorite folks in the world, that's for sure. No need in me trying to pretend he and I are bosom buddies, especially not after the way he treated my daughter. But Clarence, your father did give us you and your older brother, Knowledge. So I don't count him being in her life *all* bad."

Clarence tried to force a smile. "I told him about me being saved and about my scheduled baptism for Sunday. I asked him to come."

Gramps scratched his head. "You don't even have to tell how *that* conversation went. To him, you getting saved—and in another preacher's house at that—had to be the ultimate open-handed slap to his face. In his super-religious eyes, you are officially and publicly humiliating him. And everybody who's anybody knows your father loves the spotlight and equally detests being disgraced—intentional, accidental, or otherwise."

"That's the part of this that I don't understand. The greater point should be that I've repented of my sins and that I'm changing my ways. What difference does it make where it happened and with whom, as long as it happened? Daddy took it like I was deliberately trying to make him look bad . . . like I was purposely trying to embarrass him by getting saved under another pastor's leadership instead of his. But I heard God speak to my heart just as clearly. And in that moment, I knew I had to move right then and there. I realized where I end up spending my eternity depended on my receiving Jesus."

Gramps picked up his bishop's piece off the chess-board and held it up. He began to make air circles with it. "Are you following what God is telling you to do?" he asked.

"Yes, sir."

"Then Clarence Eugene Walker, in the end, that's all that really matters." Gramps set the bishop back in the same spot he'd picked it up from with a deliberate thud. "Marshall Walker ain't got no Heaven nor a Hell to put nobody in, 'Cause the Lord knows, if he had, I'da been in need of an eternal air conditioner ages ago. In fact, on more than a few occasions Marshall has flat-out told me which of the two places I could go, and believe me, it wasn't Heaven. But"—Gramps smiled—"as you can clearly see, I ignored both him and his hearty request. That's what *you* gonna have to do if your father is both-ering you about this. Don't let him get you off track, you hear?" Gramps struggled somewhat as he made his way to his feet with slight assistance from his grandson.

"I'm all right," Gramps said, asserting his indepen-dence to get up without help. "I've told you I can stand up fine. It just takes me a little longer to get my motor started, that's all. Eventually, I get it going, then watch out." He looked at Clarence, now shaking his head and grinning. Gramps nodded. "You can come pick me up Sunday evening," Gramps said as they left the activity room of the nursing home that he, for a year now, had called home. "If the Lord be willing and the creek don't rise, I'll be here waiting on you. There's nothing I'd love more than to see you be baptized." Gramps beamed.

They walked to Gramps's room. Inside, Gramps started grinning like a Cheshire cat as he looked down at Clarence's attaché case. "So, did you bring my stuff? I don't want you conveniently leaving here without giving it to me. I might be old, but as I just told you, my mind is still sharp. I ain't forgot, in case you're counting on me forgetting."

"Gramps, you and I both know I shouldn't be doing this."

"Boy, what did I tell you? I'm grown . . . past grown in case you've failed to notice. Now, did you bring my stuff in that fancy case of yours or not?" Gramps gingerly sat in the tan leather recliner with the built-in massager that his daughter Zenobia had given him Father's Day. He reached over and turned on the blue retro-styled radio, a modern-day replica of a 1950s automobile engine, that sat on his dresser. "Stand by Me" by Ben E. King was playing. Gramps closed his washed-out brown eyes and began to sway as he softly sang—his voice as strong as when he was twenty and just as smooth and calming as milk chocolate. There was no question where Clarence had inherited his singing voice.

"Now that's some real singing right there," Gramps said as the song trailed off. "Ben E. King, Nat King Cole, Otis Redding, Sam Cooke, Mahalia Jackson, Bessie Smith, Josephine Baker, Billie Holiday, Sarah Vaughan, Marvin Gaye, Aretha Franklin, Frankie, Ella, and Lena. And those are just a fraction of some of the greats of my time." Gramps held out a hand to let Clarence know he was still waiting on his "stuff."

Clarence opened his black case. "Gramps, we have some great singers in our time, too. Stevie Wonder,

Michael Jackson, Patti LaBelle, Janet Jackson, Beyoncé, Mariah Carey, Alicia Keys, Vickie Winans, Tramaine Hawkins, goodness! Smokie, Donnie, Kirk, Yolanda, Babyface, Raheem, Whitney, Celine . . . don't get me started." Clarence pulled out a blue, insulated lunchbox. "Then there are groups like Earth, Wind and Fire and En Vogue, who I hear are back." Clarence handed the lunchbox to Gramps. "Here. But I want to go on record that I don't feel right about this. I just want you to know."

Gramps unzipped the lunchbox, looked inside, and began to grin as he pulled out its contents as though the wrong move might cause it to explode. "Ah," he said, placing the still-warm, wax-papered-wrapped item up to his nose. He inhaled slowly and deeply, then exhaled with a sound of delight. The smoky aroma escaped into the room. "Just the way I like it, wax paper and all."

Clarence nodded. "Yeah, three rib bones with extra barbecue sauce, the sweet not vinegar kind, between two slices of white bread, wrapped in your favorite BBQ joint's signature paper." Clarence shook his head. "You *know* you're not supposed to have that."

"Yeah, well, you just make sure you keep your mouth closed about this. Don't tell your mother and we'll be fine. She's the only one trying to keep me from my barbecue rib sandwiches. Like I got these teeth, which incidentally cost a pretty penny, merely for show. Waste not, want not—I'm putting these bad boys to work." He clacked his teeth together. "You're a good grandson, Clarence. You really are. Now sing that song I love."

"You mean the one by Douglas Miller? 'My Soul Has Been Anchored'?"

"Yeah, that's the one." Gramps placed the sandwich on the dresser and handed the now-empty lunchbox back to Clarence.

Clarence put the lunchbox back in his attaché case, then began to sing—holding back his full voice so as not to disturb any neighboring or passing residents of the home.

Gramps closed his eyes briefly as he seemed to take in every note and every word with a metronome-like tick-tock of his head. When Clarence sang the final note, Gramps opened his teary eyes and nodded. "Yes," he said, pumping an open hand upward, "*my* soul's been anchored"—he swung a fisted hand while smiling—"in the Lord!"

Clarence nodded, hugged his grandfather, told him that he loved him, then left.

Chapter 2

*If thieves came to thee, if robbers by
night, (how art thou cut off!) would they
not have stolen till they had enough?
if the grape gatherers came to thee,
would they not leave some grapes?*

—Obadiah 1:5

Twenty-seven-year-old Gabrielle Mercedes and thirty-
year-old Zachary Wayne Morgan were at Gabrielle's
house in the kitchen cooking fajitas. They'd gone to a
highly acclaimed play Sunday night and had a wonderful time. Few Broadway plays made their way to Birmingham, Alabama, whenever those plays happened to
travel outside New York. Afterward, Zachary surprised
Gabrielle with tickets to "The Color Purple," scheduled
for the BJCC Concert Hall in October. Gabrielle couldn't
believe she was finally going to get to see this live
Broadway hit, after all of these years of wanting to.

The doorbell rang. Gabrielle glanced at the digital
clock on the stove. "I wonder who that could be." She
lowered the heat on the gas stove to simmer and rinsed
her hands at the sink, drying them on the large dish
towel she kept draped across the handle of the oven
door for just that purpose.

"I got it," Zachary said, turning the heat back to
medium as he took over stirring the rectangular-cut
strips of marinated steak in the large cast-iron skillet,
with plans to add fresh sliced red, yellow, and orange
sweet peppers and red onions prior to finishing it, in

order to maintain the vegetables' firmness. The doorbell rang again, this time repeatedly.

When Gabrielle saw who was standing there pressing the doorbell, she practically yanked her front door open.

"Well, it took you long enough," Aunt Cee-Cee said as she fanned her face with her right hand and stepped inside. "You must have been in the bathroom or something."

Cecelia Murphy was Gabrielle's aunt on her father's side. She'd taken Gabrielle in—raised her since she was three (close to four) years old after her mother was killed and her father convicted of her murder and sentenced to twenty-five years in prison.

"No. But I *was* busy. I have company in case you didn't notice the car parked outside when you pulled up," Gabrielle said, trying hard not to show her own frustration.

"You mean that black, two thousand and something Lincoln Town Car? I just thought you'd bought yourself another vehicle." Aunt Cee-Cee tilted her head back, nose up. "What's that I smell? Smells like it's coming from the kitchen?" She started walking in the direction of the scent. "It smells like someone's sautéeing onions and peppers."

"We're making fajitas," Gabrielle said, still holding the open door since she hadn't asked her aunt to come in. She was now hurriedly trying to figure out what she needed to do to lure her aunt back toward her and out the door.

"Well, it smells to me like I have fantastic timing," Aunt Cee-Cee said as she continued, undeterred, toward the kitchen. Gabrielle closed the front door and hurried to catch up with her now uninvited, unwelcome, and undeniably unpredictable guest.

"Seriously, Aunt Cee-Cee, this really isn't a good time right now—"

Aunt Cee-Cee stepped into the kitchen and saw Zachary just as he was turning off the stove and lifting up the large cast-iron skillet. He raked a little of the mixture of steak, onions, and colored peppers onto a flat, flour tortilla.

"Well, hello there," Aunt Cee-Cee said as she walked toward Zachary. "Well, well, aren't you some-thing? You must be the Handsome Chef." She let out a slight chuckle. "There's the Iron Chef. So I can only conclude you *have to be* the Handsome Chef who makes house calls." She scanned him from his head to his chest as she smiled.

Zachary looked at Gabrielle, who now stood next to the frumpy-looking visitor.

Zachary set the skillet back down on the stove. "No, but I thank you for the compliment. I'm Gabrielle's friend, Zachary Morgan."

"I'm Cecelia Murphy"—she extended a hand— "Gabrielle's aunt. But everybody calls me Cee-Cee."

Zachary quickly wiped his hand on the towel and shook Aunt Cee-Cee's outstretched hand. "All right then, Cee-Cee. It's a pleasure to meet you."

"Ah, that's what you say now. Give it some time." Aunt Cee-Cee laughed, then hopped up on a bar stool at the kitchen counter. "That sure does look good. I'm *starv-ing*. Gabrielle, why don't you fix me one of those things Zachary's making? Oh, and can you get me something cold to drink? I need to wet my throat." She fanned her face again with her hand. "You wouldn't happen to have a beer or wine cooler around here, would you?"

"No, I wouldn't." Gabrielle's response was stern and cold.

"I would be glad to go and get you something,"

Zachary said, obviously wanting to make a good first, impression. "There's a Quik Mart about five miles from here—"

"You don't have to do that," Gabrielle said before Zachary could finish his sentence. "I have something to drink in the refrigerator. She can drink one of those." Gabrielle turned and looked squarely at Aunt Cee-Cee. "Besides, she'll not be staying long enough for you to go get anything and make it back."

Aunt Cee-Cee glared at Gabrielle only briefly before she broke her stare with a warm (though obviously phony) smile. "Gabrielle's right. I won't be here that long. So"—Aunt Cee-Cee turned her attention back to Zachary—"are the two of you dating?"

Neither Gabrielle nor Zachary answered.

"I said are you two dating?"

"Yes," Zachary said when he realized Gabrielle wasn't planning on answering the question. "But we're actually calling it courting." He couldn't hold back his own blush.

"Courting? Oh, how cute! You don't hear that word much these days. I suppose it's better than wham, bam, thank you, ma'am." Aunt Cee-Cee slid down off the bar stool and sat in a chair at the glass-top kitchen table. She looked at Gabrielle, her way of letting her niece know that she was still waiting on both her food and something to drink.

"Gabrielle is a special woman. We want to do things right," Zachary said. He looked at Gabrielle once more, who still hadn't moved to get her aunt a plate or anything to drink.

"So, Mister Handsome Chef, what do you do for a living?"

"I'm a d—"

"Aunt Cee-Cee, why don't I fix your fajita to go?" Gabrielle promptly went and picked up the plate with the fajita Zachary had already begun making.

Aunt Cee-Cee fastened her gaze on Gabrielle like a laser. "Because I'm not *going* yet. And honestly, the quicker I get something to eat, the quicker I'll get *out* of here. I'm hungry, and I don't care to eat while I drive. Like texting, it's dangerous to drive and eat. In fact, there should be a law against both." Aunt Cee-Cee softened her face with a smile.

After rinsing her hands, Gabrielle hurried to finish rolling the fajita for her aunt.

"Now," Aunt Cee-Cee said, turning her full attention once more toward Zachary. "You were saying. What is it you do for a living? Because I hope you know I wouldn't want my niece, who's like a daughter to me . . . raised her myself, hanging out with no scrub. That's what they call a guy without a job who lives off others, right? A scrub."

Zachary laughed a little. "Well, you know, you could call me a scrub."

Aunt Cee-Cee pulled her body back and placed her right hand over her heart.

"Hold up," Zachary said with a chuckle. "Before you conclude I'm not good enough for your niece, allow me to clarify. I'm a doctor. So technically speaking, in my line of work, I wash my hands a lot, a whole lot, i.e., making me somewhat of a scrub."

"A doctor." Aunt Cee-Cee's words were flirty and sweet. "Oh, my goodness. Mercy me. My Gabrielle is courting a *doctor*, a real doctor. Well, isn't that something." She smiled at Gabrielle before turning back to Zachary. "What type of doctor are you?"

"A burn specialist. I specialize mainly in burn victims, although lately I've been spending my share of time equally in the emergency room when I've been needed."

"A multitasker," Aunt Cee-Cee said. "Gabrielle, why haven't you called and told any of us that you're *courting* a *doctor*?"

Gabrielle set the plate with the fajita and a can of Pepsi down in front of her aunt. "The last few times I've called, you haven't taken or returned my calls," Gabrielle said.

Aunt Cee-Cee eyed the can. "You got Coca-Cola instead of Pepsi? I prefer Coke."

"All I have is Pepsi. But I can give you water if you'd prefer that. Water is wet." Gabrielle smiled, knowing full well her aunt never drank water, not even with medicine.

"Oh, no. Pepsi is fine. I was just asking. I think somewhere in the Bible it says we don't have because we don't ask." Aunt Cee-Cee picked up her fajita and took a cautious bite. "This is really good," she said. "Handsome Chef, you're a great cook. The meat is so tender and moist and has such a marvelous flavor." She took a bigger bite.

"Actually, Gabrielle did all the work. The tenderness and taste is from the marinade. Lime juice breaks down the meat to make it tender and give it that flavor. She marinated it overnight. I merely stirred and added the vegetables when she went to open the door."

"I'm sure you're giving Gabrielle way too much credit. I'm willing to bet you did a lot more than you're letting on. The peppers and onions are perfect." She took another bite, then opened her can of soda. A hissing sound escaped when the cap popped. "Aren't you two going to eat before it gets cold? It's really delicious." She smacked as she spoke.

Gabrielle was about to say something when Zachary moved over to her, put his arm around her shoulders, and pulled her in close. "We *like* ours cold," he said.

"Suit yourself," Aunt Cee-Cee said. When she finished that one, she asked for another. She chatted on about how terrible things were at their house financially and her not knowing what they were going to do as she woofed down a third fajita. She then asked for yet another one. "Oh, but could you wrap that one up for me as a to-go?" she said. "Those are *so* good." She licked her fingers, then wiped her mouth with a napkin.

Both Gabrielle and Zachary looked at what remained in the skillet. Originally, there had been enough for them to have *at least* two full fajitas each. Aunt Cee-Cee had now eaten three and was asking for one more to take home with her. If they made her the one she was asking for now, there would only be enough left for one of them. Gabrielle made the last two fajitas and gave them both to her aunt.

"Oh, aren't you the sweetest thing!" Aunt Cee-Cee said when Gabrielle handed her the wrapped fajitas. "Would you mind putting them in a bag for me? And if it's not too much to ask, would you put two cans of sodas in the bag as well? Your Uncle Bubba will need something to wash his fajita down with." Aunt Cee-Cee stood up as she waited on Gabrielle to finish.

Gabrielle put the fajitas and drinks in a grocery bag and walked her to the door.

"I'll call you later tonight," Aunt Cee-Cee said. Then she whispered, "Is the doctor spending the night tonight?"

"No, Aunt Cee-Cee. We won't be doing things like that. There'll be none of that."

"You mean he's not spending the night *right* now. But you don't mean you're not planning on doing *anything* with that man until or unless you get married, now, do you?"

"You mean sex before marriage . . . fornicating?"

"Well, you don't have to be so graphic with it. But yes, that's exactly what I mean. Listen, honey, you don't need to let a man like him get away. That's a real catch you have in there." She pointed her head in the direction of the kitchen.

"Aunt Cee-Cee, I'm a Christian now. I told you that. I gave my life to the Lord. God frowns on fornication. Zachary and I agreed we want to do things God's way, and only His way. And that means keeping ourselves pure until we're married to *whom*ever."

Aunt Cee-Cee started laughing. It sounded more like an animal in severe pain than human. "Yeah, well, trust me: I know plenty of Christians, and being a Christian doesn't seem to be stopping most of them from fornicating *or* committing adultery. I'll tell you this: You'd better take care of that man and his needs or he'll find someone who will. Take it from Aunt Cee-Cee. I know how men can be. Sure, in the beginning they'll tell you they're in total agreement about something like being chaste. But men are wired totally different from women. Men don't need as much emotional bonding as we do to move to the next level. That man is tall, light-skinned enough, handsome, can cook, or at least will pick up a spoon and help out, he has a job, *and* he's a doctor to boot. Oh, you'd *better* at least let him sample the cake batter and not have to wait for the baked cake."

"Good night, Aunt Cee-Cee." Gabrielle opened the front door.

"I'm going to call you either later tonight or tomorrow. Better yet, why don't you just call me when you're free so I won't interrupt anything. You'd best heed what I just said. Call me, now. I have something I *desperately* need to talk to you about. It's important, so don't take long in getting back with me. It can't wait any longer than a day."

Gabrielle mustered up one more smile. "Good night," she said.

After Aunt Cee-Cee left, Gabrielle closed the door. She stood there for a few minutes, her forehead resting softly on the door as she quietly listened for her aunt's car to crank. Hearing the car drive away, she exhaled slowly.

"Wow, what a character," Zachary said.

Jarred slightly by Zachary's presence, Gabrielle turned around and forced herself to smile yet again. "Oh, you don't *even* know the *half* of it."

"Just from those thirty-five minutes, I believe I received a pretty good introduction," Zachary said. "So . . . where would you like to go eat?"

Gabrielle put her hands up to her face to compose herself, then took them down. "I'm so sorry. I can't believe she did that. Wait a minute; yes, I can. That's classic Aunt Cee-Cee. And the funny part is, she has no idea that what she just did was totally wrong or completely selfish. No idea at all."

"Oh, she knows," Zachary said. "I get the distinct feeling Aunt Cee-Cee knows *exactly* what she's doing. *Exactly.*"

If you enjoyed *If Memory Serves*, don't miss
Redeeming Waters

Coming in August 2011 from Dafina Books

Here's an excerpt from *Redeeming Waters* . . .

Prologue

And he shall be as the light of the
morning, when the sun riseth, even a
morning without clouds; as the tender
grass springing out of the earth by
clear shining after rain.

—2 Samuel 23:4

It was summertime, school was out, and with sky-high temperatures reaching near one hundred degrees, even the bees appeared to be chilling out from the smothering heat. Ten years old, Brianna and Alana were outside on the long, covered front porch playing a game of Monopoly—the board type, not something electronic like all the other children their age normally played. Brianna's father, Amos Wright, didn't believe children should stay cooped up in the house watching television and playing video games all day. Brianna didn't mind; she liked being outside. On the other hand, Brianna's mother, Diane, would have preferred her daughter do things inside, especially on scorching hot days like this.

Around midday, suddenly and unexpectedly, dark clouds rolled in.

"Girls, it looks like it's going to rain. You probably need to come inside now," Brianna's mother said as she stood holding the front door open.

"We're on the porch, Mother," Brianna said. "We won't get wet on the porch."

"Well, if it starts lightning, I want you to come in the house immediately. Do you two understand me?"

"Yes, ma'am," Brianna and Alana said in such perfect unison that it sounded like one voice.

"Older people sure are funny when it comes to rain," Brianna said after her mother closed the front door.

Alana loosely shook the two white dice around in her hand, then threw them on the board, rolling a double three, automatically garnering herself another turn. "I know," Alana said as she counted out loud and advanced her wheelbarrow six spaces. "Boardwalk," she said with obvious disappointment.

"Yes!" Brianna said, picking up her title deed card to that property. "Let's see now, with two houses, you owe me six hundred dollars!" Brianna held out her hand for payment.

Alana slowly counted out the money, leaving her with only a small amount of money to play with. "It's a good thing I'm close to passing go and collecting two hundred dollars," Alana said. "I just hope I don't land on any of your other properties on my next roll, or this game will pretty much be over—two hundred more dollars or not."

The rain started pouring down. And then the sun, just as quickly, came back out, brightly lighting up the sky even as the rain continued to fall.

"Look!" Brianna said. "The sun is shining while it's raining!" Brianna got up and walked over to the top step. "Wow. With the sun shining like that, all of those falling raindrops look like diamonds bouncing all over the walkway. Do you see how they're sparkling as they hit?"

Alana stood up and walked over to Brianna. "You *do* know what this means, don't you?"

"Know what *what* means?"

Alana turned and grinned at her friend. "When it's raining and the sun is shining."

"No. What?" Brianna could see that Alana was pleased, knowing something that *she* apparently didn't.

"It means that the devil is beating his wife."

"It does not," Brianna said.

"Yes, it does. If you don't believe me, then go ask your mother. She'll tell you."

"Well, I don't believe you because the devil doesn't *have* a wife."

"Apparently, he does," Alana said with a snarky shake to her head as she moved her face in toward Brianna's. "That's why the sun is shining while it's raining: to let us know that he's beating her. I feel a little sorry for her even if she *is* the devil's wife. It's got to be bad enough to be married to the devil. Then to have him beat on you like that . . . Then again, she should have known better than to hook up with a creature like him. I mean, what did she expect when she married the *devil?*"

"Well, I'm not going to let any man ever beat on me," Brianna said. "Not ever."

"They say if you stick a pin in the ground, you can hear her screaming when he's beating her."

Brianna frowned, then winced. "Who would want to hear anything like that?"

"Hey, let's go get a pin and see if we can hear her. That way, you'll see whether what I told you is the truth or not."

Brianna and Alana hurried into the house. "Wait right here while I find two pins." Brianna started upstairs to her room, then stopped and looked back. "Does it matter what kind of pin it is? A straight pin, a hat pin, a safety pin, or is it actually a writing pen . . . ?"

Alana shook her head. "As long as it pierces the ground, it should work."

Brianna came back quickly and handed Alana a large safety pin. They started toward the door.

"And just where do you two think you're going *now?*" Brianna's mother asked as she walked out of the kitchen into the den, wiping her hands on a dish towel.

"To listen to the devil beat his wife and to see if we can hear her scream," Brianna said as easily as though she were saying that they were going to the kitchen to get a glass of water.

Brianna's mother shook her head as she smiled, but didn't protest—essentially telling Brianna that she had no objections to what they were about to do or the idea of it.

Brianna opened the large, lead-glass door and allowed Alana to go out first. Brianna grinned. She saw him before he saw her, and she ran full force, straight into his arms. "Granddad!" she said.

"Hey there," sixty-year-old Pearson Wright said as he picked her up and spun her around two full turns. He set Brianna back down. The two of them now stood close to the man who had come with him. "So where are you two going in such a hurry?" he asked.

"We're going to listen to the devil as he beats his wife and to see if we can hear her screaming." Brianna held up her safety pin to prove they were serious.

"Oh, that," her grandfather said as he looked back at what he'd just come in out of. "You're talking about the rain with the sun shining. That's a beautiful sight for sure: rain and the sun shining at the same time, a phenomenon that's always fascinated folks."

The good-looking man standing next to her grandfather began to chuckle as he smiled at Brianna.

"Gracious, where are my manners," Pearson said. "This is my granddaughter"—he placed his hand on top of Brianna's head—"the lovely and talented young poet and short story writer, Miss Brianna Wright."

"And *this*"—Brianna pointed to Alana as soon as

her grandfather finished introducing her—"is my best friend in the whole wide world, Alana Norwood."

"Pleased to meet you, Miss Alana Norwood. And *this* is David R. Shepherd, aka King d.Avid," Pearson said, pronouncing it "King dee-Avid." "That's a small *d,* period, capital *A,* small *v-i-d.* You're looking at the next world-renowned recording artist."

"Are you a real king?" Brianna asked the tall man with black wavy hair and caramel-colored skin. She placed her hand in the man's waiting hand, which he'd presented to her to shake.

"No, not in the way you may be thinking," King d.Avid said. "But I do plan—with your grandfather advising and managing me—to rule the world of music someday."

"Sounds like a plan to me," Brianna said. "I plan on being the queen of something myself. Just not exactly sure what I intend to rule over. But I'm going to be somebody great, or at least produce something great one day, just like you. I promise you that. A lady at church spoke that Word over me last year. That's what she called it: 'A Word from God.' "

"I'm impressed," King d.Avid said, smiling at her as he continued to hold her young hand in his. "And I believe that." He gave Brianna a slight bow with his head, then let go of her hand. He reached over and held out his hand to Alana. "And you are the best friend of the queen to be?"

Alana walked over, shook his hand, and giggled. "Yes. Although, it's likely we'll both be queens. That's how a lot of friends roll, you know."

"Absolutely," King d.Avid said. "It's always good to be in the company of those who are going somewhere, instead of hanging around people who are going nowhere. That's precisely why I hang with Mister Wright,

here, the way I do. The man is good at what he does."
He glanced over at Pearson. "And I believe he's going
to help get me where I'm destined to be." King d.Avid
turned his attention back to Alana and gave her a slight
nod.

"So, how old are you?" Alana asked.

King d.Avid laughed. "Why, I'm twenty-five."

"You're kind of old," Alana said, turning up her nose
slightly. "Me and Brianna are only ten. Well, we don't
mean to be rude, but we need to finish before the rain
stops just as quickly as it started. Otherwise, Brianna
won't believe that the devil really is beating his wife."

"Okay." King d.Avid sang the word. "But I don't
think the devil really is beating his wife. Because I
don't *think* that the devil is married."

"That's what I told her," Brianna said triumphantly
with a grin.

Alana trotted down the steps into the rain and stood
in the grassy, manicured yard. She looked back up at
the porch, her eyes blinking with the raindrops before
she eventually shielded her eyes with her hand. "Brianna, will you come on, already!"

Brianna hurried and caught up with her friend. They
unlatched their safety pins, kneeled down, stuck their
pins into the ground, and placed their ears over their re-
spective pins with the rain drenching them and all.

Pearson shook his head, laughed, then escorted King
d.Avid into the house.

Chapter 1

The waters wear the stones: thou washest away the things which grow out of the dust of the earth; and thou destroyest the hope of man.

—Job 14:19

Brianna Bathsheba Wright Waters looked out of the window of their three-bedroom, one-and-a-half-bath house at the rain. A "starter home" is what her twenty-three-year-old (three years her senior) husband of eight months, Unzell Michael Waters, told her over two months ago when they bought it.

"Baby, I promise you, things are going to get better for us down the road," Unzell had said after they officially moved in. "I know this is not what either of us envisioned we'd be doing right about now. But I promise you, I'm *going* to get us into that mansion we talked about. I am."

She'd married Unzell at age nineteen, a year and a half after her high school graduation, as Unzell was finishing his final year at the University of Michigan. Unlike most women she knew, Brianna wanted to marry in December. The wintertime was her favorite time of the year. She loved everything about winter. It wasn't a dead period as far as she was concerned. To her, that was the time of rest, renewal, anticipation, and miracles taking place that the eyes weren't always privy to. Winter was the time when flower bulbs, trees, and other plants could establish themselves underground; developing better and stronger roots. Winter was the time when various pests and bugs were killed off; otherwise the world would be overrun with them. Brianna loved the rich colors she would be able to use in a winter wedding: deep reds and dark greens.

But she equally loved summertime. Summer was a reminder of life bursting forth in its fullness and full potential after all seemed dead not so long ago. Summer now reminded her of her days of playing carefree outside, *truly* without a care in the world.

So she and Unzell married the Saturday before Christmas. It was a beautiful ceremony; her parents had spared no expense. After all, this would be the only time they would be the parents of the bride. Her older brother, Mack, might settle down someday. But even if he did, they would merely be the parents of the groom, which was a totally different expense, experience, and responsibility.

Unzell Waters was already pretty famous, so everybody and his brother wanted to be invited to the wedding ceremony. Unzell was the star football player at the University of Michigan and a shoo-in for the NFL. As a running back, he'd broken all kinds of records, and the only question most had was whether he would be the number-one or number-two pick in the first round of the NFL draft the last Saturday in April. Unzell was on track to make millions—more millions than either he or Brianna could fathom *ever* being able to spend in *several* lifetimes.

Still best friends, Alana Norwood had been Brianna's maid of honor. Alana had grown wilder than Brianna, but Brianna understood Alana . . . and Alana understood her.

"Girlfriend, I'm glad you're settling down so early, if that's what you want," Alana had said when Brianna first told her she and Unzell were getting married in a year. "But I plan on seeing *all* that the world has to offer me before my life becomes dedicated to any one person like that."

Of course, when Alana learned *just* how famous Unzell was even *before* he was to go pro, then heard about the millions of dollars sports commentators were predicting he'd likely get when he signed—no matter which team he signed with—she said to Brianna, "God really *does* look after you! Of course, he's always looked after you. People on TV are talking eighty-six million dollars, over five years, just for one man to play . . . one man, to *play*. And you're going to be his wife? I know you used to say all the time that you were God's favorite. Well, I'm starting to believe maybe you really are."

"Alana, now you know I used to just say things like that. I don't *really* believe God has favorites," Brianna said. "The Bible tells us that God is no respecter of persons. We're all equal in his sight."

"Well, we may have the *opportunity* to be equal, but it's obvious that not all of us are walking in our opportunities. Not the way you do, anyway. So you're definitely ahead of a lot of us, not equal by any means. All I know is that you spoke that Word of Favor with a capital F over your life, and look what's happening with you so far."

The wedding was absolutely beautiful, every single detail and moment of it. But with the championship game being played the first week in January, Brianna and Unzell were only able to spend one day of a honeymoon before Unzell was off again to practice.

Michigan's team was the team to beat with number twenty-two, Unzell Waters, being one of the main obstacles standing between the other team having even a *semblance* of a chance. Brianna was at the game in Miami watching it along with her family. With two minutes remaining in the fourth quarter, Michigan was already a comfortable three touchdowns ahead. In Brianna's opinion, there really was no reason for Unzell to even be on the field. She, her grandfather Pearson Wright, and father Amos Wright were saying as much when that play happened—the play that would alter Unzell's career and life.

One of the other team's players grabbed Unzell by the leg as he ran full speed and yanked him down, pulling his leg totally out of joint. With him being down, everybody on the other team piled on him. Unzell was badly hurt. Instantly, his prospective stock for the NFL plummeted. Then came the doctor's prognosis. Even with the two necessary surgeries, Unzell would never be able to play football at that level again.

Brianna assured him things would be all right. "God still has you, Unzell."

"Yeah, but if God had me in the first place, then why would he allow something like this to happen to me . . . happen to us?" Unzell said as he lay in that hospital bed. "God knows both of us. He knows us, Brianna. He knows our hearts. God knows we would have done right when it came to me being in the NFL. So why? Why did this happen? And if God is a healer, then why can't he heal my leg completely? Why can't he make me whole again?"

"I believe that God *can* heal your leg, Unzell," Brianna said. "But right now we have to deal with reality. And from all that the doctors are saying, football is out for you, at least for now. So you and I need a new direction, that's all. We're going to be all right though." She lovingly took hold of his hand, then squeezed it. "We are." She smiled.

"So, you're not going to leave me?"

Brianna frowned as she first jerked her head back, then primped her lips before forcing a smile. "Leave *you?* Where did *that* come from?"

"Face it; I'm not going to be making millions now. In fact, I'll be doing well just to find a job, any job at all, in this economy."

"First of all, *Mister* Waters, I did not marry you for your money or your potential money. I've known you since we were in high school. You were in the twelfth grade; I was in the ninth. You didn't have any money then and I fell in love with you. So if you think I married you for your money, then maybe I *should* leave you." Brianna put her hand on her hip.

"I know, Bree-Bath-She," he said, calling her by the pet name he sometimes used. "But do you know how many women wanted me because they saw dollar signs?"

"Yeah, I know. I'm not stupid. I even think you thought about getting with a few of them. In fact, who knows, maybe you did. But still, I married you for you. And I married you for better or worse; for richer or poorer."

"Come on, Brianna. Nobody really means that part when they say it. Who truly wants to be with someone poor? Sure, we may feel that's where we are at the time, but all of us believe our lives are going to get to the better and the richer at some point—sooner rather than later—not worse or poorer."

"Well, if me staying with you now after you've lost millions of dollars—that if I'm not mistaken, you never really had anyway—means I meant what I was vowing when I said those words, then please know: I meant them when I said them. Okay, so those in the know were saying you'd likely get a contract worth eight-six million dollars over five years with a guaranteed fifty million and now it looks like you won't. So be it. I'm just glad you're okay. You could have been paralyzed on that play. You and I will do what we need to be all right. Besides, you're graduating in May. You'll get your electrical computer engineering degree. Do like most folks and either get a job or start your own business. Regardless, Unzell, I'm here to stay. So deal with it." Brianna flicked her hand.

Unzell smiled, then looked down at his hand. "God has certainly blessed me richly." He looked up. "God gave me you."

"Oh," Brianna said, all mushy as she kissed him. "That was *so* sweet."

Brianna couldn't help but think about how far she and Unzell had come since that fateful day. Following Unzell's two surgeries and the rehabilitation period, she'd suspended attending college and gotten a job as a secretary, living with her parents while he finished his final months of college in Ann Arbor. After Unzell graduated, he moved back to Montgomery, Alabama. He was relentless about getting a job, even when it felt like no one was hiring. He was diligent, beating the pavement and searching the Internet. In four weeks, he landed a job as an assistant stage manager setting up stages for music concerts, but was told if he wanted to excel in this business, he needed to be in Atlanta.

So that's what he and Brianna did: moved to Georgia.

It didn't hurt when Alana told Brianna that she was also moving to Atlanta to pursue her dream of becoming a video girl. At least now, Brianna and Alana would each have a friend in their new city. Brianna especially needed someone after quickly learning that in his position, Unzell could be gone for weeks, sometimes even months at a time.

Brianna continued to stare out of the window. She suddenly began to smile.

"And what are *you* smiling about?" Unzell said, jarring her back to the present.

Spinning around, she kissed him when he came near. "I didn't hear you come in."

He embraced her. "You were gazing out of the window. It looked like you were in deep thought; I didn't want to disturb you. Then you broke into that incredibly enchanting smile of yours, and I couldn't hold myself back any longer. Did you just think of a joke or something that made you happy?"

"Look," she said, pointing outside.

He looked out of the window and shrugged. "And what exactly am I looking for? All I see is rain, the sun shining, and trees and other things getting drenched."

"Don't you know what that's supposed to mean? Rain while the sun is shining."

He laughed. "Here we go again. Another something you learned when you were growing up? Like not stepping on a crack so you won't break your mother's back. Not walking under a ladder or splitting a pole because it will bring bad luck. Not sweeping someone's feet or you'll sweep them or someone else out of your life."

"No. Not exactly like *those* things, which are merely superstitions. This is different. I'm not saying that I believe it, but they say that when it's raining and the sun is shining, the devil is beating his wife."

"Yeah, right." Unzell smirked. "Actually, the scientific term for it is sunshower."

"Scientific term, huh? Well, people also say that if you stick a pin in the ground and listen, you can hear her screams."

"Oh. So do you want to go outside and do that so we can put that old wives' tale to the test?" Unzell's eyes

danced as he spoke. "I'm game to play in the rain if
you are."

"Nope. Alana and I tested it out when we were
younger."

He laughed. "And the verdict was?"

"I didn't hear a thing. Of course, Alana claimed that
she did. She said the scream was faint. But honestly? I
think she heard something because she wanted to believe it was true. Then she said we'd used the wrong
kind of pin and that's why it didn't work right."

"Alana is something else, that's for sure. So how is
she these days?"

"Still trying to get a contract as a video girl or whatever they're called."

"I wouldn't ever count Alana out. Before you know
it, she'll be over here forcing us to watch her DVD,
showing how she was 'doing her thing.' " He made a
quick pumping dance move followed by the long-
outdated Cabbage Patch.

Unzell wrapped his arms around Brianna. She fully
submitted, lying back into him, then rubbing one of his
hard, muscular arms that gently engulfed her.

"The devil beating his wife," he said with a sinister
giggle as they both looked out of the window. "Well,
now, I think I've heard just about everything."

Brianna broke away from his embrace and turned to
face him, playfully hitting his arm. "Just don't *you* ever
try that devil move on *me.*"

He grabbed her and lovingly locked her again into
his arms, gazing deeply into her brown eyes as they
faced each other. "Never. I promise you I will *leave* before I *ever* raise a hand to you." He hugged her. "I
would never abuse a blessing of God; I'm too afraid of
what God would do to me if I did." He gently pushed
her slightly away from him to look into her eyes again.
"Besides, I love you too much. We're one body now. So

whatever I do to you, I'll be doing to myself. And I would *never* lay a negative hand or word, for that matter, on myself. Therefore, I won't ever do anything like that to you."

"See, that's why I love you so much." She cocked her head to one side. "You really get this whole concept of loving your wife the way Christ loves the church."

"I wouldn't want our life together to be any other way. Not any other way." He pulled her to him and squeezed her as he locked her in his arms, causing her to giggle out loud. He stopped, cupped her face, and kissed her with an overflow of passion.

Look For These Other
Dafina Novels

If I Could
0-7582-0131-1

by Donna Hill
$6.99US/**$9.99**CAN

Thunderland
0-7582-0247-4

by Brandon Massey
$6.99US/**$9.99**CAN

June In Winter
0-7582-0375-6

by Pat Phillips
$6.99US/**$9.99**CAN

Yo Yo Love
0-7582-0239-3

by Daaimah S. Poole
$6.99US/**$9.99**CAN

When Twilight Comes
0-7582-0033-1

by Gwynne Forster
$6.99US/**$9.99**CAN

It's A Thin Line
0-7582-0354-3

by Kimberla Lawson Roby
$6.99US/**$9.99**CAN

Perfect Timing
0-7582-0029-3

by Brenda Jackson
$6.99US/**$9.99**CAN

Never Again Once More
0-7582-0021-8

by Mary B. Morrison
$6.99US/**$8.99**CAN

Available Wherever Books Are Sold!

Check out our website at www.kensingtonbooks.com.

HARLEM ON LOCK

KAREN WILLIAMS

URBAN
BOOKS

www.urbanbooks.net

Urban Books, LLC
78 East Industry Court
Deer Park, NY 11729

Harlem on Lock Copyright © 2008 Karen Williams

ISBN 13: 978-1-60162-441-3
ISBN 10: 1-60162-441-7

First Mass Market Printing March 2011
First Trade Paperback Printing January 2008
Printed in the United States of America

10   9   8   7   6   5   4   3   2   1

Distributed by Kensington Publishing Corp.
Submit Wholesale Orders to:
Kensington Publishing Corp.
C/O Penguin Group (USA) Inc.
Attention: Order Processing
405 Murray Hill Parkway
East Rutherford, NJ 07073-2316
Phone: 1-800-526-0275
Fax: 1-800-227-9604

Dedication

This book is dedicated to:

My daughter for being my daily inspiration;
My sister for being there every step of the way;
My mom for just being my crazy mom;
And to **my friend Ronisha**, a true angel
who always pushed me to live—
not sweat the small stuff.
Rest in peace.

Acknowledgments

Wow. This had been an incredible journey for me. A journey I don't think I would have been able to get through if I didn't believe in Him and all the blessings He had in store for me. Thanks, hugs, and kisses go out my family. My mom for showing me my book had a fighting chance by walking out of my house shaking, after I read a couple pages to her and for plain out being her crazy self. My sister for being there with me every step of the way, reading as I wrote, keep in mind, having someone like you in their life gives one a significant source of love and support. When it comes to you I can't say enough, just know that I feel extremely blessed to have a sister such as you. To my daughter, you have made this experience of being a mother so easy and joyous and I love you more than I love myself. To all my cousins and nieces, Donnie, Devin, Jabrez, Mu-Mu, Mikayla, Madison, who kept my energy up by chasing you guys around the house between breaks from writing. To my goddaughter Lanaya for watching television while your god mom slaved away on her computer. Hey Amari! Hey Faye! Thanks to my uncle Noonie, aunt Tammy, my cousin Ray, Shauntae, and Michael for believing in me.

To my friends, Lenzie, now you didn't exactly help me with the story but you made me laugh when I needed to laugh and I figured if I didn't mention you I would get cursed out. Linda, I'm so glad we reconnected, Ronisha R.I.P, Sewiaa, Cheryl, Misty, Valerie Hoyt, you've helped me so much over the years, Markeiba, Valerie Sweet, Phillopo, Shannon, Brooklyn, Christina, for your third eye, Africa, Maxine, Jennifer, Barbara, Sandra, Lydia, Lexus, I always appreciated your wisdom, Kevin you're a part of the family and Vanilla, who I know your Christian ears burned when you heard about the story. Roxie and Carla, you were one of the first to read *Harlem on Lock* and give me your feedback. In fact, *Carlita,* you read all my books! Thanks for the support and I treasure our friendships. Thanks for always lending me an ear, Pearl. Hey Victor!

Special thanks to Chanin Paige, The Evans Family, Yolanda Perdomo, and the Perdomo family for helping me make my daughter everything she is today. Keith Lily, Mrs. Bonner, Adara's and my favorite teacher! Shout out to Candis, Nashawn, Ricky, and Shana, from the Westside English Crew. Hey to Leyla, Carlos, Angelina, Maggie, Anthony, and Jason, didn't forget about you guys, keep striving. Special thanks to the teens of Carmelitos Boys and Girls Club; no matter how much time goes by I'll always reserve a spot in my heart for you guys. Hey Duncan! Hey Stone!

Thanks to all my professors who inspired and pushed me, starting with Long Beach City College.

Mr. Lastra, they need more people like you. Mr. Dominguez, you showed me I had something I didn't know I had. And Mr. Gaspar, you showed me how to let my voice come out, it's been out ever since. Thanks to California State University Dominguez Hills professors, Mr. Brueckner, you got me writing again, Dr. Turner, you kept me optimistic, Dr. Sherman, taking your class was an experience I'll never forget, and like Dr. Feuer, you really pushed me to give all I could and I still do. Dr. Becker, Dr. Oesterd, you both inspired me to write with passion and expression. And of course my favorite high school literature teacher, Mr. Conard.

Thanks to the staff of Oakwood Academy. Special thanks to Ms. Antoinette and Ms. Green for believing this day would come.

Tremendous thanks to the "veteran and new staff" of GSHU at Los Padrinos Juvenile Hall. Your encouragement and support is greatly appreciated!

Thanks to authors Victoria Christopher Murray, Mary Monroe, and Darlene Johnson, for all your help.

Thanks Fara Kearnes for your help and insight. You went far and beyond what an editor does and I appreciate everything you did for *Harlem On Lock*!

A million thanks to Candace Cottrell and Mark Anthony for believing in my vision. You gave me my start. I cannot say thanks enough; just know I strived to give you the absolute best writing that I could!

Thanks to Andrea Blackstone.

Thanks to the writers and artists that have inspired me over time, Jack Gilbert, James Baldwin, Darnella Ford, Pablo Neruda, Scotney St. James, Linda Lael Miller, Eric Jerome Dickey, Diane Mckinney-Whetstone, Mary Monroe, Jay'Z, and Tupac.

To Terrock, I love you. I believe in you. Thanks for being proud of me, loving me, making me feel like I'm important to you, listening to me whine and hugging me when I needed to be hugged.

Thanks to anyone else I didn't mention who supported me. Charge it to my mind not my heart.

In the words of Tupac: "If you believe, then you can achieve. Just look at me."

Prologue

I was tasting my own blood. It was dripping from my lip, my right cheek, and the gash on my head where he had fucked me up. But the worst wasn't over. My life was ending tonight. He had convinced me of it, after yelling it each time he attacked me. There was piss dripping down my legs, I was hoping God would be merciful and not let me shit myself. But then God hadn't been too merciful to me. Otherwise, why would I be in this fucked-up situation?

"Chief said he wanted her ass kicked so that's what we gonna do." It was that dumb bitch from the club. Damn, she sure was loyalty to Chief.

I closed my eyes briefly.

"Before the night is over Chief is gonna kill you, Harlem. And you can yell as loud as you want to. Ain't no cops going to come save you. They on his payroll. And even if they wasn't, they wouldn't give a fuck about a ho from the projects who's kin to two dope fiends anyway. Yes, bitch I know who you are."

Chapter 1

Now before I start venting, let me tell you who I am. My name is Harlem. And I'll bet you're wondering if I'm from New York. Well, sort of. I mean I was born there, but I couldn't begin to tell you shit about the town. The only damn thing I knew about New York was what I'd learned watching TV. I knew Jay-Z and Notorious B.I.G. were from New York. I'd heard they made the best pizza there, and that niggas and females from New York sometimes carried razors in their mouths. Yep, that's about all I knew about the NY.

My mama Aja and my daddy, Earl, hopped in their hooptie and set out for "killa Cali" three days after I was born. And I knew she missed Harlem—the life, the club. She longed for it; it was in her eyes.

When I was little she would sit me on the beat-up couch, get dressed in one of her old get-ups, and sing for me. Hell, by the time I was six I knew all the songs of Billie Holiday, Ella Fitzgerald, and

Nina Simone by heart and would sing right along-side her.

See, her leaving was all part of the plan, my mama's plan, that is. She wanted to do right by me and be the best mother she could be. I guess she figured if she removed herself from the environment she could get rid of her drug habit. And I'm not talking about Tylenol, Mylanta, or Orajel. I'm talking about that heavy shit—"smack"—the shit that talked to you, pleaded with you, could bring you up, bring you down, could make you shit, could make you come. It had its claws in my parents, especially my mama, and I ask myself time and time again, How did she get there?

Now, if you thought Beyoncé was fine, I wish you could have seen my mama back in the day. She had that exotic look that drove men wild—mahogany skin in the purest form, oval-shaped face, high cheekbones, chinky eyes, and long curly hair that hung down to her round ass. Delicate features. Not only did she have the ass and hips, she had big ol' titties, fat, juicy legs, and a high, small waist. My mama was a bad bitch, and she could get anything she wanted out of a man. My daddy used to say she stopped all movements even on her worst day.

I found out many things I never knew about my mama's life. A jazz singer before she had me, she used to work in a bar called Aces, a spot for high rollers. For starters the so-called club really was a cover for some big-time dope slingers. While drinks were served, people shot pool, danced, and listened to the entertainment, in the back room, which they called the "chop shop," they manufactured pure heroin. Still, when the dealers were done handling their business, they rolled up joints, got their drank on, and let my mother's sultry voice unwind them. And they let their eyes be blessed with the sight of her beauty. For the runners—Stuckey, Chisom, and Ramsey—Mama was like a little sister, and they kept her out of the chop shop. But my mama was a free spirit, a wild child who threw caution to the damn wind for a night of fun.

And so that's what heroin was to her—a night of fun one day after the club closed. A friend had introduced it to her like you would a family member or a friend. Only it wasn't like, "Hi, this is my friend, Heroin" but more like "Man, you got to try this shit. It will give you a triple orgasm."

But, hell, that night just never ended for Mama. And after she became one of Stuckey's, Chisom's, and Ramsey's biggest customers, all they could do was shake their heads and say, "Damn, Aja on that shit too? What a fucking waste. She's too talented, too fine, too sexy, too smart, and got too much potential to be doing that."

And she knew it too, what they were thinking. Soon she was too gone, too hooked, to ever come back. So she never did. It was never part of the plan. So I came to understand.

Mama had her choice of men, but she chose my daddy. Crazy part was, he was no high roller. My daddy was an auto mechanic and she was hoping that he could save her. Only, she got him caught up in the shit. She said it was his mysterious, seductive eyes, the same eyes attached to my face. The rest, I'm told, came straight from my Mama, as I am the spitting image of her, except while her hair was jet black, mine is a combination of browns. I have my daddy's full lips, a beauty mark in the corner of my mouth, and my skin is a copper-brown complexion.

They settled outside of Los Angeles, the city of low riders, Chucks, and Roscoe's House of Chicken 'n Waffles, but not the nice part. We stayed in the projects, a place I hated. We lived there since I was a baby but didn't nothing about the projects make me feel at home or that we had a better life. I always felt separate from the rest of LA, being in the projects, which was a closed-in community of violence and despair.

The place to be was Baldwin Hills, the black Beverly Hills, where wealthy black people lived in these big-ass houses that sat high up on the hills. In the projects you could live up high too, but it wasn't on no damn hill.

The apartments were so close to each other you could hear your neighbor's TV and radio through the paper-thin walls, or you knew when they were taking a shower or even a shit. In fact every Thursday I knew my neighbor Tiny got some, 'cause her headboard beat up against my wall and their screaming and moaning kept me up the whole damn night.

You shared the same yard with your neighbor and belonged to a building with six little apartments, and twelve feet away was another identical building with six more apartments. You either had to hear people stomping upstairs, or somebody was complaining 'cause you were stomping. There was a road dividing one side of the buildings from the other and a big-ass tree to every building. On a nightly basis you would see teen boys and even grown-ass men sneaking up trees, hiding from the cops. Sometimes they'd fall and bust their ass and get caught.

They did have parks for the kids, but other shit beside little kids playing went down there. People my age smoked weed there, drug dealers slanged their shit there, and dopeys found corners and bathrooms to get high in, despite the kids playing on the swings, in the sand, or on see-saws. If you were poor, which we all were, you were pretty much confined to going to the park or sitting on your stoop to entertain yourself. Most of the time I hung out on my stoop. You saw all kinds of shit there, weekly shootouts that had me running for dear life in my house, fights among the different type of gangs that wanted to run the projects, or you would see "chicken heads," young and old, out in the streets, the park, their small yard, or other people's yard fighting over a damn man. Sometimes you even saw mother and daughter fighting over a man. It was a damn shame.

When I needed an escape from the projects, I hooked up with one of my friends from school and saw how other people lived. They'd scoop me in their ride, and we'd hang out on Crenshaw, which was the spot, or Broadway. Teens and grown folks kicked it there. You just parked your car and sat in it, or stood on the street mingling with people. They had car shows, where you saw fly-ass low riders, Impalas, or Caprices, on chromed-out twenty-twos. The motorcycle clubs even came out to stunt. I had fun hanging there 'cause I didn't need no damn money.

Or we went to Baldwin Hills Plaza, or the Slauson Swap Meet, or Magic Johnson Theatre to watch movies. Most of the time I passed, when it came to hanging out at places like these, because you needed money. While my friends were buying clothes and shit, I didn't even have enough to buy me some damn French fries, so I'd sometimes take my bus fare and just ride the bus as far as it would take me before I had to get off. The bus always passed Baldwin Hills. I always wondered what it felt like to live in one of those big-ass houses with the manicured lawns and roll in the Escalade or Lexus parked out front. But after the bus ride it was back to the fucking projects.

As bad as it was, I knew why my mama and daddy came here. They came out here hoping California would give their cravings the relief they needed. It didn't. The projects was just a different place with the same old shit—addiction, sobriety, relapses, anger, frustration, fights, tears, blood— but that was our life.

Chapter 2

I don't know how it got this bad.
I sighed loudly as I watched my mama walking up and down the ho stroll located down the street from our house, or shall I say shack, 'cause that's what the fuck we lived in. It was just me and my parents, but we had visitors who didn't take their ass home—roaches. And I ain't talking about them baby ones. I'm talking about the muthafuckas that could fly and bite the shit out of you. Them bastards were so slick. If they caught you looking at them, they ass would play dead. Not to mention the fucking rats that would give birth in the cabinets and drawers. Shit, you open one up to get a spoon or a shirt and you see the little babies with their eyes closed and crying in a squeaky-ass voice, thinking I was gonna pick they ass up. Hell no. If it's one thang I can't stand it's a fucking rat. I don't care if it's a possum, hamster, squirrel, ferret, mouse, gerbil, or guinea pig. If you had whiskers and a pointed-ass nose, then you best stay the fuck away from me. And both of them took up

unlimited residency in our home among the water bugs and "daddy long leg" spiders. In the fall the rats and mice would bite through the wood in the walls, trying to ease their way into our house. They also loved to drink water out of the toilet. I always had the end of the broomstick ready to beat they ass.

We had a beat-up old couch. Our carpet was damn near black and run-down. Mama was no Martha Stewart and never made an attempt to clean it. And our walls had so many bullet holes and cracks in them, they made a pattern. Because the gas was turned off, we didn't have hot water, so I took cold showers and baths. At first it was hard as hell to get used to. I was always catching a cold or flu, but after a while my body adjusted to the temperature and cold water and hot water felt no different to me.

I usually cooked the little food we had on the electric skillet. It was the one thing besides the couch, refrigerator, and my mom's wedding ring we had left. The TV and stereo were long gone. My only entertainment was my homework, library books, my cheap little Walkman, and my thumbs that I twiddled when I got bored with my other limited fucking options.

In my room was a blow-up mattress that I slept on, and the blankets were so old, they were almost as thin as the sheets. I had nothing on my walls except sketches and various art work like plaster and metal frames, and paper-mache that I had made in art class at school and whatnot.

It wasn't the best living. Some would call it a horrible living, but it was the best my parents could do for being what they were. Junkies. And junkie or no junkie, they were my parents and they loved me. It's just that they had a problem, plain and simple, like anybody else. So who was I to beat them up? After all, I was their child, their flesh and blood. And things could've been worse. They could have thrown me in a dumpster, like some of the other dumb-ass people do to their kids, or I could've been in the system. But at least I had a roof over my head. And, hell, something, no matter how small, was better than nothing.

The block was small. On one side was the slingers, which consisted of the little hoppers, runners, lookouts, and the leader. They all worked together to make sure they got the money from the junkies, the junkies got their product, and that all of this was done without the leader touching any of the money or the product, and no cops seeing a damn thing. The action was always quick. First, the "hoppas" got the money from the "cluckheads," the runners passed the dope to them, and the lookouts made sure there were no cops coming. The leader watched the whole thing, making sure the shit went smoothly.

Then farther down the street the hoes paced the stroll for men. The traffic in this area was crazy as fuck from all the nasty-ass men that came from the east to get some cheap pussy from the hoes, half of whom would trot right up the block to get dope from the slingers with the money they just got from selling their pussy. And my mama was there, wearing some hot pink stretch pants, a faded red top with a hole in the front, along with some dirty, busted flip-flops, and a flimsy scarf covering her uncombed hair. And I knew my ass should have been embarrassed—any other teenager would have been—but I didn't give a damn. Shit, this was my mama, and I loved her. Her pain was my pain.

I know it killed my mama to have to lower herself to this, to go from having men flock to you to throwing your pussy at them for a few dollars that seemed to never be enough 'cause fifteen minutes later you back on the track, to needing something so bad you'd die to get it 'cause no matter how much of it you got in your system it never stopped calling you. I could never understand her addiction. I always wondered why and how it got my mama, but I was too scared to ask her.

The first time I caught her on the track I was ten. Back then cars flocked to her. At first I thought she was just taking rides from strangers, but eventually I learned it was more than that. I overheard my neighbor Netty, who had a son a little older than me named Bo Bo, say to the neighbor across from her, not giving a damn that I was on my stoop all up in their mouth, "You know Aja around the corner out there on that track now, girl. It's bad enough that pretty woman putting poison in her body, but now she having sex with them dirty, disgusting men."

I ran down the street and out of the projects, and sure enough I saw her. She was wearing a sexy dress and hopping into a long black Cadillac. My eyes scanned the driver, a fat, greasy-looking, white man.

"Mama!" I shouted.

She froze, and her eyes passed over me. Her face flushed instantly. "Harlem, go home!" she said.

"Mama, where you going?"

But she didn't answer. She just slid in the car and slammed the door, and they drove away.

We never discussed it, what my mama was doing in that man's car.

That night she just came in my room and curled up on my mattress with me. "Mama won't leave again," she said.

And, yeah, over the years Mama promised me she would stop, but hell I'm seventeen now, and if she ain't stopped yet, she never would.

Poor thang. Time had passed, and so had her looks. She was no longer the beauty queen that she used to be when she was in Aces. She practically chased cars down, but none of them stopped for her ass. And I couldn't blame them. Yeah, I loved my mom, but if I was the ugliest man on the fucking earth I wouldn't fuck my mama for free. That "dope overtime" had murdered her looks. She was gone, and she looked bad. But I would never tell her that though. It would hurt her feelings.

Mama slapped her beat-up purse against the fifth car that sped past her and stopped at another hoe.

I ran up to her and grabbed her thin arm before she could raise it to hit another car. "Mama, what in the world are you doing out here? Where's Daddy?"

"Oh Lord!" She gripped my face in both of her

hands. "Harlem, they got Earl, baby. You know they always fuckin' with him. There's no telling how long they going to keep him in that hellhole."

I made sure my mama didn't see me roll my eyes. Daddy was always getting locked up for trying to find illegal means to feed the ugly-ass drug habit that both of them had. He was known around the projects for jacking people. It was ridiculous how many times he got his ass whipped for doing that, but he never stopped.

"Mama, don't worry. You know they'll probably release him tomorrow, and if not, they probably won't keep him no more than a week."

Cops didn't give a damn about no dopey. There were too many of them running around for them to continue to detain them. And whether you detained them for a week or a year, the minute they got out, they were going right back to the block to buy drugs to get high.

Her hands dropped from my face, and her eyes started to water. "Why the hell did he have to take his ass out and get into some more shit?" she asked, her back to me. She turned around and faced me with a desperate look in her eyes. "Harlem, baby, you know I can't wait that long."

I stared down at the concrete. When I looked up at my mother again, she was coughing and holding her belly. Then her hands was acting like they had a mind of their own. Like she was covered in flea bites, Mama kept on scratching all over her body, making my ass itch too. I knew her withdrawal was kicking in. I started getting flashbacks of the last time this happened. Then she was throwing up and shit, pissing on herself like a baby, shivering like her body temperature had dropped, and constantly screaming.

Her voice interrupted my thoughts. "Just your hands, baby. You know that's all you need. And I promise you, baby, this will be the last time. Last time, Harlem, I promise."

I placed my hand around her shoulders and mumbled, "Come on, Mama, you know I got you."

We walked back to our house. Even though she promised this would be the last time, in the back of my mind I didn't believe her.

Once I escorted my mama to the house, I told her to lie down till I got back. I pulled my loose tee-shirt in a firm grip and tied it behind my back in a knot so it showed the shapeliness of my 30C cup breasts and my taut stomach. I pulled the rubber band out of my hair so it fell loose and cascaded down my back. I fluffed it out a little. I then took a deep breath and walked to the Property Manager's office. Once there, I knocked on the door softly and was told I could come in.

I turned the doorknob and stepped inside the office. I stood in the center of his office on his Persian rug.

"Hello, Harlem." His eyes snaked down the length of my body and froze at my breasts.

My eyes scanned the office. I did this every time I stepped foot inside, telling myself it would be the last time and mama would just have to deal with it, but I always came back. Although the projects were run-down, his office wasn't. I looked at the shine in the cherry-wood walls before my eyes passed over his degree and certificates, his employee-of-the-month plaque. A big picture of African queens and kings always had my attention. The framed photos on his desk were of a lady that sure as hell wasn't his woman. She was far too cute to piss on Mr. Barry if his monkey ass was on fire, so I know it to be a damn lie.

Front all you want, homie. Your ass is not fooling me.

Now I'm not saying Mr. Barry didn't have no woman, but the bitch was probably as butt-fucking ugly as he was. Maybe even worse. There was also a picture of his mother, who looked just as fucked up as him. Yeah, Mr. Barry didn't have a chance. And he had an 8 X 10 photo of the damn dog too sitting with his tongue slobbering, like he was his damn twin, to complete his little family.

I inhaled, and as usual, the room smelled like cinnamon potpourri, which was strange for a man. But, hell, he wasn't considered a man to most. Most considered him to be a chump. I agreed, but to me he was a dirty one. Supposedly a Christian, he was always playing gospel music. Shit, I wondered if the members of the congregation knew of this nigga's extracurricular activities, getting off on young girls and slanging "yay" on the side.

I forced myself to stare at his ugly-ass face, hiding my disgust. A short, pudgy muthafucka, his teeth were as yellow as the sun and bigger than Mr. Ed's. In fact, you could see their imprint in his cheeks before he even opened his mouth. They were so fucking big, it looked like he was always smiling. But that wasn't the worse thing about him. On the right side of his neck, the nigga had a lump the size of an apple, like someone shot him with a harpoon. And on top of all of this, the nigga had one regular arm and one stump.

I bit my bottom lip. "Hi, Mr. Barry. How you doing?"

He leaned back in his chair. "Good. What can I do for you today, Harlem?"

I forced a smile to my lips then leaned over in his face and whispered, "I need a couple caps."

He arched his right brow then nodded at me.

I watched him rise from behind his desk, his belly bumping into the edge. He walked briskly to his windows, closed the blinds, then locked his office door. He walked over to me and smacked my ass with his good hand, chuckling when it jiggled.

I bit the inside of my mouth to ward off any smart comment about this sleazy pervert touching me.

He relaxed back on his couch across from me. "Get undressed, Harlem."

As I pulled my shirt over my head, I could hear him unbuckling his belt, then pants, then zipper. What the fuck his big ass had on a belt for, I didn't know, since the nigga's belly was so big, it looked like a big-ass kid was in there trying to find his way out.

Before I could even get my pants down I heard him moan, "Oh yeah." He jerked his little dick and threw his head back, them buck-ass teeth poking out.

I posed in my bra and underwear, shaking inside, as he worked his dick like a machine.

"Goddammit!"

I held in my laugh when he tried to stroke it with his stump arm. His other hand must have gotten tired.

"Harlem, come and finish me off, baby."

I strolled over to him and curled up on the couch. *Mama, I must really love you to be doing this,* I thought.

My hand gripped his sweaty dick, and I stroked it up and down,

He howled, "Awwwww shit." His hand smacked my ass. "Moan, baby, moan!"

"Ahhhhhh."

He slapped my ass again. "My dick big, ain't it?" *Does he really want me to answer that shit?*

"Aint it?" he said louder.

"Big as King Kong, Mr. Berry." I stroked his shit faster.

Suddenly his breathing quickened and became ragged, and his voice hoarse. He gripped one of my butt cheeks as his legs started slapping against the bottom of the couch like he was choking. He howled again. "Awwww!" Then his big-ass teeth clashed into each other.

Right before his tip filled with the milky substance and it shot out, I snatched my hands away and looked in the opposite direction. When I looked his way again, it was leaking onto his pants as it hung sideways.

"Aw shit!" He leapt up from the couch and went into the small bathroom located in his office.

I took the opportunity to quickly put my clothes on.

See, Mr. Berry was a big-time joke in the projects. Word was, one time a tenant couldn't pay her rent, which was crazy 'cause rent in the projects wasn't all that much. But when people got their county and GR checks they usually fucked them off on weed or heavier dope, clothes, shoes, boost minutes for their chirps, or they drank. Or they got so far behind that the rent piled up on them. So, instead of her rent money, she offered Mr. Berry some pussy instead.

After some sucking and rubbing, the lady sat down on his dick, which went limp the moment it entered her pussy. He didn't get in one single stroke. And every woman he got with in the projects said the same damn thing. The nigga couldn't stay hard.

Whenever he would come to our doorstep if my mama was late on the rent, she always cursed him out. "Fuck you, you fat, pudgy, cripple-ass muthafucka. You'll get the rent when you get *the . . . rent*. Worry more about trying to stay hard than when you gonna get your hands on my greens."

He would never argue with her though. He was too embarrassed. He would just sigh and repeat himself, "You need to pay your rent," then walk away.

And I'd be in the corner laughing hysterically.

He never fixed his dick problem, so the nigga had no choice but to be contented with being jacked off or sucked. Mr. Berry got smart though, once he realized the women were passing on the info to each other on how to get away without paying rent. I guess he figured, if he didn't stop fucking with them like that, he'd have no damn rent to collect and it might get back to his supervisor.

So he only fucked with us minors because, for one, we wouldn't expect as much as an older woman—just a twenty or a forty—and most of all we kept our mouths shut. Plus, I also think he had a thing for young girls, probably 'cause he was a

pervert and he knew deep down money was his
only means of getting us to be in the same room
with him. Only, my mouth wasn't going anywhere
near his shit. But I'd jerk the shit out of his meat, if
it meant stopping my mama from crying or getting
sick again.

When Mr. Berry came back out, I was fully
dressed and my hair thrown back in a ponytail.

He slid me three thin plastic packets filled with
the shit my mama and daddy craved and would
break every law known to mankind to get. He
handed me an extra twenty on top of that and
said, "Maybe next time you could use that lush
mouth of yours, Harlem." He licked his lips sug-
gestively, spit all in the corners of his mouth, disgusting the shit out of me.

I tossed the twenty on his desk and rushed out
without answering. It was funny how men were
willing to pay for a pretty face.

This would have to be the last time I did that
shit. If things got really bad again a friend of mine
from school named Roslyn told me she had a way
to make extra money quick. "And it don't involve
sex, girl," she assured me.

I was glad about that, but I knew it had to be
something risky, but still I hoped Mama was telling
the truth when she said this was the last time I'd
have to do this shit. I was hoping they'd get they
shit together.

It was Christmas Eve and I made the best out of
what we had. I wasn't too worried myself, since it
was on and crackin' at school.

My homeroom class had a Christmas party, and I ate so much of that free food that my belly hurt. Students in my class brought tamales, enchiladas, fried chicken, orange chicken, boxes of pizza, chips, dip, salsa, apple cider, cakes, pies, Christmas cookies, and even eggnog. I guess I stuffed myself because I knew, once I went home, it wouldn't be much of a Christmas. And all my broke ass was able to bring was a $1.07 gallon of ghetto punch that had an acid feeling when it slid down your throat. But nobody tripped.

Now had it been a party in the projects, I would have been the laughingstock of the damn thang. It was bad enough that bitches in the projects teased me since I was a kid, 'cause while my mama took her county check and bought drugs, their parents took theirs and bought them nice clothes and shoes.

My mom said it didn't have shit to do with what I was wearing. "Come on, Harlem," she said, "think on this. You are a pretty girl. Yeah, they got clothes and shit, but they look like they belong on a chain. The little bitches look like dogs."

But the reason I think she gave such a passionate speech about how pretty I was was because she once again shot up her check in her veins and the first day of school was the following day and she couldn't afford to buy me any school clothes.

It didn't matter I didn't have the same shit they did, and it didn't matter if those females still didn't like me, because when I was in class none of that shit mattered. My brain made me popular. I was placed in a class for gifted kids, and even the work there was no challenge for me. Hell, I always finished fast and sometimes helped the other students. My intelligence took the attention away from my tacky clothes and even tackier parents. I just always made sure I did my hair in a nice style, like those twisties in the front, made sure my outfits were clean and crisp, and scrubbed my shoes till they were white.

When I got home from school and came in the house, I noticed Daddy was gone and Mama was sick, and it was only three-thirty. I found a piece of salt pork in the freezer and cooked it with some kidney beans. Shit, hopefully it would be enough to last us for Christmas Day, so we would at least have something to put on the damn table.

My friend Stacey invited me over to her house for the holidays, and just hearing her talk about turkey stuffing, sweet potato pie and making Christmas cookies had me salivating. But I couldn't leave my mama on the holidays for nobody.

Besides, Stacey said her family always did a gift exchange, and I had no money to buy her a gift. And that would be too embarrassing. I knew Stacey came from money. She was always fly—G-Unit, Ecko, True Religion—while I was wearing the same shoes I wore in the ninth grade.

I wanted to get a job somewhere to make my own money. Shit, I would have flipped burgers, cleaned up, done laundry, whatever. But my daddy wouldn't let me. And the occasional side hustles went toward feeding my mama's habit. All the same, something told me 2006 would be far better than 2005 and the years before that.

I pressed the taped-together earphones to my head and struggled with the tuner on the cheap Walkman, the one that my extra quarters bought me from the dollar store, while I stirred the beans in the pot and listened to Keyshia Cole. She knew what I was going through. As the beans began to boil, I sang "Love," as if the song was about my life.

I peered out my window and caught sight of Savior's fine ass. He looked through the blinds and nodded at me, and I nodded back.

"Get out that window looking at them niggas!"

I jumped and glanced my father's way as he slammed the living room door. "Sorry, Daddy," I said, putting my attention back on the food.

"Eddie, you got my shit?"

I shook my head. My mama didn't have no shame anymore. Wasn't any need to try to hide it from me. I knew what was going on.

He tapped his right pocket and looked back my way. "Finish them beans. Your mama and I will be back in here in ten minutes."

I nodded and continued stirring the beans as they boiled in the pot.

But they never came out of the bedroom as I sat at the table alone, listening to music with my headphones on.

After about twenty minutes, I put the beans in the fridge, cleaned up, and went to bed.

The next morning I woke up bright and early.

"Ma! Daddy! Merry Christmas, y'all!" I jogged out of my room, went past the living room, and burst in their room to find it empty. I rushed downstairs, wondering if they were outside, but they weren't there either.

Although it was still early, the sun was shining brightly. That's Cali for you. Wasn't no "Winter Wonderland" out here. Right now it felt like it was mid-spring or the beginning of summer. You could never play it safe out here. The weather was too unpredictable. It could be a heat wave in the winter or a heavy downpour of rain smack dab in the summer. But today, even though the weather was just right, everything else felt all wrong, because I was here alone.

I sat on our stoop for a while twiddling my thumbs. Then I braided my hair in some plaits, sang every song I knew, and still my mama and daddy were MIA. Kids started running outside to play with their new toys. One kid, Toby, was happily riding past me on his bike. I smiled and gave him a thumbs-up. "Nice bike, little man."

As he sped past, he yelled out, "Whatchu get, Harlem?"

"A lot of stuff."

He turned around and raced back over to me. He jumped off the curb in front of me, startling me. "Like what?"

"Boy, why you all up in my business? I said I got a lot of stuff."

He shook his head and took off.

I soon felt a pair of eyes on me and swung mine in that direction. It was Savior. Embarrassed, I looked down at my bare feet and tapped the pavement.

I had a mad crush on Savior. He wasn't much

older than I was. I think he was twenty-two or twenty-three. He was buff, tall, and dark chocolate, the way I liked them. Pearly white teeth and jet black eyes, his hair was thick and braided in corn- rows. Now, I don't know if Savior was feelin' me, but he was always lookin' out for me.

He stopped in the section of the projects I lived in to visit my nasty-ass neighbor Bo Bo, who I had to slap once or twice for slapping me on my ass. Other than that, Bo Bo's crush was harmless. Bo Bo and Savior were also dealers for some dude named Chief, who had the whole projects on lock. Which was crazy as hell, because you never saw him traveling through the projects. Yet, the nigga had a whole lot of pull. Word around the way was he'd just killed somebody for stealing a five-dollar weed sack. I ain't never seen his ass before, but I ain't never heard about no nigga standing up to him neither. And with the pull he had in the pro- jects, I knew he was making major dough.

Savior strolled over and blocked my view. He was wearing a white tee, some black jeans, a pair of clean black-and-white chucks, and a do-rag over his braids. "Why you go off on little shorty? He just wanted to know what you got for Christmas."

"He don't need to be all up in my business." I rolled my eyes.

He chuckled and bit his bottom lip. "What about me?"

"Who you?"

"Girl, you know who I am."

Yeah, I did. I wondered if he was going to bring up how I knew him.

Shit, I remember one time when my parents went on one of their binges. They'd been gone for three days, and like a damn fool, I went looking for them at the last place somebody told me they'd seen them, Keefee's house. Boy, was that a mistake.

I stepped slowly into the house, not knowing what I was walking into. The living room was dark as fuck and quiet, except for the flicker of a cigarette lighter and a constant fizzle sound, and there was a weird foul-ass odor in the room. I walked into a bedroom and found a woman bobbing up and down on a man's dick. As I rushed away, I saw a man in the bathroom sucking on a pipe like it was a woman's titty. Alarm hit me. I knew where the fuck I was—I was up in a crack house.

I turned on my heels quick and rushed past the bathroom and the bedroom. Only, two dudes were now standing in the way of my damn exit and shining a light from a cell phone on me. I took a step back.

One of them said, "Damn! What's up, shorty? You lost?"

With the little bit of light in the room from the flicker of another lighter I saw he was tall and slender, and the one laughing was short and stocky. As both dudes approached me, I shook my head nervously. "No. I mean, yeah, I was looking for somebody."

"You find them?" The short one took another step toward me.

I backed up. "No, they ain't here." When I tried to step around them, they wouldn't let me. I cleared my throat. "Excuse me."

They continued to block my path. The tall one said in a husky voice, "Shorty, you ain't gotta lie. You want some yay, then shit, you want some yay. Just say it. Only"—He flickered his cell phone down my body then held it up to my face—"what are you prepared to give us? 'Cause you damn sure lookin' right."

"Yep, yep. Ain't nothing in here fo' free," the short one said.

I hid my nervousness and glared at them both angrily. I knew these niggas were not going to rape me in a damn crack house in front of all these junkies. I placed my hand in the tall one's face and glared at the short one. "Check this out—I don't want shit from y'all niggas, and I'm not giving y'all shit, so step the fuck off, you ugly muthafuckas!"

"Girl, what the fuck you doing here? Man, I should kick your ass."

I bit my lips fearfully when they closed in and cornered me.

Before I could respond, an unfamiliar face snatched me up. He had a tight grip on my arm. He yelled, "Come on! Damn!" and we brushed past the two dudes.

Now I didn't know whether or not to trust him either, but he made me feel a hell of a lot safer than the two grimy-ass niggas in that crack house. I kept my mouth shut and followed his lead.

"Damn, Savior," the tall one said. "You never told us about her. Nigga, you came in the nick of time. It was going to go down."

As we swept past them, Savior turned and looked at them. "Nigga, wasn't nothin' goin' down with my fuckin' cousin. Y'all fuck with her again an' I'll shoot your fuckin' dicks off and feed 'em to my guppies."

I took a deep breath as the dude I now knew as Savior gave me a lashing about how stupid it was for me to run up in a drug house if I wasn't a cluckhead, a ho, or a drug dealer.

I snatched my arm away from him. "Well, I didn't know it was a fucking crack house! I was just looking for my parents. Shit!"

His face softened, and he stared down at me. "I don't mean to be harsh, shorty, but your parents are grown. If they want to stop shooting that shit in their veins they will. You can't stop 'em though. You comin' round here is just going get you caught up in some shit. Trust me, I know." Then he added, "And I know you don't want to hear this, but your parents are junkies in the worst way. And right now they just might not be ready. One day, maybe they will, but from the looks of them, they ain't checkin' in rehab no time soon."

I unpoked my lips. "You know my parents?"

He chuckled. "Aja and Earl? I've seen 'em around. Seen you too." He looked away when he talked about seeing me. "I seen you coming home from school and shit, chillin' on your stoop. You never hang out like I see a lot of females your age do, which ain't bad, by the way."

"Oh." I knew he was right about my parents, so I didn't argue with him. And it was kind of him to save my ass.

"Come on. It's kind of late. I'll walk you on back to your house."

And as we walked I was nervous. Not nervous in

a way where I felt he was going to do something to me, but nervous because I thought I would do something stupid in front of him, like trip over my own feet or say something silly, and he would think I was just a dumb little girl.

When we got to my stoop I told him, "Thank you."

"What's your name anyway, girl?"

"Harlem."

He nodded. "All right. I'll be checkin' for you in a few years."

I just laughed and went inside my house, but truth be told, I wouldn't have minded that one bit.

When I walked in the house I discovered my parents still weren't home. I went into the kitchen to watch Savior from the window as he left. Then once his tall frame vanished, I grabbed a dishrag and attacked the dishes in the sink.

Fifteen minutes later as I was sweeping up the kitchen floor, my head shot up when the living room door opened and my parents came flying in the house. Before I could ask what was going on, my mom raced to the kitchen and clung to me like she was the daughter and I was the mom. My dad, meanwhile, tried his best to close back the living room door, but some dude was still able to bust through. My dad backed away, but dude grabbed him before he could get away.

The next thing I knew, my daddy was lying flat on his back and receiving a barrage of punches from the dude, but he didn't fight back. My mom and I screamed, and she pulled away from me.

"Stay back!" my dad yelled.

"Bitch, you betta. Else, I'll fire a load in your

junkie ass 'cause I gives a fuck about a dope fiend."
The man paused the ass whipping to raise his shirt
and show my mama and me his gat.

I grabbed her before she could rush the guy because I knew in a hot second she would.

"Get out of my house, you bastard," she yelled at
the top of her lungs, jumping up and down. "And
get the hell off of my husband!"

There was nothing we could do besides watch.
We couldn't call 911. We didn't have a damn phone.

Just as quickly as the beating came, it stopped.
But that didn't mean my daddy wasn't hurt. He
was lying on the sofa groaning in a low voice.

"Nigga, going to jail don't excuse your debt. You
betta get us that money—two hundred, fool."

The man's eyes passed over my mom like she
was a piece of shit laying on the carpet. Then he
turned his eyes to me. His lips twisted to one side
in a smile. He nodded. "Yeah, nigga, you best get
that money or she'll be on the ho stroll." He
pointed at me. He continued, "Chief don't play
when it comes to his dough. He done killed niggas
for a five-dolla weed sack. What makes you think
you exempt?" He swung his foot at my daddy's
head.

I tensed up as it connected with his face, and my
mom covered her mouth with her hands and let out
a muffled cry.

Then he bowed sarcastically, tossed me a wink,
and walked out, leaving our door open.

Mama rushed over to my daddy and helped him
to his feet. "Oh Lord, how we gonna get that
money?" She turned to me. "Harlem, I'm gonna
take him to the hospital."

I sighed, knowing I would once again have to try to save the fucking day. And I hoped I could earn a little more than the two hundred to pay Daddy's debt 'cause if she was taking him to the hospital that was another damn bill. 'Cause in Cali if your ass had no private benefits, you might as well be a piece of shit lying on one of them hospital chairs in the lobby. Hell, out here, being sick didn't mean shit. People done died in lobbies and waiting rooms, and by the time they saw Daddy it would be a new day.

When I saw my friend Roslyn in the hall at school the next day, I asked her, "You still know about that little hook-up?"

She smiled and nodded, looking fly in her red Ecko jumper skirt and matching Jordans that just came out.

I stared down at them hungrily like they were a fat, juicy steak.

Roslyn was taller than me and light-skinned with some skinny braids. She had small breasts, broad hips, and a big, wide ass she loved to wiggle.

"How you think I got this tight-ass outfit, girl?" She spun around for me slowly.

I laughed and shook my head. "Naw, I just need to do it once."

"That's what I said the first time I did it, but now, girl, I'm hooked." She tore a piece of paper out of her notebook and scribbled something down on it. "Meet me at my house tomorrow morning around ten."

"But tomorrow is school."

She gave me a sharp look. "So you wanna make this money or what, girl?"

I sighed and took the paper from her. "I'll be there. What do I need to bring?"

"Nothin'. I'll hook you up, since you my girl and all."

I met Roslyn at her crib, and we left her house pretending we were both going to school. Instead, we waited at the bus stop a few blocks away.

After about forty-five minutes of waiting, some older girl named Cocoa arrived. She swooped down on us at the bus stop, music blasting in her little Honda Civic.

"Come on, Harlem," Roslyn said.

I followed her lead and hopped in the back seat.

As soon as we were buckled in, Roslyn turned to me. "Harlem, Cocoa." Then she turned to Cocoa. "Cocoa, Harlem."

The brown-skinned lady wore blue contact lenses and had a blonde weave that went down to her waist. Her face was caked with makeup, but still under all of that was a pretty lady. She punched the gas pedal and nodded at me. "What's up, girl?"

I could see her tongue was pierced, and she had a piercing above her mouth.

"Check you out, girl. You pretty. That's a good thang too. You gonna make a lot of money."

Roslyn looked back at me and laughed. Then she turned back to Cocoa. "She said she only wanna do this once. I'm trying to school her on this shit. This money is addictive. Ain't no such thing as doing it only once."

I forced a smile, not knowing what to expect.

We ended up on 109th Street and Broadway in LA in the cut at a lounge place that was used for an after-hours club Cocoa said she frequented.

"By the way, Harlem," Cocoa said as we pulled into a parking space, "this ain't a legal stripping spot, so don't be telling other bitches about it. It's by invite only."

I nodded. Shit, I figured if I can jerk Mr. Berry off without throwing up, I can do a little striptease this one time to bail my daddy out of his mess.

We got dressed in the bathroom. I had on a short-ass leopard print dress with a matching bra and thong Roslyn had given me. It was more like a shirt than anything. She said it was brand-new, and I would owe her a pair of thongs. Roslyn had on a leather cat suit, and Cocoa wore a red see-through lace get-up. You could see her nipples and shaved pussy through it.

It was still early, but by eleven the music was already bumping in the place. While we put on makeup, Cocoa was puffing on a blunt. She passed it to Roslyn, who tried to hand it to me after taking a few puffs.

I shook my head. "I'm cool."

She shrugged and gave it back to Cocoa then went back to doing her makeup.

As Roslyn lined her lips with a dark brown lip liner I said to her, "Ain't it kind of early for niggas to be comin' to a strip club?"

She gave me a look like I was silly. "Harlem, hustlas don't work a nine-to-five. Trust me, they'll be here, and with them come the *dollas.*"

At the word "dollas," Cocoa let out a scream and

bent over so her ass was in the air and wiggled so her booty, which was huge as hell, could rattle. Roslyn joined her and popped her butt. Then they high-fived each other and started laughing.

When they noticed my ass looking at them like they were crazy, Roslyn said, "The first time I did this shit I was scared too, girl. Just don't try to do too much. Relax and shake your ass like there's no damn tomorrow. Get freaky with it 'cause niggas love a nasty bitch. Be nice to all the niggas, even the ugly ones, 'cause an ugly muthafucka knows he's ugly and has more to prove. He'll give you way more money than a cute nigga."

I gave a nervous-ass laugh as my stomach twisted in knots. At least when I posed for Mr. Berry it was private, only me and him, and I only had to take off my shirt and pants to get him off. I couldn't imagine showing my half-naked ass to dozens of men, but I had no choice. *Maybe it would only be a few*, I thought, trying to comfort myself.

Cocoa added, "Oh, and another thang, don't show your pussy. Your titties and ass are enough for these niggas. We don't want them going crazy. We don't have them same rules regular ho clubs got 'cause we at an underground spot, and we damn sure ain't got no damn bouncer. So be aware, anything can go down."

"We just gotta look out for each other," Roslyn said.

"And we each give up fifty of whatever we make to the owner. That's how much he charges me to let us use the place. Now let's get these niggas' money, ladies," Cocoa chimed in.

I followed them and took a deep breath.

We exited the bathroom and walked down the long-ass hollow hallway to an area that looked like an empty dining area, except for about four round tables and chairs, a bar area, a DJ stand, and a couple of leopard-print couches.

When we stepped inside the room, the new song I had heard before on the radio from Too $hort, "Bounce That Ass," was blasting in the room. There were about fifteen niggas in the room, four at one table, six at another, and five at another.

Cocoa went to one table, leapt on top of it, and instantly started wiggling hard and fast as hell. Then Roslyn went to the other table.

I watched them both for a moment before taking my spot. My legs were wobbly in a pair of clear heels, so I didn't bother climbing up on the table. I also didn't bother looking in the niggas' eyes. In fact, I kept my head down and proceeded to move my body like Cocoa and Roslyn. The song chanted, "Bounce that ass way down to the floor." So I shook it way down to the floor and felt a few dollars slapping me gently in my face and on my back.

Then came the words, "Shake that shit till you can't no more." I wiggled my hips, quickly making my breasts and ass bounce like a damn basketball. I squeezed my eyes shut and worked my body so far into the groove of the song, I felt like I was somewhere else.

The men kept howling.

I squinted my eyes a little and saw both Cocoa and Roslyn down to their bras and thongs and men slapping dollars on their asses. When I pulled my dress over my head, the yelling and whistling

got louder from the group of niggas near me. But
all their shouts were doing was making me more
nervous. As I squeezed my eyes shut and wiggled
my booty, more dollars tickled my body.

One nigga yelled, "Shake it, bitch."

I ignored him but worked my body a little
harder, hoping the pile would have the two hundred dollars I needed.

Then 50 Cent's "Candy Shop" came on. I
squinted at Roslyn and Cocoa again. Now their titties were out, and all they were wearing were their
heels and thong. Cocoa flickered her tongue over
one of her nipples, and Roslyn was making her
butt cheeks clap together like a set of hands.

I squeezed my eyes shut again and tried to un-
snap my bra. I had it halfway off when I opened my
eyes again and almost jumped out of my skin when
I saw a dude smack dead in my damn face, making
my heart pound faster. As much as I would have
liked, he wasn't no stranger either. It was Savior.

Before I could say anything or cover up, he
yanked his jacket over me and, like he did at the
crack house, snatched me out of there with the
quickness.

One angry nigga said, "Savior, where the fuck
you taking that ho?"

Without looking, Savior tossed a hand at him,
and led me back down the long hallway I had
walked down earlier with Roslyn and Cocoa.

I was damn near naked, and his jacket was
falling off of me. It wasn't very long anyway, so you
could see the thin strip of material in the crack of
my ass, not to mention my butt cheeks. I'm sure a

nipple was hanging out, but he kept his eyes on my face, never dropping them any lower.

"Where your clothes at, Harlem?"

"Um . . . they in the bathroom," I said in a shaky voice.

"Go put them back on."

Now I know he wasn't my daddy, or my man for that matter, but something about his tone made me run in that bathroom and put my shit back on. As I stood down at the end of the hall looking like a dumb ass, Savior signaled for me to come over by jerking his head my way, then in the opposite direction.

Once I closed the distance between us, his hand went back to my arm, and he pulled me out of the warehouse. He was walking so fast, I had to jog to keep up with him.

I glanced back at Cocoa and Roslyn, who, unfazed by my departure, were still doing their thang. The men I was dancing for had split up and joined their two tables. I glanced back at the dollars resting in a pile on the floor, wishing I could go back and snatch them up.

Once we moved a few feet from the warehouse, Savior let me have it again. "Harlem, what the fuck you doin' in there?" He pointed back at the lounge.

"Makin' quick money," I fired defensively. I wanted to ask, "What were *you* doing in there?" but kept the comment to myself. For some reason I felt jealous.

"And just what do you know about quick money?"

I shrugged. I didn't know shit about it. I knew this was just my way of getting it quick.

"Girl, there were fifteen niggas in there. You know what they could have done to you?"

"Roslyn said it was safe."

"Man, who cares what she said. Let me tell you something, Harlem—You need to stop selling yourself short. Your young ass need to be at school and not with them hoes. Listen, some bitches don't want much. They impressed with money, clothes, cars, and shit. You better than this. I barely know you, and I can tell that about you. You don't need to be caught in no shit like this. Don't listen to them. All that material shit is just that. Shit. It don't have no real value. And you don't need it, if means selling a part of your soul and complicating your life."

"I didn't come here to shake my ass for some clothes."

He raised his eyebrows. "Then why you here doin' this shit?"

I crossed my arms. "To pay off a debt my daddy owes."

"Debt? What debt?"

"Some dude came to our house and beat my daddy's ass. He said my daddy owed him two hundred dollars and if he didn't get it to him I would end up on the ho stroll."

His jaw line twitched. "You know what he looked like?"

As I described him, Savior nodded as if he knew the guy. "I'll straighten it out. Come on, let me take you back home." He opened the passenger door to his Yukon for me. "Don't you ever bring your ass in here again," he barked and slammed the door.

* * *

And he did straighten things out, because the dude never bothered us again. Occasionally, when he wasn't too busy doing his hustle or hanging out with his friends, Savior would walk with me to school and home, just say what's up, or share friendly advice with me and shit. And, if I ever needed anything, he said I could always come to him. But every time his mouth moved, I was too focused on his sexy-ass lips. But that was as far as I would go. I never had a boyfriend or even kissed a dude. I just fantasized about him being my boyfriend and kissing him and sharing a tub of popcorn with him at the movies. But, hell, I was too chicken to tell him how I really felt.

Watching Savior tug his bottom lip with his teeth made my tummy quiver.

"You ain't nothing special," I told him.

He laughed. "Man, you just full of attitude today. Santa didn't put nothin' under the tree for you?"

"We don't have a fucking tree."

His smile faded, and he nodded. "Sorry to hear that. What did you have your heart set on?"

I didn't mean to snap at him, but shit, it was Christmas and I was spending it alone, just like Thanksgiving, so my parents could get dough to get high. And all I really wanted was a pair of nice sneakers. I was sick of putting white paint on my shoes so they looked halfway decent.

"Go throw some shit on and come with me."

Chapter 3

At Savior's invitation, I didn't hesitate. I dashed upstairs and threw on some jeans, a T-shirt, and my raggedy-ass tennis shoes.

We went to the Slauson Swap Meet, which was the place you went when you needed anything from a new pair of kicks, a new outfit, sounds for your ride, a tattoo, your nails done, or to even grab something to eat. I went there from time to time with friends, even though I never had money to buy shit. It was cool to look around.

Savior and I knew they'd be open because them store vendors didn't give a fuck about Christmas. Once Savior and I entered, I was like a kid in a toy store. I saw all that shit and went crazy, my eyes scanning everything.

"Since I hurt your feelings and all, I'ma buy you an outfit and a pair of sneakers."

I clapped my hands together and tried on at least ten different shoes before I settled on a pair of pink-and-white Nikes that were fly as hell. Then I chose a matching Rocawear outfit that had a jacket and skirt, the same one my friend Stacey had.

"Thank you." With tears in my eyes, I leaped on Savior and gave him a bear hug, but when I felt him stiffen, I pulled away and wiped off my face.

"No problem. You hungry?"

He knew I was. My stomach was grumbling. "Naw, I'm good."

He laughed. "Then come watch me eat this burger, girl."

We walked over to a little hut inside the Swap Meet.

He ordered two milk shakes, chicken strips, onion rings, French fries, a cheeseburger, and two hot dogs. "Girl, you better help me eat all of this."

I laughed and helped myself to the fries.

"Savior, were you born in California?"

He bit into his burger. "No. I moved out here from Jersey."

I grabbed a shake and closed my eyes as I slurped, which made him laugh. If he only knew . . . the last time I had a shake I was in pigtails.

"Why you leave Jersey for busted-ass California?"

He chewed, swallowed, and said, "Wasn't nothing in Jersey for me, 'cept my dumb-ass mama and her dude. I got sick of whipping his ass for whipping hers. Every time I turned around she was taking him back. He whipped my mama so bad one day, I couldn't take it no more. He was on that PCP and flung my mom out the kitchen window and fractured her ribs. I used to play baseball. I took my bat and broke it on his ass, and when I got through with him, I ended up breaking his arm and leg."

"Then what happened?"

"He pressed charges on me. Got charged with assault, lost my scholarship. A friend of my moms said he had a job for me." Savior stuffed an onion ring in his mouth. "But that was bullshit. And I couldn't find a job, with my record. And you see what I do, so hell, here I am." He took a sip of his shake.

"My dad ain't much better."

"Yeah, that fucker is mean as hell. Can't believe y'all came from the same family tree."

I laughed. "What he do to you?"

"He curses me out every chance he gets. I guess he don't like me too much."

"Why wouldn't he like you if he don't even know you?"

Savior's eyes locked with mine. "'Cause I won't sell to him. Kind of don't feel right selling to *your* folks."

I pulled my lips in and looked down. I didn't know why, but it felt good to know Savior wasn't the one supplying my parents with drugs. "Do you miss your mom?"

"Yeah, but it's better this way. She ain't going to leave that fool, and you can only whip on a dude for so long. If I had stayed, one of us would have ended up dead at the rate we were going."

I grabbed one of his onion rings and munched on it. And I thought my life was screwed up. Yeah, I knew what he did, but I was in no position to judge him. Both my parents were addicts, after all, and were probably getting high at that very moment, so I didn't reply. I just kept eating up all his damn food.

He shoved his half-eaten burger away and wiped his face with a napkin. "Whatchu want, Harlem? You know yet?"

"Yeah—to get the hell out of California. This may sound crazy, but I always dreamed about going to Rome or some place like that, live in a villa, smash grapes with my feet, like I saw on those *I Love Lucy* re-runs, and make wine I can sip at night and stare at some bomb-ass view. Maybe, be a social worker—That's what I want, Savior. What do you want?"

"You," he said without hesitation.

I blushed like I was a little girl, scratched my hair, and looked down. *Me? His fine ass wanted me?*

"I wanna get out this life. Slangin' ain't for me. Neither is this player shit. I wanna leave Cali too. Now, I don't know if I wanna go as far as Rome though."

I laughed.

"I'm getting out of here real soon. Maybe somewhere quiet, like Colorado. Build a life out there. How about it, Harlem? Would you leave with me?"

I looked him squarely in his eyes. "Yes."

Now it was his turn to blush. He wiped his face with a napkin, looked down at the floor, slapped his hands together, and laughed before looking at me again.

I guess he wasn't expecting that, but I never took my eyes off of him. I was serious as hell. "My mama been with one man her whole life: my daddy. I don't want no different for myself."

"And what man is that?"

"His name is Savior. He hangs around the projects. He's tall, dark as hell, and sometimes he look like he's got Down syndrome—Awww, I'm play-ing."

We both started laughing.

A chuckle still on his lips, he asked, "About which part, Harlem?"

I turned serious. "About Savior having Down syndrome. I'll be eighteen next year. You think you could wait for me?"

Out of nowhere, Savior leaned over the table and brought his lips to mine, giving me my first kiss. After the quick peck he pulled away and smiled. "Yeah, I'll wait for you, Harlem."

We continued the conversation as he walked me back to my house from his truck.

When we reached my apartment, I said, "Thanks, Savior," and lifted my free hand to wave at him as he stood still for a moment, watching me.

Suddenly the door swung open, and my daddy came out with a look of rage. He grabbed me by my shirt collar and yanked me inside. "Where the fuck you been, girl?"

"Slauson—"

"With that muthafucka?" He looked at the two bags in my hand. "Give me this shit." He grabbed them from me and ran outside. "Muthafucka, stay the hell away from my child!"

I watched from the living room window and saw him fling the outfit and shoes in the street. I winced as they hit the filthy ground.

Savior held up his hands in surrender and backed away slowly.

My daddy rushed back inside and came after me as I backed into a corner. Within an instant I was tasting my own blood, which trickled from my top lip, after he slapped the shit out of me. Then he threw me into the wall. "Keep your fast ass in this house, or you gonna get some more of this!"

I started crying loudly.

"Don't blame her 'cause we ain't got no more shit!" My mom staggered into the room, clearly loaded.

"Bitch, shut the fuck up!"

"Bitch?" She lunged at him and started pounding him in his back.

He easily threw her off of him and smacked her in the mouth too.

"Mama!" Forgetting my own pain, I rushed over to her as she hit the floor.

"You bastard!" she yelled. "We lowered ourselves to this? Now you hitting me in front of our child!"

As she struggled to stand up, I helped her by grabbing one of her arms and letting her lean on me.

He ignored us both and marched towards the door. "Like I said, Harlem, you go near that nigga again, I'ma snap your fuckin' head off," he said, an evil look in his eyes.

I looked down and nodded. "Yes, Daddy."

He slammed the door so hard, he left a crack in it.

Chapter 4

"You all right, Mama?"

She looked at me and laughed. "Girl, you always worrying about me. Shit, you took a harder punch than I did. You okay?"

"Yeah, Mama." I shrugged and went into the bathroom to grab the alcohol. There was none, so I took some tissue paper, poured some cold water on it, and held it to my lip to stop the bleeding.

Even though my cheek and lip were stinging and I wanted to cry some more, I didn't. I forced a smile on my face, grabbed another tissue, wet it, and went back in the living room so Mama could clean her face as well. "Here you go, Mama."

She took the tissue and looked towards the wall. "Damn, I bet you hate me."

I shook my head. "You my mama. I couldn't ever hate you."

"Well, you should. Hell, I hate myself."

She had that look of regret in her eyes again, all the things she should have done as a mom but didn't, and all the things she shouldn't have done as a mom that she did. As much as I wanted to take that pain away from her, I knew I couldn't. It was all mental, and I couldn't fuck with mental. I was no Dr. Phil, but still I tried.

"Don't worry. You did the best you could, Mama, the best you knew how." I winced at the pain in my mouth and blabbered out before I could stop myself, "I hate Daddy."

"You shouldn't. He does the best he can. He takes care of both of us. He really has tried to keep us together and with a roof over our heads."

Right. From where I'm looking he ain't done much. We struggle day in and day out. How does he take care of us? I don't see it.

I watched her run a hand through her patchy, thinning hair. It was so matted in the back, it looked like it was growing dreads at the nape again. Sadly, her eyes passed over my own thick, rich mane, which hung in a braid down my back. Mama had lost seven teeth, three in the back and four in the front. Her skin was sunken in, and there were blotches all over her face. And her eyes were always bloodshot red and tired looking. Her banging body was long gone and replaced with sagging skin and bones. No ass, nothing. The beauty I remembered when I was ten had long faded. The only beauty she had left was the beauty of her soul, which she'd share with me whenever she could. For once or twice, in moments like this, when she remembered I was next to her breathing and living, she put me before her drug, even if it was for a little while.

And yeah, Mama still could sing.

I buried my head in her lap, and her smoky voice filled my ears as she sang Nina Simone's "Angel of the Morning," my all-time favorite song.

She sang: *"Just call me angel of the morning. Just touch my cheek before you leave me, baby."*

Like a little kid I allowed her voice to comfort me and lull my body to sleep. I had my escape, and before the night was over, I knew she'd have hers.

I heard the shuffling of mice in the kitchen as they ransacked the cabinets for food. I ignored the sound since I was so used to it. They wasn't gonna find shit no way. My body was banged up and cramped, and I was cold on the floor. I winced and twisted my body so I could lie flat on my back, my mom's head angled at my feet.

"Ma, get up before the roaches get you." I rolled on my knees and scooted toward her head. I shook her body slightly. "Mama, wake up."

She didn't move.

I shook her body one more time, but she still didn't respond. I grabbed her arm and, for the first time, saw the syringe in it. My heart started beating rapidly. I screamed, yanked it out, threw it away, and kept shaking her. "Mama! Mama! Wake up. Daddy! Daddy!" I looked around frantically for him as I yelled at the top of my lungs.

Her whole body was cold, and there was no air going in or out. With shaking hands, I placed my hand over her heart muscle. It wasn't beating. I jumped to my feet and ran to the door. I unlocked it quickly and ran outside, screaming at the top of my lungs, "Somebody, help me! Please, oh God! Help me!"

Bo Bo and Savior were outside. When Savior saw my face, he ran over to me. "What is it, Harlem?"

"Call the police." I dashed back in the house, not wanting to leave my mother. I crouched to my knees, pulled her upper body to me, and rocked her back and forth.

Savior came busting through the door. He took one look at me and then at my mother. He peeled my fingers from her body. "Harlem, she gone. She gone, girl."

I slapped him in the face. "Shut up!"

"Calm down, your mom—"

"I'm not listening to you!" I placed my hands over my ears and sang loudly, "*Just call me angel of the morning*"—I sobbed—"*Just call me angel of the morning . . .*"

He shook me gently. "Harlem, stop. Your mom—"

"Don't say that shit again!"

I threw punches at his head until he grabbed both my hands to restrain me. Then he tried to hug me. Only, I didn't want no hug. I struggled and butted him in his mouth, so he had no choice but to release me and nurse his bottom lip.

Like a zombie, I walked past him out the house and into the street. The words of the song still on my lips. "*Just call me angel of the morning . . .*"

I kept on singing, hoping my mama would come back. Hoping that that moment she sang to me would be frozen in time. I yelled the lyrics over

and over again. Then I collapsed on the ground
and beat the pavement with my fist until pain was
pumping through me. And I didn't stop until my
skin opened up and blood gushed out, until I
passed out.

Chapter 5

I hid at the playground, sitting on a swing, while I watched through hooded eyes as they rolled my mother out of our home on a stretcher. Part of me wanted to run up and curse them out, drag my mama back in the house, and keep her body with me forever. But that other part of me knew. Man, I knew my mama was gone.

We didn't have no damn funeral. To tell the truth, I don't know what they did with my mama's body. In a way it made me mad as hell that I couldn't say goodbye to my mama properly but was still kind of okay with it because I damn sure didn't want to stand in front of people and cry my eyes out. And it wouldn't have changed anything. It wasn't going to bring her back. All I wanted to do was go home and sleep this pain away, but that seemed impossible with my daddy around. My mama's dying was slowly killing him. Well . . . that and the drugs.

He was gone day in and day out. He sold the fridge. Then he sold my mama's couch. And then he hit the lowest of the low—He sold all her old dresses from when she sang in Aces. I kept my disgust out of my eyes and buried it in the back of my throat when he went through all her shit and then left me alone without food. It didn't matter. Didn't nobody give a damn about a project kid. Not Social Services. I was one less person on their caseload. I didn't wanna be there no how. They put you in worse circumstances than where you came from.

At the end of the day, it seemed like all they were chasing was a paycheck, so my little situation wasn't shit to them. I mean, all my daddy was doing was neglecting me. I'd seen parents do worse to their kids and get away with it.

Savior looked out for me though. When my dad went on his drug runs, Savior would bring me food. The last time he brought me a burger, some fries, and a postcard he probably got at a car wash. He told me if I needed anything else to just let him know. Anything.

The card was one of those with a picture of a place, and the place was Rome. Scrawled across the back of the card in sloppy handwriting were the words, "*Keep that head up.*" It helped me a little. When it didn't, sleep helped me to forget that my mama, my friend—shit, pretty much all I had—was gone to glory.

My father re-appeared three days later early in the morning. I woke up when I heard the door open. I walked in the living room, scrubbing the sleep out of my eyes, and watched him bring in a plastic sack of food.

He glanced my way. "Hey, baby."

I couldn't name the last time he'd called me that or showed me any type of affection. Half the time he acted like he hated me, and I didn't understand why.

"Hey, daddy," I whispered with a forced smile.

"Look, it's some sandwich meat in here if you hungry."

I nodded and grabbed the bread and bologna out of the grocery bag. I put a piece of the meat between two slices of bread and sat down to eat. I bit into the sandwich, which really didn't taste like much of nothing to me. Still, I had to put something in my stomach.

My father watched me the whole time I ate, his expression pretty much unreadable. When I was done, I closed the container of meat, knotted the bag with the loaf of bread in it, sat them both on the counter, and headed back to my room.

As I walked past my father, his arm suddenly shot out and secured one of mine gently but snugly, making my heart beat faster. I narrowed my eyes in confusion.

He released me, and I continued walking to my room, feeling uneasy. He followed after me.

I stumbled over my own feet. He was standing behind me. I regained my composure and continued walking, and so did he. My lips trembled as I felt his breath on the back of my neck.

I took another step, trying to increase the small distance between us, but then I turned around slowly to face him. To my surprise, he was crying.

"Now, baby, I don't wanna do this."

Whatever it was, I wasn't waiting to see. I slipped past him and ran for the door. I hoped Savior was outside. I was gonna tell him to fuck my father up, but I didn't get the chance. Before I could take another step or scream, my daddy was on me, and he gave my head a major blow that put my ass out.

Chapter 6

The blow didn't put me out for too long. When I opened my eyes I wished to God that it had. There I was, with my daddy on top of me. When I opened my mouth to scream, he pressed a hand down on it. With his other hand, he tore my only bra. Then my underwear went next.

My words were in my eyes as I pleaded with him not to do this shit. My voice was muffled on his hand. "Daddy, don't do this. Don't rape me."

His eyes avoided mine.

My whole body cringed when he fingered my pussy in a rough manner. The first hand to ever touch me there.

"Please don't do this."

When he shed himself of his pants, I used the opportunity to try and run, rolling off the bed, jumping to my feet, and pumping my legs as hard and fast as I could. But I wasn't moving 'cause Daddy had a fistful of my hair. He dragged me back to the bed by my hair and flung me down on it. Then he forced my legs apart, pressed his weight down on me, and stabbed my virgin pussy with his dirty-ass dick. All I could do was cry before blacking out again.

When I finally came to, I heard a voice I didn't know say, "How much, man?"

Then I heard my daddy's voice. "Muthafucka, I already told you—Hand me twenty or get the fuck out!"

"All right, damn. She betta be worth the shit."

Courage made me open my eyes. I was naked on the bed, and my legs felt sticky. There was a dirty rag in my mouth, and my arms and legs were tied. I scanned the room. *Two men! Two men!* I blinked rapidly. My daddy and a stranger were standing over me.

I started shaking and shook my head when the man started unbuckling his pants. I struggled on the bed as he put his full weight on my body. I could barely breathe as his dick penetrated me clumsily, and he slobbered all over my titties. All of what he was doing was hurting me.

I closed my eyes and sobbed as he panted in my ear how good my pussy was. And my daddy, he just watched. I didn't want my first experience to ever be this way. *Daddy, please make him stop. Please get 'em off of me.*

"Hurry up, man."

The man kept jabbing me harder every time.

"What, man? I just got started. I didn't even come yet."

"Bust your shit!"

"Is she a virgin, man . . . 'cause she got a tight-ass pussy?"

"Naw, I broke her in myself. Hurry the fuck up!"

"All right, man."

He started pumping harder into me, making my insides sting. My head was hitting the headboard, and his body slamming against mine made slapping sounds. It felt like somebody was taking a stick and ramming it all the way in me. Nothing 'bout it felt good.

I felt a sticky substance enter me and slowly drip out.

He stood and adjusted his clothes. "Man, that definitely was worth the money. I'ma tell every nigga I know!"

I squeezed my eyes shut and moaned.

My daddy got smart after the first trick. After him, he made every guy wear a condom. I had never seen so many men and dicks. Black ones, white ones, Mexican, Cuban, even an Asian. I stopped counting after the seventh man, and I blacked out so many times, it was like I was taking naps instead of passing out. But my daddy didn't care. He was making that dough.

By this time my arms and legs were chafing from the rope and tearing my skin, and my breasts were raw and covered with purple marks from men sucking and biting them. Not to mention, my vagina wouldn't stop bleeding. I got to the point where I stopped pleading with my eyes.

The trade was always sex for money. And my

daddy's little operation lasted a good three days. Three days of different men sticking their dicks in my pussy, or their dick and balls in my face, coming all over my breasts, chest, pussy, ass, even my face. Or they'd just spray they shit all over me like they were holding a water hose. Thank God, Daddy kept a rag in my mouth, or else they'd stick they shit there too.

The only time Daddy untied me was to use the bathroom, and he stood in there like a guard dog and forced me back to the bed when I was done. I didn't have the strength to fight him. Most of the time I was so weak, all I could do was look blankly back at the men—young, old, and married— grinding on top of me. Hell, even the mailman wanted a piece of me.

How long was this shit gonna go down? Was it ever going to stop? I figured nobody would come looking for me 'cause we were still on Christmas break. I had to hope that it would end soon. My daddy had to have some type of love for me, but maybe he loved his dope more. Falling asleep from time to time was the only way for me to forget what my body was going through.

Suddenly, a commotion woke me up. Somebody kicked in the door, and there was a lot of yelling. Five men were on my daddy, whipping his ass.

Fuck him up, please, but don't touch me.

Two of the men held him up while he got punched and kicked. He howled in pain, but they wouldn't stop fucking him up.

Then a cloud of darkness seemed to overtake the room, as a man filled the doorway. He just stood and quietly watched. With his presence came the scent of some expensive-ass cologne, off-setting the smell of dirty dicks and my pussy. He had to be six-four and looked to be in his forties. He was a buff motherfucker, whose shoulders filled the door frame. He wore a fresh-ass suit and a trench coat, and two long braids hung down his shoulders. He looked straight up Indian with his bronze complexion, hawk-like nose, slim lips, round face, and long, neat beard.

"Fuck that nigga up!" he yelled.

The men continued to whip my daddy's ass.

The man stepped into the room. "Bring his ass over here."

When they dragged my daddy up to him, the dude grabbed him by his neck. Damn, my daddy looked so small compared to him.

"Muthafucka, you get this shit straight right now—You don't open up a ho shack in these muthafuckin' projects without my permission. I run this shit. I don't give a fuck if it's a lemonade stand. Nigga, you ask me! Got it?"

My father nodded his head and hollered out in pain, blood oozing from his nose and his right ear.

The man dropped my dad on the ground and kicked the shit out of his face. "Dirty junkie ass."

The other men went back to fucking my daddy up.

The man's eyes darted to me. Hell, I couldn't be embarrassed any more. A dozen men had seen me naked and stuck my pussy. Still, I hid my head underneath both my forearms, peeping at him as he zoomed in on me. My whole body started shaking.

"Now, let me have a look at this chick causing so much commotion in the projects."

My heart started pumping faster as he stepped toward the bed. Toward me.

"Word around town is, she got some magnetic pussy. I'm gonna make a lot of niggas mad tonight, shutting this shit down." He bent over and peered down at me, his eyes widening when he saw my face.

He made me just as nervous as my daddy, since I had no idea who he was nor what he was going to do to me. My bottom lip trembled. What if he continued where my daddy had left off?

"Boss?"

He continued to stare at me. "What?"

"Can we kill this sick muthafucka?"

Between hits to my daddy's back, another one of the dudes I recognized off the block said, "Muthafucka's prostituting his own damn daughter. That's Harlem."

He crouched down on his knees and used his silk handkerchief to wipe the combination of dried tears, snot, slobber, and cum off my face. "Let me introduce myself to you, Miss Harlem. My name is Chief."

Chapter 7

I was taken to a hospital and stayed there for a week and a half. They ran all kinds of test on me. The Lord was looking out for me that night because luckily I didn't end up with any major diseases. Nor did I get pregnant. I was almost sure that the grimy nigga who was the first to hit it had AIDS. Hell, maybe even my daddy did. But I was cool, except for the soreness and a yeast infection.

I had a hard time sleeping, with all the nightmares about men touching me, smiling at me, and licking their lips. I had never watched so much television. I looked at soap operas, talk shows, and all the sitcom marathons. And, of course, I watched *I Love Lucy* nonstop.

I hadn't seen my father since the incident and didn't want to. Deep down, I was hoping he'd burn in hell for the shit he did to me.

After two more days passed, the nurse came in the room and told me I was being discharged. She was a sweet lady with a whole lot of sympathy for me. She said she had a daughter around my age and that she couldn't imagine anyone treating someone so precious so badly. She helped me get dressed and told me, "Your brother is outside waiting for you, sweetie. Just sign the release form and you're all done. He came by and paid your bill yesterday." She handed me a clipboard and a pen.

Good, I thought, 'cause I sure as hell didn't have five cents to give her.

My eyes passed over the name, *Keisha Collins*. I signed the form and gave it back to her.

Chief had already prepped me on this part. The day he and the other dudes bust threw my bedroom after they beat my father's ass. He said if I didn't want to be stuck with my dad again I should go along with his plan. So when he passed me to some other dude and disappeared and the other dude carried me to the hospital, gave them a fake name, and told them I was his little sister who was gang raped on her way to a party, I simply nodded and played along.

. I didn't know how to react when I saw a Ford Excursion waiting outside for my ass. But there was no Chief in it. The driver, the same guy who had dropped me off there, a tall, lanky, black man with some short dreads, hopped out without a word and ushered me into the back seat. He jetted down the street playing T.I. and jumped on the 110 freeway, exiting on Crenshaw Boulevard and driving around a curved road that went round and round till we were in Baldwin Hills.

We drove up Via Leonardo to this phat-ass oakwood two-story house with big-ass picture windows. My eyes widened as he pulled in the driveway next to a candy apple low rider, and another car—I couldn't think of the name of that one—and turned off the engine. What the hell? I knew we were in Baldwin Hills, the black Beverly Hills.

I hopped out behind him, wondering if the guy was ever going to say something to me. Like the other homes on the block, the lawn was manicured. Wasn't no cigarette butts or candy wrappers on the ground. Just grass and flowers perfectly lined up along the edges of the lawn. And it was quiet. No loud-ass cars speeding past, noisy kids, and wasn't no females fighting or any gang bangers causing trouble.

He used a key to unlock the lavish house. There were high vaulted ceilings, and a big-ass flat-screen TV filled up an entire wall. My dirty tennis shoes seemed even dirtier next to the white carpet and snow-white fur couches. The walls had actual artwork that looked expensive as hell, not like the paper stencils and sketches that were stuck on the walls of my home, and all kinds of crystal gleamed on the countertops.

The driver nodded at me and vanished.

A woman came in the room. "Hello, hello." She strode up to me and extended her hand. She was tall and slender, dark-skinned with rosy cheeks, and had a gap between her teeth, and her hair was in skinny braids balled in a knot at the nape.

"I'm Kenita, and whatever it is you need, I'm here for you, girl," she said in a Jamaican accent. "Are you hungry?"

"Yeah. But I'm a little confused. Ma'am, where am I, and where is Chief?"

She looked at me for a long time and laughed. "You don't know? You home, child. You in Chief's home."

It was hard for me to fully understand the purpose of my being there, but I forgot it for the moment as she piled my plate high with jerk chicken and a spicy rice that I couldn't stop eating. It was that good. I washed it down with fresh lemon iced tea.

"Yes, Chief said he went out and got him a dime piece, whateva that means. I'm not too familiar with some of the slang Americans use. I've only been in his country for the seven months. But now I understand. You're a very pretty girl and so very young."

Her eye narrowed as if she was trying to guess my age but not comfortable flat out asking me.

"You look like that singer. What's her name? Ah . . . Phyllis Hyman. She's dead now. Drug overdose."

I didn't know if I liked the comparison.

"You want more food?"

I shook my head. "No thank you."

"You probably want to go to your room?"

I shrugged.

She laughed. "I love it. So very humble." As I followed after her, she turned her head and added, "That will change."

I didn't respond. I didn't know what she meant.

"Anyway, you will be very comfy here. I do it all. The cooking, cleaning, accountant, and the gardener so we'll be spending a lot of time together, child."

The bedroom had the same luxuries as the

other parts of the house I had just viewed. The huge bed, a California King, was covered by a very pretty pink comforter that looked like it was made out of silk. There was another huge flat-screen TV, and a vanity table and chairs like the kind my mama had always bugged my daddy to get her. I could just picture her sitting there smiling at her image and humming in that beautiful voice of hers while I brushed her silky hair. Tears starting running down my face at the thought.

"The closet is full of clothes and shoes—" She looked at me. "You okay, my dear?" She came toward me and lifted my face in her hands.

"Yeah, ma'am." I took a step back, causing her hand to drop from my face, and stared down at the carpet.

"Okay. Well, I'll let you get comfortable. You need anything, leave a list for me. I'll get it when I come next time," she said, and in a flash she was gone.

I immediately went to the closet. It was filled with clothes—dresses, blouses, jeans, skirts, velour sweat suits—in all the name brands I had seen other girls wear at school, and some I didn't know. There were also dozens of shoes, from sneakers to dressy heels. I think I tried on every outfit in the closet. Some fit me, and some were a bit too big. Then I slipped my feet in all the nice shoes. A couple were too small, but most of the heels fit me perfectly.

As nice as the items were, I wasn't enjoying any of it. And I knew why. I was alone now more than ever. I didn't care about all that shit in the closet or much of anything else. My mama was gone, and just as I was grieving, trying to make some sense of the shit, my daddy raped me. I really didn't have anyone, and the shit scared the hell out of me. I was a seventeen-year-old orphan who missed the hell out of her mama and couldn't do anything about it. Couldn't nothing I say bring her back.

I prayed to God over and over again that day she died to make her heart pump, but it seemed God just didn't hear my prayers or he just ignored them. Now it was probably only a matter of time before Chief came home and threw my ass out. All this shit was scaring me. I curled up in the bed and cried softly.

For the first time in my life I was able to eat as much food as I wanted, and I'm not talking about that shit my mama bought, like bologna. My mama would get tons of food stamps, but she spent twenty of it on food and always sold the rest. So we either had a sack of potatoes, beans, or bologna. Chief had so much damn food, every time I opened a fridge or looked on a shelf I felt I was in a grocery store. He had all kinds of meats, steaks, shrimp, crab, chicken, ham, and bacon, all kinds of bread and rolls, and fresh fruits every day, like pineapples, oranges, apples, cantaloupes, and strawberries, my favorite.

For the first couple of days I was in and out the fridge every ten minutes. Kenita was fattening me up on Jamaican dishes like curry chicken, beef patties, fried plantains, oxtails and beans, cabbage, rice and peas, and coconut shrimp. I knew in the first two weeks I was there I had easily gained ten pounds, but I didn't care.

Kenita said, "Child, I wish I had your body. I would drive men wild. Just wild."

Day to day was pretty much the same. It was a while before I caught sight of Chief. The only person I ever saw was Kenita. It was hard for me to make phone calls because there was no phone in my room. And it was always tied up by Kenita anyway. But the weird thing was, the phone never rang.

I asked her, "Could I use the phone in your room to make a call?"

She gave me a stern look. "I am not ta let ya use the phone, Harlem, so keep this among only us."

"I will."

I truly had no one to call, except for Savior, and I didn't know his number. But I was hoping to get in contact with Roslyn and then she could contact him for me to tell him where I was. I tried a couple times to get in contact with her, but she was never home. When I was finally able to speak to her, she told me she hadn't seen Savior in a minute. Damn. I wondered where he'd disappeared to. I thought if I could just get to the PJ's, I could sure as hell find him. I just had to figure out a way.

When I was of tired of eating I would dip my feet in the pool since I couldn't swim. Or if I was sick of watching television, I would sit and chat it up with Kenita because she never ran out of things to say.

She would go on and on about her boyfriend Simon who was in the Navy. She showed me pic-

tures of him and let me read all the letters he'd
sent her. "Oh, I love this man!" she exclaimed one
day, hugging one of his pictures to her chest then
kissing it. The man, for some reason, reminded
me of Savior, and it wasn't because he was dark as
hell like Savior. It was something about his eyes.
They had the same kindness that Savior's eyes had.
It made me sad because I missed him so much and
wanted to know so bad where he disappeared to.

And when she wasn't talking about her boyfriend,
she was telling me about school. Kenita was a psychology major at California State University. Once
I found that out I had a dozen questions for her—
What's college life like? What are the professors
like? What's there to do on campus?—because I
wanted to go so damn bad.

One day when we were sitting in the kitchen,
Kenita was doing her homework, and I was eating
an apple. She said to me, "Tell me someting,
Harlem—Why do you always look so sad? You're
such a pretty girl, and you seem so smart."

I shrugged. I guess her being a psychology
major, she wanted to test out some of her skills on
my ass. "I don't know, Miss Kenita."

"Did someting traumatic happen to ya, someting you don't want to say?"

I took a deep breath. "Well, my mom died not
too long ago."

"Oh." She placed a hand over her chest. Then
she touched me on my arm. "I'm so sorry to hear
that."

I offered a smile and dumped the apple core in
the trash.

"That is someting very hard to deal with, especially with you being so young. But it's God's will, and don't ever doubt that, Harlem."

I frowned. That didn't take the pain from my heart away, it being "God's will," or the crying at night, or in the morning when I woke up to the same fucked-up fate, my mama not being there. Was it God's will for me to live the way I did? Was it God's will that I be raped by my daddy and all of them triflin'-ass men? God's will . . . okay.

"Do you know the best way to deal with a loss?"

I shook my head. "No, not really."

"What I have learned about loss is that you shouldn't look at it as a loss. Maybe your mother is now in a betta place. Also think about it like this— You had seventeen beautiful years with your mother while some children don't get to spend any with theirs. They are snatched away with the blink of an eye."

I nodded. She did have a point, but when was she gonna get it that none of this shit made me feel any better?

"What made your mother so special to you? What are some of the tings she did for you?"

I thought about it. I really didn't know how to answer. For as long as I could remember, I took care of myself.

She looked confused by my silence, like she just knew I'd have a reply. "Okay, let's try this. Think of some of the positive qualities your mother had that affected you as a child in a good way."

I guess my mama was funny. And fearless. I knew she was crazy as hell too, and that was whether she was high or not. I also didn't know if that was a good thing. I guess it was good because some of the things she did cracked me up. But she also did some crazy-ass shit.

One day she took me to a parade when I was about eight years old. While we sat in the crowd, my mom was really enjoying the show, but my ass was bored. I started throwing rocks out into the crowd. My mama's eyes flashed toward me and pierced me with a look. I ignored her and kept on throwing rocks.

"Harlem, stop!"

I nodded, and as soon as she turned away I went back to throwing them. She snatched me up and slapped me on my ass.

Suddenly, out of nowhere, a cop rushed toward us yelling, "Don't you touch her!"

I tensed up and prepared for the worst, because Mama hated cops, I didn't know why.

My mom released me and got all up in that cop's face. "Listen, *Officer,* I shitted her out, and I'll do what the fuck I want to her. You ain't gonna get the chance to bust her in the head with a billy club or rape her in a dark alley at night when she sixteen."

His eyes widened. "I'll take you to jail."

"You ain't taking me to jail, muthafucka. The only way you gonna take me out of here is in a body bag, and before you can do that I'll shoot you with your own damn gun!"

There was silence for a moment.

"Yeah, what you got to say now? 'Cause I'll be damned if you get the chance to fuck with my child, get her used to jail and shit."

He looked at my mother angrily, but she just

smirked as if the uniform badge billy club, and gun were a joke.

I bit my lip nervously, knowing he was going to haul her ass right off to jail. Instead, he said, "Ma'am, have a nice day."

And we did. We kept watching the parade. I didn't throw any more rocks, and my mama kept on laughing. Every now and then I would catch the policeman casting looks our way, but my mom wasn't bothered a bit.

Just thinking about the way she talked to that cop had me cracking up in the kitchen. Kenita joined me in my laughter, even though she didn't know what the hell I was laughing about. And I wasn't going to tell her either. I didn't need nobody judging or thinking badly of my mama.

Kenita smiled and nodded as if pleased she got me to open up. "Good, Harlem. It's always good to think of your happiest moments with your mom. You have any of those memories?"

"Those were when she would dress up and sing to me."

"Oh. Was your mother a performer?"

"Something like that. A long time ago she sang in a club. She could sing her ass off."

"What was your favorite song your mom would sing for ya? Do you remember the name of it?"

"Yeah. 'Angel of the Morning' by Nina Simone."

She smiled. "Can ya sing a little for me?"

I closed my eyes and attempted to sing the lyrics: *"There will be no strings to bind your hands . . . Not if my love can't bind your heart . . ."*

Singing the song made me think of my mother.

And damn! How much I missed her. Soon my lips started trembling, and my words were smashing together because of the sob I was suppressing in the back of my throat. Finally I gave up and stopped singing. I rushed out of the room before Kenita could see the tears fall from my eyes.

I was now seventeen and living in a drug dealer's home. My mama was dead, and I had no idea where my father was. I didn't know if he was dead or alive—and I didn't care. I also knew I needed to go back to school and was wondering if Chief would grant me that wish.

"Where's Chief?" I asked Kenita one day.

"Out of town. He should be coming back real soon."

"Well, I was wondering if I would be able to go back to school."

"Hmmm, I was wondering the same thing, Harlem. That I do not know. I have been instructed to not let you leave, you know, but you can check with Chief when he comes back."

I nodded.

"But until he does, maybe I can work someting out for ya."

"Thanks."

Her solution was to get me the GED study guide. It wasn't what I had in mind, but oh well, what could I do?

I studied day by day. I did the sections one by one. I worked on the math first 'cause math was always easy for me. Then I tackled the reading, writing, then the social studies. The last section I

worked on was the science portion. I even took the
practice exams in the book.

One day we were in the kitchen, and I asked
Kenita for tidbits about Chief.

"Harlem, you very curious. Is there someting
you want to know?"

"What do you know about Chief? He seems like
a nice man, letting me stay here and all."

"That, he is." She gave me a long look. "He is
also very private too."

"Well, what type of man is he?"

"A very secretive one, miss nosy." Kenita giggled.

"I was just wondering—"

"I really don't know too much about him, Harlem."

Another month passed, and it was pretty much
the same as the last. I was allowed to leave the
house again, but it was just to go back to the doctor and take another AIDS test. Just taking that
damn thang and knowing how many men had
been inside me gave me apprehension, even
though I knew the last test I took was negative and
that I had been with no one else. Still, shit, I was
scared.

I crossed and uncrossed my legs as the doctor
flipped open the manila folder and read the re-
sults. And all that nervousness was washed away
with two words: "You're fine."

Since Kenita was the one who took me, I

begged her afterwards to take me to the projects so I could find Savior. Even though I was terrified as hell to go back to the projects and see my daddy, I was willing to take a chance and go, if it meant being able to catch sight of Savior. I wanted to say sorry for hitting him the day my mother died when he was trying to comfort me. Then I was going to tell him that if the offer he gave that day at the Swap Meet still stood then I would leave with him that very damn moment.

Kenita pierced me with a look. "Harlem, this will indeed be a one time ting," she said sternly, her hands gripping the steering wheel.

I nodded eagerly.

Once there I pulled a cap over my head, hoping that would disguise me a little. First, I went to my old apartment and walked next door to see if Bo Bo was there. Just seeing my apartment made me sick. I started shaking, and my stomach knotted up. Bo Bo was nowhere to be found.

"Shit."

I just drove around with Kenita, asking dudes I knew if they knew where Savior was or even Bo Bo. None knew. And I knew it was stupid, but I went back to Keefee's spot to figure out if they knew. That's where I spotted Bo Bo. He was sitting on their porch and smoking a blunt.

"Stop here please," I told Kenita.

Once she did, I hopped out the car and approached him.

"Harlem, where you been, girl?"

"Bo Bo, where is Savior?"

"You don't know?"

"No, nigga. Know what?"

"Savior packed his shit and hightailed it out of town, boo."

My heart damn near dropped on that stoop. Instantly Savior's words flashed in my head. *"I'm getting out of here real soon. Maybe somewhere quiet, like Colorado. Build a life out there. How about it, Harlem? Would you leave with me?"*

Damn! The nigga had left without me. That shit hurt.

I walked away, ignoring his last words about how he heard about what happened to me and that he was sorry to hear it. I didn't respond. I just slipped back into Kenita's car. I didn't even bother to ask her to take me to the projects again after that. I knew he wouldn't be there. And he sure as hell wouldn't be looking, and obviously wasn't worried about me, so I had to stop thinking about him and focus on me. And that started with me accepting my fate—I was down with Chief for the time being.

Chapter 8

Then Chief came back.

Don't get me wrong, I was living it up in his house. I had a gang of nice stylish clothes and shoes, and I was eating my ass off and hanging out by his pool. Notice I said hanging, because I still didn't know how to swim. Otherwise, I watched TV and even continued studying for the GED. I guess I was getting a little too comfortable and thought he was probably going to tell me to get the fuck out. But I soon learned he had other plans for me.

He came at an unexpected time. I had been eating chips and a seven-layer dip Kenita had taught me to make with ground beef, beans, cheese, sour cream, and jalapeños that was tearing up my asshole as I sat on the toilet when he burst through the bathroom door.

I was so embarrassed, I didn't know whether to stay seated or stand up. But there was no way I was going to stand. I was too busy dropping turds in the toilet, so I did nothing. I just sat there frozen with my eyes wide.

He poked his head in the door and zeroed in on me. "Baby girl, hurry up with that sit-down and get on out here."

I didn't know what the hell "sit-down" meant, but I hurried as fast as I could, squeezing the digested food out before wiping my ass, washing my hands, and heading nervously out to the living room, where he was waiting. I stood in the doorway wringing my fingers.

He was sitting on the couch reading a letter, one leg crossed over the other. When he felt my presence, he sat it down and beckoned me closer. "Come on in here."

He had his long silky black hair pulled back in a ponytail. His shit was damn near as long as mine. I had to admit, Chief was a very handsome man. He was dressed in some brown slacks that looked like they cost a grip, and a black silk shirt, and black shoes. On his right wrist he wore a Rolex covered with diamonds, and he had two rings on that were blinging. Just looking at them made my eyes hurt. Yeah, Chief was a balla.

With a nervous smile, I took baby steps toward Chief and sat across from him.

He smiled, licked his lips, and scanned my face. As well as my neck, shoulders, breast, waist, pussy, hips, thighs, calves, and feet. He chuckled. "You ain't gotta sit that far away, baby. I ain't gonna hurt you."

I shook my head at myself and went over to sit right next to him.

"How you doin'?"

"Good." I licked my dry lips.

He gestured toward the paper he was reading. "So you okay. Ain't got nothing, I see."

"Yeah." I clasped my hands in my lap.

"Good. Chief had to make sure . . . 'cause if you wasn't, I couldn't do nothing for ya, baby."

"Uh-huh."

"So by now, I know you know what the program is, right?"

I nodded, even though I didn't really.

"How old are you?"

"Seventeen."

"When you gonna be eighteen?"

"Next year."

"Cool. Well, you know Mr. Chief been looking out for you these past six months, right?"

I nodded. "And I really appreciate it too." I knew he was going to tell me to leave, but where was I going to go? I didn't even want to think about it.

He didn't respond. Just kept staring at me, his eyes roaming my face then my body.

"Well, can I get a ride?"

He looked at me funny. "Ride?"

"I thought my time was up here."

He laughed. "Time up? Girl, you not going nowhere. You don't get it, do you? You my woman now."

Chief clearly laid out the rules for me. I was his kept woman. Even though I wasn't a woman yet. I wasn't even eighteen yet. But I guess he didn't give a damn. His rules were simple—no drugs, no crazy-ass parties, no other niggas but him, no job. My only job, according to him, was to sit and look pretty. And I had to be accounted for at all times.

"It's hard to find a pure chick nowadays," he told me. "Most bitches in Cali fucked in, out, and over. Them niggas in the PJ's pulled some shit over on you, but you still right. And you cleaner than any ho I've met elsewhere. Shit, at least you had an excuse. You were tied to a bed and raped by them fools! Would you believe there are some women who would have done that shit voluntarily?"

I shook my head.

Chief also wasn't playing when it came to where I had to be and whatnot. "I'm a powerful man. You deal with me, you gotta work with me. No sneaking or creepin'. And the one thing I will not tolerate is a distrustful, disloyal woman." His eyes narrowed when he said that, and his mouth was frowned up like he was eating something sour.

When I asked him if I could go back to school, he told me it was out of the question.

"You want Social Services all in your business? Girl, please. Your ass will end up in some home where niggas going to be doing worse shit than what your pops did to ya. Believe that."

That scared the shit out of me. *Fuck Social Services!*

"Study that GED. You seem like a smart girl. Pass it, and in a year or maybe even less, when shit is not so hot, I'll send you on to college."

That got me extra excited. "Thanks for everything, Chief." I leaned over and embraced him. He smelled so damn good.

"No problem. Now go on and put on something nice. I'm taking you somewhere special."

* * *

Clad in a slinky black dress that stopped at the bottom of my thighs and which had an open back that went all the way to my rump, and some heels, I stepped out with Chief in a silver Benz. The car drove so smooth, I felt like I was floating as he cruised on the highway.

He took me to a fancy restaurant called Crustacean. I had never been to a restaurant that fancy. There was even someone playing the piano. It was crazy. We were served lobster and some prawns that looked like huge shrimp. I couldn't get enough, and he ordered lobster tail after lobster tail. I was sopping the meat in so much butter, my fingers were greasy.

Chief just laughed and told me to eat as much as I wanted. He didn't have to tell me twice. He poured some wine for me. I had never drank the stuff before. He said I needed it to unwind, so I allowed myself two glasses of the stuff before pushing the pretty glass away. I didn't want to make a habit of having any addictions or weaknesses. I had seen firsthand how they can ruin a person's life.

When I was too stuffed to eat anymore he took me "home." That sounded so weird to me then, but that's what it was to me now.

Once we arrived, Chief wrapped his arm around my waist and guided me into the master bedroom, his room I guessed. It was in a part of the house that I hadn't been invited to see.

It was larger than mine and had a masculine touch in the way it was decorated. Everything from the carpet to the bed and decorations were coal gray and black, from the big-ass rug that looked and felt like real fur when I rubbed my feet against it to the blankets on his bed. There was a wide-ass fish tank in the room with all types of weird-looking fish swimming around, and a fireplace. Chief must have been obsessed with those flat-screen TV's because there was another one in his room.

I smiled when I saw rose petals on the floor leading a trail to the bed.

Chief stood behind me and slipped my dress off my shoulders so I was in only my underwear and heels. I shivered slightly, a little nervous about what was about to happen.

He slipped down on both his knees, pulled off my shoes, and slipped my panties off so I was totally nude. Then he pulled me into the bathroom, where there was a huge Jacuzzi-like tub filled to the top with water and suds.

"Go ahead and get in," he told me.

I did and shyly watched him undress until he was nude like me. He was a big husky nigga, powerfully built with a muscular chest, arms bigger than my thighs, and muscular legs, tattoos on his chest and arms. One had the abbreviation for Los Angeles in big letters across his back. He had a hairy body with a trail of silky hair that started at his pecs and led a trail down his stomach to his, Lord, big-ass dick that looked like it belonged on a horse and not on a man.

Chief joined me in the tub. Like a baby, he bathed me gently, starting from my feet and going up my legs. His hands were having an effect on my body. The shit felt good too. I didn't know if it was okay for it to feel that good. He then took a shampoo that smelled like coconut and washed every inch of my hair. His hands rubbed all over my body, and where his hands stopped his kisses began. "Damn, baby, you fine as hell." He gave me gentle pecks all over my skin. Then he used his tongue. He pulled me into his lap and began kissing me slowly, first a peck, then my bottom lip was in his mouth, and he taught me how to use my tongue to play with his.

Soon, it became second nature to me. My hands curled around his neck, and I was returning his kiss with passion.

He lifted me to my feet, water splashing as he lifted me out of the tub, carried me into his room, and placed me on his bed. As I lay on my back totally nude, he stared down at me like I was a feast.

His mouth began working from my neck to my collar bone to the mounds of my breasts. He went lower and kissed my stomach and my hips. Then he raised my thighs and placed kisses on the inside of each. He placed more on my ankles. When he got to my feet he took each one and nibbled on my toes, making me squeal. Then he spread my legs apart and put his head between them. I felt his tongue enter me, setting my insides on fire. I cringed and twisted my body every which way from the pleasure.

As he licked me like I was an ice cream cone, he used his fingers in pleasurable spots then followed with his tongue. His hand kept flickering on my clit, while his tongue eased in and out of me. My legs started shaking, and I felt a weird sensation take over my body.

As cum oozed out, he lapped it up with his tongue.

"Your pussy taste good, baby," he said in a husky voice.

Then he settled between my legs and entered me.

There was no pain, just an intense pleasure as my walls stretched to accommodate his dick. His eyes bore down on mine. "You like what daddy doing to you, Harlem?"

I moaned, losing control.

He kept the tempo extra slow. He started playing with my breasts, licking them and squeezing my nipples, as he guided himself in and out of my pussy smoothly. With my legs gripped tightly around him, he thrust himself a couple more times inside of me.

I moaned loudly and clutched his back as another weird sensation came over me. I never in my wildest dreams thought that having sex could feel that good.

Chapter 9

Chief snored loudly in bed. His arm was wrapped so tightly around my waist, I had to wake him up so I could go to the bathroom.

He got up early the next morning to shower and get dressed. When he saw me watching him he winked.

When I buried my face further in the covers, he laughed, strolled over to the bed, and straddled my naked body. He kissed my lips. "Ain't no need to be shy now, baby. I done seen and felt all you got going on." He reached down and patted my rump.

"I know." I couldn't think of anything else to say.

He used the side of his hand to stroke my right cheek. "Damn, girl, you fine as hell. I can't keep my head straight. Let me get up out of here."

"Wait, Chief." I sat up in the bed and pulled the covers more firmly to my chest. "Would it be all right if I went to the mall or something?"

He stared at me a minute. "Naw. You wanna get

out the house, you wait for me to come back." And with that he left.

I didn't see him again until about four days later.

Kenita became my best friend in the house. We cooked together, I helped her clean up, and she quizzed me for the GED. But shit, there were times where I was tired of being cooped up in the house. Chief noticed.

When he came back to see me, he took one look at my moping face and told me to get dressed. He took me to the skating rink off Crenshaw and 48th Street. On Fridays it was hip-hop night, so mostly young people my age and in their early twenties came on this night. Then afterwards they went to In-N-Out to eat.

I was having a ball, but the only thing was, he wouldn't skate with me. He sat at a table on the phone but watched me as I spun around the rink dancing to the music and laughing. I wondered if Savior had ever brought girls there? Each time I stepped off the rink to sip my soda or get a bite of the food he ordered for me I begged him to join me. He waved me away and continued his phone conversation. I felt like he was babysitting me instead of being my man.

"Come on, Chief," I pleaded as I backed toward the rink.

He waved me away again. "Go on, Harlem."

I pouted and turned around and clumsily bumped into a young man, causing both of us to fall, him on his back and me on top of him. His

Lakers hat flew from his head and landed near my leg. I picked it up for him. We both laughed, and he helped me to my feet. He was a tall boy about my age with braids and braces on his teeth. As I read it I noticed him cheesing.

"Hey, you wanna skate one with me?" he asked, lingering.

I glanced back at Chief. He was back on the phone paying me no mind, so I figured it was okay. "Yeah. That's cool."

It was the new song by Snoop Dogg. I allowed him to hold my hands, and we danced to the song like we were on a regular dance floor. I had my hands in the air yelling, "Hey," and he kept up with me, bopping his upper body to the beat.

I laughed when he attempted to do the "Crip walk" in his skates. I did the "lean back" dance and then took my body all the way down to the ground, and the guy pulled me back up.

When the song ended, he continued following me. "Aye, you got a number?"

I shook my head. "I got a boyfriend."

"Aww, come on, man."

Just then Chief's head shot up and he was looking our way.

I backed away from the guy as quickly as I could because Chief didn't look too pleased. I shook my head. "No. I'm cool."

The guy kept on yapping. "Come on, baby, baby. Let me do you after school like some homework, girl!"

I laughed and kept skating away, but I noticed that Chief's expression got meaner with each step I took toward him. He had the phone to his ear, but his face told me he didn't miss a beat of what just went down.

I sat down next to him and started unlacing my skates and bopping my head to E40. Chief's eyes weren't on me, though. He was mean-mugging the dude.

I slipped away to return the skates and get my shoes. When I came back and sat down I put my shoes on and stood. "You ready to go?" I asked.

He ignored me and placed one hand in the small of my back and pushed me forward. I started walking briskly to stay ahead of him.

When we got to the exit, I paused, and he slapped my ass to propel me forward. I didn't hesitate. I jogged a couple steps to walk at his requested pace.

He handed me the car keys. "Go get in the car," he ordered.

I did as I was told, and once I was settled in the car, I watched in the rearview mirror as he strolled back inside the rink.

Five minutes later a car pulled in, and I craned my neck to follow it as it shot past me. Five guys hopped out and ran into the rink.

Chief came out at that same moment, stopped and took three drags of a blunt, ground it out with his boot, and headed to the car. He hopped in without a single word to me.

A few seconds later the five guys emerged dragging a young guy out. I heard him shout, "What's the problem, fellas?"

A fist was the only reply he got. That and a foot in his ass as they whipped on him. I looked on horrified as his hat flew off and his braids were flying every which a way. It was the guy I had danced with.

"Chief!" I shook his arm. "Make them stop hitting him!"

Chief tapped his fingers against the steering wheel while the guy got his ass tapped.

Fists and feet were flying and connecting with him, and he was screaming in horror.

I tried to reach for the door handle but felt a steely arm on my hand. I tried to pull away, but the grip was way too strong.

"He disrespected me," was all he said.

"He's just a fucking kid like me!" I yelled, tears rushing from my eyes at the pain I knew he was experiencing because of me. "Why are they doing him like that? Because he danced with me?"

He ignored me.

"Chief, it was only a dance. It didn't mean nothing. You know I'm down with you."

He turned his eyes to me. "Are you?"

"You gotta ask me?"

Chief pressed down on the middle of the steering wheel. When the horn sounded the beating stopped.

I breathed a sigh of relief and hoped he wasn't hurt too bad.

As Chief loosened his grip on my arm, I snatched it away and scooted as far from his ass as possible.

During the drive, he tried to brush his hand across my face, but I knocked it away and gave him the meanest expression I could. When he put his free hand on my knee I slapped it away, hating him in that moment.

I refused to look his way or utter a word to him the whole ride home. I wasn't so sure if this little arrangement was going to work. I didn't know if I could voluntarily be with someone with such a bad temper. Yeah, my daddy had a bad one, but I had no choice in that matter. He was my daddy.

When we got home, I snatched my body from the car with much attitude and marched toward the house. Chief tried to wrap an arm around my waist, but I moved away to prevent it.

"You still not talking to me?" He held his hands out like he didn't do anything wrong.

"You didn't have to beat him up."

Once inside I went straight into my room and closed the door, and he didn't bother me.

Chapter 10

The next morning, I almost freaked out when I felt something licking one of my feet. Then I felt teeth sink into my skin. I shrieked and fell out of the bed.

Expecting to find a rat, I yanked the covers off the bed to find something furry crawling toward me.

I laughed and scooped up the most adorable puppy I had ever seen. It had the cutest face with long floppy ears, and the little thing was covered with golden brown hair. I think it was a cocker spaniel.

"Still mad at me?" Chief asked, leaning against the door frame and puffing on a cigar.

I swallowed the reminder of my anger from last night and smiled. "No, I'm not."

"You like her, baby?"

The puppy kept licking me in my face.

"Yeah, I do."

"Good." He turned to go but stopped and said,

"Oh yeah, if you don't want what went down last night to happen again you betta keep unnecessary niggas out of your face." Then he was gone.

I blocked his words out of my head and decided on what to name the little puppy. "I'ma call you *Lady*," I told her and nuzzled her face with mine.

I couldn't wait for Kenita to come back and see Lady. And since she wasn't here, I used her excursion to my advantage.

I took a dash outside to give the puppy some air. We walked down the driveway and a little further down the street. No one was home, so I figured Chief wouldn't find out. And if he did, so what? I was only taking the puppy for a walk. What harm was it doing?

The puppy was cute but bad as hell. She kept trying to bite her collar. When I tried to gently pull her by the leash she would yank her body back. At one point she even got tangled in it. But she was so cute I couldn't get mad. I leaned over to unhook the metal leash from her neck before she strangled herself, and untangled the other end that was around one of her legs and preventing her from walking.

"You are a silly little doggy."

Once I had her free, I attached it to my belt buckle and leaned over to tickle her tummy. I laughed when she angled her body so she could try to lick my fingers.

A kick in my ass sent me flying. Before I could even get up or see my attacker I was socked in the back of my damn head. Pain clouded my vision for a minute.

"You think you can move in on my mutha-fuckin' nigga? I'm with Chief, bitch. You just a fuckin' fill-in, off-brand bitch!"

As I rose to my knees she kicked me in my side, causing me to fall on my back. "Yeah, look at me, bitch."

A very pretty, angry-looking female stared me down for a moment. Her skin tone was a shade lighter than mine, and she had "doe-brown" eyes and full lips. Her hair was short and layered and piled on top of her head, but some slipped out and hung on the side of her face. She was taller than me and slightly bigger and didn't look much older than me.

As she charged after me again, I lifted my leg and kicked her in her stomach, making her grunt and stagger backwards. I stood and instantly we both started throwing blows.

If it's the one thing my daddy taught me to do, it was to fight. I wasn't a violent person, but I could defend myself if need be. And a couple times in the PJ's I had to get down, but I always did my best to avoid it. The only time I did get down was when a bitch put her hands on me.

My mama always said, "You can call me every-thing but a child of God, but if you put your hands on me, muthafucka, that's the end of you!"

I swung like Tyson and drilled her right cheek-bone, her chest, and upside her head. Her head swung in every direction from the blows.

I knew she had to be from the projects because when she saw I was whipping her ass, she punked out and pulled out a switchblade.

I grabbed the dog chain from my belt clip and

wrapped it around my hand so half of it was hanging freely. My heart started to slam in my chest. I squatted and waited for her to make a move.

As she lunged forward and swiped her blade, I backed up and swung, bashing her in the face. The metal split her bottom lip, and blood spilled out.

"Bitch!"

I didn't have time to be calling her names. I waited for her to begin her A-game again.

She lunged forward and swiped her blade again, this time barely missing my neck.

I stepped in and struck her again. It made her weak. I moved in on her again and continued to bop her in her head with my wrapped up fist over and over until the blade fell from her hands and she hit the pavement knocked out. I stopped and took a few deep breaths to slow my heavy breathing down as the adrenaline pumped through me.

I spied Lady not too far from us in a corner chasing her tail, not bothered by what just happened. I shook my hand and scooped her into my arms. I knew one damn thing—No man was gonna get me caught up in some shit like this again. I had to get the fuck away from Chief. Far away.

I walked back to the house and let the puppy down to run around the living room.

I didn't want to steal, but I found a wad of bills in Chief's bedroom, in one of his drawers. My heart started beating when I saw the gun there too. I didn't bother it though. I just grabbed two of his twenties and five one-dollar bills. I just needed enough to catch a bus the fuck out of there. Shit, he had hundreds, fifties, and twenties. I didn't think he'd notice the small amount I had taken. And, besides, I'd be gone by the time he came back.

I didn't know where I could go. I had no family in Cali or anywhere else, but maybe if I could get back to my area I could find my friend Roslyn, who was my only hope at that point.

As bad as it sounded, I was prepared to strip at that after-hours spot for the rest of my life to escape Chief. I patted little Lady one last time. She whined and chased after me, but as much as I wanted to, I couldn't take her little butt with me. I peeked at her through the little crack in the door before I shut it completely. I could still hear her whining and scratching on the door.

I didn't feel like waiting around for a cab to come, so I walked around to find a bus stop. I walked about two blocks before I found a bus stop. I breathed a sigh of relief when I found the seat at the bus stop to be empty. *Perfect.* I didn't feel like sharing it with no wino or some pervert who hung out at bus stops asking for spare change or pussy.

According to the schedule, the next bus was set to come at four forty-five. Since I had no watch I didn't know how much longer I had to wait. I knew it had to be around four though because when I left the gas station it was three-fifty.

Traffic was speeding past me. I almost pissed when I saw Chief's driver fly by in the Excursion.

"Shit!"

I put my head down and covered my face quickly, hoping he didn't see me, but as he followed traffic and got to the end of the curve, he broke and made a U-turn.

I hopped up instantly and ran in the opposite

direction, looking over my shoulder. T.I. was blasting, his way of telling me he was close on my heels. I increased my speed and hit another street.

From the corner of my eye I saw him leap from the SUV, and he was on me in a flash the way a fucking cheetah effortlessly snatches up his prey. The fucking driver, without a single word, plucked me in the air and carried me to the truck.

Hell, I fought, though. "Get the fuck off of me!" I yelled, swinging my fist in the air and kicking. It didn't make much of a difference; it just made me tired.

He dumped me in the back seat and hopped in the front and drove back to Chief's house. I wasn't going no damn where, and I now had to face Chief.

Once we got back to Chief's house, he yanked me out the car and forced me in the house. I fell in a heap on the floor and lay there for a moment catching my breath.

Then I heard, "You trying to leave me, Harlem?"

Chapter 11

Fear slid into my face after I raised my head and saw Chief standing over me.

"Girl, I'ma ask you again—Are you trying to leave me?"

I tried to rise.

"Stay the fuck down and answer my question."

"Yes!" I rose to my feet and got all in his face, despite his order. "I don't wanna be here. Did you think I would, while you mess around with other females and get me caught up in shit? Please. You don't run me, Chief. I'll go wherever the fuck I wanna go, and I just so happen to not want to be here."

He gave my cheek a blow that sent me flying into the coffee table.

I screamed loudly as a stinging heat rushed to my face.

With a flash he pressed me into the table and grabbed me by my hair. "Listen up, miss bitch, don't ever question what the fuck I do or who I do it with. You are officially my fucking property. You belong in this muthafuckin' house, and that's where you gonna stay. You try this silly shit again and I'll blind your eyes out!"

I covered my face with my hands and cried, not bothering to tell him about the girl who had attacked me.

He was unmoved. I heard him unbuckle his belt and unzip his pants. He sat on the couch and took his dick out. "Come over here so I can show you how to suck a dick."

Being Chief's woman became my nightmare. The kindness he had originally shown was now replaced with brutality, and I dreaded living in his house. Although this was the last place I wanted to be, I knew that I was stuck from the day he'd carried me out my old house. I wasn't dumb enough to test the waters, so I just tried to stay in my place. But, damn, I sure was in a fucked-up place.

The only person in the house I could trust was Kenita, but after the shit went down with me leaving, he fired her ass, even though it wasn't her fault. Her mom was sick so she called off that day. I felt so bad for her, and I knew it was my fault. If I hadn't left, she wouldn't have been fired, but Chief didn't give a damn.

She came back one day while I was taking a shower. A little while before that Chief had made me put on some black lingerie that consisted of a nipple-less bra and some lacy thong underwear and some black boots that went all the way up to my thighs. He fucked me every way imaginable, on my back, sideways, on my knees, standing up, with one leg on the wall, standing up and the top half of my body bent over, me on the bed and hanging halfway off the bed, making my as dizzy ass hell. The last position we tried was fucking in a chair. Then he ate my pussy for what seemed like an hour and had the nerve to want me to suck his dick just as long. He had every ounce of my body sore.

As I was showering I could hear shouts coming from the living room. I threw on a towel and rushed out of the bathroom. I saw Kenita with tears in the corner of her eyes, and it seemed like she was struggling to not let them fall.

"Kenita, you heard what the hell I just said— Your lousy services are no longer needed in my crib."

"Chief, ya joking, right? I'm not going anywhere."

"Who jokin', you fuckin' foreigner bitch? I'll show you how much I'm jokin'." He snatched her purse off her arm and tossed it outside.

Kenita went off. "You should be ashamed of yourself keeping that young girl locked in here like a prisona, *bumbaclat*!"

I turned away so Chief wouldn't see me snickering silently, but turned back around quickly when I heard him raise his voice.

"Bitch, you betta get on before I have your ass deported. I know somebody who works for Immigration. One call, bitch, and your ass will be running naked through a fucking jungle with your titties bouncing and zebras chasing your ass."

Her eyes widened. She looked defeated, like she knew that waging war with Chief would be useless. "All right, Chief." Then she finally noticed me in the room. "Goodbye, Harlem."

I smiled sadly. "Bye, Kenita. Take care."

"Good luck to ya!"

She gave Chief one last glare—"Bumbaclat"—and walked out the door.

Once the door was closed Chief turned to me. He chuckled, picked me up, and carried me back to his room, where the fucking continued.

It was the last time I saw Kenita, and as time went by, I really missed her.

He replaced Kenita with the driver. From sun up to sun down the dude stayed parked in the driveway until chief came home. And he was always bumping TI!

My only friend in the house was Lady, and I treated that puppy like I gave birth to her. She ate with me, hung out with me all day, and even slept in the same bed as me. But when Chief came home, he always gave her a kick in the ass that sent her flying from the room.

Then I became his fuck slave. He used my body day in and out, taught me the way he liked it, how he wanted to be touched and fucked. I got it right because I didn't want to make him angry and have him fuck me up. And, yes, Chief was a very skillful lover. In all honesty I loved and craved his touch. I asked myself time and time again how someone I feared could make me melt the way he did when we were in bed. He took me to heights I had never been before, so I had no problem sharing my body with him. I began to wonder how many other young girls he had shacked up in beautiful houses.

When it was time for me to take my GED Exam, I was escorted there by Chief himself. He even went as far as to sit in one of the little desks next to me. Then he damn near wanted to strangle the little white lady who told him he couldn't be in the testing room and that he had to leave.

"Young lady, your father needs to wait outside while you take the exam," she said in a choppy voice.

I hid my smile.

"Let me go before I pop this bitch," he said loudly. "I'll be outside. Hurry up."

Shit, this was one request I wasn't going to grant. I took my time, like the book suggested, dividing my time evenly for each section so that I had more time for the part I struggled the most with. I read each question twice and underlined important context clues. I even did the process-of-elimination thing. The book suggested that I put a check mark by a question and come back to it later if I wasn't too sure of the answer.

Once I was done with the test, I went over each and every answer again to make sure I was okay with it and that the circles were filled in completely.

"Thank you for taking me," I told him as we were going home.

He rolled the steering in his hands as he made a right turn. "Now you know daddy been doing a lot for you, Harlem. I got you out those grimy-ass projects away from your sick-ass daddy. Keep you laced, your belly full. You live under a nice little roof, and you get this good dick too. Now I need you to do a little something for me."

I nodded, wondering if I really had a choice in the matter, and what the "little something" was.

Chapter 12

I had to make sure I didn't look nervous the next day. I thought the dress was way too short. My ass was damn near hanging out, and my nipples were poking through the top. My hair was flat-ironed and hung around my shoulders and back. And my face was packed with makeup so I looked not only sexy, but older than seventeen. Today I was Tupac, and all eyes were definitely on me. Many a man were looking my way and offered to let me cut in front of them in the long-ass line at the county jail. And, of course, the females, unless they were gay, were rolling their eyes at me and mumbling under their breath, but that's 'cause their dudes were checking me out.

The security guard with the handheld metal detector kept licking his lips at me. He looked like he wanted to scoop my titties in his hands as he swiped the wand over them. When the detector made a beeping sound, he asked, "It that your bra?" He licked his lips at me again.

It always made me cringe inside. I hated when

men licked their lips at me. It made me feel dirty, fucking impure.

"Yeah, it has a wire in it. Ain't nothing down there, see." I stepped closer to him, careful not to lift my arms, and pressed my breasts against his chest so he got a feel of my nipples. That put his mind right where it needed to be.

The fuck-off was doing a job observing all the curves and crevices of my body, and I let him, so he wouldn't suspect shit.

"Damn, baby," he whispered in my ear, "let me take you out."

"Naw." I shook my head. "I got a man in here."

"So? I don't give a fuck. These niggas in here can't do shit for you, but cause you grief, run up your phone bill, and have the damn post office out of stamps. And then when they ass get out, they gonna bring you AIDS they got from taking it up the ass."

I smiled and shook my head again.

"Girl, I'm serious. Why don't you let me save you some grief, and at the same time"—He paused and pressed his hard dick up against me—"introduce you to my johnson?"

I gave a flirtatious laugh. "Who said he was a detainee?"

"Then who is he?"

"Baby!"

The guard's head shot up toward the warden as he signaled for me at the entrance.

"Hey, boo," I said and slipped past the guard.

I really put on a show, giving him a long tongue kiss, which he returned with far too much tongue and slobber. Shit, he was old enough to be my daddy's daddy. Short, black, and fat as fuck. With dentures.

But I told myself it could be worse. I could be kissing Mr. Berry right about now. Or pushing up on the man-looking lesbian at the front gate who I couldn't get past unless I took the paper from her that had her phone number on it.

She muttered, "Damn! That muthafucka be pullin' all the fine bitches, with his ugly ass. He must be 'kickin' them down with ends.'"

I walked in behind the warden to his office, feeling like this shit was déjà vu. And though I was playing this role very well, I couldn't wait to get the shit over with.

Chief wasn't playing when he taped me up. There were places on my body I almost forgot about. One baggie of the shit was taped on the back of my neck behind my hair. One was in the valley between my breasts. One in the small of my back above where my ass dipped out. Two underneath both my arms, in my armpits. One was taped to my pussy, and one between the crack of my ass. And I had two more taped under the arch of each of my feet.

"Is it okay if I go in the bathroom and do this?" I asked him.

He sat on his desk and shook his head. "Not a chance. How I know you gonna give me all of it and not try to keep some of the stash?"

I rolled my eyes at the fat fuck. He was full of shit. He just wanted to see my bare ass. I stripped out of my clothes under his eyes, shook them one by one so he saw they were empty. I laid them flat on the floor and did the same thing to my heels. I slowly peeled each taped bag of cocaine from my body.

I was bent over, my ass all up in the air, trying to get the tape off my pussy hairs.

"Do you need any assistance?" he asked me in a husky voice.

I flicked him off. Then I shrieked as some of my hair came with the tape. I dropped the bags on his desk one by one then posed nude in front of him, so he could make sure there was no more shit on me I was trying to cop. Inside I felt like a slave at an auction.

Of course he had to be an even bigger ass and examine me "more closely," making me stand there while he lifted each of my breasts and inspected, stuck a finger in my pussy, then split apart my butt cheeks. Yet, his hands lingered a little longer than they needed to on my ass as he rolled my cheeks in his hands. The fucking pervert was making my skin crawl.

"Okay," he finally said, "you can get dressed now."

Once I was fully dressed and on my way out the door, I yelled, "You fat, black bastard. You wish you could hit this pussy!"

I cried on the way back to the house. I caught the driver looking at me, but he said nothing, just had a blank expression on his face.

Once home, I went straight to Chief's room. I would have preferred my own, but he told me when he was home that that's where he wanted me to be. I stripped out of my clothes and hopped in the shower. I scrubbed my body raw and wiped all the silly makeup off my face, as if that would rid me of my latest humiliation. Nothing could make it right. I grabbed a towel and wrapped it around me.

When I walked into the bedroom, Chief was sitting on the bed.

He nodded at me. "How it go?"

I forced a smile. "Good."

"Come here, Harlem."

I went over, and he pulled me on his lap, even though I was still wet and water was dripping on him.

"You got out without any problems, or suspicion?"

I nodded, pulling my bottom lip in.

"That ain't bad for your first time in the game, baby." He patted my rump. "You know what you are now, don't you?"

I shook my head. "What?"

"A cold piece of work—a hustlin' bitch." He threw the towel to the floor, pushed me flat on the bed, and started caressing my breasts.

Chief had me, his "hustling bitch," hit up several other jails. He took me all over the state. Only, one time I had to do the shit I almost didn't get out that muthafucka. I had to make it seem like I was seeing an inmate and when I got to the visiting unit I would pass the shit off to one of the corrections officers.

The fucking jail was no joke. I waited in line as usual in my little get-up. I had on some short shorts, which made my ass look three times bigger than it already was, and a halter-top. Chief had me put my hair up in a bun at the crown of my head, which didn't look suspicious because it was hot as hell that day. When I got inside, the security guard with the metal detector was already eyeing me in the line before I even got up to him. I had five people ahead of me, but he was already salivating.

Finally he got through the four people in front of me with the quickness. An older black woman was up next, but she turned to me and said, "Go ahead, dear. I need to find my son's booking number."

"Thank you, ma'am."

Silently I recited in my head the booking number of the dude I was supposed to be visiting. His name was Pierre, and he was supposed to be my baby's father. I stepped to the guard, my sexy smile already planted on my face.

The security officer was looking impatiently out the window. He shook his head and muttered, "Fucking pigs and department of justice always trying to step in, like we don't do our fucking job right."

I turned my head slightly and almost shitted on myself when a police truck slowly pulled up in the parking structure. But that wasn't what alarmed me. It was the type of police vehicle. The one that carried drug-sniffing K9's.

I continued to watch them as the officer jumped out and went to let the damn dog out the back. I thought quickly.

"Oh shit!" I clutched my stomach desperately. "I gotta use the bathroom."

He looked at me funny and pointed across from him. "The ladies restroom is that way."

"Thank you." I rushed past him, pretending I had the shits.

Once there, tears shot out of my eyes as I locked

the door, and hoped no one would come knocking and catch me before I got rid of the shit I had on me. I went into the vacant stall, pulled off my clothes, and yanked the taped baggies off my body, ignoring the pain. Once I had all eight of them, I ripped each bag open, careful not to spill any of it, and dumped the contents in the toilet. I flushed it quickly, and then again, to make sure all the coke went down the drain. I stood at the sink naked and rinsed the baggies out. When all the white powder residue was washed off each bag, I wrapped the bags in about ten paper towels before dropping them in the trash.

But I wasn't done yet. I turned off the cold water and turned the hot water on full blast, took more paper towels and some soap from the dispenser, and scrubbed my body. I scrubbed so hard I wanted to cry. I scrubbed until my skin was damn near bruised and the paper towels were shredding on my skin. I ignored how painful the hot water was on my body, and slapped more water all over until I was convinced there was no cocaine residue anywhere on my person. Then I lightly scrubbed my clothes. Thank God, I'd learned at school from the D.A.R.E. officer that a dope dog can pick up even the smallest amount of the drug.

When I walked back out, the security guard offered to let me get back in my spot in line. I looked around for the police and K9 and saw them walking through the jail entrance about ten feet away from me.

I glanced at the prisoner's name on the sign-in sheet. When I saw another woman's name scribbled across the first line and the time 12PM, I thought of something slick. "Oh hell, no, this muthafucka did not have this bitch for a visitor! And he knew I was coming. Fuck that nigga. Let that bitch put some money on his books." In a huff, I turned and walked past the guard, and the crowd, which was staring at me like I was crazy. I walked out the lobby and continued walking until I was at the pick-up spot.

A few minutes later the driver pulled up. It seemed I had stopped breathing from the moment I had entered that bathroom. I climbed in and leaned back in the seat so relieved that I was sucking in air, almost hyperventilating. Now the only problem was explaining to Chief what happened to his shit.

My legs were shaking as I stood in the doorway and bit my lip, not knowing what kind of a reaction I was going to get from him once I told him I flushed his dope down a toilet. I doubted that if I explained the situation to him he would give a damn about my fear. All he wanted to hear was that I got the job done right.

I stepped into the house and slowly walked up the stairs to Chief's room. He was on his chirp phone and sitting on his bed. I guess he used that chirp all the time because it was a prepaid phone and couldn't be traced back to him. I never saw him use the phone we had in the house, and I never heard that muthafucka ring either. The only person who ever used it was Kenita.

He studied me for a moment, an amused look on his face. I knew that look would vanish the moment he found out what went down.

"What's up, Harlem?" he said as he sat the phone down, not hanging up.

"I have to tell you something."

He patted the bed next to him. "Sit down."

I obeyed.

"Aye, dawg, let me hit you back." He sat the phone down and looked back at me. "How did the run go?"

I took a deep breath and scratched at my scalp nervously. "Well, that's what I want to talk to you about. See . . . umm—"

"Spit the shit out! What happened? I got shit to do." He knocked a fist into his open palm, making a loud sound and making me jump.

"I couldn't bring the drugs in. I got to the door and a police officer with a K9 dog was coming in, so I had to dump them down a toilet. I'm so sorry, Chief." I closed my eyes, waiting for my body to be filled with pain—either a smack across my face or a punch in my stomach.

Chief busted up laughing. "That was only a test, Harlem. That's a hard jail to bring drugs into. Ever since an inmate went AWOL, security been tight like a muthafucka. I just wanted to see if you could do it. Don't trip. It wasn't real shit. That was just flour. I figured if you could get that in, you can get the real thing in. I guess you can't. You not as slick as I thought you were. Don't worry, I got somebody else for the job."

He dismissed me and went back to his phone conversation.

* * *

Although he never made me go back to any jails, I damn sure was put in another risky situation.

The next time he had me dress up, the driver dropped me off at a fancy-ass hotel to meet some nigga named Rico.

I walked inside carrying a big-ass Dooney & Bourke bag filled with cash. This time I was getting the pick-up. I met the dude downstairs at the small café. The deal was he was under tough-ass surveillance from the cops, so I had to make it look like he was my man, who I was meeting for a light dinner then a little romp in one of the rooms upstairs. I was dressed conservative that time in a white blouse, a pearl necklace, and a pair of black slacks, and my hair was brushed back in a neat ponytail that was braided. I strolled into the hotel and went straight into the little restaurant inside. The only thing was, Chief didn't tell me what the nigga looked like, but he would know what I would be wearing.

I almost went to the wrong dude, a guy who was seated and eating dinner alone. When I heard, "Lola," the code name, I immediately turned on my heels and walked over to a man who looked like he was Costa Rican.

Rico was a handsome man, tall, with a muscular body. He had curly hair and a neatly groomed goatee. He wore a suit and wasn't the type of dude I expected to be involved in this line of work. But underneath that suit he was no better than Chief. He was a fucking criminal too. He grabbed me, and I was forced to give him a long kiss. Only, I didn't mind so much because he wasn't bad to look at. Not at all.

He pulled out the chair for me. Since we didn't know where the narcs could be, we played lovey-dovey and continued to kiss and hold hands during the whole meal. We ordered pasta, which we shared from one plate, for effect.

For dessert, I fed a slice of raspberry cheesecake to him before leaning over and kissing him again. It seemed by the glazed look in his eyes and the way he was eyeing my titties that he didn't mind too much about making out with me either.

After he paid the check he got up and pulled back my chair. I stood up, and he wrapped his arm around my waist. We smiled at each other and walked up the stairs to our room.

Once we made it to the second floor, anxiety hit me. Yeah, he was playing a role in the restaurant during dinner, but what if he was thinking about flipping the script and maybe trying to do something crazy to me. Like try to get the dough in the bag without giving up the dope, and killing me if need be. I had no way of protecting myself. No gun, no knife, nothing.

He opened the door, and my smile faded when I saw the dark room.

"Hit the fucking light switch," I ordered, like I was somebody.

He chuckled. "Anything for you, *chica.*" He walked a few feet away from me and flipped them on.

I nearly jumped out of my skin when I saw another man lounging in a chair in the room facing the door. But that's not what scared me the most. It was the big-ass bazooka he had pointed at me.

I placed my hand over my chest and demanded in the most confident and pissed-off voice I could find, "What the fuck is going on, Rico? Do Chief know about this?"

Rico laughed again, as did his heavily-armed friend.

"We're not afraid of Chief."

Well, that was a first. I almost wanted to shake their hands.

"Now, lessee what you got in the bag."

As he took a couple steps toward me, I took a couple back. "You ain't seeing shit until he stops pointing that goddamn gun at me." I didn't have much to lose. If they were gonna kill me they would have done it already.

They both stared me down with menacing looks.

I glared up at Rico. "I'm not playing."

After a pregnant pause, they both turned to each other and burst out laughing again.

"You know what," Rico said, "I like you, *chica*."

You ain't gotta like me. Just have your boy put that fucking gun down.

Even though Rico's man laid the gun on the bed behind him, I wasn't gonna relax until I was the fuck up and out of there.

I handed them the bag and leaned against the wall while they went to work. Within five minutes they had counted the twenty G's in there and re-stuffed the bag with their shit for me to take back to Chief. At a glance I could see it was some type of weird-looking pills.

When he tossed the bag back, I casually pushed myself off the wall and followed Rico out the door.

Behind us the other dude yelled something in Spanish.

My head shot around, but before I could say something smart, Rico said, "Don't worry. He said he likes you, and that maybe, just maybe, a beautiful *chica* like you would consider coming and working for us."

Chapter 13

I had been counting down the days until my GED test score would come. Maybe finishing school didn't make a difference to some, but shit, getting my diploma and going to college meant something to me. Just because I was from the hood didn't mean I didn't see the importance of getting an education and knowing how much having a college degree would help me.

When I saw the white envelope with my name on it, I squealed and ripped it open. My eyes flew over my scores. Not only did I pass the shit, but my scores were higher than the damn passing scores!

I wished my mom was alive so I could show her. I was anxious to share my news with someone, so I ran into the entertainment room where Chief was. He'd been entertaining guests the night before. I didn't know they were still there though.

"Chief! Chief!"

Seven sets of eyes swung to me, making me feel self-conscious in my little shorts that read on the booty, "CUTE," and I had on my hot pink tank top with no bra underneath and no shoes on my feet.

This was the place Chief came to unwind, and my ass was rarely invited in there. Chief's entertainment room was the biggest room in the whole house. There was a pool table in there, a big-ass stereo system so loud that when he played music you could feel the vibrations from the bass all over the damn house. Must have shaken the block too, 'cause once a neighbor came banging on our door, telling us to turn the music down.

Chief went to answer the door with his gun. He yanked it open and pointed the gun directly at the neighbor and said coldly, "Muthafucka, you trespassing. I could blow your ass away and get away with it."

The neighbor never came to our door again. But, I guess, to avoid any other neighbor from getting the balls to come to his door, he had some soundproof walls installed. The entertainment room had not one, but three flat-screen TV's, and it was stocked with a DVD player, an Xbox, and PlayStation. Across from the biggest TV were two red suede couches, the other two TV's were on the walls. There was also a stocked bar and bar stools in the back, and chains divided the bar from the small dance floor, where there was a DJ stand. Chief also had a portable stripper pole set up in the room, which I didn't remember seeing in there before. It was like a mini-club. Whenever I went in the room when Chief was there, it always smelled like weed, and today was no exception.

My eyes flew around the room. There was cups of drink all around, and niggas was smoking blunts.

There were even lines of coke laid out on the glass coffee table, along with some of those weird-looking pills.

Chief, Solomon, and a dude named Nicky were seated at the table. Two dudes were shooting pool, and two others were seated at the bar.

Chief stared at me through glazed eyes. He was high as fuck. He sat down his dominoes. "Harlem, you know what I always wanted to ask you?"

"What?"

He grinned. "Can you play dominoes, baby?"

I shrugged. "Yeah, I guess, but no better than anybody else."

"Girl, as smart as you are you mean to tell me you not good at slapping bones?"

"No, not really."

"Well, let us be the judge of that. Sit down over there."

I sat at the round table at the empty chair.

Chief chuckled. "Now this is the catch to the game, Harlem, 'cause we bored as fuck with the usual game and we wanna spice it up, and just when we was thinking of a way to liven up thangs, here you come along."

I bit my bottom lip, wondering if it was such a good move to barge in on them.

"Now here's the catch—For every game you lose, you have to take off something. Cool?"

I narrowed my eyes at him, as I took in what he was asking me to do.

All the niggas at the table were frozen, waiting for my next move. Ugly-ass Solomon was smirking 'cause it was just up his alley to see me naked so he could lush on me.

I could not stand Solomon. Whenever Chief wasn't looking, he was winking at me and eyeing me in a sexual manner. The look I always gave him told him I wouldn't spit on his cross-eyed ass. Hell, when he was staring at my titties he was probably seeing four of them. And he was real sneaky about it. He made sure he never did it when Chief was looking. Once, he even went as far as to rub up against me and then pretended like he bumped into me by accident.

I scooted away from him and muttered, "I'll tell you about a cross-eyed muthafucka—Half the time they can't see where the fuck they goin'."

His reply back was, "I'll tell you about a ho— Half the time they can't keep their mouth shut."

But he was Chief's boy, and they were close. So I doubt Chief would've believed me if I told him he made passes at me.

"Chief—"

"You ain't gotta do nothing that's a big deal. Hell, we all high, so you probably win any damn way."

I tilted my head to the side and tried to keep the annoyance off my face. After a moment of silence I said, "Just one game, you promise, Chief?"

"One game."

I closed my eyes and pretended I was at home with my mother, when we used to play together. I watched him throw a couple pills in his mouth that he washed down with a small bottle of Hennessy, while Solomon put the dominoes on the table face down. My heart sped up as he shuffled them.

Solomon shoved seven dominoes to everybody

at the table to start the game. Nicky's whole face lit up, and I knew why. He probably got the big six.

I bit my bottom lip as he put it in the middle of the table.

I looked down at my dominoes. I didn't have a six or anything to make six. Solomon had one, and Chief had one, so I tried to pass.

"It ain't fair for you to get away with passing, Harlem," Chief told me.

"What?"

"I consider passing losing, so every time you pass, you need to take off something. Nicky, since you picked the lucky six, pick what she takes off."

My eyes burned into Chief's. Then they shot to Nicky's. I prayed he'd refuse to go along with this shit.

He licked his lips at me. "Take off your blouse."

"Chief—"

"A game's a game, Harlem. You agreed, so take that shit off." His eyes bore into mine, making me drop the dominoes out of my hands and lift my tank top over my head.

If I had to pass again or if I lose, I'd be assed out, because all I had left on was my underwear and shorts.

Chief started laughing and saying, "Tickled bitties!"

Nicky whistled.

Embarrassed, I kept my head down. I wanted to cross my arms over my chest.

"Pick up your bones, Harlem, and let's finish the game."

I did as he told me.

The next person to go was Solomon. He made six again with two dominoes. Chief followed. Then Nicky. This time I was cool. I put it down a match to what Solomon put down, like the rest of them did.

Now Chief put down two more dominoes, one with a six, another with a three.

I took a deep breath as Nicky was able to put something down to match it and Solomon, but I didn't.

"Go on, Harlem. Let's keep this game going."

I put down two dominoes, hoping Chief would be too drunk to know that they didn't match.

Chief took one look at the two I put down and shoved them away. "Get that bullshit off the table, Harlem, and take them ass shorts off."

The two dominoes fell to the floor.

I pleaded with his eyes. But he was too busy looking at his remaining dominoes.

At this point a few of the other men in the room were crowding around us, and all their eyes were on my titties. Now they were watching as I stripped out of my shorts.

Chief just looked at me and chuckled. "Now play your hand right, Harlem."

I tried to bend over to retrieve the other two dominoes.

Chief barked, "Naw, your cheating ass lost them. Use what the fuck is on the table."

That meant I only had one domino left to play. I looked down at my hands to avoid all the eyes lushing on me.

"Play your shit, Harlem!" Chief slapped the table, making the dominoes rattle.

I looked down at the only domino in my hand. My hand started shaking. The board had sixes and threes, and I had a five. I had to pass again. I paused nervously, hoping Chief would let me go. "I pass, Chief," I said quietly.

"What?"

"I got a five."

"You know what that means."

"No, Chief."

"Take your shit off!"

Now all the men were crowded around the table, and I had no choice but to stand up to my feet and take off my underwear. Then I stood naked in front of all of his friends. All side conversations had stopped.

Chief stared me down. "Sit over there where everybody can see you."

I walked slowly to the small couch across from the table, wishing I could sink into the cushions. I'd never felt so uncomfortable and embarrassed as I sat there waiting for him to tell me I could leave.

He didn't. Instead he forced me to remain seated on the couch, ass buck-naked, until the game was over.

Nicky won.

I kept my eyes on the floor, not wanting to meet anybody's gaze.

Then I heard Chief say, "A deal's a deal, man. Fuck it."

He looked even higher than he was when I first walked in the room.

I heard him ask Nicky, "What you want her to do, dawg?"

Nicky whispered something.

The next thing I knew, Chief pointed a finger at me. "Play with yourself, Harlem."

I looked at his friend, who was taking a long drag from a blunt. "Huh?"

"Nicky won. He get to pick what you do."

My eyes widened. "No, Chief, I don't wanna do that. You said play a game of dominoes. You are really tripping." *To hell with my clothes.* I stood, turned my back on him, and rushed to the door. Then I heard a click that made me stop in my tracks.

"Don't do that, Harlem. Don't fuck up my high. Do what the fuck I tell you to do." The muthafucka had a gun pointed directly at me. "Give my nigga a show. You act like I'm asking you to give him your damn liver."

Them fucking tears came pouring down again. I hesitated as I begged Chief with my eyes not to make me do something like this. So degrading, so embarrassing. So nasty! But he never dropped the gun. Just raised it to my head and repeated his order.

I walked back over to the couch and sat down facing them. Shame filled me.

"Cock open them legs," Chief said.

His friends stood still as statues as I revealed my pussy.

"Do it right for Daddy, and do it slow," Chief urged.

I closed my eyes and placed my shaking hand over my pussy. Then I stuck my finger in myself and pulled it out. It was making the men yell and laugh like I was really entertaining them.

"Look how tight her pussy is," Nicky said.

"Slide in some more fingers," Chief ordered.

I obeyed by plunging two fingers into myself.

"Now lick them."

Dudes in the room grunted, moaned, and whistled as I slipped my finger in my mouth and tasted myself. I wanted to throw the fuck up.

"Tell her what to do, Nicky," Chief yelled. "Damn! It's your fantasy, ugly muthafucka."

"Play with your clit," Nicky said in a nervous voice.

I tried to keep my tears in the corner of my eyes, as I rubbed my hands over my clit.

Then Chief told me to use my other hand to fondle my titties, and the grunting continued.

I was feeling sick at all the men I knew were leering at me. My hands were making my own skin crawl.

Then I was told to open my pussy lips wide, so they could see the inside.

They went crazy.

"Stroke it until it get wet," Chief said to me.

I stroked myself for a little longer.

"Okay, Harlem," Chief said, "that's enough. Get the fuck out!"

I hopped up off the couch silently and, in a quick pace, left the entertainment room. I went into the bathroom to rinse my mouth off and wash myself off of my hands. Then I tossed on a nightgown, and lay in the bed and cried until I dozed off.

A few hours later Chief's loud voice woke me up. "Bitch, what the fuck is wrong with you, getting naked and acting like a freak in front of my homeboys?" He punched me in my stomach, knocking the breath out of me.

I had my mouth wide open, but no sound came out. Tears ran down my cheeks at the pain.

Without another word he walked out of the room.

Okay, it was official. I hated Chief. Everything about him. The way he walked, the way he talked. How he used his height and power to make me do the most humiliating and fucked-up shit. He told me constantly how he thought I was so precious, fine. Beautiful even. Smart. But yet he treated me like I was some ho out in the street, pretty much making me his drug mule, then making me blow his punk-ass friend. That shit was not love. No nigga ever showed me love, except for Savior. But the feeling that he was gonna some day rescue me like he did before were long-gone thoughts. No matter how much I thought about him, I came to the conclusion that he didn't give a fuck about me either. That's how I felt. Or more so, I forced myself to feel that way.

From where I was looking I may have been young, but I'd lived a fucked-up life and was on my way to a fucked-up future. I truly didn't know how to get myself out of that mess.

After a three-day hiatus, Chief popped up. I sighed inside because I wished the big bastard had stayed where the fuck he was.

I was sitting on my bed brushing Lady's hair. When she saw Chief, she snarled at him, making her cute little face look so vicious and ugly. I held my lips in to hide my laugh. When he tried to pet her, she snapped her head back and nicked one of his fingers.

He leaned over and smacked her so hard, she fell from the bed. "You little bitch!"

As she whimpered and ran out the room, I cut my eyes at him.

"Okay, I'm sorry. Damn! You act like you love that dog more than you love me? Why is that, Harlem? Huh?"

"She never hurt me, Chief, and lately it seems like that's all you do."

"Is that how you feel? I hurt you?"

My look said it all.

"Look, the other night I was fucked up off that X, out of it, baby, else that shit would have never went down. Them niggas knew I was out of it, and they let it go down anyway."

"Yeah, whatever." *Because you popped ecstasy that makes it okay? Shiiit.*

He chuckled. "You ain't letting that shit go, are you?"

I ignored him and pulled strands of Lady's hair out of the brush.

He stroked his beard and studied me carefully. "Here then, baby girl. Damn!" He sat two velvet boxes in my lap. "Look at them."

I huffed out a deep breath and opened both the boxes. One had a beautiful tennis bracelet. The other was a matching necklace, and they were blinging! Despite their beauty, I handed them back to him. "I don't want them."

Now he took a deep breath. "You know it's a lot

I can deal with, but not with you being mad at me,
or that silent treatment shit y'all silly women like
to do."

    Get the fuck over it! I wanted to yell. *I don't like
having to perform like a porno star!*

    "Well, get dressed. Something real pretty. I'm
taking you to a party."

Chapter 14

Stepping out with Chief to the Century Club, I was dressed in a cream-colored dress that slinked over my curves and had a slit that went all the way up my thigh, and some flashy-ass heels by Jimmy Choo—whoever that was. I styled my hair in a side ponytail that hung over one shoulder. Chief had on a fly, cream-colored suit with matching hat, his hair hanging down underneath. And, yeah, he looked handsome. All the females were checking him out, and the males were checking me out. But what those females didn't know was that he was no knight in shining armor. And, as for me, hey, I was pretty, but I was damaged goods.

We went right in the club. No line for us. As we walked around, I noticed a lot of people from the projects in there. Girls I knew were pulling me each and every way, asking if I was okay after what went down, and if my daddy was locked up, and did I still miss my mom.

Chief shoved them out of my way. "She don't wanna hear that shit. Bitches, move!"

Chief led me right to the VIP section, which was filled with his friends and their lady friends, some of whom were their hoes. In all, there were about twenty different guys and their dates. This twenty included all those who were at his house the day I had to play with myself, including Solomon. I wondered how his date could look at him in his fucked-up eyes without cracking up. Did she wonder if he was looking at her or someone else? I always did. And when he was having sex with her and on the verge of coming, did his one eye cross more, roll up in the back of his head, or straighten out? The guy who won the domino game, Nicky, was there too, and the dude was fucked up. One of his eyes was closed shut and damn near purple, his bottom lip was huge, and one of his arms was in a sling. Every time I looked his way, he avoided my gaze, but every now and then I caught him mean-mugging me. I simply smirked and looked the other way.

They sipped Moet, Hennessy, and Hpnotiq and chalked it up.

Chief said, "Fuck Cristal," and kept downing glasses of all kinds of shit, but when he offered me some, I declined. I sipped on a soda instead.

I was bored. I wanted to get up and dance to get rid of this pressure in my chest. I was dressed to kill and I knew I looked nice, and being Chief's lady, I had more clothes than I could've ever imagined having when I lived in the projects. And I knew all the other women in there wanted this spot. But I didn't.

Project life, the violence, not knowing if when you walked out your front door you'd ever come back, or the chance of getting your head blown off, just sitting on your stoop, I'd take that back any day. Still, you took a chance and you sat out there anyway. All of it—I'd take it all back in a minute if I could escape the life I lived now, never mind the roaches, rodents, the cold-ass house in the winter, barely having food, and not having clothes while all my friends were decked out. Only thing was, I just didn't know how to get away.

I was so absorbed in my own thoughts I didn't know what the sudden chatter was all about. Voices grew louder, and I heard a lot of laughter.

Chief jumped up and yelled, "My nigga! About fucking time." He embraced a tall guy.

Chief's shoulders were so broad, I couldn't see past them to see who the guy was, but when Chief pulled away my heart skipped a beat. It was Savior! All the other dudes followed suit, giving him hugs.

I simply sat and stared at him, but I made sure my face didn't show what I was really feeling.

When he turned his head, his eyes connected with mine. He lost his composure for a moment, but his smile came back instantly when another dude gave him a bear hug. But his eyes were still on me. He was bigger than the last time I saw him, his shoulders broader, his chest wider. Shit, he was almost as big as Chief. And now his braids were replaced with a bald head.

I put my head down for a moment and nervously pulled my bottom lip in.

"Here, muthafucka. Come and get a drink, man. Where the fuck is that waitress?" Chief shoved him down next to me and pushed a drink in his hand.

When his thigh came into contact with mine, I jumped up from my seat. "I'm going to the bathroom, Chief," I said, and slid past them both.

"Harlem, tell that sorry-ass waitress to bring up some more bottles of Moet. It's a celebration, bitches!"

Everyone laughed, except for Savior, who continued to watch me.

I stumbled out of the room and down the stairs to the restroom, which was packed with females, touching up their makeup and messing in their hair. I assumed they were hoping to score a man or a damn sugar daddy. I didn't really need to use the bathroom, so I stood and watched them for a moment, waiting for a stall to be empty. When one was available, I stepped in and sat on the toilet seat, trying to catch my breath.

Savior was here. *After a year he fucking reappears. Did he get another job, go back home to see his mom, get another woman? Maybe he got married. And what is he doing back here? And more importantly, why did he leave without me?* A dozen more questions filled my head, and I had no answer to any of them bitches. One thing was for sure; he never came to see me again after my mom passed, so maybe that was the confirmation I needed that he really didn't care what I was doing. I mean, I wanted him to punch out Chief and say he was taking me away from there. Even shoot his ass if he had too. I wouldn't be hurt. No, sir. I know the shit sounds corny, but I was hoping he would pick me up in his arms and carry me out of that club and into a new life, no worries about the future. We'd go somewhere like Paris, or where I would love to go—Rome.

Harlem, kill those thoughts. It's good to dream, but it's just not going down.

I left the restroom and went to the bar to get the waitress' attention. She was serving someone at the other end, so I drummed my fingers on a bar counter that held an abandoned drink. I was in no hurry. Any time wasted at the bar kept me out of the fucking VIP section and away from Chief and Savior.

I felt someone was standing behind me. I turned my head, and my heart started beating again. I acted indifferently, like I didn't care if Savior was in the room when, deep down, shit, I did. I wanted to leap into his arms and hug him and cry my eyes out about what I'd been through. About what I was still going through. And here it was again, I was thinking that maybe, just maybe, he could get me out of it. But my voice of reason came back in my head.

Harlem, Savior ain't thinking 'bout you. I glanced at him.

He just stared at me with a blank, unreadable expression. He twisted his lips twisted to one side then to the other side of his face.

"What the fuck you looking at?" I yelled.

He just laughed, making me madder. It wasn't one of them laughs when someone is laughing with you, 'cause I wasn't laughing. It was one of those laughs when you knew they were laughing *at* you.

"Well?" I snapped my head to the side then rolled it around in a circle. "What do you want?"

"Chief told me to check on you to make sure

you was okay down here and to make sure no dude was all over you."

"Gee, what a nice little puppy dog you are, Savior."

He aimed a finger at me. "Bitch, I know you not talking."

That got me for a minute. The color drained from my face. Still, I pretended I didn't care. I made barking sounds at him and rolled my eyes to the ceiling.

He took my right arm and pulled me closer to him, causing me to wince a little at the pain of his grip. He whispered furiously, "I ain't nobody's fucking flunkie! You the one who shacking up with the nigga, giving him pussy at his beck and call. For what? So you can lay up on your ass and wear this kinda shit, like some gold-digging tramp? Harlem, that's exactly what the fuck you are. I been watching you for the past ten minutes. You just like the rest of these bitches in here. You enjoying this shit"—He yanked at my dress—"not me, so let's get that shit straight right fucking now." He shoved me away so hard, I almost fell off the bar stool.

"And what the fuck you know about what I do and what I want, Savior?"

"I know enough. I used to think you were different than those project chickens. I thought you had some substance to you. I was wrong. You ain't got no integrity in you. Hell, you don't even have self-respect. And it seems to me you right where you wanna be—somebody's kept ho." He pulled me by the collar of my shirt.

"Fuck you, nigga. You ain't shit no way." I picked

up the glass of half-filled drink and flung it directly in his face.

Savior scowled when the brown liquid hit him. He stood up to me like he wanted to slap the shit out of me, but he simply grabbed a napkin, wiped his face, and backed away from me.

I slid off the bar stool and sauntered off in the opposite direction, although we were heading back to the same place. I wanted to stop him, tell him the truth. But would he really give a damn? He did, after all, leave without me, despite his promise, and it wasn't just that my pride got in the way. *Fuck Savior.*

But even as I walked away, my eyes began to water because of what he said. Damn, it hurt. Imagine, the one you loved all that time fucking hated you. And I didn't know why. What I also didn't know was why I didn't hate him, even though I wanted to. Damn, I wanted to.

Chief didn't pay me no mind when I went back to the VIP section and sat down. He continued downing his drink and entertaining his friends. He thought he was a real comedian, and they laughed at him like he was. He acting like he was Nino Brown and shit, with his shirt unbuttoned and a Hennessy bottle in his hand, singing "Super Freak" like he was Rick James.

When Savior came back, he smirked at me then sat across from me, making me shift my body and face the other way to avoid his mocking gaze.

"Sorry it took me so long," he said, his eyes on me. "I had to tell some simple-ass bitch about herself."

I bit the inside of my mouth to fight the urge to go off on him.

"That's right," Chief said. "Tell these bitches!"

Chief bumped into me. He turned around. "I'm sorry, baby." Then he bent over and started kissing me, using extra tongue and slobber, with his drunk ass.

I spied Savor's eyes on us, and his look of disgust. I guess this was my time to smirk, but I didn't.

By two AM my ass was ready to go, but people were still partying. Chief had disappeared with Solomon and three other dudes to smoke some weed. They said they'd be in the parking lot.

I was stuck there, forced to sit under the evil glare of Savior. And when he wasn't mean-mugging me, Nicky was still shooting evil stares my way. I rose and walked past both of them and the other people partying and went out on the balcony to get some air from all the heat in the damn room. I was hoping Chief would hurry the hell up so we could go home. I took a deep breath of the fresh air but exhaled quickly when I suddenly heard what sounded like a woman crying.

I walked over to the opposite edge of the balcony and stared down at Chief and his other four flunkies. There was a girl down there too standing in front of Chief. She looked familiar as hell.

"Chief," she whined.

Solomon snuck up behind her and kicked her in her ass, making her fall forward.

She stood up quickly and got all in his face. "Don't touch me, you cross-eyed fucker!"

One of the other dudes raised up her skirt, revealing her thong.

"Stop!" She turned and slapped his hand.

Chief leaned against one of the cars and laughed louder.

"Chief, why you doing me like this?" She rushed toward him again. "You know how I feel."

"How you feel, girl?"

"I love you."

I heard the heels of his shoes slid against the gravel on the concrete as he got in her face. "What? Love? Y'all hear this ho?"

"I do," she said in a shaky voice.

"Shit, you was a jump-off ho. You got the game twisted."

"What about all the shit I did for you—bringing dope up in the county jail for you, the fucking transports I did, and entertaining your punk-ass friends?" She was flinging her arms as she spoke.

Chief stepped to her and gripped his hands around her throat. "Look, bitch, you was the one who wanted to get crazy and pop up where I rest my head, getting in my damn business."

"But I was just jealous," she said in a high-pitched voice. "Bitches in the projects was saying a new girl had stepped to my man and was laying up with him. I was just going after what was mine."

He shoved her away. "What was yours? Bitch, you think you runnin' me? You crazy."

She came running right back up to him. "No, Chief, I thought I was your chick. I been down with you for over a year."

"Yeah? Well now your pussy is tired to me. It lacks 'lasticity."

She was now crying hysterically at his cold-ass

words, but his buddies were busting up laughing at his comments.

"But me and my family ain't got nowhere else to go now. You know they threw all our shit in the street."

Chief studied the girl and stroked his beard. "Let me ask you a question, Tina—Are you loyal?"

"You know I am, Chief. Whatever you want, you know I'm down."

In that next moment I watched horrified as she bent over against Savior's car and Solomon and the other three dudes ran a train on her, fucking her one by one.

Chief just laughed and watched, singing between each chuckle, "It ain't no fun if the homies can't have none."

She looked like she was being tortured. Solomon was the roughest with her, yanking on her hair and smacking her on the ass as he rode her.

I felt a chill run down my back as one dude after the other jammed their dick into her and she let out moans of pain, not pleasure, that I later couldn't get out of my head. I stepped away from the balcony rail and turned away with tears in my eyes for the girl, even though she was the one who had attacked me with a switchblade.

Chapter 15

I sat by the side of the pool in my bikini soaking up all the sun the next day, trying to forget about the night before and how embarrassed I was seeing Savior and him seeing me with Chief. His words had been coming and going through my head all night and day: "... *you right where you wanna be—somebody's kept ho!*"

I shook my head, but the thoughts weren't going anywhere. I felt like shit. And in all honesty, I was a well-kept ho. Didn't want to be, but hell, that was my title. And that wasn't the only thing on my mind. I thought about that girl and the nasty shit she had to do to prove her loyalty to Chief. I wondered if I would ever be in her position. It wasn't as if I hadn't degraded myself already.

I heard Chief calling my name.

I wrapped my sarong around my hips and went to his room, where he was lying on his bed, ass buck-naked and stroking his dick. I lowered my gaze, not in the mood for no fucking with his nasty ass.

As much as I enjoyed sex with him before, I hated it two times over with him now. It got to the point that he made my skin crawl. I knew I had no choice though. Before the night was over I'd either be on my knees or on my back, but never on top though. It seemed to me that Chief had some serious power issues. Once I tried to get on top of him while we were having sex, and he body slammed me so hard on the bed, he knocked the breath out of me. Crazy ass.

"Come in, baby. I got a surprise for you."

I stepped in the room.

"Come on and give Chief a kiss."

I slipped on the bed, crawled to him on my knees, and did as he requested.

His hands gripped my ass and massaged my butt cheeks as he slipped his tongue in my mouth.

I closed my eyes and continued to kiss him the way I knew he liked to be kissed.

He pulled off my sarong, slid my bikini bottom off, and began slipping a finger in my pussy. His kissing became rougher, and I know, when I felt someone slip their tongue in the crack of my ass, that I wasn't imagining things.

I pulled away from Chief and turned on my back to find a young girl about my age crouched on her knees less than a foot away from me. "Chief, what the f—"

"Relax, baby." He pulled me back on top of him. "Remember I said I had a surprise for you?"

I twisted my head and mad "dogged" the girl. She was black with beautiful mahogany-colored skin and a short haircut that framed her pretty face. She was real skinny too. She had a tongue piercing and was ass buck-naked, with a facial expression that said, "Down for anything."

Well, I wasn't! When she tried to touch me again, I backed away to the edge of the bed.

Chief laughed. "Relax, baby. Let's have a good day."

I shook my head. "I can't do that!"

"You really ain't got no choice in the matter, so lay the fuck back," he growled, gripping the back of my ponytail.

As I lay back on the bed, my heart was in my throat as she slowly approached me like a cat. Chief sat up and watched, fascinated, as she crouched between my legs. First, she started rubbing all over me, cupping my buttocks in her hands and kissing me all over my neck. Then her hands snaked up to my titties. Then more kisses to my stomach. She scooted her body up, and her tongue flickered over my nipples, while her dark eyes held me, wide-set, penetrating. Then her hands started stroking my face.

I resisted the urge to knock them away.

Chief grunted, and I looked his way. He was sitting there stroking his dick so hard, I thought the outer skin was going to slide right off. When Chief felt the girl (who I wouldn't dare touch voluntarily) was giving me too much attention, he started tripping and wanted us all over him.

I had the top of his body, and she the bottom. I kissed him, while she sucked his dick. As I was bent over, one of her hands slinked over my ass, and she slid a finger in my pussy and started to stroke it rapidly. While Chief wasn't looking, I pushed the bitch's hands away from me. I was disgusted as fuck, but I had no choice. Never fucking did. Either it was perform a threesome or probably get fucked up.

He wanted her to stroke his back as he fucked me. Then, between fucking me, he wanted her to suck his dick again, which she did with a whole lot of enjoyment. Then he wanted me to sit on his face so he could eat my pussy in front of her.

She lay back on the bed, watching and finger-fucking the hell out of her pussy, as Chief's tongue slid into me.

Nasty bitch!

She then crawled over to Chief and pulled one of his hands to her so he could penetrate her with his finger. As he did it, she started screaming and grabbing her titties.

Chief slapped me on my ass. "Get on your knees, Harlem." He followed behind me on his knees and slid his dick in my pussy.

She positioned herself underneath me and started raising her head and licking on my titties and squeezing my clit between her fingers. Chief pumped into me hard and came like I never felt him come before.

But we weren't done. With him you're never done till he said so. Next, he made the girl dry-hump me while he watched and continued to rub his dick up and down, until cum shot from his dick to the damn wall.

Still, we weren't done.

In the bathroom, he sat on the toilet and watched while me and the girl took a shower together. Then he hopped in too and had me hold on to the shower head while he fucked me. Meanwhile, she crawled out of the tub, lay on the floor, and once again finger-fucked herself.

Chapter 16

I woke up the next day to find Chief watching a tape of the three-way. That made me wonder what else his sneaky ass filmed. But I doubted he would voluntarily tell me. He was sitting there relaxing and smoking a cigar, while my pussy and the girl's head were on the widescreen in the entertainment room. I hid in the corner as he watched.

His cell phone rang. He used the remote to turn the TV off. "This Chief, man. What's up, Savior? Oh, that's going down in a few days, man. Yeah."

I snuck back into his room, but I could still hear the conversation.

"What house got stuck up? Awww, shit! Man, I'm on my way."

I jumped back into his bed, my mind made up.

Once I saw his Benz speed out the driveway, I snuck back into the entertainment room and pulled the tape out the VCR. Then I struggled to find a spot to put it in my room. *Hopefully Chief won't notice it missing.*

* * *

Later that night as I was in bed dozing off, I felt a sharp pain in my neck. I opened my sleepy eyes to find Chief's angry face hovering over me.

"I'm going to ask you one time and one time only—Where the fuck is my tape?"

"Chief—"

Bam! He threw me from the bed into a wall.

As I fell to the floor, pain shot threw my right shoulder.

Chief came behind me, grabbed me by my hair, and bashed my forehead into the carpeted floor.

I screamed again and pointed underneath the bed, hoping that would stop his assault on me.

"Get the muthafucka."

I crawled on the floor in such a hurry to grab it, I banged my own head into my bed. I shook it and reached under the bed for the tape.

"Hurry the fuck up!"

I stretched my fingers until I felt the edge of the tape. I curved my fingers around its edge and pulled it toward me. I stood back on my feet and handed it to him.

He wouldn't take it though. Instead he pulled off his belt, held me by one of my arms, and started swatting my ass with it. I kept screaming over and over again, telling him that I was sorry, but he kept whipping my ass until there were welts crisscrossed all over my behind.

When he got tired he shoved me on the bed. "Don't ever touch shit that belongs to me!" He scooped up the tape.

For the next ten minutes I had to lie in bed on my side because my ass was on fire. Meanwhile,

Chief went back into the entertainment room. The door was closed, and I didn't dare enter it. I did, however, sneak over and put my ear to the door. I couldn't hear much, but one thing was for sure—Chief wasn't gonna let go of that tape.

I was soaking my sore ass in a tub filled with warm water and Epsom salts when Chief barged in the bathroom, no smile or apology for what went down the night before, just a cold-ass nod. .

I nodded back.

"Aye, when you get out of that tub, I got something for you to try on in the room." With that, he shut the door behind him.

I got out of the tub quickly, grabbed a towel, and dried my body off. I was extra careful and gentle when it came to my behind because it was still sore from that ass-beating he gave me the night before.

When I walked into the bedroom, I was expecting to find some hoochie mama dress or a sexy outfit he wanted me to wear. Instead I noticed there was a big sweatshirt on the bed and a pair of jeans in my size. I read the lettering on the shirt and smiled—*California State University Dominguez Hills.*

My heart started to pound and I was hit with a rush of excitement. Did this mean Chief was going to let me start college? It had been some time since I had passed the GED. I smiled and hugged the sweatshirt to my chest. I wanted to study social work. I was going to join all the clubs they had on campus: drama, art, dance, an Afro-centric club, a club for helping the environment, and a club for big sisters (if there was one). Count my black ass in. I was going to do sports. Hell, maybe I'd even join a sorority.

With Chief doing this shit for me, maybe he wasn't so damn bad after all. He just needed to work on his temper.

He walked into the room. "Try the shit on, Harlem."

I dropped the towel, put on a bra and panties, and slipped into the sweatshirt and jeans. I knew there was excitement in my eyes. Once I was done, I stood in front of him silently.

He examined me for a long time, twisting one of the rings on his finger. Then he nodded to himself and said, "Yeah."

"Thank you, Chief. When do I start?" I asked breathlessly.

His eyes narrowed. "Start what?"

I gestured toward the shirt. "The college."

"What the fuck you talkin' 'bout, Harlem? You ain't startin' no college. You goin' to Vegas to do a drug run. The sweater is just a decoy to make y'all look like some college students hanging out there for spring break. Now throw some shoes on, pack you some shit, and march your ass downstairs. And you betta hurry. Savior gonna drop you off at the Greyhound."

Chapter 17

I sighed when I found Savior sitting in the living room sipping a soda. He had a mocking kind of look on his face when I stood in front of them.

Chief smiled. "Aye, dawg, don't she look like one of them *edjamacated* bitches that go to that school?"

Savior shrugged. "Yeah, she'll do, I guess." He was dressed like a college student too in a plaid Ecko shirt, a pair of dark blue jeans, and Timberland boots. He even wore a pair of glasses, which took the edge off his normal thuggish look.

"Y'all make sure you don't just drop the shit off and jet. Y'all need to lay low when y'all get out there and shit."

Great, *I had to be with this bastard, who for some reason hated me.* And at the moment, I hated him just as much as I hated Chief. And yeah, we wouldn't be together for a long time but still even two minutes in his company was too much for me. I wondered why Chief didn't take me himself. But then I figured it was probably a risk he was not willing to take but he was willing to have me take it. That man wasn't shit.

Chief watched us pull out of his driveway like he was some proud, doting father, when he really gave a fuck only about himself and was sending us like lambs to the slaughter. What if we got caught and never came back? Did he think about that or even care?

The truck was filled with silence, and I kept shifting my weight from my sore bottom to my thighs, to ease some of the pressure.

Savior ignored me, and just blasted the stereo. He was playing Anita Baker. *Weird*. I expected him to be blasting some gangsta rap, but that's what he chose, and I had no problem with it.

After an hour had passed I asked him, "How long is it going to take to get there?"

"Look, don't start asking me twenty-one questions. We get there when we get there, so sit tight and shut the fuck up."

I sucked my teeth and turned my body in the opposite direction. "Why do you have to be so fucking mean to me, Savior?"

"How do you expect me to be?"

"Shit! Nice."

"To you? Hell no. I can barely stand you. The driver was out making rounds and I did it out of love for Chief, he can't be out there like that no more. Truth be told I can't stand your trifling ass—"

"Fuck you! Fuck you! Fuck you!"

"You know what, let's fix this now—Don't say nothing else to me!"

I looked out the window and wiped the tears

that started running down my cheeks. I caught Savior looking at me too. He looked a little sad even, but he didn't respond.

He got out the car and I watched him walk into the Greyhound station to get my ticket.

About three minutes later he walked back to the car. He was on his cell phone, I assumed he was talking to Chief. I couldn't hear what they were talking about.

He hopped in the car quickly and started the ignition. In a distracted voice he said, "Change in plans. We driving out to Vegas."

I had to block the view even though it was pitch dark at the restaurant. Savior had gave the manager one hundred dollars to let us park in the back by the dumpsters. The dude looked out and made sure no one came out there. One by one Savior loaded the dope that was shaped into bricks and wrapped in thick plastic underneath the fender of the car. I counted eight of them.

Once done, the manager opened the gate and we rolled out. Once we made it safely down to the freeway, Savior turned the radio up as far as it would go and put his concentration on the road.

When his cell phone rang, he turned down his radio and answered the call. "Hello?"

I knew it was a female on the other end because his whole demeanor changed. He smiled instantly, and his voice turned from being harsh to husky and sexy, hurting my feelings even more. Why couldn't he be nice to me? Why couldn't he talk to me in a husky, sexy voice?

"What's up, mama?" He paused for her to respond then said, "I'm cool, just working." He paused again and gave me that evil-ass look again. He turned back to the road, and the look faded. "Yeah, I can talk. So what are you doing?" Pause. "Oh, you in bed? What are you wearing?" He chuckled. "The pink? That's the one I bought for you."

I gritted my teeth and rolled my eyes.

"You better behave yourself and wait for daddy to get back. Yeah. Make sure you have that shit on when I come home too. Yeah, baby. You know I like to see you in that. It's my favorite on you." He paused again.

Whatever the bitch said made him chuckle, a sexy chuckle that rolled off the back of his throat.

"I miss you too. All right, baby. I'll be home soon. Be good. I don't want to have to spank you. Bye."

I was tempted to snatch his phone and call Chief just to show him how the shit felt, but I figured Chief would say something like, "Harlem, what the fuck you callin' me for?" and hang up. And, plus, there was a fucking lump the size of a mango in my throat, preventing me from saying anything. Not to mention, I couldn't stop myself from crying again.

After another hour had passed, my back was hurting from the position I was in, and my ass was aching from the welts.

Savior noticed my pain. "You wanna stop and eat somewhere?"

"No, I'll be okay." I knew we needed to dump that shit as soon as possible.

Once we drove through Vegas, we passed all the

nice hotels. I saw the MGM, Stratosphere, Caesar's, and whatnot, but we wasn't going to any of those. He drove past it all into a seedy part of Vegas that looked ran down as fuck to a raggedy-ass hotel, our drop-off spot. And it wasn't like you saw in the movies where you go into a warehouse and dudes come out with guns, holding briefcases and shit, testing the product to see if it is legit and exchanging the product for the money. It was more cool, more sophisticated. Hell, we simply left the truck outside with the keys in it in the parking lot, took our shit out like we were traveling, and got a hotel room. The guy working there didn't have to utter a word. He just made a quick phone call and got us a room. There was nothing else to do after that, other than wait till they brought the car back.

The only thing I didn't like was being in the same room as Savior. But it had double beds, so we were cool.

Once we went to the room, Savior went into the bathroom. I used the time to slip off the sweat-shirt, pull off my jeans, and slip under the covers in my bra and underwear. I got as comfortable as I could on my stomach and wished I had bought some painkillers, but my pride prevented me from asking Savior to get me some. Hell no.

Later that night, I woke up to see the room light on and Savior pacing back and forth across the room. I put my hand over my eyes to shield the bright light.

When he saw I was awake, he marched in front of me and yelled out, "What the fuck you doin' with my boss?"

I sucked my teeth and gave him an ugly look, rolling my eyes, and twisting my lips to one side, not knowing where a comment like that came from. Without answering him, I lay back down on the bed and presented him with my back.

"No, you gonna answer my question, Harlem." He reached over and grabbed me by one of my shoulders.

"Get your ass off of me, Savior."

"Answer my question!"

I was sick of muthafuckas demanding shit from me, putting their fucking hands on me without my permission too. "Here's an answer, muthafucka— 'Cause I don't owe you shit." I balled up my fist and knocked the fuck out of him.

He fell back and almost hit the floor. His eyes widened, and he came after me again.

I slapped him right across his face this time. Then I pounced on him and tossed more blows until he was covering his face and telling me to calm down. But I wouldn't. I just kept on hitting him as hard as I could until he grabbed both of my hands in his. But he couldn't control my mouth.

"Savior, do you have any idea what I been through? After I lost my mother, huh? You wanna know what happened to me? My daddy knocked the shit out of me, ripped my fucking clothes off of me, and raped me. And it didn't stop there, he tied me to my bed, ass buck-naked and let fucking men rape me for twenty dollars a pop. Not once, not twice, but over and over again, until my pussy started bleeding. Until it wouldn't stop. Let me give you a damn visual—I had men on top of me, sticking their nasty, dirty, grimy-ass dicks inside of

my pussy and busting nuts all over me while my
daddy watched. Was you there? Did you come save
me? Hell no. You boned the fuck out without me!
I didn't have nobody. And every day I prayed you
would come back and get me out of that fucked-up
house. I kept that stupid-ass postcard you gave me.
And all that time when you didn't come, guess
who did? Chief. He came and got me, he whipped
my daddy's ass, he cleaned me up and gave me a
place to stay, food, and clothes. And for that I am
very fucking grateful. So before you start running
your fucking mouth about me and calling me hoes
and bitches, think on that shit. 'Cause when the
shit went down with my father, you were nowhere
to be found. And for the record, I'm not with
Chief for money. I'm with Chief because I have
nowhere else to go. And since you got all the fucking questions for me answer this—Where were
you, huh, Savior? Where the fuck was you?"

Then as I started crying, I mean, really bawling
like I was a baby, his hold loosened a little more
with each sob, until he was holding me and
stroking my hair like I was a little girl.

In my ear he was telling me, "Shush. I'm home
now. Everything's gonna be okay.

Savior held me for a long time. We didn't talk or
nothing. He just gave me the hug I had been needing for the past year.

"Go ahead and go back to sleep. We'll figure
this out in the morning," he told me.

I nodded, sniffed a couple times, and lay on my
stomach. The movement caused my underwear to
ride up in my butt, giving me a Murphy.

"What's this all over your ass?" he asked me.

I didn't answer. If I told him Chief had spanked me like I was a child, he would have asked why he spanked me. And I'd have to tell him I hid Chief's tape. And then he'd want to know why I hid the tape and then I'd have to tell him the tape was me with Chief and another girl fucking. I would be too embarrassed. And Savior would probably bounce on me then, let alone the other shit I had done.

"Don't tell me—naw, tell me. Did Chief do this to you, Harlem?"

I looked away and wouldn't answer him.

"Harlem!"

I thought of a quick lie. "It got pretty wild one night when Chief and me were havin—"

"You know what"—He rose to his feet and raised a hand, halting the last bit of my sentence—"don't bother telling me about you and Chief's sex life. I got something for that swelling though."

He left and came back about ten minutes later.

I felt fingertips on my bottom. I turned my head and saw Savior rubbing something on it. "What are you doing?" I demanded, trying to get up.

"Relax, baby."

I was marveling at the fact that he called me *baby*.

"Are you sure 'Mama' is okay with you rubbing on another girl's ass?"

He chuckled and continued massaging the cream into my butt cheeks. "I didn't know if you were going to fall for that or not. That wasn't no girl, Harlem, it was somebody that had the wrong number. I just said all that shit to piss you off." He laughed again. "I see it worked."

I tried to pull away, but he placed a hand down on my waist, gently pressing me into the bed so I couldn't get away.

The laughter was still in his voice. "Girl, stop tripping. I said I was just playing with your ass. Ever since I saw *her*, the only woman I've had on my mind is *Harlem*. Ain't nothing changed that."

"Whatever," I said, but I wasn't really mad. In fact his words had me cheesing from ear to ear. I buried my face in the pillow so he wouldn't see that.

"Anyhow," he continued, "they say this stuff is supposed to work quick. Does it feel a little better now?"

I nodded, busy thinking about how his hands had my coochie tingling.

Chapter 18

Savior took a deep breath. "Look, Harlem, we are going to have to talk about a lot of shit."

I sighed. "Like?"

"Like where I been all this time. You know it hurts me to know that you think I would just up and leave you like that."

"You did," I shot back.

"I didn't. I was locked up. So whoever told you I went out of town is a damn lie."

"Bo Bo told me and that's your boy, so why would he lie?"

"Because Bo Bo liked you too and shit. Obviously Bo Bo is a hater. Look, a couple days after your mom died, I tried to come and see you, despite your daddy's warning for me to stay the fuck away. I wanted to see how you were and I knew your daddy wasn't doing much of nothing for you. So I offered to kick him down with some bills to at least get you some food and shit."

"Did he take it?"

"You know he did. But he also warned me to still

stay the fuck away, or I would fucking regret it. And I did. I think it was your pops that dropped a dime on me. Cops got me. I did this big-ass transport—a transport that sets niggas up for life. That's what I was doing for Chief."

I was confused. "Then why are you still doing transports, Savior?"

"Chief never said it, but me getting arrested for a little baggie and shit, the decoy? Harlem, you don't know how a hustler's mind works. Chief thinks I'm soft right about now, that my mind wasn't completely on the job at hand. And it wasn't. So I have to prove myself to him again. That's why we here."

"I don't get it. What was the decoy?"

He calmly explained it, which made me love him more for his patience with me. It made me think of all the times Chief prepped me for the drug runs about the way each institution operated, and if I didn't understand right away, he would yell at me so loud, I would jump.

"I got arrested because the cops found a baggie in the front seat. That was the decoy. We always do have a decoy if we got some heavier shit. Then once you dump the heavier shit, you get rid of the decoy and you smooth sailing. Only thing was, after I dropped off the big shit, my mind was so on getting back to you, I forgot to get rid of the decoy. I ended up getting pulled over, and cops found it in the front seat. But one thing I swear to you is that I wrote you letters and shit. I sent you cards. What you don't understand is that you were the only thing I looked forward to while I was in that fucking box. Getting out and seeing you. And not

He traced my bottom lip with his finger. "A lot f stuff. Let's see, we can go to brunch, then gam- le. There are places for you to go horseback rid- ing while I'll chill—I ain't getting on no damn horse."

I laughed and snuggled under the covers.

"Or we can go to the arcade at Circus Circus, go ride an ATV, go on a helicopter ride. What? What- ever you wanna do, Harlem, this is your day."

"Wherever. Just out of this ugly-ass hotel."

"Girl, I just got my tour guide on and that's all you got to say?"

I laughed again. "Boy, you crazy."

He joined in on it. "Okay. Go get dressed."

I rose to go jump in the shower. Whatever med- ication Savior had given me worked. The welts were slowly fading from my bottom.

I had just washed my hair when I noticed Savior knocking on the sliding shower door. "What's wrong?" I asked him, opening the shower door slightly and slipping my head out.

He had a weird look on his face, like he was fighting himself. He had a small container in his hand. "I wanted to know if you still had welts."

For some reason I wasn't shy about my nudity in front of him. I turned the water off, slid open the shower door completely, and showed him the marks on my behind. He stepped in the shower in his boxers in an attempt to put some medication n me, but I pulled it out of his hands, set it aside, nd started kissing him. I rubbed his head and ipped my tongue deep into his mouth, tasting ery crevice.

His hands gripped my hips, and he was return-

just seeing you, being with you." He paused before adding, "There's something about *Harlem* that makes me want to be an honest man. Something about you that makes me want to give you the world, or as close as I can to it and hope that it's enough."

I closed my eyes briefly before opening them and looking at him.

"So after I did that year, the first thing I did be- fore I changed clothes—anything—was to come and see you. I told myself, if your pops got in my way, I was gonna knock him the fuck out, get you out of there. I didn't care about nothing else but that. I risked everything when I did the transport. Had I not been able to deliver that shit and the cops got to me sooner, I would be buried under- neath the jail. But, hell, I did the shit for you. I got sick of seeing you there, seeing people fester off your hope and give you despair in return. That shit you was dealing with, you didn't deserve it. Shit, and I knew we were both young. Hell, we're still young. But I just wanted to get you out of there, out of that project life before you made yourself at home. I was hoping we could get away. Maybe get a place far out, and you could go to school or some shit. Maybe we could have opened up a business. Now, I'm not very book-smart, but I could have put the money up. Plus, I'm good with my hands."

He was reminiscing like he thought this shit was still possible, even with Chief and the way things were now. And I didn't have the heart to tell him it wasn't, not without a time machine.

He leaned forward and rested his hands be- tween his legs. "I'm telling you, I had my speech all planned on what I was going to tell you and I had fifty *G's* waiting for me. The only other missing piece was you. So when I came back to the projects to find out you was gone and down with Chief I was"—He shook his head, reliving the moment—"Man, I can't even describe how I felt."

"I'm sorry it had to be like that, Savior."

"I was too. And I've been angry with you for a long time. But, baby, to know what they did to you, Harlem, it kills me." He started crying.

I reached over and wiped the tears off of his face. "I don't want you to hate me no more, Savior."

He grabbed my hands in his and kissed my fingers. "Baby, I don't hate you. I never hated you. I was just covering up because I loved you and it was killing me to know you were with Chief. I never stopped loving you, Harlem."

Damn. Never stopped loving me? Who would have thought anyone was capable of loving me after everything I had done? But then again Savior didn't know about all the stuff that I had done.

So he didn't ask for nothing from me. There was no pressure for me to do anything that night with Savior. We just talked. I told him about that night, how I met Chief to all the men who hurt me that day. It made him so mad. It was the first time I had talked about the incident since it happened. And Savior hung on to every word and as I cried, he cried right along with me. Then he held me until I drifted off into the calmest sleep I had in a long time.

Chapter 19

"**W**ake up, baby."
I felt lips on my eyelids, and I opened them slowly to find Savior staring down on me, a smile on his face.

"We got a problem baby."

Alarmed, my eyes widened. "What?"

"The dude ain't brought the car back yet. They said some shit about a delay."

"So what does that mean?"

"That they got another twenty-four hours to deliver it or I will be at that door with my Glock demanding payment."

That made my heart speed up. "So then why you smiling."

" 'Cause that gives me a little more time spend with you. They know better than t over Chief. They just fucking around 'cau don't like him."

I yawned, rubbed the sleep out of my thought about it. What did I know ab "What is there to do out here?"

ing the kiss fiercely. He leaned my head back and started kissing on my neck. Wet, hot kisses that trailed down to my breasts. He rubbed them in his hands first, allowing his fingers to rub over my nipples, making me whimper in pleasure. Then he tasted them with his mouth, kissing them with the same intensity as he did my mouth. His hands rubbed and gently stroked every inch of my body. Then he made me hold on to the shower head while he crouched down on his knees and tasted my pussy, while rubbing a finger over my clit repeatedly.

I moaned out load and gripped the shower head as tight as I could because I felt my knees growing weak and I started shivering. My juices flowed out of me and into Savior's mouth.

"Come here, baby." He sat on the edge of the tub and pulled me into his lap.

I was confused at first, but he showed me how to ride him slowly and how to take him all the way inside of me.

He kissed me and moaned against my mouth, "I love you."

And I was getting turned on all the more. I started moving faster on top of him as he guided me, stroke after stroke, until both our bodies grew weak and we came together.

I held onto to Savior's hand like he was my man, as we strolled down the Strip and took in all that Vegas had to offer. We went into shop after shop, but I wasn't interested. I just enjoyed walking with him. He made me feel so damn safe.

We gambled for a bit. I only played the quarter and nickel machines, even though Savior was feeding my hands with dollars after dollars. Shit, I wasn't crazy. I wasn't giving the machines money like that.

"Go ahead, baby," he told me, "try your luck."

As we stood near the craps table, Savior pressed behind me, his arm around my waist. He kissed my neck and placed the dice in my hands.

"Savior, how much you gambling?"

He chuckled. "A *G.*"

My eyes widened. "You trust me with gambling that much money?"

"I trust you. Wherever you wanna throw it to, you do it."

I placed the dice to his lips to let him kiss them. Then, with my eyes closed, I threw them. I kept my eyes closed tight.

Savior screamed, "You won it, baby!" He kissed me on my neck.

I squealed in delight at the sight of all the chips the dealer was pushing my way.

Then we went to Circus Circus, where Savior and I got on all the crazy rides. Then we went to the arcade and played games for a couple of hours. I had to drag Savior to the Dance Dance Revolution game. They had it at arcades in Cali, and the line to play it was always long. It was a dancing game that had a screen full of different-colored arrows, and whatever arrow came on the screen, your feet had to step on it. And it played music that kind of sounded techno.

"Come on, Savior," I pleaded, trying to pull him by his arm.

"Naw, Harlem, I said I'm cool."

I laughed. "What? You too hard to dance?"

"Gangstas don't dance."

"You know damn well you ain't no gangsta, your heart too good. So come your ass on."

He huffed out an impatient breath and stepped on the machine. To him it was a very "unthug" like thing to do, but I was starting to see he had a hard time saying no to me.

The music came on, and the lights flashed, telling us where to put our feet. Although I caught on quick, Savior didn't. I cracked up at his stumbling over the pedals on the machine.

Then we went to another casino, where they had lions chilling.

The last stop was the MGM. As we walked through it, I asked Savior, "Ain't this the one where Tupac was killed?"

He smirked. "Yeah. But that nigga ain't dead."

We dined at Morton's Steakhouse, where I had one of the best steaks I ever tasted.

On the way back to our room, Savior asked me, "You still on that Rome kick?"

I laughed. "Always."

"Well, I was thinking, why not somewhere more local? Like maybe here."

I stopped walking. "Savior, stop playing."

"I ain't playing, baby. We don't have to go back to Cali."

I cut him off, waving my free hand.

"What? You wanna go back to Chief?"

"Believe me, Savior, I don't. But we can't just settle somewhere. I'm thinking about you."

"Don't think about me, think about what you want. You love me, don't you? Or do you love

Chief? Seems like he wants to be your daddy, as opposed to your man."

"You should know what I want, and who I want to be with. And the only person that has ever been is you. That ain't changed, so don't even think like that."

Savior was jealous, but believe me, he didn't have to be.

"Anyway, baby, if you say you care about me and you want to be with me, shit, I'm offering you that now. I know it's not a lot, but that offer I had way back when, hell, Harlem, it still stands."

I smiled and brushed my knuckled across his face. "Savior, we need to think this through, and now ain't the time to make no big moves either. He'll come looking for us. And you know he don't play when it comes to his money."

His lips were poking out as he looked at me. He was mad I wasn't saying yes. He kissed my fingers.

We continued to walk back to the room. "Remember this. I got a crib in Chino that Chief don't know nothing about. It's on Adams. The only gray house on the block."

"Okay." I hoped I could remember the street name, just in case.

Chapter 20

He got a phone call. It was three in the morning, and I had a pretty good idea who it was. I knew they had brought the car back and we were safe to go on back to L.A. It made my heart sink.

Savior flicked on the light, confirming my fears and my dread. In a husky voice he said, "I got the call. You know what that means. We gotta leave now."

Without much talking, I got up and pulled on some clothes.

Savior watched me with a defeated look on his face. He was sitting on the bed and watched me slip on some pants. He pulled me by my waist and buried his face in my stomach. "Don't make me send you back to him."

"Just until we figure something out, Savior, only until then." But deep down I knew I should have stayed with him. I was going back into a war zone with Chief.

Before we left, I made love to Savior one last time.

I knew it was a stupid thing to do because Chief could find out about it, but we both couldn't resist. It was bad enough that when he came home, before he did anything else, he would come straight to my pussy, sniff it, then stick a cold-ass finger in it. He said it was to make sure I wasn't fucking around.

So I douched afterwards and made sure Savior's smell wasn't on me before we set out for the long ride home.

Savior held on to my hand as we pulled into the driveway.

I stared at him a long time, wanting to kiss him, hold him, and have him make love to me again, because when we made love, not only did it feel good, it felt right. Like that's where I was always supposed to be. With him. But he let my hand slip from his, and we both went into the house to meet up with Chief.

Chief grabbed me and placed a long, wet kiss on my lips while he rubbed on my ass. I felt embarrassed and bad for Savior. His jaw was poking out, and there was an evil look in his eyes, like he wanted to rush Chief.

"Damn, man, let the girl get in the house halfway before you attack her."

Chief chuckled and let me slip past. "Shit, man, if you had a woman that fine, you'd be all over her ass too."

Little did he know.

* * *

I found out a little secret about our maid. Ms. Gladys liked to steal from Chief. All that money he left around his room seemed to be too much of a temptation for her. The first time I caught her, she was packing a twenty in her bra as she vacuumed his room. I said nothing though.

The next time he went away and I saw her slipping dollars in her clothes, I was ready. While she was in Chief's room, I yelled out, "Gladys!"

She sucked in a breath, and her eyes shot up to the ceiling. They were buck as hell. All I could see was white.

"You fast-ass girl, why you sneaking up on me?"

With both my hands on my hips, I said, "I'm telling Chief."

"Why, Harlem?" She adjusted her wig, but her eyes were still wide.

"Because I want Chief to see what kind of staff he got working for him."

She squinted her nose up and snarled, "I knew your ass was a troublemaker."

I laughed. "You the troublemaker, old woman." I clutched my chin in my hand, like I was in serious thought. "Hmmm . . . and I wonder if we take this to Chief who he would think is the real troublemaker?"

Her evil look was replaced with fear. "No, please don't tell him."

"Oh, now you begging, huh? You wasn't begging or being nice to me when you were spying and trying to get me in trouble. Now I'ma tell you what—

You betta lay off of me. No more spying on me, stay out my room, and most important, stop running back and telling Chief my every move. You got that? Or I'm snitching on you."

"Yes, yes." She started wringing her fingers and smiling at me.

That was a first for that shit. I shook my head at her.

"You hungry?"

"No. But do you have a phone in your room? 'Cause I need to use it. In fact, I'm gonna need to use it often. Is that okay with you?"

She nodded and rushed out of the room, without putting the money back.

I ignored her and went into the room to call Savior.

Chapter 21

I wasn't too stupid though. I stayed extra slick with mine when it came to Savior. Chief was slowly loosening his tight hold on me. But only a bit. While he was home he let me take Lady for a walk, but only to the corner. And I was able to go to the grocery store with his driver. He even gave me some spending money to buy some of the goodies that I liked. I really didn't want to go, but it was a chance for me to get out the house. I kept most of the fifty he gave me and bought Chief a jar of macadamia nuts. I knew he liked them. And I was hoping if I was nice to him, he'd be nice to me.

All it did was get me a fuck from him I could have done without.

The next weekend he surprised me by coming into the kitchen while I was making some baked chicken. He sat down at the table.

He studied me for a moment.

I stared down at my feet.

"How you been feeling about your situation, Harlem?"

"Good, Chief." *I fucking hate you and everything else about this life.*

He licked his lips slowly, curving the tip of his tongue around his edge of his mouth. "I got some shit going on this weekend so you gonna be here alone 'cause I got some shit to do that can't wait. Hassam ain't going to be here on Saturday either." He locked eyes with mine. "But your punk-ass is not to leave this house."

I nodded.

He aimed a finger at me. "Don't take the kindness I been showing you as a weakness 'cause Chief ain't hardly a weak nigga."

I nodded again.

"Be a good girl, Harlem."

"Okay, Chief."

I know I promised Chief I'd be a good girl, but hell, I lied. I wasn't perfect. Every five minutes I was peeking out the window to see if the driver was there and calling Savior. I finally found out his name was Hassam. I wanted to meet his ass so bad but I was scared that any moment Savior or his driver would catch me gone.

We were conversing so much it got to the point that Savior was calling the house for me. We learned so much about each other in those phone calls. But that Saturday I almost got caught. I had just got out the shower when the phone rang. I just knew it was Savior 'cause the home phone rarely rang, so I snatched it up and said, "Hey, baby."

"Baby? You ain't ever called me that shit before?"

I gasped and almost dropped the phone. It was Chief. Thank God I didn't say Savior.

I recovered quickly. "I know but I miss you."

"Yeah, all right. I may be gone a little longer."

"Ahh." I swung my fist down in celebration.

"Yeah, you miss this dick huh?"

"Yes, Chief."

"Play with your pussy for me, Harlem."

"Chief—"

"Do what the fuck I say."

I sat down on the bed, parted my legs and did as he requested.

"You stroking it baby?"

"Yes."

"Moan."

I did.

"Rub your clit baby."

I closed my legs. He couldn't see me.

"You rubbing it?" he was breathing hard.

"Yes," I lied.

"Okay, now stop. Have that shit ready for when I come home." Then he hung up the phone.

The only man I wanted to rub myself for was Savior.

Chapter 22

Since it was so hot I was sleeping in my underwear that night. I wasn't expecting Chief until
the next day.

"Where the fuck you been?"

I froze. I didn't even bother to look at Chief,
who I knew was standing in the doorway.

The muthafucka was big as hell, but moved like a
mouse. Within seconds, he was towering over me.

"No where—"

Wham! He punched me right in my face.

I fell to the floor, and my legs and hands shot up
to ward him off. This didn't help though.

I got a look at his eyes. They were glazed and he
blew out spit. He was high and it was probably off
something worse than coke or ex. I had never saw
him like this before and he scared the fuck out of
me.

He slapped me hard across one cheek and then
the other.

I started crying and begging him to stop.

He grabbed my ponytail and dragged my ass from the bed.

"Chief, I didn't do nothing I swear!"

My lie was so whack. And I had no stuff to support it. And even if I did, he'd told me not to leave.

My head was throbbing, but he wouldn't let up as my head thumped on each stair, and my body was going every which way as he continued to drag me. I landed in a loud thump on the bottom stair.

"You wanna be out in the street? Bitch, you can go out and make me some money."

"No, Chief. I'm sorry."

He pulled me to the door then marched me outside to his car. "Get your ass in the car."

"Please," I sobbed, not knowing what he was going to do, and also because I only had on my panties and bra.

He held me in one arm, opened the passenger door with his other, and shoved me inside.

I cried and sunk as low in the seat as I could while he got in the car and sped out the driveway and down the highway. As he drove, I noticed the big, beautiful houses disappear. He drove down Crenshaw, past Slauson, and made a left on Manchester. He drove down a little ways, and I had never seen so many liquor stores, motels, and churches. The farther he drove, the uglier the neighborhood got.

Soon we were on the dirty-ass block of Figueroa, where a cluckhead was walking back and forth and prostitutes were hanging out. And this is exactly where the car slowed down, on the ho stroll. This spot was fucking famous for hoes. Young hoes.

And this is where we stopped. I curled into a ball and kept my eyes closed.

The next thing I knew Chief was getting out the car and yanking me from it. "Get out!"

I fell on the curb beside the car and shot to my feet quickly. Despite my pleading and crying, he drove the fuck away, leaving me there. I shivered and wrapped my arms around myself to ward off the cold, goose bumps suddenly surging and forming on my skin.

I backed up into a corner in front of a liquor store that was closed. I really didn't know what to do. I didn't want to walk because that would have drawn attention to myself, and I didn't want to wait there because it would seem that I was a ho like the rest of the girls on the street. The prostitutes were on the other end on the street, and one of them saw me and started pointing at me.

Soon one of them came flying over to me, titties bouncing in the air and yelling, "Bitch, back the fuck off our block! Yeah, bitch, I'm coming and I'm talking to you!" She got all up in my face.

I could see she was tore the fuck up. One of her two front teeth was missing, her cheeks were sunken, and her lips were purple. But, even still, through all of that, I recognized her, and she recognized me.

When our faces were inches from each other, she froze for a moment, and the anger in her face left and was replaced with fear. She backed away from me and ran back to her group. It was the girl who had attacked me that day. The one who was also at the Century club that night. And now she was a ho? Tricking for money? And, man, she looked bad. Nothing like when I first saw her. Damn! I wanted to ask her, "What happened to you? Was it Chief?"

I started crying even more at that point and praying God would get me out of this mess. All I could do was wish this was a pure nightmare and that Chief would have some type of decency and come back to get me.

A car pulled up nice and slow. The passenger next to the driver poked his head out the window and asked, "You trying to get fucked, baby?"

I shook my head.

"Come on, man, 'cause them bitches down there are tired."

I waved them away.

"Damn, you fine. And I like that outfit. Step closer to the car, baby."

"Naw."

"Awww, come on, cutie."

The driver leaned over the passenger and winked at me.

I ignored them both. I stared down at the dirty-ass ground that had new spit, dried-up spit, old black gum, trash, and shit. I was out there barefoot.

In a flash, before I could even blink, one of the dudes from the car ambushed me and tried to drag me to the car like Chief did earlier.

I started kicking and screaming at the top of my lungs, fighting for my life that didn't mean much of shit, but I didn't wanna go out like this. As I struggled, my hair in my face blinding me, I fought him as best I could, but he held on tight like I was a rag doll.

I had flashbacks of my daddy forcing himself on me, and all those other men too, and it made me fight all the harder. I yelled Chief's name over and over again until my throat ached.

The man had me in front of him and an arm hooked around my neck, so I couldn't get away. "Damn she got ass."

One of his hands reached down to touch my butt. That move caused his grip to loosen on me a little. That's when I snapped my head back and butted him in his mouth.

He dropped me to the ground. "Trampy-ass bitch!"

I crawled to my feet and took off running, leaving him to nurse his mouth. I ran down the block and turned the corner, my heart pumping wildly in my chest. I quickly looked behind me to see if he was anywhere near me and suddenly collided with a large frame. I screamed again when an arm shot out and grabbed me.

"Relax, Harlem."

It was Chief.

Behind me, the dude had just hit the corner and was coming toward us. "Muthafucka, I seen her ass first!"

Chief secured me to his body, with one arm, then aimed his gun at the guy with the other.

"Aww, shit, man." He stood as still as a statue. "My bad, dawg."

Calmly, Chief said, "Get on, nigga, before you get wet."

Terrified out of my mind, I squeezed my eyes shut and buried my face into Chief's wide chest. When I opened them, I saw the guy pivot on his heel and run away like he was in a marathon. I cried and clung to Chief, my whole body shaking. My tears and snot smeared his shirt.

"See what happens when you disobey me?"

I nodded.

"You lucky I got a little love for you, else I'd let them niggas run a train on you just on strength."

"Yes, Chief."

"Shut up! You need to appreciate what the fuck you got and just how good your little ass got it."

I nodded over and over again.

"Now come on."

I followed him back to the car.

Chapter 23

When we got home he ordered, "Go get in the shower." I slipped past Lady, who was scratching at my feet. I hopped in naked and let the water cascade down on me. I couldn't stop the tears from falling and mingling with the drops of water. I crouched down low in the tub and wished the water would just swallow me up. I would have stayed that way, if it wasn't for Chief banging on the door and telling me to get my ass out before my pussy shriveled up. I turned the water off and wrapped my body in a towel.

At the mirror, I stared at my face for a moment. Both of my cheeks had red marks of them, and my ears were still ringing. A patch of my hair was ripped out, and a couple of strands in that patch were still hanging on for dear life to my bleeding scalp. I went ahead and tore it from my head and dumped it in the trash.

In my mind I tried to think of a way to get the hell out, but every time the thought came, the repercussions of leaving had me too fucking scared.

I dried off quickly, put on a robe, and stepped into Chief's room.

I had never seen a man more obsessed with his dick. He would sit in the bed and stare and stroke it like you'd pet a dog or a child. And that's exactly what he was doing.

Without taking his eyes off of it, he asked, "What are you going to do for daddy?"

I dropped my robe and crawled into the bed fully naked. I slipped between his knees and proceeded to suck his dick. I wanted to bite his shit or bend it backwards until it popped off.

He moved his hand through my hair and forced me to take him fully in my mouth. I felt him on the back of my throat. He got impatient and flipped me on my back and started playing with my breasts.

I was dying inside. I didn't want any man, except for Savior, to touch me like this.

He tongued my nipples, and I was getting really sick. But I moaned like it was the best feeling in the world. He went down to my pussy and tongued it, and I felt nothing at all.

"Why you not wet?"

"I am, daddy," I lied.

When he started licking my clit, I started screaming and thrashing my body from side to side so he'd think I was getting off. But my love for Savior and hate for Chief wouldn't let me.

He climbed astride me, pushed his dick in me, and started pumping. Only, I was so dry, my pussy started making farting sounds.

I tightened my legs around him, dug my fingers in his back, and yelled, "Fuck me harder, daddy!"

And he did. So hard, in fact, my head was hitting the headboard, and yet, I still wasn't wet.

The more he pumped, the more he noticed. "Why the fuck you not comin'?"

"I am, baby."

"Why you lyin', bitch? Daddy's dick ain't good enough for ya any more, ho?"

"It is, it is!" I was trying to come, but I couldn't.

My eyes bucked to the ceiling when he reached for my neck and started choking me. "Harlem, you tryin' to mess with my manhood?"

I couldn't get any air in my mouth. It felt like my lungs were sewn together and I was going to throw up, as I struggled with Chief. I gripped his hands with mine, but he was way stronger, and on a mission. He pumped and choked. Each time he entered me, his hands got tighter on my neck.

I felt weak, and my hands dropped. I was damn near passing out when he bust a fat nut into me and shoved me away and left me struggling for breath. I couldn't stop my hands from shaking as I rubbed my sore neck. I couldn't stop coughing, and my eyes were leaking a fluid. My nose was also running.

He went into the bathroom, expressionless, and came back wiping his dick with a towel, which he dropped on the floor, and got back in bed. "Sleep your ass on the floor with the dog."

I curled up next to my puppy and did exactly as I was told. And as humiliating as it was, I would have slept on the floor with Lady every day to avoid sleeping with that evil, dirty muthafucka.

Chapter 24

The next month, Chief was in one hell of a good mood. He got a new operation going. I heard him telling someone on the phone. He was branching out of the projects and over to another side of town.

"Yeah, man, this shit sounds very lucrative ta me," he said into the phone.

Ghetto fabulous ass. And a friend of his was fresh out and coming through soon.

One afternoon we got a knock at the door, which didn't happen often. Since Chief was in the bathroom taking a shit, I went to answer it. The man standing on the porch was as tall as Chief and buffer. He was dark-skinned with brown eyes, very handsome, except for the long scar across his right cheek. He wore his hair like Chief did, long, pressed, and hanging down his back. He also dressed the same way. He wore a black shirt with some brown slacks, and his shoes looked expensive as hell. Looked like they were made out of alligator. And there was something about his eyes that looked familiar, but I didn't really give it any thought. I figured it was just the fact that his style reminded me so much of Chief's style that maybe that was why he seemed so familiar.

When he lowered his head to look at my face it was like he was seeing a ghost. "What the fuck?"

My head snapped back confused as he continued to stare at me. When he wouldn't respond I asked, "Can I help you?"

"Man . . . ahhh . . . you—?"

I cleared my throat. "Huh?"

"I'm sorry but you look like someone I used to know."

I narrowed my eyes at him. "Who?" I knew I should have asked him what his name was, or allowed him to come in, but curiosity got the better of me.

Just then, an arm curved around my waist and jerked me out of the way.

"What's up, nigga?" Chief exclaimed.

Chief and the man hugged. When they released each other, both men turned to me, noticing I was still standing there being nosy.

"Go somewhere, Harlem," Chief ordered.

I hesitated. I was still observing the guy, and silently my eyes were asking him to answer the question I had asked previously. I rushed away when Chief swatted my butt.

I heard the man say, "She looks familiar."

Chief didn't respond. And I was wondering who the man was talking about.

They stayed in Chief's office for a long time. First, I heard laughter. Then I heard shouting and cursing. Next thing I knew, things were being slammed into the wall, and I heard the sounds of glass shattering. Although I couldn't hear exactly what they were saying over shit being thrown, the one word I did hear used over and over by both men was "spot."

Finally they left the office, and the guy had an angry scowl on his face as he walked to the door. Once there, he passed one final look my way. Chief came out the office next with a blunt in his mouth, obviously unfazed by whatever just transpired. His face nowhere as heated as the guy at the door.

The anger then faded, and the man looked at me with a kind look on his face, like he was looking at his own daughter. "Good-bye, young lady."

It seemed like he wanted to say more, like he was struggling to get something out. I gave him a little time before I smiled and said, "Bye."

He turned back to Chief, changing his expression to a more evil one. "Seems to me you can't follow the codes. I'm home, and these streets are mine, Chief, and you know it. I was kind enough to give you the Ap's, but now you getting too greedy. You know damn well Jordan Downs is mine. Give that idea up or lose both. This is my last warning. You swoop in on my shit, and I'm tearing your shit down. The smartest thing you can do is be content with what you got, 'cause no matter how hard you think your operation is, I don't think you that. But the choice is yours."

Chief calmly puffed on his blunt. He blew out a cloud of smoke before saying in a quiet hiss, "Get the fuck out my house, Stuckey."

And I knew for sure I knew that name from somewhere. I just couldn't remember where.

The next day I couldn't resist calling Savior from Gladys' room and telling everything that went down. I told him what the guy looked like, how he was dressed, and the exact conversation he had with Chief. I even told him what the man said to me.

"Why do you think he stared at me like he did, Savior?"

He chuckled into the phone. "You don't know by now? All men stare at you like that because you're a gorgeous woman, Harlem."

The compliment had me blushing. "That's not what I mean. He looked at me like he knew me."

"It's probably because you heard about him from around the projects. Long before Chief had the shit on lock, he did. He was running things. But he went in for ten years. During that time, Chief came into power and took over where Stuckey left off. Now that Stuckey is home he wants his spot back. Only, Chief ain't being so accommodating to him. Chief's trying to take over territory Stuckey claimed, instead of allowing him to set up shop there."

I wasn't listening. *The name Stuckey . . . where the fuck have I heard that name?* I thought back to the look on his face when he saw me and what he said. *"I know someone who looks just like you. Looks just like . . ."* Then I thought about his name again. *Stuckey. Who had mentioned that name before?* I gasped. Mama did!

"Savior, I think my mom knew Stuckey."

"It's possible. You don't hear the name *Stuckey* too often. .

"Wow! What a small world." I then digested Savior's words about Chief and Stuckey feuding over Jordan Downs. "So what does this all mean?"

"It means that Chief and Stuckey are about to go to war and a lot of niggas are about to get wet."

Chapter 25

I didn't have the time to figure out the relationship my mother had with Stuckey. I was hit with a whammy of shock. I was late. Try almost two months late. What if . . . Then I thought about it. There was no what if. With the symptoms I was having my ass had to be pregnant.

I wondered whose baby it could be, Chief's or Savior's.

I counted down the date. Judging from how late my period was, it would seem that the baby was conceived when I went on the trip with Savior because when I came back home Chief had disappeared again and I didn't see him for another two weeks. So, if it was Chief's, I wouldn't have been so late. Deep down, I hoped the baby was Savior's. Having a baby with Chief would trap me forever. But then again, if it was Savior's baby and Chief found out about it, he would kill us both. Despite this, I still hoped the baby was Savior's.

Maybe this was a sign from God and my opportunity for me to leave Chief for good. Or maybe I was just a damn fool to be happy about having a baby. And regardless of whose baby it was, I was going to keep it. Hell, this baby was now my inspiration to really leave Chief like I had been planning to.

I smiled thinking about holding a baby in my arms. I would be the best mother that I could possibly be. I would never mess with drugs, I would eat healthy, walk, play music for my baby, even while he or she was in my belly. I would read to them when they were small and take them to the park. Yep, I was convinced I would be a good mother. I was prepared to give that child everything they needed to be happy.

I took a quick look in the mirror and just like I saw in those movies where women would look in the mirror at themselves and imagine how they would look once their bellies poked out, I did the same. I imagined eating all that crazy shit women ate and wondered if I'd have those same crazy cravings for things like pickles and ice cream like I saw on *I Love Lucy*. Or would I be throwing up and unable to keep any food down? Maybe I'd blow up like a pig, eating everything in sight.

Baby names tumbled over in my head. If it was a girl, I would probably name her something like Naya, Adara, Mikayla, or Keya. But then I thought of an even better name. I could name the baby after my mama. Aja. And if it was a boy, something powerful like King or even Malcolm. I liked the name Ashanti too. I learned in school in my history class that it was the name of an African tribe in Ghana.

Then I thought about Savior. In that moment I

knew for sure I was leaving Chief. I was going to tell Savior I would leave Chief, had to get out now. I had too much to lose, and I wanted this baby more than I ever wanted anything.

I rushed into Chief's room and grabbed the phone, and dialed Savior's number. I put the phone to my ear.

"Who you callin', Harlem?"

Shit. My voice was caught in my throat as I hung up the phone. Chief was standing in the doorway of his bedroom.

"I was ordering a pizza." My heart started pounding.

"When it's comin'?" he demanded.

"I—I—in twen—"

"Why you stutterin'?"

The phone rang in my hand. I closed my eyes and couldn't stop shaking.

Chief sat down next to me on the bed and snatched up the phone. "Who in the fuck is this?"

No one said anything, so I knew it was Savior calling me back.

Chief slammed the phone down. He started rubbing his beard, studying me slowly. "What I'm trying to figure out is who the fuck is calling my damn phone. 'Cause don't nobody got the number to that muthafucka. So it's gotta be somebody you talking to. But the question is, Who the fuck you talking to? You don't go out unless it's with me, so you don't have nobody to call. Unless you calling party lines. Is that what you doing, Harlem, when you get bored? You know I'm a jealous man, baby, so tell me the truth so I can go on about my business."

He asked me in such a calm way I thought, if I agreed, he would lay off me and I would get away with a simple chastisement.

After a pregnant pause, I nodded at him, beads of sweat on my forehead.

He nodded back at me. "I figured that's what it was."

I sighed in relief when he rose from the bed. But he rose only halfway and took his elbow and slammed it directly into my stomach. I fell back on the bed as the sharpest pain I ever felt spread into my abdomen and back. I opened my mouth to scream, but no sound came out.

Chief leaned over and whispered in my ear. "Bitch, what I tell you about lying to me?" He slammed his elbow into me again.

I couldn't breathe for a moment. Paralyzed with pain, I was choking and gasping. I prayed he didn't kill my baby.

Chief rose from the bed and walked out of the room.

By the next morning, I wasn't pregnant any more. I woke up with severe cramps in my stomach, a pain in my lower back, and a warm liquid in my crotch. Matter of fact, the sheets were soaked with blood.

I knew without a doubt Chief had killed my baby. My heart beat loudly in my chest. I examined the substance between my legs and saw a thick glob of blood, and after an even closer inspection, I saw little clot-like particles in it. I clutched my stomach. When I stood up, more blood shot out of me.

I went into the bathroom to run some bath water and sat in the tub, hoping the warm water would stop me from bleeding, but it didn't. It snaked out of me and reddened the water in the tub.

I bled the whole day. That baby was long gone. At that point there really was nothing left for me to live for. I couldn't deal with this, all this shit. Some way, it had to end. I slid my fingers over the razor blade, wishing I wasn't so scared and could slice through my flesh. It seemed like that would be the easiest thing to do. Just fill a tub with water. Yeah, it would be the punk's way out. But try as I might, I couldn't use that shit, so I did the next best thing.

I found pills in Chief's medicine cabinet. It was the Vicodin he had left over when he had one of his teeth pulled. I remembered he cried like a baby, the hardest nigga in L.A. crying because his tooth was pulled. I shoved them one by one down my throat. I lost count after the ninth pill.

Once the bottle was empty, I cupped water from the faucet in the palm of my hands and washed the pills down. I thought about my mama and how long it had been since I saw her. How much I missed her. How much I needed her.

The telephone rang.

I walked into the bedroom and picked it up. I put it to my ear without bothering to say hello.

"Baby . . ."

I recognized Savior's voice instantly. I wouldn't answer, so he continued to talk.

"Miss you. Listen, I got a plan. Remember what we was talking about the other day?"

I gave a long sigh into the phone.

"I just have to find a way to get to you."

My heart started giving my body long, slow pumps, like a flower budding suddenly, or a cake puffing up in an oven over and over. I'm sure that's how my heart looked inside my body. I hung up the phone and ignored it when it rang again.

My head was spinning, and my body felt like it was floating. My legs felt like jelly. I walked out of the room and attempted to go down the staircase. I struggled at first and felt so weak, I had to grip the railing with both my hands.

As I made it to the bottom steps, my legs gave out, and I collapsed. And my body rolled down the remaining steps before I felt the hardness of the floor.

My body felt so weak. I couldn't move my arms, and my head felt heavy. My body was like dead weight. All I wanted to do was sleep.

Then before I knew it I had I descended into blackness..

Chapter 26

I was dreaming. I had to be.

"Come on, baby, I have a surprise for you."

I smiled as Chief took my hand and guided me through a door. I stepped inside and saw my old apartment, the one I had lived in with both my parents, and everything looked the same. I tried to pull away from Chief, but he held me in a tight grip and pushed me into my old bedroom, where my father was standing. I looked at him like he was shit, and my eyes widened when I saw a needle hanging from his arm. When he stepped aside, I saw ten more men behind him, and they were licking their lips at me 'till they were all moist and shiny with saliva.

Someone shoved me onto the bed, and instantly my daddy climbed on top of me. I struggled under his weight and screamed. He started ripping my clothes off. I was yelling like crazy and swinging my fists at him wildly, pulling his hair, trying to scratch his face.

Suddenly, the door burst open, and Savior came running toward me and my father. He lunged after my father, but Chief pulled out his gun and fired it into Savior's chest. Blood leaked from his body, and he collapsed on the floor.

"Savior! Savior! Don't die! Please don't die!"

"Harlem? Harlem? You having a dream. Wake up." Someone was shaking my body gently.

My eyelids fluttered open, and once they came into focus, I stared into Savior's face.

He leaned over, looked behind him, hugged me, and whispered, "Baby, I have been losing my mind over you. What were you thinking?"

I looked away.

"You gotta answer me, Harlem. What made you do that?"

I cleared my dry-ass throat and rubbed the sleep out of my eyes. "Don't hate me," I pleaded in a hoarse whisper.

"Aye, what I tell you about that?"

I touched his bottom lip with one of my fingers, happy he still loved me.

"I made up some bullshit excuse as to how I found you over there and that I had to rush you to the hospital. I'm glad you okay."

I looked down embarrassed. But I guess I wasn't thinking straight after I lost the baby and realized I would never get the chance to feel it grow inside of me and truly love him or her. I felt like shit. I felt hopeless, like there was nothing for me to look forward to. I wanted to live a regular life, go to school, be able to be with who I wanted be with. And without a doubt I knew that person was Savior. And

194   *Karen Williams*

most of all I wanted to feel safe, not feel like every other day I would have to do all kinds of nasty shit to satisfy my so-called man, or do illegal stuff, or feel like at any given moment I would get my head bashed in. I didn't like the life I was living at all, despite the luxuries.

And most of all, I didn't feel like I had anything to offer anyone, including Savior. Yeah, I was cute, but shit, that's all I truly was, a cute face with good pussy for men to fuck. How far can you get on that? And what the hell can you accomplish with it? Shit, I was a ho, trash, a damaged package. I done shit I still have trouble looking in the mirror about. I knew Savior cared about me, but would he after he knew all the shit I had done for Chief?

And I couldn't really get free of Chief to be with Savior the way I wanted to be. Truth be told, I didn't think I'd ever truly be free from Chief.

I stretched my body and moaned. My stomach was sore as hell.

"You can't look at me, Harlem?"

"I'm ashamed."

"You ain't ever got to feel like that. You just made a mistake."

There was a tap on the door. A doctor, a white man who looked like he was in his late twenties, slipped in the room. He had to be twenty-eight, I thought.

"Hello. Harlem, right?"

I nodded.

"I'll give you some privacy, Harlem." Savior walked out the door and quietly closed it.

The doctor flipped through my chart and pulled

a pen out of his jacket pocket. "You took a large amount of pills, young lady. You want to tell me why?"

"I wasn't feeling good."

He bit on the tip of his pen. "We had to perform a D and C on you, not to mention we had to pump your stomach. Well, were you aware that you had a miscarriage the day before?"

I nodded.

"I see."

Duh. "What's your point, doctor? You got one?"

"Well, young lady, if you took these pills because you miscarried—"

"I didn't."

"I was going to say, you're a very young girl, you'll have plenty of chances to have—"

"No disrespect, doc, but I don't want to hear this shit. You and me come from totally different worlds. While your mother and father were teaching you how to ride a bike, mine were both shooting up. Now, all I want to know is if my information is confidential, and if you can burn my file?"

He stuttered over his words. "Yes, yes, it's all confidential."

"Good. When my boyfriend comes, don't bother telling him I lost a baby . . . unless you wanna see me carried out of here in a body bag."

After all, I wasn't one hundred percent sure who the baby's father was.

He reddened in the face, but he looked like he felt sorry for me. "I won't. Who is your boyfriend?"

There was loud yelling outside. "What fuckin' room she in? 'Cause the bitch up front said room ten. Y'all need to get your shit straight. Y'all stupid muthafuckas getting all this money in vain." Chief swept through the room like a hurricane.

"That's my boyfriend."

"Go on an' leave us for a few, *doctor*." Chief looked at the young dude like he was covered in shit.

"Certainly." He took one look at Chief's tall, buff, thugged-out ass and nearly ran out the room.

Chief approached me slowly. His eyes scanned my face as he leaned down and stroked my hair, something he never did even when we were fucking. "Baby, was it that bad? I'm sorry you felt like you had to do this to yourself."

Chief saying sorry? What the fuck is this?

"I know what the problem is. I have been neglecting you. Ain't been home giving you the time and affection you need." He nodded to himself. "You wanna go out and shit, be around people your age you can have fun with. You're like a caged bird right now. You couldn't take the loneliness any longer, huh? Between you and me, if I had to stay up in that house day in and day out I would have taken them pills a whole lot sooner than you did."

I laughed softly.

"That's why you went on the party line, right?"

I nodded, lying for the second time about that damn party line.

"Well, it's over now. I'm not gonna make you feel like shit. Let's just put this behind us."

Dear God, now I know I'm not the most spiritual, but please let this man have a little decency. Enough decency to free me and send me on my merry way so I can have a

*chance of a halfway normal fucking life. Sorry for curs-
ing, God,* I prayed silently.

Chief pierced me with an evil look. "Harlem,
are you listening to me?"

I nodded. That was the Chief I knew.

"I know just what you need. You want a little
freedom, right? Well, we gonna have a little fun
this weekend to take your mind off of all this shit.
I'm throwing you a pool party for your eighteenth
birthday, and, baby, it's gonna be off the chain!"

Chief spared no expense for my party. He hired
a DJ, had a full bar for the guests, had the shit
catered. The menu was lobster, shrimp scampi,
crab legs, shrimp cocktail and salads, potatoes,
and various fruits dipped in alcohol. There were
all kinds of drinks for the guests to get fucked up
on, and they were served in huge, carved-out
pineapples and coconuts. He made the theme a
luau, a Hawaiian feast. He even had a hair stylist
come in and do my hair. She flat-ironed it so it was
silky and hung down my back.

When my makeup was done, I was given a
Hawaiian skirt that wrapped around me and tied
in the corner of my waist in a knot. My bikini top
was made out of two coconuts that hid my titties
and were attached to strings that crisscrossed on
my back. The rest of the women were dressed in
the same way I was, and the guys wore Hawaiian
shirts, pants or shorts, and sandals.

The party was nice, and under different circumstances, I would have enjoyed it, but because of my

fucked-up situation, I just couldn't. I sat on a lounge chair by myself watching people have a good time.

Chief was getting his drink on too. In fact, the nigga was fucked up. Twice I saw him pop pills in his mouth. It was that ecstasy he had used the night he made me masturbate in front of his friends. I saw him take them before he disappeared inside the house with a dude who had been over a couple a times, and his girl. She was very pretty, I noted, with a very curvy frame, and her hair was bleached blonde and looked nice on her. She wore a thong bathing suit, with no skirt, cover top, or sarong covering up her ass.

I hoped they stayed in there. Chief was very unpredictable when he popped that shit. Sometimes when he took it, he would leap on me and fuck me roughly for hours. Afterward I couldn't walk straight, and my coochie would be sore as hell. Usually, I'd end up soaking in the tub.

I watched the partygoers dancing. I imagined it was me freaking the hell out of Savior, like one girl was doing to this guy. I had seen Savior earlier playing cards inside with Chief and some other dudes, looking like this was the last place he wanted to be. He even brought me a gift, but he kept his distance.

I rose to go to the buffet table and drown my sorrows in some lobster and butter. I hadn't been eating well since the day I tried to kill myself. I put a couple of tails on a plate and grabbed a small container of butter and some salad. I tasted the food standing up. The lobster didn't taste as good as it did that day Chief took me out, but that's because I wasn't as excited as before about eating lobster. Back then my nose was wide open. Now there was nothing to be wide open about. I had seen too fucking much to be considered young, even though I had just turned eighteen. I was an old soul. I may not have been aging on the outside, but I had aged on the inside for sure.

I stabbed some salad with my fork and dipped it into my mouth. All the vegetables in the salad were fresh, as well as the salad dressing, but I wasn't tasting a damn thing. I threw the plate in the trash.

"Harlem, Chief want you." Chief's driver said.

My stomach started knotting up. I nodded, scratched my head, and went into the house. The door to his bedroom was closed. I opened the door blindly. When I saw what he was doing, I gasped and took a step back.

The lady who earlier had walked in with Chief and the other dude was on the floor, ass bucknaked on her back, and Chief was crouched over her, sniffing white powder laid out in skinny lines off of her stomach.

She giggled and tilted her head back so she could see me. "We switching today, Harlem. You got my man, and I got yours. He's in your room waiting for you." Then she added, "Go easy on him, girl."

I narrowed my eyes at her as she threw her head back and sighed, like she was anticipating something. Then I looked at Chief. He wasn't even looking my way. He was too busy using his nose like a vacuum and sniffing the white powder off her abdomen.

Sure enough, her man was in my room. The door was slightly open. From the small crack I could see his nasty ass sprawled across my bed, ass buck-naked, touching his dick, and obviously waiting for me.

Well, I hate to burst your bubble, buddy, but you not bursting a damn thing in me. I ran from the house and went back outside to the party. I knew I might be in trouble for not going to his friend, but I was willing to take a chance that day. I couldn't go through with that shit, no fucking way. I would deal with the consequences later.

Chapter 27

I was lying on a lounge chair talking to some girl who I'd met at the party. She was telling me that she had just graduated high school and was on her way to college. She was going away to some school in Georgia. I was so envious of her and it seemed she was envious of me.

"I'm going to take up social work. I want to be a social worker." She stuffed shrimp cocktail in her mouth.

"That's good. There are a lot of kids out there who could use people who care about them." I know I could have. I didn't bother telling her that I shared the same dream to be a social worker.

She nodded excitedly. "Yeah, you're right. Aye, this is a bomb-ass party. My friend over there in the pool said your man Chief paid for everything. You are so lucky to have a man like that, girl!"

"Looks can be deceiving," I commented dryly. 'Cause nothing was lucky about being with a man like Chief.

"Girl, I can't even get a man to take me out to Denny's."

We both laughed at that comment. I knew, without a doubt, I'd take her life in a heartbeat. And the sad part was, she would probably take mine too.

I glanced up in time to see Chief making his way over to me. Boy, if looks could kill, I'd be sliced and diced, laying in that salad.

He took one look at the young girl who was staring at him in awe like he was a King Kong or something and said, "Get on, bitch."

Her eyes bucked as she took a sharp intake of breath and scurried away.

Now folks stopped dancing, people stopped eating and talking, and all the attention was on us.

"Go on in there with old boy like I told you. You owe me."

The closer he got to me, the more I smelled the pussy on his breath.

Since there were more people around, I figured he wouldn't try anything stupid. "Why I owe you, Chief?"

"Why? 'Cause nothing in this world is free, Harlem. I spent a grip on this party, and you gonna have to work it off. You should know by now you don't get shit voluntarily from me. And, more importantly, this is your fucking position, my pleasure, whatever it may be, so play it, bitch."

"I ain't going in that room, Chief. That dude looks nasty. And, besides, he has a damn woman. I'm sure one of these other girls will be willing to do it. But I'm cool."

His eyes were shooting fire my way. "You gettin'

a real smart-ass mouth. I ain't ask no other ho, I asked you. Get the fuck in the room."

I backed away from him. If I had to fight, if he threw me out, oh fucking well, but I wasn't going to sex his friend. Enough was enough. "I'm not go—"

I didn't get to finish the words. Chief lifted me up and threw me over his shoulder, my hair hanging in my eyes and my head banging against his hard shoulder as he carried me.

I pushed the hair out my face and looked in dread as he paused in front of the swimming pool.

"Maybe this will bring you back to the real world. In that world, Harlem, you don't ever say no to me. I'll kill you, and I don't give a fuck who's around."

"Chief, don't drop me! I can't swim!" I clutched his shoulders, then his shirt, to stop him from throwing me in the pool, but this didn't help.

He released me, and I fell straight in. I struggled as soon as my body came into contact with the water. I was kicking my legs and flinging my arms. Water was rising, or I was sinking, because it quickly crept up to my neck. I struggled to float, but couldn't.

"Help me, somebody!" I managed to get out before water seeped into my mouth.

"Naw, bitch, you bad. Swim the fuck out. Aye, muthafucka, did I say touch her?"

My head snapped to a girl who had extended a hand to me. At Chief's words, she pulled it back.

I couldn't hold myself up any longer. My eyes were blinded by my tears, and the chlorine in the water was stinging them. I slid my body up, only for it to ease right back down. And nobody would help me.

The music had stopped, and people were leaving. Some crowded around the pool and looked at me like I was the entertainment.

"Help me!" I screamed, struggling to stay afloat.

No one did. Then I was completely under. Water had filled up my nostrils, and it felt like my lungs were closing in. Still, I was fighting, but it felt like my body was sinking rapidly to the bottom.

Somebody dived in. I held my arms out, and they effortlessly swam to me, yanked me, and pulled me up out of the water.

Once I could breathe, I took in a mouthful of air. Then I started coughing and belching and found myself looking into the concerned eyes of Savior.

As I clung to him, Savior held on to one of my arms and leaped out the pool. Then he pulled me out.

Chief laughed. "She ain't talkin' shit now, is she?"

Savior ignored him and continued walking, carrying me in his arms. People were brushing past us and leaving, while others continued to watch. Some looked on with pity, some had blank expressions, some looked anxious to see what was gonna pop off next. And some went right back to partying, like what just went down didn't. Chief didn't follow after us.

Once inside Savior lay me down on the couch.

My breathing was still ragged, my eyes were red, my nose was burning, and snot was running out of it.

"You okay?" Savior asked me.

I nodded, but I really wasn't.

"Good." He rose and stalked angrily to the door. "Savior!"

He turned around and said, "You need to leave before he kills your ass. Because when he does, I'll be in jail, 'cause I'll kill him." He slammed out the house.

I lay there for a while, not knowing what my next step in the shit was. One thing was clear, I had to get the fuck up out of there. I couldn't stay another day. I just didn't know how to leave. Could I say, "We're just not compatible," or "Chief, we have come as far as we can. Now I think it's time?" Hell no! There was only one way I could do it and that was to escape. I just needed to figure out how.

But I didn't have to. Someone tapped me on my shoulder. It the girl I had been talking to earlier and in a couple of words she made the decision for me. "If you wanna get away from that psycho girl take this. I can swoop by and pick you up tonight at nine," she said firmly.

She slipped something in my hand and dashed away.

I looked down at a small can of pepper spray.

Chief never came to me and said he was sorry for nearly letting me drown. I was in his room, like usual, when he was home.

He barged in the room with two females. One was looking at me like she wanted to fuck me, and the other was mean-mugging me for real.

"Get the fuck out," Chief ordered.

I did gladly, and with a hidden smile. He just made it easier for me to escape, because I wouldn't have to be under him.

Chapter 28

That girl had my nerves on edge. Was she really going to help me, or was she setting me up? I couldn't be too sure, and with every passing second I wanted to reconsider my decision and apologize to Chief. Because I knew when his high came down he was going to tear my ass up. Since he had the bitches in the house, we couldn't leave until they left. We wanted to make sure he was asleep before I stepped out of the house.

I peeked out the crack of my door as a naked Chief and the two chicks passed my room and he escorted them down the stairs and to the front door. I heard the creaking of the wood as they walked down the staircase. The females were giggling.

I snuck out of my room and hid in a corner of the small space just above the top step. I could hear a smacking sound. I saw Chief kissing one girl, then the other, and grabbing on their asses, as he did it. I looked away disgusted.

"Bye, Chief," they chorused. Then they slipped out the door.

As soon as I heard it close, I rushed back to my room, jumped in my bed, and partly hid under my covers. But, damn, I forgot to turn off the light.

Chief came back up the stairs, his thundering footsteps pounding every stair on the way up. Then after a few seconds, the sounds of his heavy-ass feet stopped.

I froze, and my heart started pounding. I squinted my right eye to a slit to see him standing in my doorway, his dick hanging limp and cum leaking from it and dripping on the carpet.

He reached down and grabbed it, studied it for a moment, then scratched his balls. His head shot back up to me again.

I shut both my eyes again quickly and pretended I was asleep.

His feet slid across the carpet, and soon I felt myself being pushed into the bed, and the bed being pressed into the floor.

When I opened my eyes, Chief's dick and balls were all up in my face, and I could smell pussy all over them. He was standing up in the bed, strad-dling me between both his legs. "Suck my dick," he ordered.

The thought of doing that made me want to gag, but when he punched me in my neck, making me unable to breathe for a moment, my mouth shot open.

He jammed in so far into my mouth, I had to breathe out of my nose.

"Suck it right, Harlem, or, bitch, I'm gonna hurt you."

Now I knew what pussy tasted like, although I would have preferred not to, as I deep-throated him and was forced to lick around every crevice of his dick. He pulled his dick in and out of my mouth like he was fucking my pussy. My head hit the back of the headboard, and tears were stinging my eyes as I tried to keep up with him or risk making him angry.

"Lick my balls."

I obeyed, although there was barely any saliva left on my tongue. I had to rub it against the roof of my mouth to moisten it before I swirled it all around them.

Chief had his head tilted back. "Yeah, bitch, you know who the boss is around here. You know who runnin' shit. That pussy, mouth, and ass is mine." He kneeled on the bed, snatched me up by my ponytail, and rammed his dick right back in my mouth. He shoved it in and out in quick inserts, at the same time rubbing his fist against it like he was jacking himself off. And each time he did, it was hitting me in my face. He released it and gripped my breast underneath my shirt and twisted it so painfully, I wanted to scream. But I didn't.

"Now there it go. I'm about to bust, and you betta swallow all of it." His legs started shaking, and he released a nut in my mouth.

I coughed but swallowed it as it eased down my throat.

"Swallow that shit and love it!"

I was swallowing not only his cum, but the dried-up leftover cum from the pussy that was on his dick.

He pulled out of my mouth, pumped his shit some more, and as more oozed out, he let it drip all over my face, neck, and breast. Then he stood and stared down at me like I wasn't shit.

I didn't move an inch until he exited my room.

After I cleaned myself up, I let a little more time pass before I crept up to his bedroom door. I slid closer to it and pressed my ear to it. I could hear him snoring. I relaxed a little and went back into my room.

Pure relief was what I felt when I saw the beams on the girl's Volkswagen flash. It was the signal to get my ass out of the house as fast as I could.

I tucked the spray in my pocket and exited my bedroom as quietly as I could. My hands wouldn't stop shaking, and my kneecaps were bumping into each other. I was sure after the fuck-fest Chief had with those tramps he was asleep now. Still, I tip-toed down the stairs. The target, the living room door, was in my sights after I had passed the sixth step. I had about nine more steps to go.

I was glad the stairs were carpeted and didn't make a sound as I descended them. I didn't hold on to the rail because it would have made a sound as I went down. Once I reached the bottom, I made even smaller steps toward the door on my tippy-toes, because there was no carpet there and it was possible to hear my feet hitting the floor. I had half a foot of distance left. I took a deep breath and extended my hand to reach the door handle.

"Harlem!"

I jumped, and my eyes flew to the bottom of the stairs where Chief was standing. I froze up only for a second. Then I turned back around to unlock the door, but my shaking fingers kept slipping off the knob. By the time I managed to get it unlocked, Chief had already closed the distance between us and snatched me up by my ponytail.

"How many fucking times do you think you can pull stupid shit like this?"

I closed my eyes briefly.

"You are giving me a dozen reasons to butcher your ass." He shoved his fist into the side of my face, catching my nose and causing me to fall backwards into the door.

Blood spilled from my nostrils. The pain was intense, but I ignored it. I was watching for his next move. I slid the pepper spray out of my pocket. I felt for the safety catch on the small canister, flipped it off, and hoped the nozzle was fully open.

When he lunged at me again, I held the can up to his face and sprayed it like a wild woman. The first blast hit his forehead before running down into his eyes. I never saw him howl like he did when that combination of peppers clouded his vision.

He started running around the room, like a blind man, bumping into shit, and I took off, out the house, down the porch steps, and flew into her car. She put her foot to the gas pedal and got out of there like a bat out of hell.

I let out a moan. I forgot to grab Lady.

* * *

Despite the girl I now knew as Tammy was urging me, I refused to stay with her at her cousin's house in Ontario. She didn't need any more drama. I had got her caught up in enough. There was only one place I was going to go, and couldn't nothing change that.

"This is it," I told her as her car pulled up on the street next to a small gray house. I looked at the windows. All the lights were off. But Savior's truck was outside, so I knew he was home.

I turned to her and said, "Thanks, Tammy. You really looked out for me back there."

She leaned over and hugged me, and I hugged her right back. And I didn't let her go. I started to cry. Then the crying turned to sobbing on her shoulder. I clung to her tightly. When I finally pulled away, I saw tears running down her face.

"Call me, Harlem." She handed me a paper with her address and a phone number.

I waved at her one last time before I stepped out the car. Then I walked up the steps to the door and knocked.

Savior opened the door and looked half-'sleep. He just stood there staring down at me looking surprised as hell to see me on his doorstep. He was a shirtless with a pair of sweats on.

I heard Tammy start her car and drive away.

I bit my lip, knowing I looked a mess. My nose was swollen, and there was dried-up blood on my face. I smelled like pepper spray. "Ahh, Savior, you said—"

He stepped over his threshold, grabbed my hands in his, and hugged me deep and long. Then he pulled away to get a closer look at the bruises on my face. His eyes teared up. "Baby, what happened to you? Tell me."

That was when I lost it. I broke down and mumbled through the crying, "I'm sorry I didn't try to get out sooner."

He carried me inside to his bedroom, where he lay me on his bed and stripped me out of my clothes. He came back with a warm face towel and washed my face.

"Savior, I gotta tell you something."

"Sssh. Come on and let me put this shirt on you."

I held my arms up, while he slipped a long white tee-shirt over my head.

"Get some sleep, and we'll talk in the morning."

I nodded and relaxed on his bed. I had never felt safer.

When I woke up in the morning, Savior was wide-awake on the couch, with gun in hand.

I approached him slowly. "Hi."

He smiled and tucked the gun underneath a pillow, but I had already seen it. "Hey."

I sat down next to him. "Did you get any sleep last night?"

"Yeah."

"Don't lie, Savior."

He chuckled. "It don't matter. What matters is that *you* got some sleep. What matters even more is that you finally left Chief."

"Yeah, I finally did." I folded my legs underneath me and looked around his apartment. It didn't have all that fancy shit Chief had, just a comfortable long brown couch with a lot of pillows, a TV, DVD player, a coffee table, stereo system, and Xbox. That was it.

He rubbed my right thigh. "Whatchu thinking about?"

I looked down. "That I got you in some deep-ass shit, Savior. Chief might try to kill you."

"He don't know I got this place, for starters, and by the time he does realize you here, we'll be long gone."

I raised my head back up. "What do you mean?"

"It don't take a fool to know that Chief did that shit to you. Or to know that once he figures out you left him and that you with me it's gonna be some shit. So we're leaving. I'm getting you the fuck up out of here."

"Where are we going?"

"Far away from here, that's for sure." He slid me an envelope.

I opened it quickly. Inside was a deed to a house located in Colorado. I lit up with excitement then breathed a sigh of relief. "Can we leave today?" I asked. Despite Savior's coolness, I still felt we weren't safe from Chief, not for even a second. I knew he was going to be gunning for my black ass.

"Not today, but soon. I got one last transport to do, then we can go." He took one look at my worried face and kissed me. "Aye, don't worry. Now what did you want to tell me?" He stroked my cheek softly and stared at me, and the fear was there again.

The way he looked at me, so gentle, with his

eyes shining every time they swung in my direction and his lips always curved like they were going to crack into a smile, I loved it. But what if I told him all the shit Chief had made me do, would he still look at me that way? Would he still want to be with me and make love to me?

I had been battling this fear ever since we went to Vegas and made love. But I couldn't hold on to these secrets any more. If he really loved me, he had to love all of me, accept me and all the shit I had done and went through, or else it wasn't real love.

I took a deep breath and told him everything, from jerking off Mr. Berry, to all the foul shit Chief had done to me, the strip dominoes and masturbation shit I did in front of his friends, taking drugs into a jail, what happened at the hotel, the threesome with another girl, how he threw me out in the street half-naked, and the latest incident from the night before. Each time I told him something else he had this crazy look on his face.

The last thing I told him was about the beating Chief gave me that led to the miscarriage. Just speaking of the miscarriage made my voice crack, and I ended up crying again.

After what seemed like five minutes of silence, Savior said, "Why you just now telling me this stuff, Harlem?"

"I was scared if I told you all the shit I had done, you would be ashamed of me and wouldn't want me, Savior. And I was scared that if I told you about the miscarriage, you would try to do something crazy to Chief."

He shook his head angrily then he blew out a

blast of air. He whispered, "Muthafucka. You know what, Harlem, that shit is over with, but I ain't gonna lie. I wanna kill that fool for treating you that way."

"See, Savior, don't do anything crazy."

"About that miscarriage . . . is that why you tried to kill yourself?"

I nodded.

"Baby, I wish I had known." He rubbed my tummy as if there was still a baby in there.

I smiled letting him know it was okay.

"Damn, Harlem, what can I say to make this right? Nothing. I'm sorry you had to go through all of that shit. It wasn't your fault, and believe me when I say it's over now. I'm not going to let anybody else do any more foul shit to you."

I believed him. After a couple seconds of silence, I asked, "What do we do now?"

"We wait till I get the call."

The call came a couple days later.

We were living it up being together. Only thing was, we had to lay low. Even though we were a little ways from Chief in some city called Chino Hills, Savior said it didn't take but a hot minute to hop on a freeway and find us. It had been a couple days, and the hiding-out shit was driving me crazy. I couldn't leave the house. Savior or his friend, Bam, went out and got whatever I needed, even some clothes, underwear, bras, and whatnot.

To pass the time, Savior and I had sex like three times a day, played his Xbox, and watched TV. I read a couple of the books Savior had lying around. I expected him to only have dumb chick and car magazines, but he had books by James Baldwin, Cornel West, Lisa Delpit, and Bell Hooks. We also talked all through the night and made plans on our future together and shit.

"Damn, I miss Lady," I whined, all hugged up on Savior as he was lying on his back on the couch and I lay face down on his chest.

He kissed my forehead. "I'll get you another dog."

"Savior, it won't be the same. I love Lady."

"I know, but you can't go back there. Which means you can't get her," he said gently.

I sighed and snuggled closer. "I know."

As Savior's cell phone went off, I bit my bottom lip nervously.

"Hello. What's up, Chief?"

Since they were both using a chirp phone, I could hear the whole conversation. My hands started shaking, and I felt my stomach knot up. But I kept quiet. I didn't want Chief to hear me.

"What up, man? We got more important shit to deal with. Two apartments been robbed. Muthafuckas got me for about four bricks."

"Shit!"

"Stuckey behind the shit," Chief said calmly. "But I'm not concerned with that faggot now. I won't have to deal with him much longer anyway. I'ma get this shit straightened and take care of him at the same time. So I need to take a little trip. That's why I'm sending you to a new connect in Oakland. We gonna use half of the product to take over Jordan Downs. Don't fuck up this time."

"I won't. How much you puttin' up?"

"Two hundred and fifty Gs, a hundred for the

supply, fifty for you taking the drive, and another hundred to take out Stuckey."

I held my hand over my mouth to stop my gasp from being heard.

"Tate riding with you. You can pick up the dough from Solomon and swing by to get Tate on the way to Oakland. Call me when you make it out there. I'm expecting you back in two days."

"All right."

"Oh and another thang, Harlem ran away. If I wasn't so busy trying to get my operation under control and dealing with Stuckey, I would have put you on it, since you so good at tracking mutha-fuckas down. But money is first, and hoes are always last. And, nigga, you betta remember that, fucking with these hoes in L.A. So when you get back from Oakland, I need you to find her dumb ass."

Savior winked at me. "Shit, with all the trouble she giving you, you want her back?".

"Yeah."

"Why?"

"So I can fuck the bitch one last time before I kill the bitch."

I closed my eyes and gripped my hands over my heart to stop it from pounding so hard. I walked out of the room so I wouldn't have to hear any more of the phone call.

Chapter 29

All that night I couldn't stop thinking about what Chief had said. His words rang in my head over and over: "So I can fuck the bitch one last time before I kill her." And maybe, just fucking maybe, all of this shit was a set-up. Maybe Chief knew that I was here and was toying with us. He could have the trap ready and waiting for us to fall in.

I sat in the living room nibbling on my nails and waited for Savior to pull up. His friend Bam wasn't too far from me, and having him around was irking my nerves, even if it was for my protection. Once he saw Savior pull up and approach me, he retreated to the back yard.

Savior was smiling big at me, a couple of bags in hand. "Hey."

I didn't respond.

He stood in front of me, staring down at my face and holding the bags. "I went to Marie Callender's to get you some food. I know you sick of junk, so I got the chicken fried steak, potatoes, and steamed vegetables. They had all these desserts."

He disregarded the look on my face and continued talking.

"When we went to Medieval Times I know your greedy ass was crazy about that apple pie *a la* whatever, so I got you one. We still have ice cream and—"

"I don't want you to go on that transport, Savior."

"What? Come on now, don't start that shit. You know I gotta go."

"No, you don't!"

"Come on, baby. Matter of fact, change the conversation before this food gets cold. Get up and let's go eat."

"No! I'm not stupid." I slapped at the bags in his hand. "I know what you up to. You gonna try to steal that money. You ain't going on no real transport, are you?"

"Harlem"—He put the bags down and pulled me to my feet—"listen, I'm doing this for us. It's the last thing I'm doing for Chief, I promise. Then we outta here. We jettin', baby, I promise."

Since he avoided the question, I figured I must have been right on track. But I knew deep down whether or not he was doing the transport or stealing the money wasn't important, and that wasn't what was bothering me. I didn't give a damn what he did with Chief's money. The truth was, I didn't want him to have any more dealings with Chief. Period. It was too risky. I would have been scared either way.

Through my tears I blinked and yelled, "What if it's a set-up? What if he tries to kill you, or the people you going to see do it? Don't be stupid about this." My words were coming out broken up, because every time I uttered a word a sob came after it. "You are all I have left, Savior. All . . . I . . . have. I can't lose you. Damn, Savior, don't you understand? I love you too much." The thought of him never coming back made my knees crumble, and I kept sobbing.

Savior swung an arm underneath my legs, and an arm around my waist. He then carried me into the bedroom.

Over and over I said, "You are all I have, Savior."

I made love to Savior that night like I never made love to him before. I kissed every crevice of his body, making him scream. I went down on him and sucked his dick so long and hard, he growled. I pleasured it until his sweet cream filled my mouth. Then I exchanged his for mine as I spread my legs and let him taste me until I whined and scratched at his arms while I came over and over again. I fucked him so hard, we were both panting. Then I let him ride me as rough as he wanted to until I came like I never came before, and it seemed like he did too. It was a scheme, though, to get him to not leave. I guess, I thought if I filled him up on lovin', he wouldn't.

In the morning when I felt his movement, I rolled over quickly and looked at him. He opened his eyes slowly. My eyes looked hopeful, I guess.

"Last night was good, Harlem, but I'm still going on the transport."

I sucked my teeth and turned away from him, giving him my back. He slipped closer to me and spooned me from behind, rubbing my waist. I tried to slip away, but he gripped an arm around me in a snug, gentle hold.

"I can't promise I'll be here when you come back," I said in a snappy voice.

"Girl, I'll whip your butt if you leave this house."

"Savior, you said you'd never lay a fuckin' hand on me!"

His low laughter rumbled in my right ear.

"I'm just messing with you. You right. I would never lay a hand on you. Any man who hits a woman is a fuckin' coward. I'm not that. And I love you too much."

I was getting real weak because tears were flowing from my damn eyes again. What was this man doing to me? "If you love me, then why don't you do what I say and keep your ass here?"

He sighed and released me. "I already told you what I have to do, Harlem. In this situation, you are just going to have to trust me."

I exhaled and stared at the ceiling. *It's not you I don't trust.*

My nerves were messing with me that whole day. I couldn't eat shit. I didn't bother trying to get any sleep either. I just sat on the couch and waited to hear boots hit the mat, telling me my man was home and not lying in a pool of blood somewhere, his head blown off.

By two in the morning I finally dozed off, but I was waking up every five minutes and checking to see if he'd made it back home. At one point I even put some clothes on and was gonna go out to find him, which was silly because I had no idea where he was and couldn't even drive. But, hell, sometimes love made you stupid.

Bam put a stop to my silliness. He blocked me from leaving the house by standing in front of the door. I sucked my teeth at him, rolled my eyes, and stomped into the bedroom, where I lay awake that whole night.

It wasn't till late that next night that Savior made it back home. And you better believe that before his arrival, that whole day I gave Bam hell. That morning when I found Bam eating cereal in the kitchen, I snatched it out of his hands, with tears in my eyes. "Savior is supposed to be back today. Today. How can you sit here and eat fuckin' Fruity Pebbles when he could be lyin' dead some-fuckin'-where, Bam?"

He stayed calm, kept his usual poker face. I never knew what the hell he was really thinking.

"It's still early, Harlem. Give him time."

I huffed out an impatient breath, shoved the bowl back on the kitchen table, and slammed into the bedroom.

With every hour that passed I would stomp to wherever Bam was. "Is it still fuckin' early? He ain't here."

He simple nodded.

When it reached nightfall, I couldn't take any more. I attacked Bam as he sat on the couch watching TV, taking my frustrations out on him.

He sat there quietly as I swung my fist at him.

"Why the fuck won't you do something?" I yelled threw my tears.

He let me vent on his ass until my body got tired of fighting him, and sleep. I went into the room and took my emotional ass to bed.

My sleep was interrupted by someone kissing me on my mouth passionately. When I opened my eyes, Savior's face came into full view.

I smiled. "What time is it?"

"Eleven-thirty." He pecked me one more time and exclaimed. "Baby, I did it!"

I inhaled deeply and reached over and hugged him

"No more transports, Savior? No more dealings with Chief?"

"No more transports, no more Chief. Did you hear what I said, baby? We done. Now we can get the fuck up out of here. And since Chief don't expect me until two more days, by that time we'll be long gone. Our plane leaves tomorrow, and we can be out."

Yes! I didn't care what he did or how he did it. I was just glad this shit would be over in one more day.

The next morning Savior was watching the news, and I was curled up in his lap on the couch. I didn't get enough sleep the night before and was dozing off and on when someone knocked on the door. Since the worst was almost over for us, I wasn't tripping.

Savior was, though. He pulled out his gun, making me nervous, and cocked it. "Go in the room," he ordered, not looking at me.

I rose quickly and rushed out the room. Only, I

didn't go into the bedroom like he ordered. Instead, I hid in the hallway, so I could get a view of the visitor.

When he yanked the door open and pointed the gun directly at them, my heart damn near jumped out my chest and onto the floor.

"What the fuck you want?" Savior demanded.

Chief's friend, Solomon, smirked as if Savior's gun was a joke. He raised his hands. "Relax, Sav. I didn't come here to kill you. You know Chief got more class than that. It's Sunday. There are rules to this shit, remember? Naw, you wouldn't. You are, after all, fucking the boss's woman. That was some low shit, Savior. I mean, I can understand why, she is fine and all—"

"Get to the fuckin' point before I forget the code and blow your ass off these steps." Savior held the gun sideways.

I watched Bam slip past me and hide on the other side of the door, his gun drawn.

"Well, first of all, did you really think you were going to be able to bail the fuck out with Chief's dough? That was some silly shit to do. The connect called us and told us you never showed up. It don't take that long to get to Oakland. In fact, Chief was being generous in giving you a two-day grace period. And to top that off you were supposed to roll with Tate, dumb ass. Leaving him hanging added even more suspicion. You sure ain't no natural criminal. How the hell you get on Chief's payroll? Nigga, you been trailed. You think you slick too, huh?" He laughed. "Chief also know about your other indiscretion. So therefore, nigga, I just came

here to give you a message. Chief said y'all, meaning you and Harlem—he know she's here—y'all
walk the streets, both of y'all dead men. Chief also
want his money, and you ain't got too long to give
it to him."

He looked over Savior's shoulders and spied me
hiding in the hallway. My eyes widened. Then he
winked at me, shoved a medium-sized box into
Savior's hands, and left.

Savior didn't reply. He just slammed the door
and locked it, while Bam continued to watch the
bastard from the window.

I rushed back in the living room on legs that felt
like jelly, my eyes as wide as golf balls. Shit, I was
scared as hell now. "We can't leave now, Savior.
The moment we step out the door we might be
killed."

"Calm down, Harlem."

"Hell, I can't. I'm scared for our lives now." I
sank down on the couch and stared off into space.

"Don't trip. We'll figure something out."

But I couldn't be too convinced.

Savior sat next to me and put the box on the
table. When I reached for it, he placed a hand over
mine silently.

"We might as well open it," I said, curious to see
what was inside the box. "Shit, we know it's not a
bomb 'cause we'd be dead by now."

It was probably a picture of me with a knife
through it. Or one of those letters with cut-out
magazine words spelling out shit like, "You're dead,
bitch."

I tore off the pink ribbon and lifted the lid. As

soon as my eyes got a view of the contents in the box, my stomach lurched, and I threw up all over the floor. When I was done vomiting, I let out a horrific scream.

The box contained the limbs, head, tail, heart, and intestines of Lady.

Chapter 30

I counted the tiny cracks in the ceiling. My eyes were red and my throat was dry and strained from screaming. Despite how much I loved Savior, this morning was a wake-up call that he wasn't strong enough to take on Chief alone. The fact of the matter was, it had to be either Chief or us. One of us would have to be taken out. There was no way I wanted to walk the earth looking over my shoulders, wondering if and when he would find me. I'd rather be dead than live my life that way.

Savior stepped in the doorway and stared at me for a moment. I held his gaze briefly and smiled slightly to let him know I was partially okay then put my head down.

"If you wan—"

"Before you say anything, I been doing some thinking about this situation, and I think I know a better way to go about it, besides just up and leaving," I began. "And most of all, I don't want to spend the rest of my life in fear that one day Chief is going to find me or you. So, before we leave, there's somebody I want to go see."

"Who?"

"Stuckey. I want to go talk to him. You said they have beef. And when he was at Chief's, he didn't look too happy with whatever had went down between the two of them. Maybe he would be willing to help us take Chief out before he does us first. What other options do we have?"

Stuckey wasn't hard to find at all. He was in a little hobby shop located in Long Beach called The Spot, where they sold and taught people how to make model cars and airplanes. It seemed like a popular place 'cause it was filled with kids and adults. But it probably was a damn cover for a drug house. That's what they usually did. They put the drug money into businesses so they seemed legit and put it in other people's names, or they used it as a cover.

Chief himself owned three different liquor stores and a laundromat. Only, I could never fully understand, if you had money to buy businesses, why you didn't walk away from the drug game completely? It was greed, plain and simple, and I couldn't think of anybody greedier than Chief.

We found Stuckey in the office seated behind a desk, looking at some papers like he was a legit businessman, as opposed to what the fuck he really was—a drug dealer, gangster, and a murderer.

I'd told Savior to wait outside for me, that this was something I had to handle on my own. He didn't want to leave me in there with that man, but I insisted. He slipped me a small gun, which I stuck in the new purse he'd bought me to cheer me up. But I thought the smarter thing to do was put it in my bra. I made a note to do that later and planned to never ever go anywhere again without a gat.

On the way over we had dropped Bam at the airport. He was getting the hell out of Cali too, headed to Chicago. I couldn't blame him. The shit was getting too hot for all of us.

Stuckey looked me over, which was what most men did when they saw me, checking out my face and body, appraising me, whatever. I was used to it, but it was a different look in his eyes. It wasn't the same lust I was used to.

"What is it I can do for you, young lady?"

I relaxed back in the chair and stared at him for a long time. "A few things. For starters, you can tell me how you knew my mother, Aja."

"It's a touchy subject."

"Why?"

"I hoped the day would come that I'd have the opportunity to tell you that I was in love with your mother. And it's just possible that you, Harlem, are my daughter."

I got all up in his face. "Wait a minute! Hold the fuck up! My daddy is Earl Scott, and, yeah, he's a fucked-up junkie, but he's my daddy, not you." I sat back down.

He chuckled. "I know you hurt, but just listen. If your mom talked about me—"

"She didn't really, so you must not have been too damn important to her."

He ignored my smart comment and continued, "I know she talked about Aces, the club. That's where she met me. She was looking for a job, and frankly, I thought she was the finest woman I'd ever seen. I hired her as a singer and fell in love with her, and she knew it too. But I learned I wasn't the only man in love with her. She wasn't just fine, she had a spirit about her that you could just soak up, Harlem. You got it too. And when she sang them songs . . . Whew!" He closed his eyes. "It could've been a hundred guys in the room, and the woman could've been blind, but you would've sworn she was singing that song just for you. But your mama was also a flower child. I know she probably told you that. She didn't have inhibitions. She was a thrill-seeker. And I couldn't keep her in one place, no matter how much I tried. She wanted to be out and about and getting into shit she had no business getting her ass into."

"So? That don't make you my damn daddy."

"Listen, she was pregnant by me, four months to be exact. We were doing so good. She was doing her singing and entertaining, and me, Chisom, and Ramsey were running the chop shop. We were brothers. But there were always fucking issues with a nigga like Chisom. No amount of control was enough for him, no amount of money was enough. He wanted to run everything. When you got two business partners, shit, just don't go like that. And when you got other muthafuckas in the same line of work as you, you have to respect their shit and their territory like they respect yours. But Chisom never wanted to hear any of that. The nigga thought he ran New York. He didn't. None of us did, and though me and Ramsey were content with what we had, Chisom wasn't.

"And one day Chisom did something really stupid that cost us a lot. He called it being ambitious, I called it being greedy and stupid. He threatened one of them Italians across town. Told him who he was and that he was taking over that area, an area no nigga should ever enter. Them Italians never entered ours. Then, to show his ambition, he robbed him, and the Italian called him a 'nigger.' Now Chisom had a temper and a hard time walking away from shit, so he pistol-whipped that Italian and ran off, thinking it wasn't going to get back to him at that time of night. Without a witness, it probably wouldn't have. Since his dumb ass gave the dude his name and he already had a reputation, they knew exactly where to find him. At the club."

His eyes started to water.

"Anyway, when they came looking for Chisom, they found Ramsey instead. When he wouldn't tell them where Chisom was, they shot him execution-style in the parking lot. The guilt was fucking with Chisom, who blamed himself for Ramsey's death. As sure as the sun is shining, the shit was his fault. And my silence, I guess, was the confirmation he needed. It was then that Chisom started using off and on when the pain of Ramsey being gone hit him. He did it recreational only, and I think it was then that your mother flirted with it too. She had an ache in her heart sometimes. It came and went. And when she had it, she wanted me around. But I couldn't, because the club came first to me. She knew it, and she hated me for that. So when I couldn't be there, Chisom, it seemed, could. And he showed her that heroin could too. And I know deep down that Aja never thought it would take her to the places she went to. It hooked her, and so she wasn't the same. I was so blinded by the club and my grief over Ramsey, I couldn't see it.

"Chisom was always envious of me. But the way he did it was fucked-up. He introduced her to something he knew none of us should've ever used. He did it to lower her, humble her, so they'd have something in common. We never used our real names back then, only our middle names. Chisom's first name was Earl."

I gasped. The room was suddenly very quiet.

"You telling me that my—Earl—is your brother?"

He nodded. "And Ramsey is our little brother. And Earl and I were both in love with the same woman. So after Ramsey's death, we made plans to get the fuck out of Harlem. It was right after she found out she was pregnant with you. And she was a lot further along than she thought. She felt you would be the salvation she needed to get clean.

"We sold the club and had the money to get a good connect. But, let's just say, we didn't all travel together. Aja and my brother ran off with the money, and by the time I found them, she was strung the fuck out, and so was he. It wasn't no need for me to kill them. He was my brother and I still loved her. And they were dying on their feet, so I moved on."

I was trying to convince myself that his ass was lying, but the eyes I was staring into were the same as the eyes on my face. And the beauty mark in the corner of his mouth was identical to the one I had on my face. "That still don't explain how you are my father."

"My brother can't have kids, and it's the main reason he hated me. I was born with the looks and the ability to procreate and he was born with a high-ass IQ and the ability to influence. So I know, without a doubt, you're mine."

"Well, if you knew all this time you had a fuckin' daughter, why didn't you come get me?"

"I didn't know, Harlem. All this shit is new to me. Your mother told me you had died. And I never set foot in the projects so, Harlem, how was I supposed to know? And I been locked down for twelve years. But when Chief told me where he found you, it all made sense. And I even went a step further. I found out where Earl was, and that wasn't too hard. Shit, my brother got a rep in the projects. They say he's the one who goes around the projects stealing shit. That didn't surprise me.

"Anyway, I went to see his ass, and he admitted what I suspected . . . that you are my child. And, believe it or not, I did go looking for you. But you gotta understand, Chief and I are at war now. I can't walk up to the nigga's house and ask for you or snatch you away. Not now. But my plan was to do it when this shit is over. Me telling him now, that you are my seed, would have given him more ammunition against me, and not to mention what he could have possibly done to you, Harlem. But I still had niggas casing his place for the past two weeks. They claim they never caught sight of you, so my back was against the wall."

I sat back shocked. All this time the man that raised me didn't have a damn thing to do with my conception. What the fuck was wrong with my mama, passing a man off as my daddy? But Mr.

Earl wasn't innocent in this shit either. *Mechanic, my ass.* "Just out of curiosity, where is my father—I mean uncle?"

"He's in rehab, trying to get his life together. He said he found God. He even sounds like a different person. And, yes, he told me what he did to you. The shit was horrible to hear. I'm not going to lie, I wanted to blast his ass away when he told me about that sick shit. I even pulled out my gat and pointed it at him. Something in me felt like he almost wanted me to pull the trigger. He begged for forgiveness, not just from me, but from you."

Fuck his forgiveness.

After a short silence, I said coldly, "You should have blasted him away."

He studied me for a moment. Then he said softly, "That's your anger talking."

"You should have blasted his ass away."

"It's fucked up what you had to go through. No one should have endured what you endured. But—"

"What the fuck you want me to say, Stuckey? I have no sympathy for his ass and probably never fucking will, despite the fact that 'he found God.' And if you wanna blame someone for all the years you missed out on being in my life and seeing me grow up, blame his punk ass 'cause as sure as the sun is shining, it's his fault."

"Seems to me that you will never be able to put this behind you until you have closure. Seeing him one last time and telling him how you feel just might give you that. He's over at that home on Cedar Avenue in Compton. Don't wait eighteen years like I did. Go and see him to put this out of your heart and mind, Harlem."

For a thug, Stuckey sure was philosophical.

"You'll be at peace, Harlem."

"I doubt it." I looked away and wiped the tears off my face.

What he didn't understand was that Earl had mistreated me all of my life, like he hated the damn sight of me. I made straight A's in school, he didn't give a fuck. I never got a high-five or pat on the back from him. I was even on the honor roll. You think he cared? I excelled at everything I tried, and it didn't mean shit to him, because for some reason, he despised my ass.

Once I even brought it up to him. I was six years old. He was sitting in the living room, and I came inside. I ran up to him and pressed my palms against his cheeks. "Daddy," I said, "how come you don't do stuff with me like the other daddies around here? The other kids' daddies ride bikes with them, they take them up to the park to go play, they get them ice cream off the ice cream truck." I went on and on about what I had seen other fathers do for their own kids. "Why we don't do none of that, Daddy?"

First he placed his hands on mine, making me smile. Then, in the next instant, he applied pressure, making me scream in surprise, and I started crying. He had this evil look on his face when he told me, "Don't ever put your fuckin' hands on me again, girl." Then he swatted my ass so hard, he left a mark.

I ran out the room crying and buried my head in my mama's lap. I never said more than two words to my daddy again. Stuckey would never understand any of that, because I didn't.

"I know I can't change the past, but I can start making up all the time we lost now. Whatever you need, Harlem."

I paused and clasped my hands together, raised them to my lips. "I do need your help, Stuckey."

"With money? You want to go away to college? What?"

"I need you to help me kill Chief."

He was speechless for a moment.

"Harlem, I have a hit on Chief. It just ain't possible for you to be there when the shit goes down."

"I want to see him die."

All Stuckey did was smile. "Now what would a young lady want to see that for? You supposed to be sugar and spice."

"Cut that bullshit out right now. You have no idea about the shit I been through in my life. Ain't shit about me sugar, and ain't shit about me spice. It was never an option for me. I didn't have no tea parties or dollhouses. I had two addicts for parents that were torn between two worlds, the real one you and me live in, and the one they entered when they were high. Either way, either world didn't have no room for me. I done seen my mom prostitute herself for dope, jerked men off for dope, stripped to pay off debts. And that ain't the worst of the shit I done had to do just to breathe. Stuckey, a part of my soul is gone and can't nothing get it back. Can't nothing replace it. And I am what I am. I had a fucked-up life, and I'm just playing the hand I was dealt."

He looked at me for a long time before saying, "If you like, I'll let you know when the nigga's heart stops. Matter of fact, you and Savior are welcome to stay at my crib until this shit blows over. I got security around the clock. It's safer for you to chill there than run the streets."

I jumped in his face. "How do you know about Savior and me?"

"*Baby*, everybody in the projects knows about that shit. You gotta be my daughter, pulling some cold shit like that over on a nigga like Chief, running off with his favorite soldier and stealing his dough. Girl, you got some balls *fo sho*. That's from my blood running through you."

I sat back down and wiped the sweat off my brow, sweat that wasn't from any damn heat, but from nervousness. Because Chief's evil-ass face flashed before me.

"Of course I would like you to stay, Harlem. Believe me when I say I loved your mother. I would have loved you just the same. But I didn't get the chance. But I'm here now. Maybe we could work on having a relationship. We could spend time together and do the types of things fathers and daughters do. I always wanted a daughter, Harlem. And it would have been a blessing to watch you grow up. Girl, you look like your mama spit you out."

I shook my head. "I gotta get up and out of Cali. I seen and went through too much horrible shit out here. I want a fresh start and as normal a life as I can get. And with a hustler for a daddy, I just don't think that's possible."

He nodded his understanding but looked disappointed. Even hurt.

"But I will take you up on the offer to stay in your house. And once you tell me the black-hearted muthafucka is dead, I wanna go spit on his fuckin' corpse."

He looked at me for a long time and smiled. "That's my daughter."

Savior and I stayed on the 60 freeway for what seemed like an hour. I told him everything Stuckey had just told me about my mother and how the man I grew up thinking was my daddy wasn't, and how a damn near stranger, Stuckey, was really my father.

All Savior could say throughout the conversation was, "Whoa!"

I shook my head. "I know, my mom was a real fuckin' trip, huh?" *Mama*, I thought, *you need your ass whipped for this one.*

"People make mistakes."

"Yeah. I know all about that. I was raised by two walking mistakes."

We exited the freeway, which was practically empty due to it being so late. Once off, we stopped at a red light. Savior took the opportunity to kiss me.

And I know I wasn't hearing things when T.I. blared in my ears, making my heart speed up rapidly. But it wasn't coming from our car. My hands gripped one of Savior's as I peered out the rearview mirror.

"Damn, baby! You got a tight-ass grip."

I didn't reply, just kept looking at the side mirror at the Excursion behind us that had Chief's driver inside of it.

"Harlem, you okay?"

My breathing had become shallow. I pointed behind me with a shaking finger. Savior looked out his side mirror. My lips trembled, and my knees began to shake.

"Damn," he muttered.

The SUV honked at us, but Savior ignored it and took off as soon as the light changed to green. As the truck trailed behind us, Savior increased his speed.

My eyes shot back to the mirror. They were close. Right on our heels.

He made a quick right. "Harlem, I'm gonna get us out of this shit."

I didn't respond. My stomach was twisting in knots, and I couldn't stop my body from trembling.

He punched it to sixty and shot past a stop sign, took a quick left, then a quick right, and drove down another street. I gripped the armrest on the car door as he skidded to a stop at a red light.

When it turned green, Savior sped off again and quickly turned down an alley. I craned my neck to see the Excursion pause at the alley opening as if it was going to let us go. Then the driver busted a U-turn and went the other way.

Savior paused for a minute, put the car in reverse, and backed up to go the opposite way.

I looked wildly behind me through the back window as he closed the distance and we were about to dip out of the alley. But just as we reached the end and Savior was about to make a quick right, the Excursion, along with a black car, were on us and we were caged the fuck in.

"Harlem, duck!" Savior shoved my head down as glass shattered into the car from the impact from a bat one of the dudes swung at it.

A fist swept through the window and punched Savior in his face. Then three guys dragged him from the car and threw him on the pissy-ass alley ground and commenced to whipping on him.

I screamed loudly and cursed them bastards for putting their hands on him.

Suddenly, Solomon's ugly-ass face filled the broken car window. "Come here, bitch."

"Fuck you!" I scooted my body as far toward the passenger side as possible and swung my foot at his head.

He ducked and leaned further in the car, grabbed my arm, and dragged my ass out. I grimaced as broken glass prickled my skin.

He held my arms behind me, making it impossible for me to move them, and he leaned my body backwards to keep me off balance, so I was on the balls of my feet and leaning against him.

"Let me go, you cross-eyed muthafucka."

He tongue-teased my right earlobe and whispered, "You know you talk a lot of shit. Maybe I'm gonna have to stuff your mouth with my dick, just to shut you up."

I threw my head back and tried to spit on him.

He used his other hand to push my face away and laughed.

"You put your shit in my mouth, you gonna end up with a stump for a dick."

"Relax, boo. We'll have time for that later. Chief wanted you to see this."

I sobbed and shook my head as Solomon forced me to watch the three men continue to beat on Savior. One held him up, while another continued to pound his flesh with his fist, making Savior groan. The third one joined in the attack, swinging his bat at Savior, hitting him in his back and side. Blood was running down Savior's face as he still tried to fight back, but he couldn't. The dude holding the bat swung it again and hit Savior in the mouth, making me scream at the top of my lungs and struggle against Solomon. Blood sprayed from Savior's mouth, and he dropped to the ground.

They continued to hit and stomp his body until he stopped moving and his blood was splattered all over the ground at their feet.

"Savior! Savior!" I sobbed over and over again. A pain rose in my chest, seeing him lying there like that and I couldn't do anything to help him.

The three men hopped in the Excursion, but Solomon didn't move an inch. His feet remained rooted in the spot we were both in.

One of the dudes in the passenger seat next to Chief's driver yelled, "What the fuck you waiting for? Let's go!"

"Ahhh . . . fellas, I'm about to make a quick detour."

When Solomon rubbed his dick against the crack of my ass, I knew just what *detour* he meant.

I screamed for help as loud as I could, but it didn't stop him from dragging me to his car, throwing me in the back seat, and trying to pull my pants and panties down. I used all the power I possessed to get his ass off of me. I scratched his face, kicked him in the nuts, bit one of his fingers, but still, some way he managed to get my pants down to my ankles.

He planted his knees into my thighs so I couldn't escape and held my hands over my head in one of his hands. Then, with the other, he unzipped his pants and yanked out his raggedy, little dick.

"I been waitin' to do his shit for the longest, but Savior's ass beat me to it." He stuck a finger in my pussy, making me close my eyes and squirm. "Let me get this shit wet and ready for me." He wiggled his finger around inside of me.

I cried again and kept yelling.

Just as he was about to stick his shit into me, he was plucked off of me and pushed aside by Chief's driver.

"Man, what the fuck are you doing?" Solomon yelled, pulling away from him and stomping his feet on the concrete like a damn kid.

The driver said simply, "You know what the orders were."

It was the first time I heard him speak. And his words were like music to my ears. Because those words saved me from getting raped by Solomon.

"Man, I was just trying to get me a little piece. He's going to kill the bitch anyway. What fuckin' harm would it have done?"

When Solomon caught sight of the look of murder in the driver's eyes, he backed up slightly and said, "Okay, big man, it's your call."

Without another word, Chief's driver leaned over me and yanked my pants up around my waist and pulled me from out of the car. He held me in a tight grip and swept past Solomon. He didn't release me until me made it to the truck, where he shoved me in the back seat near one of the three guys that had whipped on Savior.

I stared out the window at Savior's body. He was coughing and spitting up blood, and I started crying all over again as they, without the least bit of concern, drove right by him, leaving him to die out there. Even Solomon sped away in the opposite direction in the black car. I kept sobbing and loudly sniffing and calling out Savior's name.

One of the dudes said, "Shut that bitch up."

Then one of them reached over and punched me in the mouth, knocking me out cold.

Okay. This is one of them situations where you don't wanna wake up, but with my head being kicked repeatedly, I really had no choice.

"Wake up, bitch," I heard from a soft, singsong voice.

And when I did, I was surprised as hell to see a girl looking back at me. It was that dumb bitch from the club. Damn she sure was loyalty to Chief.

I looked around. I wasn't in the car no more. I was at somebody's house I didn't know.

I heard murmurs in the room.

There were two more girls seated across from me on the couch.

And yes they were all young like me and very

pretty. Except the bitch I had beat up. She still looked as bad as she did the day I saw her on the corner.

"You didn't think it was just you did you?" she asked me.

I didn't respond.

"I'm down with Chief. Yeah, I fell off no doubt but as soon as your ass is gone Chief is putting me up in that crib. I'm next in line. And Chief said he wanted your ass kicked so that's what we gonna do."

I closed my eyes briefly.

"Before the night is over Chief is going to kill you, Harlem. And you can yell as loud as you want to. Ain't no cops going to come save you. They on his pay roll. And even if they wasn't, they wouldn't give a fuck about a ho from the projects whose kin is two dope fiends anyway. Yes, bitch, I know who you are."

I looked at the other two chicks, one light skin with spiky hair and the other dark with a curly ponytail. The light skin girl rolled their eyes. I caught it. The dark skin girl looked more scared than me.

"Let me do the introductions. I'm Tina. The redbone is Yvette and the dark chick is Keya. And in case you wanna know. We all got pads that Chief run dope out of. And I'm his chick on the side. 'Bout to be the main chick."

Yvette rolled her eyes again. "Why the fuck we here anyway?"

"Y'all know what's up." Tina dialed Chief's number. "Y'all getting paid for this shit so chill!"

I heard Chief on the speaker phone. "Yo."

"Hey, baby. Your goons dropped the little princess off not too long ago."

"Well, I'm waiting for Savior to bring my paper. I'll be there soon. "Go on and do to her what I said."

Before I could even run for the door they were on me. The other two chicks grabbed both my hands and Tina's fist slammed directly into my forehead, giving me a big ass coconut. I fell to the floor on impact.

"Get up." With a grip on my hair, she swung delivering punch after punch to my abdomen. She then slapped me across the face so hard my head flew in the opposite direction. Then she kicked me over and over again in my stomach 'till I was lying flat on the ground.

"You didn't realize how good you had it ho. You were in Chief's crib. Then you go out and you fuck his favorite solider. How fucking disrespectful."

She lifted my head and repeatedly bashed it into the hardwood floor until the ground sliced through my flesh and created a deep gash on my forehead.

"Turn around and look at me bitch. Remember this?"

She flipped open the same knife she had tried to attacked me with. I winced as she grabbed handfuls of my hair and went to work on slicing it off of my head. She then tossed it at me and went back to punching me all over my body. I was too weak to fight back and it was a battle I couldn't win, especially since the other girls went in on fucking me up also. But Tina was vicious with it. Lighting cigarettes and burning me all on my face.

"Yeah, you ugly now bitch. You ugly just like me." Then I felt the sting of warm fluid. The bitch was pissing on me.

Then she went back to beating my ass. Yvette was going in on me too while Keya just held me up with shaking fingers.

By the time they finished I was spitting up blood, barely breathing out of my bloody nose and one of my eyes would not open up. It was from the kick Tina had delivered to it.

From my good eye I watched Tina snap pictures of me on her camera phone.

"Why the fuck y'all bitches resting? Finish fucking her up!" she ordered.

"Look Tina I'm getting tired of you bossing me around like you running shit."

"I am running shit. Once this bitch is dead, Chief moving me in his crib and I'm gonna be his main bitch."

"How the fuck you figure that?"

Tina tossed the phone and rushed up to Yvette and placed the gun all up in her face. "Why the fuck you throwing shade bitch? You supposed to be my girl and you supposed to show appreciation about the fact that I put you on with my nigga. Your muthafucking ass would be on the ho stroll if it wasn't for me."

"You woofing. Get that gun out my face. Guns don't scare me Tina."

As best as I could I pulled myself up slightly and tried to drag myself to a corner. 'Cause they were both standing over me arguing with a gun that I was pretty sure was loaded.

"Naw, bitch. You taking too much credit. It was

something Chief saw in me that made him want to put me on!"

Keya gasped. So did Tina. If I could breathe correctly I would have also gasped at what Yvette was saying.

Tina moved the gun out of Yvette's face, by dropping her hand to her side and back up. "So what the fuck you trying to say Yvette? Huh?"

Yvette shook her head and smirked. "Nothing Tina."

"No, fuck that!" she screamed at the top of her lungs. "What the fuck you trying to say? You fucking Chief bitch?"

"Naw, bitch! He fucking me! And from what he told me. I'm moving in that muthafucka!"

Before she could get another word out a bullet pierced her in her neck. She flew with the impact. Blood spurted from her neck and she put a hand over it while more blood spilled from her mouth and tears started flowing from her eyes as she seem to struggle with her own life. But Tina wasn't done.

Her eyes were cold. "Bitch, you gonna betray me like that! You was supposed to be my girl and you fucking Chief all along behind my back? I'm gonna split your head in half!" She pulled the trigger again. But nothing came out. The gun simply made a clicking sound. Yvette removed her hands from her neck and her arms started flapping at her sides.

Keya stood frozen.

Tina pulled the barrel of the gun to her face to examine why the gun didn't go off again. "This shit must be jammed. Chief gave me this sorry ass gun." She pulled the trigger again and before she could remove it from her face a bullet pierced her temple!

Keya screamed. Yvette's arms stopped flapping and her eyes became glassy.

Tina fell back. She wasn't moving.

Despite my fear of seeing two dead bodies in front of me I thought quick. I rushed over to Tina and grabbed the gun out of her hand before Keya could get it.

She gasped and her hands immediately went up as I aimed the gun at her.

"Was you fucking Chief too?"

She nodded and started crying with her shoulders shaking.

"Then you know where he lives. Can you drive?"

She nodded.

"Come on."

As we slipped in the car and headed to Chief's house I thought quick. I can't battle Chief alone to get Savior back. I needed help.

"Hit the 710 freeway," I ordered. I needed my father's help.

Once we arrived at his little shop I aimed the gun at her. "Get the fuck on."

She opened the driver's door and ran off.

I hopped out of the car and rushed inside.

Stuckey was in his office with the some dudes.

"Stuckey I need your help. Chief got Savior and he just tried to have me killed."

Stuckey pulled a gun out of his drawer placed in his pants and rushed me outside with him.

Chapter 31

With my dad by my side I had enough guts to face Chief. I needed to see if he had Savior and I wanted to watch my daddy kill him.

I stood behind Stuckey and his goons when they rushed into Chief's house into his game room.

"What the fuck is this, niggas? Y'all know who the fuck I am? I know y'all not trying to rob me!" Chief stood from the chair and pulled out his gat so did his goons.

"Like *you* robbed me."

All the heads shot toward the voice at the door.

Stuckey stood in a doorway for a second, then walked in slowly while aiming his gat at Chief. He stood next to the dudes who were facing Chief and his men.

When Chief shook his head and lowered his gun, all his niggas lowered theirs as well.

"Stuckey, what the fuck you want now?" he spied me behind him and he looked confused. He thought I was dead.

"I hired somebody to kill you in exactly four hours, but I thought the shit is a waste of dough when I can do the shit myself. And I don't give a fuck who is here. I warned you what I was gonna do if your monkey ass got too ambitious and tried to take over Jordon Downs, and you ignored that warning. So it's on now. You done fucked with the two things I value, Chief—my streets and my seed."

Chief narrowed his eyes to slits. "Nigga, what? Your seed?" He turned around and looked at the men behind him. "What the fuck he talkin' about?" He turned back around. "You want a blunt, Stuckey? 'Cause prison made your ass fuckin' coo-coo, man."

"Harlem is my daughter, nigga, and you been fucking her and abusing her, you sick muthafucka. I know you kidnapped her too. I'm getting her back, and today is your last day."

Chief shook his head and laughed in disbelief. "Ain't this some soap opera shit!" He spun around in a circle, his arms wide, before turning back to face Stuckey. "Harlem is your daughter?

"Yeah, muthafucka."

"Well, I'll tell you what, man your daughter got some good-ass pussy." Chief cupped his balls and shook them. "And she about to make a whole lot of money for me—"

Bam!

My daddy fired his shit! It made a loud popping sound that exploded in my ears so loud I screamed. Smoke instantly filled the room. Another bullet pierced one of the flat screens, making it explode. Within seconds shots were fired all over the room. All the TV screens busted and exploded, the walls

were covered in bullets, tables and chairs were toppling over, and shit was flying. The niggas acted
like they were on a mission, and kept shooting at
one another.

I squinted and saw Chief fire a shot that went
through a window and shattered the glass. A guy
from Chief's crew screamed as a bullet came out of
nowhere and pierced him in his chest. Blood colored his shirt as he flew backward.

Chief's crew started firing more rapidly, but the
bullets continued to spray all over the place, on
the huge stereo system with the expensive speakers along the walls, and the DJ stand. Bullets penetrated the wall above, bringing down clouds of
plaster all over me.

I screamed again over the horrifying blasts and
curled my body into a ball as I shielded my head
with my arms. A body fell heavily beside me, dead,
and I scooted back from it, trying to avoid the
growing pool of dark red blood spreading toward
me across the floor.

As gun smoke filled my lungs, I tried to cough
into my hands, but I wanted to keep my arms over
my head, praying a bullet wouldn't hit me or flying
glass cut me in the face. The bottles of alcohol on
top of the counter flew every which way, flopped
over, rolled off, and exploded in small pieces when
they hit the floor, liquor spewing out and splattering everywhere.

I was in a panic. Should I try to run and get out
of there? I wiped plaster from my eyes and took another quick peek. A nigga was struggling to stand
after several bullets from Stuckey's boys ripped his

body. Blood gurgled from his mouth, and he dropped to the ground before he could fire another shot.

Out of the corner of my eye, I saw a bullet managed to strike Chief in his leg and shoulder. Despite my terror, that shit was encouraging. I clenched my fists and prayed another bullet would hit him. In his moment of weakness I picked up the somewhat intact bottle and threw it in his direction. I missed. I ducked back down, so he wouldn't see I was the one who threw it. I wanted to do more, but I was scared he'd catch me.

One of Stuckey's boys went down when a shot hit him in his head. He was leaning back against the DJ stand, fighting the hell out of death as blood escaped from his mouth. He struggled to rise, only to slide back down and stay slumped over.

I gripped my arms tighter around my head, blocking out all the flying shit. And while the shooting had only been on for not half a minute, I felt like I was gonna go fucking crazy from the horror taking place on the other side of the counter. The noise was loud, and both my ears were ringing.

There was a brief lull in the firing and I looked up again, just in time to see one of Stuckey's boys take out Chief's third man. He would have been the last one standing, until the one lying on the ground raised his gun and struck him in his chest. The bullet ricocheted through him and hit Stuckey in his shoulder, making his body spin around and his voice howl. It weakened him, and he crouched down on one knee as blood poured from the wound.

Chief saw it and took the opportunity to fire at least six more times at Stuckey, but only hit him once. But the one shot was fatal. I watched horrified as Stuckey dropped to the floor on his other knee. Then he slumped on his side and stayed motionless.

And for a moment, the only person that was standing was Chief. Which scared the shit out of me. How could he be the last muthafucka standing? I crouched again behind the bar, my heart beating wildly. The puddle of blood from the dead body had reached me, and when I lost my balance on the balls of my feet, I stuck a hand down in the red liquid to keep from falling, my other hand covering my mouth for fear that Chief might hear my crying.

Just then, a rapid series of bullets was fired from the doorway and got closer as the shooter entered. I stood up in a half-crouch but I couldn't make out who came in. The room was dark to begin with, and many of the lights had been shot out as well.

Not far from me, Chief jerked left and right as bullets hit him, and the remaining windows that weren't broken were broke now as glass continued to cascade on the floor.

I screamed again and felt my ears ringing, knowing, just knowing, one of those bullets was for me. I ducked completely down again and didn't raise my head again for fear the shooter would see me and blast my ass away.

Then it was real quiet.

All of the men in the room lay dead. It was the craziest shit I had ever seen. Chief was dead. Stuckey was dead. I looked, horrified, at the dead man lying on the floor next to me covered in broken glass and splintered wood, alcohol dripping from the counter.

Plaster continued to sprinkle over us, and in the angled light, I could see it covering the body and the pool of blood. When I took a deep breath, I inhaled the plaster and nearly coughed. I covered my mouth, still wondering if I was the next to be killed.

"Harlem? Oh shit, Harlem!"

I knew that voice. I lifted my head and smiled with joy. I tried to stand, but once I got to my feet, I fell right back down. "Savior! I'm over here."

The smoke in the room had me coughing again, and I could barely see him through the haze.

Savior stepped over the dead bodies and limped his way over to me, grimacing in pain with each step he took. He looked pissed when he saw how bad I looked.

I wanted to freak out too. I had just seen seven men murdered. "Let's get out of here, Savior."

He helped me to my feet, and I limped alongside him. He took small and slow steps so I could keep up with him. We went around the bodies, avoiding the blood that was all over the floor.

When we made it halfway to the door, I heard my name called and a chill ran up my back. We turned just in time to see Chief raise his gun and aim it at me.

Savior pushed me out of the way and claimed the bullet with his body.

I screamed as it ripped into him and he fell to the floor. "Savior!"

Chief aimed his gun at me again.

I froze when he cocked it.

He fired, but it made a clicking sound—the chamber was empty.

I quickly inspected Savior's wound. It was nowhere vital, just in his shoulder, but he was bleeding pretty badly. His heart was still beating, but he couldn't move. I kissed him on his mouth.

He mumbled, "I'm okay. But you gonna have to save us this time, Harlem. Get that muthafucka."

He slipped something heavy in my hands—a knife—and in that moment I knew enough was enough.

Disregarding my tears and the soreness in my body, I tucked the knife in the waistband of my pants and, with fear running in my chest, I rose up to face Chief, who was struggling to stand because of the shot that wounded him in one leg and another shot that had mangled his right arm. He had holes in his side and shoulder too where Savior's shots had hit him, but he acted like they were nothing more than flesh wounds.

As I faced him defiantly, he took one look at me and laughed. "Oh, you wanna fight me, Harlem? Is that it? Okay, you crazy bitch, I'll tell you what—I'll do this shit without a weapon." He tossed his gun aside.

I eyed the chains that stretched across the bar area and divided it from the dance floor. I figured I would need some type of weapon to beat Chief's ass. So, with all my might, and without taking my eyes off of Chief, I yanked one chain off the wall and wrapped it around one of my fists.

Coldly, I said, "Come on, Chief." I stood up as upright as I could in order to at least reach his neck.

He staggered toward me and chuckled.

I stepped in and swung my fist, hitting him in his jaw.

He just laughed and slapped me across my face, causing me to almost fall.

I ignored the sting that rushed to my face and kept my balance.

"What you gonna do now, Har—?"

Adrenaline pumping through me and making me forget about the pain I was feeling, I sidestepped his next swing, refusing to give up, leapt and connected with his nose. "This is what, you punk muthafucka!" Some of his hair had gotten tangled in the chain. I knew it was going to piss him off so I snatched it away swiftly pulling some of the silky strands with me.

He howled and swung wildly at me.

"This is for all the fucking times you put your damn hands on me!" I kicked him in his fucking nuts.

He screamed and lashed out again, this time catching my shoulder and smacking me to the ground. Shaking his head, he turned his back on me for a moment, rubbing his eye with one hand and holding his nuts in the other.

I jumped up quickly and moved backwards on the tip of my toes so I wasn't getting too close to him and he couldn't reach out and grab me again.

When the back of my legs bumped into something sturdy, I bent back and reached with one hand, keeping my eyes on him and feeling around. It was a heavy vase. I grabbed it and swung it with all my might, connecting with the back of his head with a loud thud.

"That's for making me go on them damn drug runs!"

He grunted, hunched over in pain. "Bitch."

I had to be quick as fuck on my feet because I knew Chief could crush me with one hand.

After shaking his head for a couple of seconds he lurched after me, but he could only see out of one eye, the other one was bleeding and leaking a fluid. He kept trying to wipe it all away, and there was blood flowing out the back of his head.

I probably didn't look much better myself. Every part of my body was in pain. I had several bruises, and my asshole was still bleeding. But I wasn't going to stop until the nigga was dead.

Despite the ache in my joints, and the combination of sweat and blood dripping down my face, I climbed up on a table to reach his height, and before he could swing on me, I bashed his other eye and socked him in the chest, knocking the wind out of him. "That's for throwing me out in the street!"

I jumped on him and continued to punch him in the face with my fist, causing his skin to tear and bleed. "This is for throwing me in the pool and leaving me in there to drown!"

When I tried to jump down, he grabbed my forearms then quickly grabbed my throat with both his hands. "You had your fun, bitch, but now I'm going to kill you for betraying me." His hands squeezed tighter, and he started choking me.

I twisted my body and struggled, hoping he would get weak and drop me. When it didn't work and his hold became stronger, I head butted Chief in his nose over and over until I saw blood pour from it. He still wouldn't release me, so I took my middle finger and as hard as I could, dug my nail into the bullet wound on his arm.

He yelled at that and released his hold on me.

I fell down painfully onto my back and was surprised to see him lunging at me again, with murder in his eyes.

I reached in my waistband for the knife Savior had handed me. "And this is just because I can't stand your evil, black-hearted ass!" I aimed it high, hiding it slightly.

As soon as he rushed toward me, I drove it with as much force as I could into his chest. Then as he froze, I leaned back, slid it out, and slammed it back into his chest as deep as it would go, till all I saw was the handle, the whole while screaming.

As blood poured out like red wine from the gaping hole, he collapsed on his knees, blood oozing from his lips. His eyes got glassy, and he fell backwards, powerless to stop my attack.

As he lay there shaking, I kneeled over him and continued to stab him all over chest as far in as I could, still screaming in rage. His head was twitching back and forth, but nothing else on his body was moving.

Then all of a sudden the twitching stopped.

Chief was dead. Hell, I killed him. Me. Li'l ol' Harlem.

My heart was pounding in my chest as I checked to make sure nothing was moving on his ass. As I stared at his lifeless body laying in that pool of blood that continued to ooze out of his body. He didn't look so powerful or scary anymore.

Then, for the first time since the shootout, I looked down at my dead father. I wished things could have been different. I wish that I had really gotten the chance to know him. Maybe have a relationship, even. We were both put in a position that prevented that. But like I had learned, you can't change the past. You can only hope and work toward a better future. And that's what I was on my way to.

I stumbled over to Savior. "Come on, baby." I helped him to his feet.

Funny how crisis situations could give a woman so much strength.

Once he was up and my body supported half of his, we walked out of that place, Chief no longer a threat to us.

Epilogue

I held onto Savior as we entered the concourse at Colorado Springs Airport. We had just checked in our bags. We always traveled light because wherever we went we always wanted to bring back souvenirs. So when we sat and reminisced over those moments we had something to look at.

"Baby," I said, pulling my hand away, "I have to pee before we get on the plane. The last place I wanna be is on the toilet when the plane is in the air."

He grabbed it back. "I'm going in with you."

I laughed. "Savior, stop playing."

"I'm not. I don't want to let you out of my sight ever again."

I laughed. He was always this way when we went somewhere, and I didn't mind one bit.

Those words brought me back to all that had gone down this past year. Losing my mother, being brutalized by a man who I thought was my father, being victimized by Chief, losing the man who was my real father, almost losing Savior twice, and having to take a man's life. In the midst off all I had been through, Savior said the thing he admired about me the most was my spirit. He said my spirit wasn't like any other he'd ever seen, and that I had way too much damn courage and way too much forgiveness in me. But he said having way too much was not a bad thing at all.

Well, I needed way too much of both of those for my final move in Cali. I had decided to make a trip to Cedar Avenue in Compton to see my father before we headed to Colorado.

I went to the front desk of the establishment and waited patiently as the nurse talked into the phone. Behind her I could see a room through glass windows. The people inside were watching TV, playing ping-pong, or reading. I scanned the rec room for sight of my father. None of the faces in there looked familiar to me. I thought maybe he was in his room, or outside.

"Can I help you, young lady?"

I smiled. "Yes. I'm looking for Earl Scott."

The nurse narrowed her eyes at me. "And you are?"

I held on to Savior's hand tightly. "His dau— um, his niece. Harlem Scott."

She stared at me for a long moment. "You weren't notified about Mr. Scott's departure?"

"Departure?"

The corners of her cheeks rose in a half-smile, and she looked down briefly before saying. "You really don't know, do you, dear? Mr. Scott left for home about a week ago. Shortly after, because the hospital didn't know who to contact, they contacted us and said that he was taken to the hospital. He had overdosed and went into cardiac arrest. The last time we checked, he was still there.

"We have an open-door policy. He is allowed to leave on his own recognizance and is allowed to come back when he's ready. We really liked your uncle. In the time he was here, he made such great progress. But the addiction he had was just too strong for him to fight it. He said nice things about you too."

She scribbled an address down on a piece of paper and handed it to me. "This is the location of the hospital. He's on the fifth floor in intensive care. The last time I checked he still hadn't pulled out, but with God there's always hope."

"Thank you, ma'am." I took the paper from her and walked away with tears in my eyes, Savior rubbing my back all the way to the car.

I guess it was too much to hope Earl would finally get his life together.

"Take me to the hospital." I handed Savior the paper with the address.

I felt like I was being stabbed with pain when I saw the man all my life I thought was my father in that hospital bed hooked up to all those machines. If it wasn't for Savior holding my body halfway up, I would have collapsed on the floor. See, it was one of them things where as much as I hated him, I loved him all the more, 'cause he and my mama were all I'd ever known. The only family I ever had.

"Harlem, you gonna be okay?"

I wiped tears away and nodded. "Yeah. You can wait for me outside, Savior."

He released me and slipped out the door, leaving me alone.

I turned back to Earl. He wasn't moving an inch. His eyes were closed, and I didn't know whether the machine was making his heart pump or if it was doing the shit on it's own.

Some people say even if a person is brain-dead they can hear you. Some people even say sometimes a loved one's voice can bring someone out of a coma. I didn't know if I really bought the shit, but I tried.

The sound of the machine's beeping put my nerves on edge as I approached the bed slowly and peered down at his face. Nothing.

"It's me. It's Harlem. To be honest this is the last place I ever expected you to be. I met Stuckey, and he told me what the deal is. He said you were trying to get your life together. And now you're here." I grabbed one of his hands in mine. "And I know it seems like you messed up, but it's not too late for you to try again. It ain't ever too late. Stuckey said you felt bad about what happened in the projects. When you . . ." I paused, unable to get the words out.

"If you still stressing over what you did to me, don't worry about it. It's over." I sobbed on the words. "It took a lot for me to get to this point, but

I forgive you. I realized I can't be at peace with you and even myself if I don't get past this, and this is my way of doing that. You can have your redemption. And I hope you come out of this. I hope everything works out for you."

I backed away from the bed, from Earl and the heart monitor with the slow beat, and sat in a chair and began to cry. I cried until no sound came out, until my knees balled up in my chest, and I let out a sob. I needed to get this out.

Ten minutes later, I kissed his cheek and walked out of the hospital. He never moved an inch.

Savior and I decided to relocate anyway, despite Chief being gone. There was nothing more in L.A. to see or do. No matter how pretty Cali was, and no matter how much people talked about it being the place to be, the land of the wealthy and of movie stars, it would always be tainted to me. I had much too much history there, which I wanted to put behind me.

We went ahead and moved to Colorado, although I would have preferred Rome.

We didn't rush into anything stupid like marriage or having kids. Although I wanted to have a child, I figured if Savior was my true soul mate, like I felt in my heart he was, those things would happen later on. Right now, I wanted to live my life.

I started college like I'd always dreamed, majoring in social work, just like that girl I'd met at my birthday party when I was with Chief. I still wanted to be a social worker and help out as many kids as I could.

And, yes, I enrolled in nearly all the clubs on

campus. I was a social butterfly, dancing at the step shows, marching for children's rights, and sitting in on ciphers.

Savior enrolled in school too. He was considering trying out for the baseball team at school, or maybe even coaching.

I told him both were good ideas, because I knew he could do whatever he wanted to do. We both could. There was nothing holding us back now.

Every day with Savior was a pure blessing. Of course, we had our problems. Everybody did. Sometimes he didn't put his clothes away, or cap the toothpaste, or he left the fucking toilet seat up so I always damn near fell in. But these things weren't half as bad as the shit I had to deal with when I lived with Chief.

Savior never raised his voice at me, called me out, or hit me, and when we made love, it was so gentle, I always ended up purring when we were done. He treated me better than I ever thought I could be treated or deserved to be treated.

He told me, "Get used to it."

Eventually I began to see my worth. It was a lot higher than I thought it was.

Savior made me realize all that shit that happened to me, all the shit Chief forced me to do hadn't tainted me in any way. In fact, all it did was make me stronger, to never sweat the small stuff.

When girls at my school stressed about gaining weight or being too fat, I laughed. 'Cause Savior loved the hell out of me and an extra pound or two wasn't gonna change that, or who I was on the inside. It just gave me more cushion.

When the girls worried about failing a class, I

would just shake my head. I knew I could always retake it.

One day a girl asked me, "Damn, Harlem, does anything ever stress you out?"

I shook my head. "No, girl. I've had enough stress to last me a lifetime. Life is way too short to worry. I'm living my life."

She sucked her teeth. "Um-hmm. What have you ever had to worry about? Having to balance time between school, all them damn clubs you in, and that fine-ass boyfriend of yours?"

"Something like that."

I kept the real deal to myself. The only people I talked about my issues with were my therapist and Savior. That girl could think whatever she wanted to.

Savior and I tried to live a normal life. We've craved it. We vacationed often, and we'd been back to Vegas to gamble. We'd been to Florida, Texas, and even cold-ass Alaska. Going to all those places made us more knowledgeable about the world, more cultured.

I wished a lot more kids were able to get out of the projects like I did. It would show them there's a whole 'nother world outside those gates.

On this trip, we were going to Rome and staying for a whole month. And I was gonna kill Savior if he didn't crush grapes with me like I'd always dreamed of doing at one of those vineyards.

I still thought about my mom. The one thing I always wanted to ask her before she died was, "Did I make you proud?"

And I wanted to let her know that no matter what she did or how much she failed, I would always love her and see her as the same mama. I guess I'll never know if she was proud of me.

Sometimes, when the house was real quiet and I was alone, if I listened carefully I'd hear her voice. She wasn't fussin 'cause she didn't get no fix, or hassling my daddy for one neither. Nor was she crying. She'd be singing in that beautiful voice of hers:

Just call me angel of the morning
Just touch my cheek before you leave me, baby

The voice was a sign that she was right there with me. And despite all the pain I had been through, the ache her death brought me, all of this happened for a reason. It gave me strength to endure anything that came my way, and a love that nothing can break. And I guess that made everything okay.

COMING SOON 2011

THUG IN ME

BY KAREN WILLIAMS

Prologue

Blood leaked from a gash on my cheek. But it didn't stop the punches as four police officers continued to give me. One minute I was getting out of my shower after hearing a banging on the door. The next minute, I was getting fucked up. I was now lying on the floor while they all delivered punches and kicks to my head and body, wherever they could land a punch or kick.

I placed my hands around my head to block some of the blows.

"You fucking cop killer!" one of them yelled, stomping his black boot into my face.

I winced from the pain as he continued to slam it down on my face. When he finally retracted his foot, I cracked one of my eyelids open to get a peek at his badge. Swarovski was his name. Another cop took his baton and started hitting me in my back with it, all the while Swarovski continued to bring his foot down with the weight on his entire body onto my face.

I grunted from the pain being a black man from

the projects you couldn't escape getting beat by racist police but I had never experienced a beating like this before. And most of all, I didn't know why they were attacking me or even why they were in my house.

But it only got worse.

Swarovski flipped me over and over on my back.

The others paused their assault.

Swaroski took the other officers baton and jammed me in my stomach with so much force I started choking and coughed up blood. He then took the same baton and placed it around my neck and started choking me.

I placed my hand on his, hoping I could stop his assault. Because yeah, I didn't stop the cops from beating my ass but I was gonna try and stop them from killing my me!

"Get your fucking hands off of me!" His grip on the baton on my neck tightened.

Snot flew from my nose and I felt like I was going to vomit, but he continued.

I felt myself getting weak and going out. My hands started flapping at me sides and I knew in that moment I was going to die.

Spit flew from his mouth as he continued to call me out of my name. The baton came down one more good time, hitting me in the back of my neck. Suddenly my body started feeling weak fuzzy, the way I felt just the night before when I popped an Ambia so I could get some rest.

And like the Ambia put me out, so did that blow.

Chapter 1

And now I'm here. Two days later, after getting my ass whipped, I sat in front of the judge and had a hard time standing to my feet, when the prosecutor laid out my crime: Murder of Devin Johnson: A police officer. A man I had never seen or heard of before. I damn near shitted on myself when I heard the charge and how much time the DA was asking for. All my fucking time: Life, plain and simple.

Without even looking my way, the Judge looked over his glasses and asked my lawyer, "How does the defendant plead?"

I stood with my Public defender, angry as fuck and scared.

"The defendant pleads not guilty, your honor."

I nodded and tried to keep calm, when inside I was dying. I ran the risk of losing everything I had, my mom, my job, my home, my girl, everything… And it pissed me the fuck off, and more importantly what pissed me of more was that I didn't do shit.

How in the fuck did I get here?

Three days ago. March 2003

I turned my Suburban down my street bumping Too Short. I then pulled into my drive way. I had just bought that bad boy. It was on point too. Ivory white and fully loaded with a couple TVs, iPod, and leather seats. My ride was a grown and sexy ride. And it was sitting on some twenty-four inch rims and that were shining on a daily. It was a gift to myself for all the hard work I had been putting in. And when I say hard work, no I'm not talking about nothing illegal. I did the shit the legal way. I'm not going to say I was never tempted to get in the game. Growing up in the Springdales, illegal shit was all around me and so was the opportunity to involve myself in it. But I saw way too many niggas get arrested over bullshit and too many killed over bullshit. I was cool.

And with the stress my mama had to bear from trying to raise my black ass alone, due to the fact that my punk ass father, who lived in the Springdale's just not with us, wouldn't help her or give her squat. And if it wasn't enough that my mama had to squander to make a life for us, she had to deal with a lot of unnecessary bullshit from my daddy, Curtis Redding. He was so uninvolved my mama gave me her last name. He refused to claim me and his various women always harassed and would even jump on my mama 'cause she had something they just didn't have: me. Funny. The thing he didn't give a fuck about. But the one thing my daddy did teach me indirectly was your dirt always catches up with you. Case in point, my daddy ended up with full blown AIDS. Sticking your dick in a hole just because it is open is not always a good thing. I didn't care too much when he died and I told my mother that he got what he deserved. But she always told me that it is always better to forgive if not for anybody else, for yourself.

After seeing my mom go through all of that, the last thing I wanted to do was cause her any trouble.

So by the time I was seventeen I finished high school, at the age of twenty graduated from ITT Tech with a Bachelors Degree in Computer Network Systems. I knew the computer like the back of my hand, and could do any and everything to it.

A few months after graduating from college, I landed a job as a Computer Analyst at Microsoft Word, making 50,000 a year. Within my first year of employment, I bought my first home. It wasn't anything special, just a two bedroom. But it was enough for me to move my mama out of the projects and enough for her to stop working like a slave. But she still managed to hold on to one of her jobs, being an In-Home Care Aide, for some elderly white woman. Time and time again I told her to quit and that there was no need for her to work. But she always said, that working for her wasn't like a job because they were so close. Like best friends.

I'm sure to most men, living with their mother would probably cramp their style but not me.

I wouldn't have it any other way. My mom was why I was everything that I was. I wanted her to be comfortable and have peace of mind. My mom was the most supportive person in my small inner circle. And I wasn't done accomplishing stuff. I still had a ways to go. The thing about me is this: I didn't wait for nobody to give me shit, I took it. I was in the process of getting a loan to open up my own business. Fuck the American Dream. I had been off that since I saw how people in the projects never got out, the shit just became a generational thing. Shit, I was living Chance's dream. And when my business opens up, I will be living that shit fully. And I knew the rules to the game, no felonies and no bad credit.

I downed the last bottle of my vitamin water and put my truck in park. I had just come back from the gym. I had done cardio for forty-five minutes and lifted weights for an hour. It was my usual schedule when I left my nine to five.

I hopped out of the car just as my cell phone started ringing. I pulled it out of my sweats pocket and recognized my baby Toi's number.

"Yeah baby?" I answered. I grabbed my gym bag out of the passenger side of the car.

"Hello?" was all she said.

I smiled. Toi. She was everything a brotha could ask for. She was fine, with that small waist and apple bottom booty, juicy lips, smoky bedroom eyes. She was sweet, could cook and even hold down a job. The only flaw as she was too high maintenance, wanted me to kick my mama out and move her ass right on in. It wasn't enough that I had also moved her out of the projects and into her own pad. That shit wasn't cheap. I had to work a day of overtime a week to do so.

"What's going on baby?"

"Not much just wondering if I could swing by," she said.

"Yeah. Ma probably cooking now."

"I meant for later. Is your mom gonna be there?"

"She lives here. What do you think?"

"But it's your house."

"What does that have to do with anything? It's my mom. She ain't tripping off you why you tripping off of her?"

She sucked her teeth.

"If you talking about later I can swing by your house baby."

"Chance, we been together for over three years. I love you don't you love me?"

I sighed. Oh Lord here she go. "Toi, I wouldn't have said it if I didn't."

"Then why aren't you treating me like you do?"

"How am I not? I take you out, I'm faithful, I'm damn near paying all your bills."

"I want to move in."

"You're not my-"

She hung up before I could finish.

I chuckled. I closed the passenger side door and slung my gym bag over my shoulder. I knew what that was about. Yeah, I loved Toi even when she had her attitude because she sure as hell could jump ghetto when she wanted to. I had learned to adjust to it. But what she wanted at that time I just didn't. Yeah I grew up in the projects, where guys went from girl to girl and had multiple babies, like my boy Calhoun, who had two kids, he rarely saw because he was always roaming the streets, chasing dirty money and pussy, or in jail. Time and time again, I pondered over both he and my situation. Calhoun grew up on the Westside of Long Beach too, but not in the Springdales. He had a mom and dad. You couldn't get more normal than his family. Calhoun's dad worked a nine to five as the principal of Cabrillo High School. And his mother stopped teaching to stay at home and raise Calhoun. Despite the upbringing Calhoun had, he joined a gang, smoked weed like it was going out of style and sometimes sherm. Time after time, Calhoun's father tried to be that ideal father to him, the kind of father I had always craved. Calhoun never listened. He dropped out of high school in tenth grade and has been in and out of jail for things like selling drugs to beating up his baby mamas, and refusing to pay child support. And he was an all around fuck up. A few years ago, he talked his parents into paying off the child support debt and when they loaned him the money, instead of paying for it, he went and bought a brick of cocaine that somebody robbed his dumb ass for.

I, on the other hand, had bigger plans for my life. I didn't have a problem settling down, I just wanted to make sure I was financially set. While I was sure Toi was the one, I was willing to marry her once everything in my life was in the order I wanted it in. The last thing I wanted was to bring a baby into the world and not be able to give him everything, that meant quality time as well as a stable, functional home. A father in every sense of the word father. Something I didn't have growing up. The last thing I wanted was to have to struggle and for my child to see me struggle. If Toi would just be a little more patient, I saw himself proposing to her in another year. A nigga was only twenty-one. By that time my business should be a go. I had been taking additional business classes and learned how to draft my own business plan.

I spied Calhoun sitting on my porch, puffing on something as I turned towards my house.

I sniffed and knew it was some weed.

He hopped off my porch and walked up to me.

I ignored him as he raised his free fist to give me a pound.

"What I tell you about smoking that shit near my house?"

"My bad. You wanna hit it before I put it out dawg?"

"No." My job tested us for weed religiously. And the last thing I needed was to get caught up. And the funny part was it seemed they always randomly tested all the brothas.

He smirked and wet the tip of his joint with his tongue and slipped it behind his right ear, and asked, "Aye man, what you getting into tonight?" For the life of me I couldn't understand why Calhoun of all the things chose to be a gangsta. Yeah he was a big dude like me, with the same height, complexion and build as me. Some people could say he could pass as my brother. But I was a lot more handsome and the nigga hated on me about it and was always calling me a pretty boy. I couldn't help it cause all his front teeth were gone his mouth from all the times niggas done knocked him out for running his mouth. And he looked aged past his years. They say that's what a wild life will do to you.

"Sleep." I jogged up my steps. I had worked a sixteen hour shift the day before, came right back in my normal time. I was tired. But I never turn down overtime. Now all I wanted to do was get something good to eat, pop an Ambia and get some sleep. I could hang on the weekend. It was only Friday. And when I did hang it wasn't going to be with Calhoun unless his ass was sober and not on any type of crime sprees.

I had loyalty to Calhoun only because we pretty much grew up together. When we were younger, he was always in the Springdales visiting his cousin Paul who was the same age as us but in a wheelchair. Paul and his mom lived right next door to me. So was his dad's younger sister. So Calhoun was always running with me and Paul was always trying to keep up in his chair. And yeah, Paul was half our size cause his legs wasn't long enough but he could roll with the punches. We did all kinds of shit together. Stuff that you would expect young boys to do but with a little more edge to it. If boys our age were pulling up girl's skirts, me and Calhoun were smacking their asses after Paul rolled by in his wheel chair and pulled their skirts or dresses up. When niggas was stealing candy from the store, we thought smarter, we would sell candy for the Boy Scouts and then lie and say some bigger dudes robbed us. But instead we took the money and bought skate boards. When niggas our age playing hide and go get it, we were actually getting the pussy while Paul was the look out. A couple times, we even talked the girls into letting Paul stick a finger in their young pussy. See, Paul couldn't fuck, something wasn't right down there and he sure as fuck didn't want to talk about it. Sometimes I wondered if he even had a dick but I was always

too scared to ask. But he was satisfied with us getting some.

We ran the lot we lived in and ran the other
niggas our age off. They answered to us. And yeah,
Paul was in a wheelchair but he was definitely with
the business. Whenever we had an disagreement
we fought it out amongst each other, Paul included. To be fair, depending on which one of us
had the problem, if it was with Paul, we got on our
knees so that we were the same height as his wheelchair and we got down. Whoever the winner was,
what they said was how it was going to be. Truthfully we all got down. I beat Calhoun's ass, me and
Paul tied and Paul packed Calhoun out. Calhoun
didn't come around for a few days after Paul gave
him a whipping. But when he did come around it
was just like it used to be. And our relationship
had its benefits. Calhoun couldn't fight worth a
damn so when he got into it with boys in the hood
I was always there to jump in and pack the dude
out. Paul would lean over his wheelchair and
throw a couple punches too. And when I didn't
have decent shoes and clothes because my mama
struggled with money, Calhoun would hook me
up. Paul's mama got social security for him so he
always looked fresh. And Paul was nothing nice on
his wheel chair he could pop wheelies and do the
same tricks we did. We build a skate board ramp
and Paul wasn't even scared to jump off that shit!

I remember one day we thought we had lost
Paul for good. Me and Calhoun had went to the
grocery store. Calhoun had came to me and said
he had got forty dollars in food stamps from this

crack head for only ten bucks. So we went looking for Paul but he was no where to be found so we went to the store without him As we walked back to the Springdales with everything from frozen burritos to Hot Pockets, rainbow sherbet ice cream, Hostess Cupcakes and bottles of Mountain Dew that we planned on eating with Paul.

Yeah, Calhoun had shit like this all the time, I didn't. He wanted to get us some liquor instead. I was cool on that. My mama would beat my ass.

As we walked home, a girl who lived in my lot rushed up to us.

She was breathing hard and her eyes were wide. "Aye! Paul got hit by a car and I think he dead!"

"What?" we both screamed in unison.

Instantly tears started falling from our eyes as we rushed back to the Springdales crying all the way.

The front of the building was blocked off. And me and Calhoun both sobbed uncontrollably as we though our friend was being wheeled out on a stretcher.

Then out of no where someone tapped me on my back saying, "What happened?"

I jumped and turned to see Paul behind me.

"Awwww! Nigga! We thought that was you!" I exclaimed.

"Yeah man!" Calhoun yelled, "Where you been?"

"I went to the doctor with my mama today."

We both leaped on top of his wheelchair and started punching him, happy our friend wasn't dead.

But it turned out our good times didn't last long before we were hit with the real tragedy. Whatever that shit was that he had that caused him not to walk took, his life a couple months later. We were all the same age . . . Twelve.

Me and Calhoun never got over it. And me and Calhoun were never the same. Things were never the same and our fun was never the fun it used to be either.

I chuckled thinking about all the crazy stuff we used to do. We were inseparable. But now I just wasn't fucking with him Calhoun like that, like we used to. I grew up, he never did. Truthfully, I didn't have many male friends because I didn't have time to be dealing with hate or no nigga being thirsty in regards to what I had. Jealousy was not just reserved for women.

I half listened to Calhoun as he went on the subject of stuff I cared very little about. Finally I told him, "I'm going to sleep."

He looked at me like I was crazy. "Sleep? Its Friday. What I fuck you going to sleep for?"

When I didn't answer he said, "Come on let's go out and have some fun."

I grabbed the keys and inserted it in the lock. "I don't have your kind of fun. You for some reason keep walking around acting like they can't lock your black ass up again."

He waved me off with a hand. "Man you sound like my pops. I don't need to hear this shit."

"Well you should listen to it." I pushed open my door all while shaking my head at him.

"Man I just wanna go ride, get some pussy."

"I'm good on that." I walked inside Calhoun followed after me.

I turned around just in time to see Calhoun

shake his head at me. "You still stuck on Toi. I don't blame you though. That bitch got a—."

I grabbed Calhoun by his neck. "Don't use that language in my house you know my mom lives here and don't call my girl out her name. You gonna make me fuck you up," I whispered.

He pulled away from me. "Sorry man. But you know a nigga saw her first."

I ignored him.

I dropped my stuff on the couch. "Ma, you home?" The smell of cooked food wafted to the living room and made my stomach grumble.

"I'm here in the kitchen Chance."

I walked to the kitchen to see what my mama cooked. She was mixing a pot on the stove.

"Hey boys," she said to me and Calhoun. "Chance, I made some pork chops, rice, gravy, and some cabbage with hot water cornbread. Y'all want me to fix you two a plate?"

My mama had me at the age of twenty. She was now forty two and she could easily pass for someone in her thirties. But that is usually how black women were. That "Black Don't Crack" shit was true. My mom was dark skin with full lips and an oval shaped face. She always had her long hair pulled back into a ponytail and simple clothes like sweat suits, that always covered her body, while I took my dad's strong jaw line, height and build. I was six feet two and had always been a big dude. I had well toned arms and was blessed with a six pack I tried to maintain by working out four times a week. My dark skin, silky, curly hair, light brown eyes, full lips and my set of dimples all came from my mama. I wore my hair in a set of natural curls and sported a goat tee. I didn't have a problem favoring my mother more than my father. To me my mama was the prettiest woman in the world. Often other men took notice of her beauty too. A couple times I had to slap Calhoun upside his head for lushing on my mother. And even though she wasn't aging on the outside she was on the inside. Years of stress affected my mama's health. She had high blood pressure and had already had two strokes in her life. That's why I was trying to take as much stress off of her as much as possible.

I kissed her on her cheek. "Naw, mama I'll get it."

"Okay, well everything is ready." She grabbed a towel and wiped her hands on it. As she walked away she stopped and said "Before I forget. Toi called and said to call her back, that it was important."

I chuckled as my mom walked away. I frowned at my friend. "You want a plate man?"

"You know I do."

"Come on."

I scooped two pork chips with dark brown grave and onions, white rice and cabbage with bacon onto a plate for me and one for Calhoun. I topped them off with hot watered corn bread.

We both sat down at the kitchen table to dig in the food.

My mom came back in the room. "Well that's my ride baby."

"Where you going mama?" Calhoun asked, jokingly.

"Me and one of my friends are going down to Pechanga to do a little gambling."

"I need to be going with you, na'mean?" he joked.

She chuckled. But said nothing else. She was never really social with Calhoun. I thought it was because he was always a nuisance and a bad influence on me. When I was a kid his dad was always knocking on our door and yanking Calhoun to his car and telling my mother to keep her son away from his. But it didn't matter Calhoun always came back.

I swallowed the food in my mouth. "You need some money?" I asked.

"No. I got my quarters I been saving for the past couple months."

"How you expect to gamble with only quarters?" Calhoun asked.

My mom ignored him, so did I.

I reached in his wallet and grabbed two hundred dollar bills and handed to her. "Have fun Ma."

"I will. I'll be back on Sunday." She pecked my cheek and was out the door.

"Play the nickel machines for me!" Calhoun joked.

I ignored him, got up, grabbed two cups and filled them with some cranberry juice I had in the fridge.

I sat a cup in front of him and downed the juice in mine.

Calhoun, out of nowhere, started chuckling. "Aye remember that time we broke into Fred Sanford's house?"

I chuckled despite myself thinking back to that day.

Christmas had just passed and my mom and

worked crazy hours to have a surprise for me under the Christmas tree. A bike. I was happy as hell to have one and made sure I took extra care of it. While Calhoun had already lost two bikes and was already on his third one. But his father told him that if that one came up missing, he wouldn't replace it. During that time, a lot of kids' bikes in the Springdales were coming up missing. And no one could figure out who was taking them. Then finally is was discovered that a dude who stayed in the house across the street from the Springdales's would drive around and if he saw a bike outside he would get out his beat up old truck hobble to the bike, grab it and put in the back of his truck and drive away. So I made sure that I kept my bike with me at all times. I always had an eerie feeling when I saw him driving around the neighborhood. My bike meant something to me and I knew my mom got this not only for Christmas but because she saw how much Paul's death had affected me.

One day me day Calhoun was over my house and all we had to snack on was some Fritos. It was the end of the month so food was always scarce in my house around this time. Calhoun only had a dollar left from his allowance so we rode our bikes and took the bag of chips to the local store that sold chili-cheese nachos and instead of paying two dollars for them, we bought the Fritos and had them at the store put cheese and chili on them. For a dollar they did it with no problem.

We grubbed them down quickly.

I paused my eating watched Calhoun and said, "You probably got all kinds of snacks at home."

Calhoun didn't respond, just kept smacking. It

was just something about this hood life that he liked. I didn't get it at all.

As we rode our bikes back to the Springdales, my stomach started bubbling like I had to take a shit. I looked to see if maybe Calhoun was having the same problem as me. And sure enough, he was clutching his stomach too.

"I gotta shit," I said.

"Me too. They must have gave us some fucking bad chili!" Calhoun yelled.

We pedaled as fast as we could, back to Springdales and without thinking threw our bikes down and raced inside to use the bathroom.

I sat on my toilet and let loose while Calhoun bammed on the door. When liquid shit wouldn't stop pouring from me, Calhoun gave up and I figured he went next door to his aunt's house to use it.

When we came back outside our bikes were gone.

I sat on my porch trying not to cry while Calhoun paced in front of me. "I know that mothafucka got our bikes man."

I didn't say anything.

"My daddy said if I lost this bike he's not going to give me another one."

I nodded. "My mama can't afford to buy me another one if she wanted to."

He slapped his hand into the palm of his other hand. "Fuck that! We need to get our bikes back."

"How we gonna do that? You know he ain't gonna admit he took em."

"We need to get inside his house somehow."

So over the next few days . . . We watched that

man. We named him Fred Sanford because everyday, when he came home that's what he watched
on TV and nothing else not even the news. My
mama said everyone should watch the news.

He didn't.

He always had his bedroom window open. And
he left every morning at seven thirty. Every morning. Probably to go to other cities and look for
other bikes to steal with his thieving old ass.

But it never failed: He never forgot to leave his
bedroom window opened.

That is until one day when he left out running
late.

We watched it all through some expensive binoculars Calhoun took from his dad. We were upstairs
in my bedroom window.

"Are my fucking eyes deceiving me?" Calhoun
asked.

We could see him backing out of his driveway.
Usually he lets that piece of shit warm up. Not
today. Cause he was running late.

Calhoun shoved the binoculars to the right.
That's when we saw it he left his bedroom window
open.

We rushed out of my house and snuck to the
back side of his house then crept to the backyard.
We hopped over his fence and tiptoed to his bedroom window. Good thing he ain't had no dog or
we would have been fucked.

As soon as we stepped foot in that mans' house
my nose was hit with the funkiest smells in my life.
I glanced at his TV that had Fred Sanford on. Fred
was doing that, "Elizabeth" line he always did. I

chuckled then pulled my tee shirt over my nose as we walked around the bedroom. Nigga had shit everywhere. You could barely walk in the room for all the boxes and papers, plates with food on them dirty cups and shit, dirty clothes. I scanned the room and nothing but roaches clung to the wall. His closet door had a chair pushed upside it and the top of the chair was hooked under the door knob. I started to open it but when a rat sped past my feet I rushed to the living room. Calhoun was already ahead of me. This nigga had stacks of bikes all over his house, mine and Calhoun along with a lot of other kids, even bikes that belonged to girls.

"Yo. He a rotten mothafucka," Calhoun said.

"Yes," I responded as I looked all around his house.

He even had skate boards. What the fuck did he plan on doing with all that shit I thought.

He had, kids toys they probably left outside like trucks, girls' baby dolls and Barbie dolls.

Calhoun came back from the kitchen with two trash bags and we loaded them up with as many toys as we could.

When were done, we were sweating.

We crept back to the bedroom planning on going back out the window. But then we figured we couldn't get our bikes out the window so we were going to go out the front.

We paused in front of the closet door.

"What you think he got in there?" I asked Calhoun.

He shrugged sat his bag down and tugged at the chair until it gave way.

Then I grabbed the door knob and opened the door.

Suddenly something flew out of the room screeching.

"What the fuck is that!" Calhoun yelled.

Me and Calhoun dropped to the floor as fucking monkey went crazy in the bedroom flying all around and grabbing shit and throwing it at us, from the plates and cups to clothes and boxes he was going wild in the room.

"Come on!" I grabbed the bags and tossed them out the door. Then the bikes.

Calhoun was crouched in a corner terrified.

"Come on man!" I pulled him up and we rushed out of the room while the monkey continued to go crazy.

"Yeah that man was crazy." Images of the monkey flew in my head.

I added, Your bitch ass was shook by that monkey."

Calhoun shoved a piece of corn bread in his mouth and said "Yeah, whatever nigga."

I finished up the last of my food and stood to dump the plate in the sink.

"So you really don't wanna go anywhere huh?"

"I already told you."

"Can I use your truck then?"

"Hell no." I stood from the table. "And lock the door on your way out."

I pulled out my cell phone and dialed Toi's number while placing my plate in the sink.

"What?" she snapped.

"Mom said you called. What's so important baby?" I walked out of the kitchen ignoring Calhoun as he continued to beg me.

"I'm busy. Never mind." She hung up in my face.

I chuckled again and went upstairs to get some much needed rest. I wouldn't mine getting some from Toi but I didn't have time for all her drama.

About the Author

Karen Williams is a native of Long Beach, California. She has a B.A. in Literature and Communications and works as a corrections officer. *Harlem on Lock* is her debut title.